To [illegible]

CW01637299

Cherry Pie Lies

Lynne Whelon

Hope you enjoy
'Cherry Pie Lies'
Love from
Lynne xx

December 2013

Published in 2013 by FeedARead.com Publishing – Arts Council funded

A CIP catalogue record for this title is available from the British Library.

PROLOGUE

I'm not lying. Not this time.

I was in the garden. Not sure how old I was but it was a long time ago. I'd always liked birds and there was this robin. He was really tame. Sometimes, if I'd had a bad day I'd sit behind the shed where no-one could see me and he would sit on the little privet hedge just a couple of feet away.

I began to take him out some bits and pieces of food. A bit of greasy old bacon or some stale bread. I just got stuff out of the bin. And do you know it wasn't long before he was jumping on to my hand. He even let me stroke him. I was very gentle, I can be sometimes. He calmed me down that robin, made me feel better. Made me feel warm and cosy inside. Then, one day, when something really bad had happened at school, he wasn't there. He wasn't there when I really needed him. I don't even remember what had upset me so much but when the bird didn't turn up I went in to a rage. It's true when they call it a 'red mist'. That's just what it's like. I loved that bird. I could feel the pain charging and pumping through my body. I kicked everything over in the back garden that I could find and then I stamped on all the flowers and weeds. That was when I found him. In a clump of nettles. Dead. I was crying like a girl and when I looked up the cat was sitting on the wall. Spitting coppery coloured feathers from it's mouth...

1

Summer in the City – Lovin' Spoonful

JULY 1966 – Plaistow, East London

Jimmy stood at the bottom of the street. He didn't want anyone to see him, not yet. And no-one would know who he was. It had been ten years since the family had left for their new life in Australia.

The first thing he noticed was the cars, parked all along the road. In 1955 there had hardly been any. When Auntie Molly had been staying, the kids used to gather around her black Ford Anglia and just stare at it. Funny, the things you remembered.

As he gazed at his past and the street where he had lived for the first eleven years of his life, he saw that there were banners, posters and union jacks everywhere. Pictures of the England team gazed down from upstairs windows and red and white bunting stretched the whole way up Churchill Street, flapping lazily in the light breeze. That's why they were here.

Him and his dad were back, for the World Cup Final. It had taken thirty two hours to fly from Brisbane.

'Look at all them West Ham players in the England squad son,' his dad had said. 'It's our time, we've got to go.'

Jimmy hadn't been so sure. Yes, the team was playing well but they hadn't got into the finals yet. His dad had been so confident that he had got the tickets and booked the flight before Jimmy had known anything about it.

His dad had cried as the plane touched down at Heathrow Airport. He had always missed home more than Jimmy and his mum had and, of course, he wasn't well. Jimmy pushed those thoughts from his mind.

It had been good for him to go to Australia although he had hated it at first, they all had. The heat was oppressive and no air conditioning in the little huts for ten pound poms, not until they could afford to move on. But his mum and dad had both worked, all hours. They didn't give up and go back to England like many of the others had. He'd got on alright with some of the kids in the huts but he still missed his mates. And everyone was always moaning.

'We'll get out of here Jimmy,' his dad had said. 'There's loads of money if you work hard. Won't be long son. Don't you be listening to them whinging poms. God, no wonder the Aussies call us names.'

Well, thought Jimmy, the name calling hadn't stopped when they had left the huts. Some of the kids at his new school in Southport, near Brisbane just used to spit at him. Didn't even speak except to tell him to get back to his own country.

'I thought they wanted us out here,' he had said to his dad.

'No Jimmy. The Australian government *needs* us, they ain't got enough workers. The Aussies don't really want us but we'll prove 'em wrong mate. Nah, it's all propaganda. Just like in the West Indies. Remember Winston, me mate on the docks?'

Jimmy had nodded.

'He was told they was all wanted in England. '*You'll be welcomed with open arms'*, they told him. That used to make him laugh. It'll get better son.'

And it *had* got better for Jimmy. The teachers out there had discovered that he had a problem working out letters. The way he saw them was different, they were all in the wrong order. He was put on an experimental reading scheme and a new world had just opened up for him. His mum and dad had saved enough to buy a little plot of land and they had started a second- hand car business. He had some good mates in Southport, practically lived on Mainbridge beach and he had almost forgotten his old life in London. Almost, but not quite.

A warm feeling crept through his bones now as he watched two kids, both wearing West Ham United kit, kicking a football around.

'Who are you then? Ain't seen you round here before.'

The ball had rolled over to where he stood, he kicked it gently back to the kid with floppy ginger hair and a freckly face. The kid held the ball under his foot while he stared at Jimmy, hands on his hips.

'I used to live here,' said Jimmy, nodding towards their old house, 'at number four.'

The other one walked towards him now, eyeing him up and down. Blond hair, good looking kid but an arrogant face.

‘That’s my house,’ he said, glaring at Jimmy.

‘Yeah,’ said the other one. ‘That’s Jason’s house, ain’t yours.’

Jimmy tried not to laugh. ‘We moved ten years ago,’ he said, ‘when I was about your age, to Australia. Me and my dad have just come over to watch the Final at Wembley.’

‘Wow that’s groovy,’ said Jason. ‘That must’ve cost you some dosh an’ I s’pose that must be why you talk funny. Coming from Australia.’

The other one picked up the ball and sniffed. ‘Don’t s’pose you’ve got tellies over there yet so you’d have to come here.’

Jimmy smiled.

‘Must be hot in Australia an’ all,’ the kid carried on talking. ‘You look like a Paki. You must know me mum. She’s lived ‘ere for hundreds of years, her name’s Sally.’

‘Are you one of the twins? I remember them.’

‘Nah, they’re older than me, I’m the baby. He walked over to Jimmy, the ball tucked under his arm. Then he spat on his hand and held it out. Jimmy grimaced slightly but shook the hand that was offered.

‘I’m John,’ he said. ‘John Pattinson. Seeing as you lived ‘ere before, you can call me Tonk.’

‘Jimmy,’ he introduced himself. ‘Jimmy Potter.’

Jimmy looked past them to the end of the street and grinned. ‘We used to have our den on the waste ground up there,’ he said, ‘when we were your age. Me, Josie, Del and Legs. Have you got one?’

Tonk looked miserable for a second. ‘They’re building two more houses,’ he said. ‘See the diggers? That’ll be the end of *our* den. I’ve heard about you,’ he grinned. ‘Josie’s me big sister. She ain’t in but me mum is. You could come over, she won’t mind.’

Jimmy felt a wave of apprehension. No, he didn’t want to meet them all yet, he wasn’t ready. It was all so long ago. He felt scared, like he was a little kid again himself.

‘No, you’re alright. I’ve got to go now but I’ll come back, maybe in a couple of days, bring my dad. Have you got a phone?’ He wrote the number down and the boys moved away, dribbling the football between them.

Jimmy waved to them and walked up towards Plaistow Station. What changes there had been in London since they had left for Australia ten years ago, he thought. His dad Billy hadn’t been impressed when the taxi driver had given them a quick tour of central London on their way back from Heathrow to their hotel in Victoria.

‘God, look at the length of them girls’ skirts!’ he had exclaimed. ‘They might as well have nothing on.’

This was the great revolution in Jimmy’s home country. They’d seen it all on television and in the papers in Australia. England in 1966 was where it was all happening. Everyone wanted to be in London. Of course it had been The Beatles who had started it all off and the fact that the Americans had fallen in love with them had really set the ball rolling. Him and his dad had stared out of the taxi windows, quite amazed at what they had seen. Skyscrapers where there had been bombed out buildings, the young people all wearing purples, pinks and yellows. Legs everywhere. Men with hair down to their shoulders. Jimmy's dad had clucked his disapproval.

'Men wiv long hair an' wearing pink shirts,' he laughed, 'They wouldn't last five minutes in Brisbane. They'd all be tarred and feathered.'

The taxi driver had laughed. 'Yeah, there's been a few changes mate. Some good, some bad. What part of London you from?'

'Plaistow mate.'

'You won't notice too much difference there yet. Don't mean working class lives have changed much just cos the Americans love England at the moment. You won't see no men in pink shirts in Plaistow. Few black ones though. That causes a bit of bother.'

He hooted his horn as two giggling mini-skirted girls danced out in front of the cab.

'Come on girls,' he shouted, 'get your arses out me way. I can see your knickers you know. No idea,' he shook his head. 'They have no idea what that does to men. An' then they wonder why they get into trouble.'

Jimmy and his dad had booked into their hotel, his dad had gone to bed but Jimmy hadn't been able to sleep, not yet. He had wanted to go back. Back to Churchill Street.

Plaistow didn't look much different. This certainly wasn't the West End. There seemed to be a lot more litter on the streets and there was a more neglected air than he remembered. Everything looked old and shabby. He noticed several tower blocks on the skyline.

He had heard that they were clearing a lot of the old slums and moving people into them. He didn't think he would have liked to have lived in one when he was a kid. As he approached the station he noticed a lot of black and brown faces. The taxi driver had been right. He only remembered one West Indian family on the estate when he had been there. Oh, and Winston, his dad's mate down the docks. He was shocked as he passed a large Victorian house to see a notice in the window, written on a piece of torn off cardboard. ROOM TO RENT. NO WOGS OR DOGS. He shivered, even on this hot and humid day. This wasn't how he remembered it. He turned when he reached the spot at the station where him and the gang had collected money for their guy every year. Everything seemed a lot smaller now. He sighed as he made his way into the station.

***

Billy Potter woke up suddenly. He wasn't quite sure where he was for a moment and then he remembered. Suddenly overcome by a bout of coughing, a sliver of fear rippled through his body, almost taking his breath away. He was alone in a strange hotel in Victoria, London. Kate, the girl he had married over twenty years ago, was on the other side of the world and Jimmy, his son, had gone off for a walk.

It was these times, he thought, when you just couldn't ignore things that were happening to your body. When you were on your own and there was no-one there to take away that fear.

'Hey dad, how you doing?'

Jimmy burst in the door and Billy was transported back ten years. His son hadn't changed, not really. Same floppy fair hair, cheeky grin and love of life. It was infectious.

'Guess where I've just been?' Jimmy laughed.

'Surprise me son.'

'Churchill Street. We'll have to go dad, see everyone again. Sally's had another baby, I met him. I didn't see any of the others though. It seemed a bit strange somehow, everything looked a lot smaller.'

'You was only a little kid, that's why,' Billy laughed. 'I'm surprised you remember any of it.'

He coughed again and pulled his hankie out from under the pillow. Kate had told him that Sally had had another boy. Sally, that took him back. His life would have been very different if he had done what his body had wanted to, ten years ago. He remembered that night, when he had almost been unfaithful to Kate. Funny how you could look back and know. The times that you made those life changing decisions. God, she had been a looker though. Sally. Memories of running his hands through her silky, blonde hair. For a few seconds he smelt roses and young, soft skin. His body responded to his memories in a way that hadn't happened for months now, he wasn't sure that he really wanted to see her again.

'Is that blood dad? On your hankie?'

Billy coughed quickly and tucked the hankie up his sleeve. He hadn't told his son how ill he really was, though he supposed he had probably guessed. The weight was just dropping off him. Sometimes now, when he looked in the mirror, he scarcely recognised himself.

'No son, just cut meself shaving that's all. Anyway we'd best get downstairs an' get something to eat. Semi- finals tonight on telly.' He coughed again. 'We have to win son. We'll not be able to face them all in Oz if we don't at least get to the Final. An' it's West Ham that's gonna win it for 'em. Some of our lads will be there.'

Jimmy laughed. 'Just got to beat Portugal first dad, Eusebio's on form.'

Billy shook his head. 'Believe me son, I ain't come all this way to watch Germany against Portugal in the Final. Now come on, let's get some grub while the telly warms up.'

'It ain't 1955 dad. They don't take that long to come on.'

Billy laughed. 'Pity it ain't 1970. We'd be watching it in colour.'

***

Sally had just plated up the fish fingers and chips and was staring out of the window. Memories were flooding back after what Tonk had just told her. Billy was back. Oh, how she had loved him even though she had always known that he hadn't felt the same way about her. She remembered that one night when they had almost made love. Now, here they were in the 'swinging sixties' and the new contraceptive pill. There were no longer any consequences to sex and everything was out in the open. Oh you had to pretend to be engaged at the surgery but no-one expected any longer that you should wait until you got married, not like in the fifties. Sally sighed and just wished for a moment that she had been born twenty years later.

She watched Tonk as he wolfed down his tea, he grinned back at her. All teeth, freckles and juggy ears but what a character he was. He caused her no end of worry with his escapades but when he smiled...

She had got quite a shock when he had come in and told her that he had just met someone called Jimmy who used to live here.

'Not Jimmy Potter?'

'Who's Jimmy Potter?' the twins asked in unison.

Sally put her plate on the table and sat down with them.

'Him an' his dad have come to see the Cup Final,' said Tonk. 'They ain't got tellies in Australia.'

'*Suffering seagulls*,' said Chris, one of the twins. 'What do they do if they got no telly?'

'They don't go round talking about *suffering seagulls* and *plundering porpoises*,' Sally laughed. 'You're too old to be watching Captain Pugwash now, it drives me round the twist.'

'Go on then mum,' said Tonk, 'tell us who Jimmy Potter is.'

'They lived at number four,' she began. She was interrupted by the instantly recognisable sound of the Beatles '*Help I need somebody...*' at full volume. Just about sums up my life, she thought, smiling to herself.

'Josie!' she screamed. 'Your tea's ready and turn that down. May and George will have heart attacks.'

The music died and Josie came clumping down the stairs, sliding into her place at the table.

'Thought you liked the Beatles,' she muttered.

'Not that loud.'

'I'm more of a Stones man meself,' said eleven year old Chris who stood up and did a quick impression of Mick Jagger's swivelling hips. They all laughed. Chris was the joker, everyone loved him. Sally looked across the table at Pete, the other twin. Quiet and studious, he had just got in to the grammar, she had been so proud. Maybe at last someone was going to make something of themselves in her family.

'You'll lose him,' her friend and neighbour Maggie Tyler had told her. 'If you let him go to that school. He'll have all posh mates an' he'll be ashamed. Ashamed of all of youse.'

Sally had just laughed. Pete had always been different. He thought more about things, he went his own way. Going to the grammar wouldn't change that. She knew he wouldn't hang around in Churchill Street and if that was what was going to make him happy, that was good enough for her.

'Hey Jose,' she looked at her only daughter now. In her mind she remembered when she had been nine and the Potter family had still lived here. She had looked like a boy with an ugly little elfin face then, she was beautiful now. Slim, golden hair cut into the mod style, it swung and shone when she walked. And those beautiful grey eyes when she smiled. Well, she could have been a model, could have been. That would never happen now.

'Guess who Tonk just met?' Sally asked her. 'Remember Jimmy Potter?'

'Course I remember him.'

'He was your boyfriend weren't he Jose?' Chris laughed, pinging a pea with his fork and aiming at his younger brother, 'before Del I mean.'

Sally saw Josie's expression change. Flinging her knife and fork on to her, almost full plate, she scraped her chair back, glaring at her younger brother.

'We was just kids,' she hissed at him. 'So just shut up Chris.'

'Josie, that's enough,' Sally snapped, but her daughter had stomped back upstairs and the Beatles resounded through the house even louder than before.

'I'd say you hit a bit of a nerve there Chris,' said Pete quietly.

***

Well, I've heard you're back Billy boy. It doesn't take long for news to travel round here, remember?

I wasn't expecting this. I'm not happy about it at all. I mean - have you just come home to watch England get knocked out of the World Cup or have you got other unfinished business on your mind as well? It's nothing personal you know that. You're a good man but can I take a chance that you'll keep quiet? You see you're the only one left now, who knows what I did. I might just have to shut you up before you start mouthing off. Know what I mean?

And you know exactly what I'm capable of Billy, I'd be very careful if I was you. BANG BANG. *That's all it takes. You won't be able to resist coming back to Churchill Street. It's your roots ain't it? It's where you belong. And I'll be waiting.*

So I'm off to Romford now to see a man. And it ain't about a dog.

***

2

Keep on Running – Spencer Davis Group

WORLD CUP FINAL 30th July 1966

'Where the hell have you been dad? We'll miss the first half of the most important game in England's history if we don't get a move on.'

'We're alright son. It's only just gone twelve, we've got hours yet. You look a right prat in that hat by the way.'

Jimmy laughed. He had to admit, the red and white striped bowler that he'd bought outside in the street wasn't really him.

'You look like a right ponce,' his dad laughed. 'Never mind eh. Bet there'll be a few strange looking supporters today. Turn the telly on son and let's see if they've picked the team yet, I know Greavsie ain't playing. Ain't never gonna get over that is he?'

'We haven't got time dad,' said Jimmy. 'We need to get there before the rush. You're not well, remember?'

'Well, I ain't feeling no pain today son.' He rubbed his hands together. 'Can't remember the last time I was this excited about anything.'

'What, not even me being born?' Jimmy laughed. He had heard the story of his birth hundreds of times. How his dad had been called over the tannoy at Upton Park in the middle of a cup game. '*Would Mr Billy Potter, please make your way home where your wife is about to give birth.*'

The whole crowd had erupted with a huge roar, even some of the players had clapped apparently and his dad had been left with a face the colour of a beetroot.

'You can't go yet Billy,' his mate Loopy had said. 'We're winning.'

'*Hardest decision I ever had to make in me life*,' he always said. But not today.

He was looking at Jimmy with a strange smile on his face. 'Nothing beats you being born son,' he said quietly.

It was so unlike him that Jimmy felt embarrassed. It hung in the air between them for what seemed like hours.

'We were losing by half-time anyway mate,' said his dad eventually and laughed. 'Come on, let's get going. Got the tickets in me pocket.' He took them out, kissed them, then put his arm around his son's shoulder. 'This is going to be a great day. They'll talk about it for years and you and me mate, we were there.'

The streets were heaving with people. Laughing, smiling, all headed for the tube. Rattling rattles, blowing horns, waving union jacks. Cars, buses and taxis all hooting. A rich cacophony of sound on a beautiful, blue sky, end of July day.

'Let's get the bus,' said Billy. 'We can't see nothing underground.'

From the top deck they could see it all happening around them. Banners and ribbons hanging from windows. 'COME ON ENGLAND' signs everywhere.

Jimmy felt like he was in a bubble about to explode. The excitement was contagious and it was difficult to keep still. Everyone on the bus started singing. '*We're gonna win the Cup, we're gonna win the Cup, ee aye addio, we're gonna win the cup.*' The England supporters began to stamp on the floor until the bus almost seemed to be in danger of collapsing in on itself. The bus conductor got so carried away singing that he completely forgot to collect any fares.

The roads to Wembley were choked with traffic. Many of the passengers jumped off and ran the rest of the way. Jimmy only just managed to stop his dad doing the same.

'Stay on till we get there dad,' he shouted over the noise. 'Save your energy for the match!'

Walking up to the stadium was just magical. Everyone laughing and singing and the constant banter between supporters. Jimmy wanted to hold it all in his head, he was scared that it would slip away over the years. How he wished that he could write it all down. Writing had never been his strong point. Anyway, how could you put these feelings into words? Oh, the newspaper reporters would try but they'd never get it. You had to be here to understand. The optimism, excitement and comradeship, everyone in the whole country wanting to be here and he was. Something great was about to happen, it was like being a part of history. They *would* win today, Jimmy thought to himself, they just *had* to.

The Germans were all laughing as well. They walked past a gang of them, clowning around and joking.

'Good luck English,' one shouted after them. Jimmy and his dad grinned. Two of the Germans came running over, one was waving his camera around.

'You want me to take photo of you?' Jimmy mouthed very slowly. They shook their heads and put out their hands towards them. 'Might the best team win,' one of them laughed as he shook Jimmy's hand. He, too, was obviously with his dad. The two dads looked at each other, smiled and shook hands.

'No war today,' German dad laughed.

'What war?' his dad smiled. 'I'll forgive you for the war mate,' he laughed, 'but only if you let us win the Cup.'

They seemed to understand, kept clapping Jimmy and his dad on the back which brought on a serious bout of coughing from his dad. They insisted on taking jolly photos of them with the German crowd before they set off to their different ends of the ground.

'I think this could be the day when I finally forgive the Germans,' his dad shouted, adjusting the West Ham and England rosettes on the front of his shirt. 'As long as we beat 'em of course.'

When they finally sat down in their seats in the South Stand Jimmy could see the relief on his dad's face. This was taking it out of him, he thought but one look at his dad's beaming grin, as he took in the hallowed turf below him, made Jimmy realise that the effort was worth it. He was in his element.

‘You stay here dad, I’ll get us a programme. Do you want a Bovril and a pie?’ he shouted.

His dad nodded. ‘That would be good son. Ta. Wish we was standing though, don’t seem the same sitting down at a football match.’ He reached for his hankie and coughed into it. Jimmy looked away. He didn’t want to see anything bad today.

The noise, the chanting, carried on through the band playing. The air was choking with cigarette smoke and the occasional farts and belches that always followed Wembley pies.

The teams were announced.

‘Yeah,’ West Ham supporters all cheered when they heard that three of their players were going to be in the Final squad.

There was a small chorus of ‘I’m Forever Blowing Bubbles,’ to the general amusement of the Arsenal, Chelsea and Spurs supporters in the crowd.

But it was England’s day, no time for local rivalries. The noise as the teams came out was the loudest sound of people en masse that Jimmy had ever heard. If that didn’t get the team going, he thought, nothing would.

‘Look at Bobby,’ his dad nudged him. ‘Our Bobby Moore, leading out the England team in a World Cup Final. I’m so proud I could cry.’

Well, Jimmy thought, as the Queen came out to be introduced to the teams, they’d probably *all* be crying at the end, either with joy or despair.

‘Remember what she’s wearing Jimmy,’ his dad said. ‘The Queen. Your mum will want to know.’

And so it began. The ball backwards and forwards, the game flowing from one end to the other. Ooohs and aaahs when either side came close to scoring. 'England! England!' The crowd roared, willing their heroes on to victory. Wembley became a little world of its own. Nothing else mattered to those inside and by half-time the score was one all.

Then they all sang along to '*Colonel Bogey'* and '*A Life on the Ocean Wave*,' as the Royal Marines played and marched up and down the pitch. Time for a breather, a release from the tension and ferment that had filled the air for the last forty five minutes.

'Alright dad?' Jimmy asked as he came back from the toilet. His dad nodded, he was in a deep conversation with the boys sitting in front of them and laughing like a drain.

There was an almighty roar as Geoff Hurst scored again for England in the second half. Jimmy and his dad threw their arms around each other in delirious joy. A memory flashed into Jimmy's head. Hugging his dad after a cup goal at Upton Park when he had only came up to his dad's waist. The smell of his coat. Tobacco and mints. How he had snuggled into it and how safe and warm he had felt. He remembered that it had been snowing and he could almost feel the soft flakes melting on his cheeks.

The ninety minutes was almost up. Everyone started whistling, an eerie sound all around the ground and then suddenly all the England supporters were stunned into silence.

‘Fucking bastard Germans,’ shouted the man in front. Hands went on to heads. Drained faces, no-one wanting to believe what had just happened on the pitch below.

‘Extra time,’ said Billy quietly. ‘I should never have had my photo taken wiv ‘em’

Shortly after Weber of West Germany had scored and run joyfully around the pitch, the whistle went for full-time. For a few minutes there were no cheers except from the Germans in the East Stand. This wasn’t meant to happen, Jimmy thought. They had been all ready to start celebrating and now it felt like his guts had dropped out. His dad was shivering, even though it was a warm day and he was wearing a thick jacket. He had dropped his rattle, the one his mum had put special ribbons on. The same rattle Jimmy remembered from all those matches at Upton Park when he had been a little kid. He picked it up. There were tears in his dad’s eyes again.

‘They’re all knackered Jimmy, all cramped up. Look at ‘em. We can’t lose now, we just can’t.’

Jimmy picked up the rattle and handed it back to him. ‘Dad, this isn’t West Ham. This is England and we *are* going to win so stop bloody bawling and rattle that rattle.’

As the teams started to play extra time, the crowd responded and the sound grew louder until it just filled their whole beings. The players tired legs seemed to refill with energy. Inspired by the crowd they kept running, kept fighting. When Geoff Hurst volleyed the ball in towards goal, the cheers stopped as the ball rebounded.

'That crossed the bloody line!' They were all screaming, shouting.

The referee agreed with the England supporters and it was only the Germans who knew it wasn't a goal. Even Jimmy, who had sneezed at that precise moment and missed it altogether, was positive that it had crossed the line. Everyone was jumping up and down. Jimmy, in a moment of fierce patriotism, ripped off his T-shirt and flung it up into the air as the referee pointed to the centre spot.

The West Germans were devastated and when Geoff Hurst saw an empty space and made it 4-2 to England, it really *was* all over.

Jimmy wanted to stay in Wembley Stadium for ever. To wrap himself up in that world of ecstasy, warmth and laughter. He had never seen his dad look so happy though tears streamed down his face, just like Bobby Charlton below them on the pitch. A world full of skipping, toothless Nobby Stiles. A world where Bobby Moore was being carried aloft with the Jules Rimet trophy. A world where everyone was hugging strangers and jumping up and down and singing '*Rule Brittania,*' '*When the Reds Go Marching In*' and anything else they could think of. A world of total happiness and delight.

'Is this your T shirt mate?' A young boy handed over the crumpled shirt to Jimmy. 'It landed on me head.'

‘Cheers,’ Jimmy laughed and shook his hand. ‘Don’t you ever forget this day,’ he said to the wide-eyed child in front of him.

‘Oh, I won’t,’ he replied. ‘I won’t forget it ever. It’s the best day of me life.’

Jimmy watched as the little boy raced off into his future. ‘Good luck,’ he whispered after him.

***

Arthur, the landlord of *The King’s Head,* looked around his pub and felt so proud to be English that he was almost bursting with it. Sweat poured down his ruddy face and into his greying beard. The punters were all well on the way to getting seriously drunk, singing and waving their scarves, he couldn’t remember a time when everyone was so full of joy. He looked over towards the door.

‘I don’t bleedin’ believe it,’ he shouted over the hysteria. He almost dropped the beer he was holding as he saw his old mate Billy Potter coming in through the door. Even though England had just won the Cup and the pub was heaving with smiley faces and drunkenness, everyone trying to get drinks in, Arthur ran out from behind the bar and threw his arms around his old mate.

‘Are you pissed or what?’ Billy laughed. ‘You couldn’t wait to get rid of us.’

‘Going soft in me old age,’ Arthur laughed. ‘Come on mate. We heard you was back, knew you wouldn’t be able to resist seeing your old mates and what a day, what a match! An’ Bobby, Geoff an’ Martin eh? West Ham won it for ‘em.’

'Since when was you a West Ham supporter?'

'Since the quarter finals mate. Right, let's get you a drink. Usual?'

'Silly not to.'

'Dad.'

Billy looked at his son and grinned. Jimmy had that look of disapproval on his face, he was good at that.

'Look son, I know I ain't s'posed to drink. Bloody hell, I've given up the fags. We've just won the World Cup for Christ's sake an' I'm back home at *The King's Head.* Give me a break will yer?'

'I promised mum.'

Billy pushed his way to the bar, ignoring his son. If he was going to go he would do it *his* way. He had come home and he knew that he probably would never see Australia again, that flight had really taken it out of him. He had liked it out there. Oh, it hadn't been easy at first but they'd had a great time. Him and Kate had worked hard, made enough money to start up his business. Kate and Auntie Molly did all the paperwork and he had some good lads working for him, plenty of time to spend days on the beach, fishing and swimming, barbecues by the pool. Yes, he even had a swimming pool! He had to pinch himself sometimes.

Billy had watched his son grow up swimming, scuba diving, surfing and getting clever. He still didn't think it was that important when Jimmy had got to university but Kate had been ecstatic. She had been relaxed and happy out there, so different to the troubled girl he had married who had been haunted by the war. Losing her mum and little sister in the Bethnal Green disaster, being attacked in Victoria Park and then losing their baby girl. Yes, they *had* done the right thing. Especially after what had happened just before they left Churchill Street. That was what had finally made him decide to go. He couldn't have stayed around here after that, which reminded him. He must give Jimmy the letter. And soon.

He looked around the pub. Nothing much had changed though he noticed a jukebox installed in the corner where the dartboard used to be. Arthur certainly hadn't done much to improve the decor. The faded wallpaper was the same, just more faded and nicotine stained than it had been before.

But, he thought, all that time in Queensland there *had* been a part of him missing. A hole that no amount of money or sunny days on the beach could fill and the answer was here. He was back where he belonged. He couldn't stop grinning when he saw all the old familiar faces. The word had spread, like ripples through a lake on a stormy day.

Billy Potter was back. Not looking too good but he was here and then he was overwhelmed with people clapping him on the back, shaking his hand, hugging him. His old football mates, well drunk by now, all gathered around. He *did* still belong here. He had been scared, truth be told, that they would have forgotten him. This feeling was better than any amount of money and what would make it absolutely perfect was a few beers and maybe even a fag, just the one.

***

Jimmy turned away from the bar, he didn't want to watch his dad drinking.

'Hey Jimmy!' his dad was shouting. 'What you having?'

His dad was beaming. This was probably the best day of his life. He couldn't spoil it for him, not now. They were all looking at him.

'Oh, go on then, I'll have a pint with you dad. Then I might just go up Churchill Street and see if any of the old gang are around.'

There was silence around the bar, sudden and cutting.

'Well,' his dad's mate Loopy whispered to him. 'You've opened a whole can of worms there mate.'

'Why, what's happened? Is it Del?'

Jimmy knocked back his pint in twenty seconds and gave his dad a thumbs up.

As the noise and banter in the bar returned to normal, Loopy ushered him outside.

Jimmy had often wondered what would happen to Del. Would he end up an alky like his dad Mick? And nasty with it? He hadn't had much of a life, not when they'd lived in Churchill Street anyway. He didn't think he really wanted to hear what Loopy had to say, he knew it wouldn't be good.

'I'd best tell you Jimmy, before you go up there.'

'What's happened to Del?'

'Oh no, Del's good as gold, once his dad was out of the way, no, it ain't Del. It's the other two. Well, Legs mainly. Ain't no easy way to say it mate. He's doing time in the Scrubs, he should be out soon.'

Jimmy swallowed hard, he couldn't believe this. Legs in prison? No, not Legs.

'Why– what happened?' he asked.

Loopy shuffled his feet and lit a cigarette.

'Well, I reckon I'll let Del tell you about that, here he is now.'

Loopy moved back into the pub as Jimmy looked up the road. Funny, how you could recognise someone just from the way they walk. Del Tyler would be twenty now, just like him. He watched, as Del swaggered towards him, sweating in a mod green parka and grinning all over his face, his dark hair swinging into his eyes. Jimmy didn't remember him smiling much in the old days and, truth be told, he had been worried how he would turn out. His mum had always said that Del was a born hooligan yet here he was, standing in front of him looking positively confident and relaxed.

'Heard you was in town,' he clapped Jimmy on the back. 'We got a lot of catching up to do mate. Come on, I'll get you one in.'

As they both moved towards the door, Del stopped and turned to face Jimmy. They both grinned as if neither could really believe that the other was there, then, simultaneously, they spat on their hands and shook them.

'To the gang,' said Del, lifting his bottle of beer and clinking it with Jimmy's.

'Yeah, to the gang,' laughed Jimmy. 'D'you remember the witch?' he asked as they leant against the bar.

Del lit up a cigarette and nodded. 'Well, she's still alive. Getting on a bit now though, still see her around. Old Bones lived wiv her till he died. We give him a good send-off though.'

'Yeah I heard he'd died. Mum and the witch write to each other you know,' he laughed. 'Doesn't sound right does it?'

'God, we had some laughs didn't we eh? We was right little bastards. I missed you mate, we all did. Weren't the same after you left.'

Jimmy had so many questions, everything was coming flooding back to him now. All those old memories, faces, just like it had been yesterday. It was really weird, he almost felt like crying. He looked over towards his dad who was still laughing and smiling.

'Alright son?' he shouted across. Jimmy nodded.

'Your old man don't look too good mate,' said Del. 'He was a real good-looking geezer, I remember.'

Jimmy looked over at his dad, saw the lines etched on his face, the grey pallor of his skin, the pain in his eyes, no amount of laughter could hide that. And then he knew.

'I don't think he's got long Del.'

His old friend put his arm around his shoulders. 'Good job he's come home then mate.'

'What happened to *your* dad?' Jimmy asked, swallowing hard.

'Ain't seen him since that night. You remember? When he run off after he'd set fire to the witch's house.'

Jimmy noticed a flicker of pain in his friend's eyes.

‘I still miss him sometimes, me dad.’

Jimmy couldn’t think why he would. Even though it was years ago he could still remember the stink of Mick Tyler. The booze and the sweat, the fights. The bruises on Del’s mum’s face. No, from what he remembered it had been a good thing that he had never come back to Churchill Street.

‘They built her house again, the witch,’ Del was saying. ‘It was just the roof really. They saved the rest of it, she still gives me the creeps though.’

‘So how’s your mum doing?’ Jimmy asked.

‘She’s alright, been living wiv Winston for nine years now. There he is over there, talking to your dad.’

Jimmy looked over to the other end of the bar. ‘But Winston’s black Del.’

‘Well spotted mate. Nah, he’s alright. He’s taught me to play the drums an’ stuff, I’m in a group now you know, you’ll have to come an’ watch us play. We ain’t quite as good as the Stones yet but we’re getting there.’

Jimmy was sure that the shock must have shown on his face. ‘But you hated coloured people, you always said they were worse than the Germans. I remember that.’

‘Well yeah, but Winston’s alright. An’ there’s loads round ‘ere now. Everyone moans about ‘em. Still, they’re good for getting hold of a bit of ganja, know what I mean? And they know a bit about music an’ all. Hey,’ he punched Jimmy on the arm lightly. ‘When did you start talking so posh? You sound like a cross between a bleedin’ newsreader an’ Skippy the kangaroo. An’ you look like a fucking film star wiv that tan an' all. You look – you look just like your dad used to.'

As they talked about old times Jimmy noticed that Otis Redding singing '*Respect*' was playing on the jukebox.

Del was shaking his head to the music. 'You can keep all that Beatles rubbish, this is the real music man.'

'So' Jimmy took a deep breath, scared of what Del was going to say. 'Loopy said Legs was doing time. What happened to him?'

Del looked down at his feet and took a deep breath. 'Well, it was about two years ago,' he began. 'We was just mucking about on that night, in Victoria Park, bored out of our brains. We'd started nicking cars, just now an' then, you know. Sometimes just me an' Legsy, sometimes a few of us. I usually did the driving, Legsy never had the bottle. Remember what he was like?'

Jimmy nodded.

'Anyway, we'd had a bit of a blow in the park, just me an' Legsy. I'd nicked some dope off Winston, never done it before. I think it got to Legsy more than me cos suddenly he decided he wanted to nick a car an' *he* wanted to drive. We was laughing like drains, just couldn't stop bleedin' laughing. He thought he could do anything I s'pose.'

'Jesus,' said Jimmy. 'I don't know if I want to hear what happened next.'

'Well, we found a little mini, parked up, he'd even left the door open for us. Managed to get it started but Legsy wanted a go. I drove it round the corner, you know into a quiet road and showed him what to do. I blame meself Jimmy, I still blame meself. I shouldn't have let him drive.'

He took a drag on his cigarette and looked down at the floor. 'Anyway, he was useless, he was all over the place. I was trying to stop the car and shouting at him but the handbrake had jammed. That was all I could think of doing. She was just walking across the road, an old lady on the crossing. She'd just been to bingo and won ten quid. Then she was dead, blood everywhere. Just like that.'

'Christ,' said Jimmy. 'What a nightmare.'

'He won't talk about it, I tried. Went to see him a couple of times before he got sent down but he won't see no-one now except his mum an' dad.'

The noise in the pub seemed to roar in Jimmy's ears. Singing, shouting, laughter. It didn't fit in with what they were talking about at all, as if it were two separate worlds. He noticed that Del was shaking and put his hand on his mate's arm.

'Wasn't your fault Del,' he said gently.

'No, but it feels like it is. Anyway,' he smiled at Jimmy, 'let's forget all that for now mate an' celebrate you being home. Oh, and of course the fact that England just won the World Cup for the first time ever.' He grinned.

'I think you'll find,' Loopy stuck his head between them, 'that *West Ham* won the World Cup actually!'

Del walked slowly over to the jukebox and the Stones boomed out, mingling with all the World Cup celebratory singing.

'This could be the last time, this could be the last time, maybe the last time I don't know...'

His dad was laughing at the bar. 'That's a good song for today. I'll bet it will be the bloody last time we win the World Cup lads,' he shouted. 'Best make the most of it.'

The laughter all around just seemed to fade in to the background, like when the radio was on but you weren't really listening. Jimmy stood at the bar and felt stunned, as if someone had hit him. Legsy in prison. He wanted to ask Del about Josie but he was scared that might not be good news either. What on earth had he come back to? What had happened to the gang while he had been away?

***

God, they'd all aged, Billy thought, looking at his wise old friend George. George looked weary, not surprising after what Arthur had told him. His son doing porridge, didn't bear thinking about.

'Sorry mate, about your troubles,' he clapped George on the back. 'I can't believe that of your Legsy.'

'Well, he was in the wrong, at least he admitted it and he does feel very guilty. There's nowt we can do except support him now. Tell you what though, he's passing all sorts of exams in there, be qualified to run the country when he comes out and your Jimmy at university, I'll bet Kate's proud. Who would have thought it eh? None of them could hardly read when there was all that business with Greta Broncowiez.' He chuckled.

‘Oh you mean the witch,’ Billy laughed. ‘Those kids were real little shits weren’t they? Good old days.’

‘Oh, I don’t know Billy, but everything is changing here now. Can’t keep up with it, it’s like a whole new world. Laws and rules all being turned upside down. The old and the new. No-one knows how to behave any more. All these pop stars doing drugs and smashing up hotel rooms and then there’s us ordinary folk, well, we haven’t got a clue what’s going on.’ He laughed. ‘The swinging sixties, they’re calling it but there’s still kids round here whose shoes are falling to pieces.’

‘I’ve noticed there’s a lot more foreigners,’ said Billy. ‘Is there much trouble?’

George nodded sadly. ‘You know me Billy, I’m not a prejudiced man but people are scared. Scared for their jobs, their homes, their way of life. Sometimes it’s not very pretty or civilised. But take our Joe. The street in Forest Gate where he lived, there’s only two white families left. The shops sell Indian food and clothes, the cinema shows Indian films. You can understand how it gets to people. Families who’ve lived here for generations.’

‘Don’t sound very fair to me.’

‘Oh I don’t blame the immigrants,’ said George. ‘They just want a better life like your mum and dad did. It’s the politicians living in their leafy suburbs, they don’t have to deal with any of the problems. I don’t know how it’s going to end, if it ever does. There’s always been immigrants, probably always will be.’

They looked over to where Jimmy and Del were engrossed in conversation.

‘How’s Del been?’ Billy asked quietly. ‘Without his dad?’

George took a long gulp of his beer. ‘He’s not bad, much better than he should’ve turned out from that family. He really tried to help my son after he’d been arrested, he just didn’t want to be helped. He’s playing in a group now, Del. They’re quite good. I went to see them a few months ago, made me feel my age though. In a dancehall with all those kids.’

He smiled and looked at his old friend, put his hand on Billy’s arm, saw tears in his eyes.

‘I’m sorry I shouted at you this morning Billy when you came round. That letter, it was just such a shock, I still can’t believe it.’ He was shaking his head. ‘I don’t understand why you did what you did but I trust you, I won’t let you down.’

‘I don’t wanna talk about it anymore George, I still have nightmares. I’m giving the letter to Jimmy tomorrow. Watch him for me won’t you? I know I’m leaving you to face the flak an’ I’m sorry. Anyway,’ he sighed as he started coughing violently. ‘They might never find him.’

Billy smiled at his old friend and took a drag from the cigarette that Loopy had given him. He immediately began to cough again and had to hold onto the bar. George took the cigarette away from him and stubbed it out on the floor. He looked sadly at his old friend. But he wasn’t old, he wasn’t even forty.

‘It’s too late now George, ain’t nothing more they can do for me,’ Billy gasped, ‘but I tell you something, at least I've been to Wembley wiv me son and seen us win the World Cup, it don't get any better than that.'

Loopy started a chorus of '*I'm Forever Blowing Bubbles'* and it echoed around the pub, bouncing off the walls.

Billy looked around him. He wanted to hold on to this memory with all his old mates. He had come home.

***

He wheezed and coughed as he half fell into the hotel room. He really shouldn't have had that last pint or that fag. Sod it, what did it matter. He switched on the radio, opened the window and sat in the armchair looking out at the sprawl of London in front of him. Getting dark now, lights going on. His city, his home. The hum of the traffic, the hooting cars. Some laughter from below and glasses clinking.

He barely heard the news announcer on the radio, it became part of all the other sounds and merged into one.

'So, tonight we bring you wonderful news. In a year that has been a fearful one for our country. Tensions between Russia and our allies the United States are at an all-time high, the threat of nuclear war has never been greater. Earlier this month we have seen the violent protests outside the U.S Embassy in Grosvenor Square against the Vietnam War. Chaos and carnage.

And we must never forget the dreadful and heartrending trial of the Moors Murderers and the taped cries of one of their victims which will be etched in our minds forever.

But at last, today, on the 30th July 1966, there is good news and no-one can say that we don't deserve it. The whole country has come together and supported our fantastic football team. It is estimated that 32,000,000 British television viewers watched as England won the World Cup for the first time in history. Our country has come back to life and out of the dark shadows a miracle has taken place. The hearts in our towns, cities and villages have been lightened today by these extraordinary men. We salute them all and their manager Alf Ramsey, may they never be forgotten.'

Today had been one of the best days of Billy Potter's life but he didn't have any energy left now except to crawl into bed. His hand closed around a sliver of paper in his jacket pocket, probably one of his mates giving him their phone number or something. He took it out and noticed that his hands were shaking. He stared at it, looked again, shook his head. There were just seven words. Capital letters.

I KNOW WHAT HAPPENED TO MICK TYLER

And then Billy couldn't breathe.

3

(Fa fa fa fa fa fa fa fa) Sad Song – Otis Redding

Jimmy was woken by a loud, rasping noise coming from the other bed.

'Dad?' he called out fearfully. He switched the bedside light on. 3.10 a.m. Looking over to the other bed, he saw that his dad was having trouble breathing, there was blood on the pillow. His skin was ash white and he was trying desperately to speak, his mouth working.

Jimmy leapt out of bed and over to him. He plumped up the pillows and pulled him into a sitting up position. His dad nodded, tried to smile and managed to speak.

'Jimmy,' he gasped. 'Something... I've... got... to... give... you.'

'Not till I've phoned for help dad.'

He got through to the reception desk and shouted at them to get an ambulance, his hands trembling as he put the receiver down. No, this couldn't be happening, not when England had just won the World Cup. He sat on the bed, he could see his dad was agitated.

'In... that... top... drawer... son... there's... a...a letter.'

His breathing was getting worse, Jimmy could see the effort it was costing him to sound out every word.

'Alright dad, alright, I'll get it later. Don't say anything else now, you'll be alright. The ambulance won't be long, they'll sort you out. You're not going to die dad, you don't need to be leaving me letters just yet.'

His dad tried to smile. 'Just... promise... me... son. Promise... me. It... ain't... nothing... to... do... wiv... me... dying...but... something... might... 'appen... soon I think... You'll... know... son . You'll... know... when... you... have... to ...deal... wiv... it. I'm... sorry... Jimmy... I... didn't... want... you...to...have...to...sort...it... I'm ... sorry. Talk... to...to George...if...you...need -'

'You're not dying dad, don't start scaring me like this. Just stop talking, you're not helping yourself.'

His dad's face was screwed up in pain. 'You're... a... worse... fucking... nag... than... your... mother.'

Jimmy saw tears in his dad's eyes. He heard the sirens, the ambulance approaching. Please don't let him die, he thought, please God. A picture of Josie flashed into his mind, praying. When they were little kids, praying about silly things, witches and stuff. And then he remembered her praying for his mum when she had been poorly, and at Bethnal Green Station where his gran and his auntie had died in an accident during the war. He remembered everything, he wanted her to be here, *she* would know what to do. As the ambulancemen knocked and burst into the room, Jimmy felt tears almost drowning his face.

'Come on mate,' said one of the men, patting him on the shoulder, 'we'll sort him out.'

'Jimmy...' his dad gasped. 'I... think... you'd... best... phone... your... mum.'

***

It was very serious, the doctor had told Jimmy. Lung cancer and it was the final stages.

'I knew he wasn't right,' Jimmy had mumbled, 'but he never said.'

'Well we've been in touch with Australia,' said the doctor, 'and your dad knows there's nothing we can do, he left it too late I'm afraid. He should never have attempted that journey, let alone go to watch a World Cup Final.'

'He had to,' said Jimmy. 'It was the best day of his life.'

'I know,' the doctor smiled, 'so he keeps telling me but I'm afraid it's shortened his time on this earth considerably. When will your mother be here?'

'Later today, she's got the first flight she could. She didn't seem very surprised, I think she knew.'

The doctor patted his arm. 'I'm sure she did,' he said. 'We'll look after him. Just try and keep him as comfortable as we can, I can only give him a few days I'm afraid.'

Jimmy turned away and bit his lip, he'd been sitting with his dad all night. Sometimes he had woken up and tried to say something but mostly he had just slept. Jimmy had sat and listened to the sounds of the ward. The coughs, the sighs, the cheery nurses and his dad's laboured breathing through the oxygen mask. He squeezed his dad's hand. The nurses had said he should try and talk to him even when he seemed to be sleeping but Jimmy just felt daft doing that. He couldn't do it, so he just thought about all the stuff they had done together, all the football matches at Upton Park when he had been a kid. Standing in the chicken run singing '*I'm Forever Blowing Bubbles.*' That was something he could do, he could sing to him. He started quietly '*I'm forever blowing bubbles, pretty bubbles in the air*'.

'Sing up mate,' said the man in the next bed, I can't hear yer.'

He joined in and soon all those in the beds who could were singing along too, even the nurses joined in. Jimmy closed his eyes and he was back at Upton Park sitting on his dad's shoulders in the chicken run.

'*Fortune's always hiding I've looked everywhere. I'm forever blowing bubbles, pretty bubbles in the air.*'

His dad had opened his eyes and was smiling.

'Thought... I'd... gone... to... heaven... then... son... never... mind... eh. Best... wait... for...your...mum... or... I'll... be... in... real... trouble.'

'Dad that's horrible.'

'No... it...ain't... son. You've... got...to...laugh, ain't... no...other...way. An'... I... want... me... ashes...done...at...Upton...Park... in... the......'

His dad's face was looking pale and agitated, his breathing laboured and rasping.

'Chicken run?' Jimmy finished the sentence for him.

His dad nodded. 'Now...need...to...sleep...so... piss... off.'

His eyes closed again.

***

After going back to the hotel and booking his mum and his Auntie Molly a room, Jimmy got on the underground and made his way to Plaistow Station. He had phoned Josie's house, she had been out but Sally, her mum, had told him to come over any time. She had sounded really upset when he had told her about his dad. He almost ran from the station to Churchill Street and knocked on the door at number eight, the blue paint was peeling and the whole house had an air of neglect about it.

As the door opened, it was Josie's stunning grey-green eyes he noticed first, they hadn't changed at all. Her fair hair tumbled on to her shoulders. He couldn't believe this was the same little girl who had been his mate, the little tomboy who was as brave as a lion and always wore dungarees. She was beautiful now, except for one thing. She put her hand up and covered her left cheek but he had already seen it, a deep, livid scar from just under her eye down to her mouth. And then they were hugging each other as if it had only been yesterday, not ten years ago, that he had left for Australia.

So Josie told him everything that had happened since he left. About her mum having another baby and how they had all felt like a proper family until Tonk's dad Joe had walked out of their lives. She told him about Maggie Tyler meeting Winston, Legs going to prison, Del joining the rock group. In fact everything except the most obvious. All the time Jimmy was conscious of the clock ticking, of having to leave soon to get to the airport and then back to the hospital with his mum and Auntie Molly. The doctor had told him that his dad didn't have long. At least, hopefully, his mum would be here in time.

‘Listen to me rabbiting on,’ Josie laughed as she poured him another cup of tea. They were sitting opposite each other at the kitchen table, Radio Caroline jingles playing in the background. Josie sighed and cupped her head in her hands. She looked at him and smiled, those beautiful eyes.

‘So how did it happen?’ he asked, touching the scar on her face gently with his fingertip. Tears welled in her eyes. He didn’t want to ask but he had to know, no point trying to ignore it.

She looked down at the table.

‘I was just walking home from me mate’s house,’ she began. ‘It was quite late, there wasn’t anyone about. I was just under the railway tunnel when I heard footsteps behind me, running. When I tried to turn around his hand was over me face, he must have used chloroform or something. All I can remember was another smell, Brut aftershave. It was really strong, made me feel sick. I never saw his face. When I come round I was lying in a pool of blood. I didn’t know it was my blood but it didn’t hurt, I just felt so happy to be alive. I laughed, I can remember that. And then a couple come up the alleyway and seen me lying there. I couldn’t move an’ I didn’t know why. I remember me back was all wet, it was raining and I just kept laughing and the rain was trickling into my mouth. He hadn’t touched me, not in that way, but he’d cut me Jimmy. Why would he have done that? I hadn’t done nothing to no-one. He nicked me purse, there was only two shillings an’ sixpence in it.’

She put her hand over the scar. ‘He did this for half a crown.’

Jimmy looked at the tears coursing down her cheeks. ‘And they never caught him?’ he asked, holding her hand.

She shook her head. ‘They did sort of try but you know what they’re like, not that bothered. They thought he’d probably cut me because there was only shrapnel in me purse. Oh I know I’m lucky it wasn’t worse. Del and a lot of the other lads went out trying to find out who done it but there was nothing. Just a weirdo I suppose. I’d just got a modelling job an’ all,’ she laughed. ‘Still, I couldn’t really see meself as a model could you?’

‘You were going to be a train driver,’ Jimmy laughed. ‘I remember that. No, I can’t imagine you’d have enjoyed all that hanging around and smiling.’

‘And I’d have had to wear bleeding dresses all the time.’

They laughed together. ‘So what are you doing now?’ he asked.

‘I’m working in an old people’s home, just till I’ve taken me A Levels. I’m doing them in evening classes. I want to be a social worker Jimmy, gawd knows why, that’s what I really want to do. I started at mum’s factory when I left school, only lasted two days, I hated it. Anyway, that bloke probably did me a favour. Made me realise I’ve got to do what I want to do now, not keep putting things off. You’ve only got one life an’ I nearly lost mine.’

‘And is Del OK?’

'Yeah, we're going steady now. Well, we were sort of going out together before the – accident, we weren't serious or anything. We were both too young, the time wasn't right really I suppose and he was getting the group together so we – well – me really, I finished it. He didn't seem bothered though.'

As Josie spoke the back door flew open and Del stood there grinning.

Josie laughed. 'Talk of the devil.'

'That's me,' Del laughed.

He came over to the table and ruffled Josie's hair. He planted a kiss gently on her scarred cheek. 'Alright doll? I'll get us all a cuppa shall I? How's your dad doing mate?' He turned to Jimmy and punched him lightly on the arm.

'He's not good Del. He -' Jimmy could feel himself choking up. He looked at the kitchen clock. 'He's not got long. I need to get back, got to meet mum at the airport first.' He scraped back his chair and stood up.

'D'you want a lift on me scooter?' Del asked. 'Ain't no trouble.'

Jimmy shook his head. 'No thanks mate, I'll get the tube, I've got time.'

'D'you remember,' Josie smiled sadly at Jimmy. 'When we prayed on the tube at Bethnal Green? It just come back to me then, I'll pray for your dad Jimmy.'

Jimmy knew he had to get out before he started crying. Del clapped him on the shoulder.

'Don't be a stranger mate. We're here for you, you know that don't yer?'

Jimmy nodded. 'Yeah, I'll phone. I'll let you know what happens. Ta mate.' The years flooded away. Him and Del spat on their hands and shook them, like they were nine years old again.

'We'll always be your mates Jimmy,' said Josie. 'Now go on sod off before we all start bawling.'

As Jimmy walked back down Churchill Street, to meet his mum and Auntie Molly at the airport, he felt a mixture of emotions, sad about his dad, worried about how his mum was going to be. Angry about Josie's face. Who could do that to a beautiful young girl? He could see how pretty she must have been before that happened and Del, who had been there for her, who obviously didn't care about the scarring of her face. There was something else as well though.

It should have been him. As soon as he had seen Josie and talked to her it was like the last ten years had just melted away. She had been his best mate all that time ago but he felt more than that now. He knew what that other emotion was and he knew he had to forget it, she was with Del now, end of story.

***

Kate tried to stay calm as the plane came in to land at Heathrow. She had begged Billy not to fly back to England, she had known that he didn't have much time.

'I'll be alright love,' he kept saying. 'An' if I am poorly over there I won't bloody have to pay like you do here, disgusting, charging people when they're sick.'

She had gone to see his doctor and he had told her that there was nothing he could do, that Billy had refused any treatment at all. He had also added that, in his opinion, it would have been too late to save him anyway.

And his cough had just got worse and worse. In the back of her mind she wondered whether he had just gone home to England to die. There had always been a little bit of him that had never been quite there in Australia with them. He had been fine while they had worked their way up to where they were now but recently he had started talking a lot about the old days, the old places. When West Ham had won the F.A. Cup two years ago he had been beside himself that he couldn't be there. Since then the business had really taken off, they had three second hand car showrooms now and he'd made it back to England for the World Cup. But only just.

Kate felt free in Queensland. Free of all the pain in the past and there were so many immigrants who were now just like her and had no parents to support them. She had seemed to make friends much more easily, it was as if her life had started again and she had watched Jimmy grow. Tanned and healthy, making friends and spending all his time outdoors. He had got on so well at school too and now already he had done a year at university in Sydney. *Her* son, at university, she was so proud. Of course she had missed him, there had been an empty space inside ever since he had left but she was working all the time with the business and all the other interests she had. She had even learned to swim and play tennis. Kate hadn't told Jimmy that his dad was ill so he had been shocked when he had come home last

Christmas and seen him, thin and gaunt. He had been so angry then.

'Why didn't you tell me mum, he's not going to die is he?'

There had been a lot of shouting, it hadn't been a good time. Billy just refused to discuss it with either of them.

Tears came to her eyes as she remembered the wonderful last Christmas they had spent in Churchill Street, she almost laughed out loud but ended up spluttering.

Auntie Molly patted her on the arm. 'We'll soon be down Kate, not long now. I know you don't like landings.'

'I was just thinking about that last Christmas in Churchill Street,' Kate smiled weakly. 'Do you remember that ferret running up your legs and the tree falling over?'

'Yes dear. It belonged to Old Bones didn't it, smelly old man.'

'He was a good man though Molly. I was quite upset when I heard he'd died. I want to see them all in Churchill Street while we're here, especially Greta.'

Tears suddenly erupted from her eyes, and panic seized her suddenly. She thought of her friend Greta and her healing hands and how much she needed them now. Auntie Molly squeezed her arm.

'I – I don't know how I'm going to live without him Molly.'

The plane banked sharply and Kate gasped. She tried to concentrate on the mundane piped music that always accompanied landings and gripped Molly's hand even more tightly. Molly. What would they have done without her? She certainly couldn't have coped with this on her own. And Jimmy, he would be waiting for them at the airport. She was dreading what lay ahead but her heart warmed at the thought of seeing her son again. She forced herself to stop crying, there would be time for that later. An empty time, she thought, for the rest of her life. Because there had only ever been Billy, she had never loved another man. It hadn't always been easy but eventually they had had a gentle yet passionate marriage and she knew he felt the same. Now it was almost over and she would carry on because she had no choice but there would never, ever be another man in her life.

It seemed an age but finally they had collected their bags and had cleared passport control and customs.

'I can't believe we're really back in England Kate,' said Molly, 'I wish it wasn't in these circumstances though.'

Kate gasped as she saw Billy running towards them, the years melted away. She was sure it was him. The shock stunned her whole body and then she realised that it was her son. Just for a second she had thought - Jimmy looked so much like his dad.

And then, Jimmy had held her so tightly she thought she might break.

'How is he?' she asked, as they moved towards the exit.

‘Not good mum but he’ll be pleased to see you. We’ll just dump the cases at the hotel and get to the hospital. I think that’s best.’

How am I going to get through this, Kate wondered as panic almost engulfed her again. She stumbled and Jimmy held her arm.

‘You’ll be alright Kate,’ said Auntie Molly. ‘We’re here for you.’

‘I know,’ said Kate, smiling gratefully at both of them, ‘you always are.’

***

Billy couldn’t quite open his eyes but he was thinking as clear as a bell. He could hear bustling sounds in the background like the crackling on the radio. God, he thought, I’d love one last fag. He couldn’t feel his body. Everything seemed to be concentrated in his head. It was like his body was lost and he just couldn’t find it. But he didn’t mind. It didn’t seem to matter anymore. And, almost like a slide show with accompanying fireworks, the pictures started coming. He knew what that meant. His mum was smiling at him and tickling his toes. First day at school, crying, hiding behind her skirts and closing his eyes. If you closed your eyes no-one could see you.

His dad. Stinking of whisky and perfume but it wasn’t his mum’s perfume. Fast forward. Bastard. The belt, hanging on the doornail, that fear was worse than the bombs. The sun shone for the first time in his life the day his father had left home.

The crackling was louder now in his head but the pictures kept coming. Quite scary, he thought. Not knowing what's going to come next. But exciting too. He discovered that he could move forward or hold the pictures as long as he wanted, he was in control. This was a bad bit, Evacuation. His mum crying. Waving his hankie out of the train window, tears running down his face. It had toughened him up though. Fields and trees, what did he want with them?

Kate. Her smile. He knew straightaway that he loved her, that was it. Not easy though, her pain became his pain and here was Jimmy, his son, his life, his little football mate. In his head he sang '*I'm Forever Blowing Bubbles*' and they were back in the Chicken Run together. He could feel the skinny little legs and the warmth of his son's body as he sat on his shoulders. Fast forward to his little girl. No, don't move on . She was beautiful, Dawn, she deserves to stay a bit longer. Everyone crying and following the tiny coffin of grief. And then, from somewhere, the big white ship hooting, sunshine and Australia. Warm, lazy days.

So why was he so desperate to move on quickly? To miss what other people would think was the best bit of his life. The bit where he got to make money and have nice stuff and where the sun shone all day, he knew why.

Because he wanted to come home, to the *Kings Head* and to all his mates, still there, holding up their glasses and Kate, running towards him and smiling. How much he had loved her. He felt a moment of regret, that he had never really told her that.

Sorry love, he tried to say but I can't hold on any longer. Told you we shouldn't have bloody gone to

Australia, ain't my fault. And the pictures were fading now, the sounds and crackles disappearing. But he could still see Geoff Hurst, running up the wing. They think it's all over. Well, it is now.

4

Reach out I'll be there – Four Tops

This was like being in the middle of a nightmare, Jimmy thought. They'd ended up getting caught in the rush hour from the airport. In the end he had been left with the bags to take to the hotel and his mum and Auntie Molly had carried straight on to the hospital. He threw the bags in to their room and then quickly went to his for a wash. I just have to get through this, he whispered to himself. I have to get through it and look after mum. His eyes were drawn to the drawer where he had put the note from his dad. He opened it quickly and took the envelope out. On the front it just said 'TO BE OPENED BY JIMMY ONLY. YOU'LL KNOW WHEN.' What was that supposed to mean? He put it back quickly, he needed to get to the hospital as soon as he could. The doctor had said that his dad had a few days left but Jimmy wasn't so sure. Please, he prayed to a God that he didn't even believe existed, please, let my mum get there in time.

He quickly changed his shirt, it was hot out there today, though he had scarcely noticed until now. Jimmy ran down the stairs and headed for the tube. He thought that he had planned for the worst thing, in his head but it was the worst thing, and he hadn't.

He was taken to a small room that smelt of peppermints and smoke. There were four threadbare armchairs and in one of them sat his Auntie Molly. She was crying softly, Jimmy didn't know what to do.

'Is he -?' His great auntie nodded. 'Your mum's sitting with him Jimmy. Go and see her, I'm alright. They're bringing me a cup of tea.'

Jimmy suddenly felt a wave of pain washing through him. Not just for himself, his dad and his mum. For Auntie Molly. She had always looked after them all, sometimes he had hated her, especially when she had made him wash about ten times a day when he had been a little kid, but she had never faltered in her support for them all. He had never seen her cry before and who did she have to look after her? No-one. Her husband had died during the war and she had never looked at another man, tears rolled down Jimmy's cheeks as he put his arms around her. She clung to him for a few seconds and then pushed him away.

'Go on Jimmy. Go and see your mum and tell her he said nice things. You know, when you last spoke to him. She's so upset he died alone.'

A nurse had come in with a cup of tea while they had been talking. 'Can I just say,' she said, as she put the cup on the table, 'and I say this to everyone who doesn't get here in time. Often patients actually choose to die alone. Usually when the relatives leave the room, that's when they go. I know I'm a bit fanciful but I think it's their last act of love.'

'Hmm, well, thank you for the tea dear, not sure my niece would agree with you though.'

'Sorry,' said the nurse, leaving the room. 'I know you've come a long way, it must be awful for you.'

Jimmy sat next to his mum by the bed. She was holding his dad's lifeless hand. Jimmy wished she would cry or scream or anything, she just didn't speak. He couldn't stop crying but it helped him to look at his dad. He looked peaceful and the sun was shining warmly on his face, a soft breeze blew in from the open window.

'He's at peace now mum. No more pain.'

'Did he say anything Jimmy, you know when you talked to him earlier?' She sounded very calm.

'He said how much he loved you and he didn't regret anything,' he said softly, remembering Molly's words.

She smiled wistfully. 'That doesn't sound like him,' she said. 'What else did he say?'

Jimmy squeezed her hand. 'Said he wanted his ashes scattered at Upton Park. Then he told me to piss off,' he laughed through his tears.

'That's more like it. Don't you dare tell Molly that those were his last words,' she said. And then her body began to heave and tremble. And she wept.

***

Back in the hotel, Molly was fussing around and criticising everything. She was really starting to get on Jimmy's nerves. She was like that Auntie Molly. One minute you loved her and the next you could throttle her. He tried to stay calm.

'I think they could have done more for him,' she was saying. 'I'm sure they could have kept him alive a bit longer just until we got there.'

His eyes met his mum's. She shot him a warning look and put her fingers to her lips.

'And what's this about having his ashes scattered at that dreadful football ground, that's ridiculous. Honestly Kate, you can't agree to that.'

The phone rang at that moment. Jimmy answered it then held it out to his mum. 'It's May mum. May from Churchill Street, for you.'

Molly was still going on about his dad's ashes.

'Look Auntie Molly,' Jimmy snapped. 'It's what he wanted. Loads of people do it, we can just scatter them in front of the chicken run.'

'Well you won't get me going to a football ground, I'm sorry Jimmy but I draw the line at that.'

'You don't have to go,' said Jimmy, trying not to raise his voice. 'I'll do it with his mates. We'll have had the service at the crem, what difference does it make to you?'

They both turned towards Kate as she put the phone down. 'May wants us to stay with them until after the funeral,' she said, tears welling in her eyes. 'I think I'd like that Jimmy.'

'Well, I certainly would rather stay in this comfy hotel,' Molly sniffed.' You two must do what you want. Personally speaking, I can't wait to get back to Brisbane.'

Jimmy could feel a ball of anger careering through his body. It grew and grew until he thought he might explode, he was powerless to stop it. He took two steps towards Molly and began to shout, his voice echoing around the small room. 'My dad died three hours ago

Molly. Now will you please piss off back to Australia right now if that's how you feel, you're doing my fucking head in. You never cared about him so he wouldn't want you here anyway. You never thought he was good enough, why don't you –'

'Jimmy!' his mum exclaimed as he turned on his heel and walked towards the door. 'How dare you be so rude to your Auntie Molly. Come back here and say you're sorry.'

As he slammed the door, Jimmy shouted. 'I'm going for a walk!'

He stood outside the door, slid down the wall and cradled his head in his knees, then he wept.

After a few minutes, the door behind him opened and then he was in his Auntie Molly's arms.

'I'm sorry Jimmy,' she cried, 'I was out of order.' They held on to each other for a long time.

'I shouldn't have shouted at you,' Jimmy said, sniffing. 'We can't be falling out we're family, we need each other.'

'Right,' said Auntie Molly, pulling away from him at last. 'Go on, off you go, you'll feel better if you get a bit of fresh air.'

Jimmy kissed her on the cheek. He had never kissed her before.

***

'Thank you so much for letting us stay May. It's been so much nicer than being in that hotel.'

Kate sat at the table in May Pattinson's kitchen.

'It's been lovely having you and Jimmy here,' May smiled at her friend as she poured her another cup of tea. 'You need your old friends around you at times like this. We'll give Billy a good send-off on Friday and you're welcome to stay as long as you like.'

'Jimmy's talking about stopping on for a bit longer. I think I want to get back to Australia, after I've seen everyone of course. I'll pop up and see Greta later today, if that's alright with you.'

May patted her friend's hand. 'She'll be pleased to see you. Old Bones dying really knocked her for six.'

'He was such a smelly old man until he met her,' Kate laughed. 'God May, it just seems like the other day all that was going on. And Maggie, how's Maggie? Jimmy told me she'd met someone else.'

'He's lovely, Winston, a real gentleman. He was a mate of your Billy's, they worked together.'

'Yes I think I remember Billy talking about him.' Tears came to Kate's eyes, every time she spoke his name. Billy, Billy, Billy. It was as if it was the only word in the world that mattered, in her head all the time. It was almost like when she had first fallen in love with him. Her devastation now was as extreme as her happiness had been then. She knew that she would probably cry for him every day of her life. And now, she was being reminded again of his kindness.

He had been really angry at some of the dockers who had refused to speak to Winston just because he was black. Well, she thought, they had certainly learnt themselves in Australia about prejudice. As Billy had said, you just have to keep your head down and rise above it, that was easier said than done. One day, when Jimmy had come home from school for the third day in a row with a battered face, Kate had gone straight round to see the bully's mother.

She remembered that it had been a wet, muggy afternoon as she had stood at the front door and rung the bell, the rain had felt like it was drowning her face. The woman had opened the door, her face bloated, her eyes hard and dark. Before Kate had even opened her mouth the woman had simply spat in her face and told her to get back to England. 'We don't want you poms over here,' she had shouted as she slammed the door. Thank God it had only been a few Aussies who had treated them like that but it had been something that no-one had prepared them for. Now those times were in the past but Kate had never forgotten.

As they were chatting away they barely noticed the police siren. When they heard another and another, they looked at each other.

'This is the Churchill Street I remember,' Kate laughed.

'This is a lot of police cars, even for Churchill Street,' said May seriously. 'What on earth's going on?'

***

Her white friends had started by calling her Coffee, because of the colour of her skin. She didn't seem to mind. 'Better than you calling me a wog or a nigger,' she had said.

The name Coffee soon became Nescaff and now they just called her Nessie, it seemed to suit her. Her real name was actually Hayley, after Hayley Mills the film star and she was the youngest child of Maggie

Tyler, a woman who had changed her life and found peace at last with Nessie's dad Winston.

'Whatcha Nessie.'

'She ain't bad for a girl,' Tonk whispered.

'Ain't joining our gang though,' said Jason quickly. 'No girls remember.'

'Well Jason, we ain't gonna get no-one else in our gang at this rate. There's only you an' me. It's all your bloody rules. No gingers, no blacks, no girls, no-one who don't live in the street.'

'We can't just have anyone Tonk.'

'Oh and I forgot the one about no-one who's bigger than us.'

They laughed together.

'Anyway,' Tonk whispered. '*I* think she's alright so I'm gonna ask her.'

Jason shrugged his shoulders and sighed. 'I hope you two ain't whispering about me,' Nessie smiled. 'An' where are you off to?' she asked as if she wasn't really bothered.

'Nowhere you'd wanna go,' Jason muttered sulkily. 'We're doing man stuff.'

'I can play football you know,' she said.

'It weren't women what won the World Cup Ness,' Tonk laughed. 'Nah, we're just going up the waste. Come wiv us if you like, it ain't gonna be there much longer.'

The three of them looked over towards the waste, the builders had started on the foundations.

'It ain't over yet,' said Jason. 'We'll think of another way to stop 'em.'

'Hey!' Tonk shouted. 'It looks like they've even dug up our den already. *Blistering barnacles*!'

'Will you stop watching that Captain Pugwash thing, can't you be a dalek or something more manly?' Jason shouted as all three began to run towards the noise of the diggers and drills. They ran over to the far end of the waste, in the corner were the remains of their rather neglected den. Bits of wood, bricks and tarpaulin lay scattered around, the earth surrounding it had been freshly dug.

'Hoy!' Tonk shouted at the nearest builder he could see. He stood up and grinned, he was huge. Tonk shrank back a bit behind Jason but Nessie kept right on going until she was stood right in front of the builder. She was only up to his waist and pointed a finger accusingly at him.

'What do you think you're doing?' she shouted. 'That's their den.'

'Well it ain't now is it? Just give up kids, we know it's you that's been nicking bricks an' stuff.'

Another man came up to join him. 'Yeah, get off now kids, this is private property. There's a fence going up tomorrow.'

The first builder spoke again, the drill had stopped. 'We found some bits and pieces in your den. We've put 'em over in the corner, we ain't that heartless you know. So just get your stuff and sod off.' He nudged his mate, whispered something and they both laughed.

'Bastards,' said Tonk under his breath as he started shifting through the stuff the builders had found. The Stanley knife that Del Tyler had given them was there, that was something. And half a packet of fags. Out of the corner of his eye Tonk saw Jason pick up a plank of wood and throw it half-heartedly at the men, they just laughed as they jumped out of the way.

'What's that?' Nessie was looking down at the ground where the plank had been. Lying on top of the freshly dug earth was a bone, quite a large bone. Long with knobbly bits.

'Dog,' said Jason, not looking very interested. 'Big one though.'

'Let's see if there's any more,' said Nessie. They all dug around in the earth for a few moments.

'It feels like...lots of bones,' said Tonk fearfully. '*Jumping jellyfish,* you don't think -'

Nessie stood up quickly. 'Most of 'em are joined together,' she said. 'Hoy!' she ran towards the builders holding the first bone they had found.

The men came running over and moved the earth back with their spades.

'Shit,' said one of them. 'Shit, that's me overtime gone.'

***

'Come on you two, out me way.' Sally bustled into the kitchen carrying bags full of food. 'I need to get your tea started. Are you stopping Del?'

'Nah, group practise tonight Sal.'

Josie, who had been sitting on his knee at the table, got up and stretched. 'Jimmy came round,' she said, 'you just missed him.'

Sally stopped putting the tins in the cupboard. 'Oh, that's a shame,' she said. 'I'd have liked to have seen him, I must pop over to May's. How are they coping, him and Kate?

'Alright I think,' said Josie. 'It's upset you an' all mum hasn't it? Billy dying.'

'He was a good man,' said Sally, tears pricking at the back of her eyes. 'Yeah, it has upset me.'

She remembered back to that night again when her and Billy had been getting passionate on the settee and Julie Tyler had walked in. She wondered, just for a second, what would have happened if her and Billy *had* made love that night. Would it have changed everything?

'Poor Kate,' she whispered and carried on unpacking the bags. 'An' where have those boys got to? They've been out all day.'

As if on cue Chris and Pete appeared at the door on their roller skates.

'Take 'em off outside,' Sally shouted. 'And where's Tonk?'

'Up at the waste I expect,' Del laughed as he stood up, pecked Josie on the cheek and headed for the door. 'Throwing stones at the diggers.'

'I hope they're bloody not,' Sally exclaimed.

No-one was happy about them building two houses on the bit of space at the end of the road but especially the kids. There was nowhere else much for them to play. Victoria Park was a good walk away and there was so much more traffic on the roads now. The coppers had already been round about bricks that had disappeared overnight. Sally loved her three boys but she wouldn't be surprised if they had something to do with it. Well, except Pete.

'They do right,' said Josie. 'We'd have fought tooth and nail if they'd tried to bulldoze our den when we was kids wouldn't we Del?'

'I'm going,' Del laughed. 'I ain't gonna get in to that argument. See youse later. Hey, watch it Tonk, crashing into me like that.'

Sally's youngest son came charging in. He looked as if he had seen a ghost. A police car went past, screeching to a halt, sirens screaming.

'What's going on?' Sally shouted. 'What have you been up to?'

Tonk collapsed onto a chair. 'I can't talk, ain't got no breath.'

'Well, that's a first,' said Josie.

'We found something,' Tonk said quietly as they heard another police car racing past. 'Up on the waste. Me, Jason an' Nessie, we have to go an' talk to the coppers. You've got to come wiv us mum please.' There were tears in his eyes.

Oh, what on earth had they been up to now, Sally thought, why couldn't there ever be a bit of peace in her life?

'Before I come anywhere just tell me, tell me what's going on. What have you done?'

'We've found a skellington,' said Tonk, 'an' it ain't alive.'

5

We Can Work It Out – The Beatles

'We need to talk to everyone in Churchill Street again,' said DCI John Paradise. He took a bite from his bacon roll as he spoke slowly to his team. 'Forensics have confirmed that it was a murder, that's why we're all here, fractured skull caused by a heavy blunt instrument. Now remember lads, this all happened a long time ago, about ten years and my gut instinct tells me it's someone local. I think we need to concentrate most on the people who lived here then.'

'No I.D. yet then guv?' asked one of the Murder Team.

'Give us a chance, it's only been four hours but no, not yet and no-one reported missing at that time. Not in this area anyway and none that fits the description. We might get somewhere with dental records, he'd lost a few teeth.'

One of the detectives laughed. 'Well, if he was a local, he'd have lost them in a punch-up probably.'

'Dunno Doug,' John Paradise laughed. 'He was a big man. I think he could have looked after himself, whoever he was.'

He began handing out sheets of information to his men. 'Right, get out there lads. Let's find out who this bugger was. Charlie, you go and interview everyone in Churchill Street to start with. The rest of you get round your snouts and start sniffing, amazing what they'll remember when you flash a fiver at 'em. Everyone back here at eight in the morning, we might have some news about the dental checks by then.'

The team all filed out, they weren't in any rush. The body had been there for ten years, it wasn't as if there was a hot trail to follow.

John Paradise stood looking out of the window. Plaistow, his patch. He hadn't even been a detective ten years ago but he *had* been here and something was niggling in his mind. 1955. He was sure that was the year. It had been around Christmas time. Something had happened near Churchill Street, he couldn't think what it was but he had a feeling it could be relevant. He made his way quickly to the records office to check *everything* as he always did. Everything that had happened that year and the years either side of it until he found what it was that was nagging in his brain. He knew it would be there somewhere. By the end of the day he probably wouldn't have got his murderer but he would know the victim and then the fun would really begin.

***

'I thought I'd escape from all the police activity and come and see you Greta.'

Greta smiled but looked tense. 'You've not come back at a good time Kate. This skeleton is going to cause a great deal of upset.'

Kate sat in Greta's house in a cosy chair in the sitting room. 'I can't believe your house looks exactly how it was before the fire,' she whispered to her old friend.

'Oh, the shell was still left,' said Greta, pouring Kate a cup of tea. 'It was mainly the roof. That was completely destroyed.'

It had been a tearful reunion. Greta had helped Kate so much before they had gone to Australia, she had changed her life.

'You look so much better than when you left here,' Greta said. 'I know this is a dreadful time for you and Billy was so young, but it was his time. Nothing can change that you know.'

'Are you not going to move Greta, now that Bones has died?'

'No Kate, he's still here. Oh I know he's still everywhere to me but he enjoyed his time living in this house and we met so late in life, I just want to hold on to it. When I sit in this room I can still feel him, smell him – almost touch him.' She laughed, suddenly. 'I made him wash twice a day after we moved in together. Remember how he used to smell?'

'And that ferret,' Kate found herself laughing too. 'What was his name? I don't know who smelt worse!'

'Chuck,' Greta laughed, 'he was named after Chuck Berry, he didn't live that long. Run over by a number 147 bus. I must admit, I didn't miss *him* much.'

'And Bones, how did he - you didn't say a lot in your letter.'

'I've not talked about it Kate and you must never say anything. In the papers it just said he was found in the river, washed ashore at Tilbury. That he was drunk and must have fallen in.'

Kate stared intently into her friend's eyes. 'But you don't believe that?'

Greta shook her head. 'No, I don't. He hadn't had a drink since his daughter died forty years before. He'd left her on her own to go to the pub and she choked on a sweet, he never forgave himself. There was no reason why he would have started drinking again. Not unless he was forced to.'

'But why would anyone –?'

'I don't know why, but I'm too old now to try and find out, my instinct tells me that it would be very dangerous if I did. He's crossed over and I can't bring him back whatever I do.'

Kate held the old lady's hand and squeezed it. She wondered whether her psychic friend was going a bit senile. No-one would have wanted to harm Bones.

'There are people out there who let the evil come through,' Greta was saying. 'They'll always be around Kate,' she sighed. 'Anyway, please don't repeat anything I've told you, let's talk about happier things. Tell me about Australia.'

'I love it,' said Kate simply. 'Oh, it was hard at first. You know, fitting in but once they realised we were there to work we got on alright. I don't know how it's going to be now without -'

Greta stroked Kate's arm gently. 'But I will go back. I feel it's my home now, it just feels right and I've made some good friends.'

'And Jimmy? He seems to have done well.'

'Yes,' Kate smiled. 'Oh, it's not just that he's got into university, he's still the same Jimmy inside. I know he wasn't very kind to you when he was little.'

'That's all in the past now,' Greta laughed. 'It was all in their imaginations. I'm glad he's doing well, he's the only one out of that little gang who seems to have prospered.'

'Yes,' Kate's eyes widened. 'I can't believe that Legs, I mean Clive, is in prison. It just seems so out of character and poor Josie, having her face cut like that. Jimmy's had a bit of a shock coming back to it all. Thank God we left when we did.'

'Yes,' Greta nodded. 'You definitely did the right thing there Kate. Well, I've told you that time and time again in my letters and maybe I should have told you about the bad things that were happening. You just sounded so happy, I didn't want to spoil that for you.'

Kate took a sip of her tea. 'And now this skeleton. You must know who it is.'

Greta gazed out of the window. 'I think I can guess,' she said.

***

'We've got a name,' John Paradise announced. 'Dental records have confirmed it. Some of you may remember him. Mick Tyler.'

He had guessed long before that confirmation. He had looked through all the records. Rumours that he had started the fire at Greta Broncowiez's house and that he hadn't been seen since. John Paradise had been in touch with the Merchant Navy pool and the shipping companies. Mick Tyler had been on a cargo ship out of

Tilbury from January 1956 for five months and had signed off in May. It fitted the timescale perfectly.

At six o'clock the previous day a dentist in Poplar had confirmed that he had extracted five damaged teeth from a Michael Tyler of Churchill Street at various times up to January 1955. They matched exactly the empty sockets on the skeleton. Forensics were working on some fibre samples they had found at the scene but John Paradise knew that he had found his victim.

There was some muttering around the room from those who did remember him.

'Don't think there'll be much grieving for him,' said one.

'I've questioned Maggie Tyler this afternoon with Charlie,' John Paradise continued. 'She's saying that she hasn't seen him since December 1955.' He looked around the room at some puzzled faces.

'So why didn't she report him missing then guv?' asked a young detective.

Another laughed out loud. 'You obviously didn't know him.'

John Paradise held up his hand. 'Alright, that's enough. Mick Tyler wasn't the nicest of men but we've still got to find out who wanted him dead. His wife had as good a reason as any, he was always beating her up. He did a lot of time for burglary, stolen goods and GBH. In and out of the Scrubs when he was younger, they had six kids. One of them, Julie, died after a botched abortion. Sent him a bit mad and he set fire to a house, we could never prove it of course. He thought the woman who lived in the house, Greta Broncowiez, was the abortionist. She wasn't, but as I say, he just went mental. He was seen running when the house was well alight. We think he believed that he'd killed Greta. As it happens she was safe but he didn't know that. From there we know that he got a job on a cargo ship out of Tilbury, the last entry in his seamans discharge book would have been May 28th 1956 when he signed off.

'That's when he must have come back here then,' said Charlie.

'Yeah and I'm sure he would have gone straight home. There's something Maggie's not telling us. I've asked her not to say anything. She swore she wouldn't even tell the kids yet. That the skeleton is Mick Tyler. She doesn't seem bothered. In fact I'd say she looked quite relieved. We'll get there lads but I don't want the name getting out until Saturday. There's a big funeral in Churchill Street tomorrow, Billy Potter. Used to live there and knew Mick well. It'll be a good opportunity to watch and listen before we release the name.'

'How long has Maggie been living with that nigger?' Charlie asked.

'Yeah, she's been with him a long time,' said another. 'It could have been him.'

'I don't believe you lot,' said John Paradise angrily. He had seen a massive increase in racial tension in the last ten years. Why did politicians never think things through? Oh, we'll just get people over here from the colonies to clean the toilets and drive the buses. Tell them everyone wants them here, just don't tell them about the fucking weather. Well, it wasn't the weather that had caused the problems and it had infiltrated into the police, this prejudice. His own mates and the young ones, losing their girlfriends to young black guys. Out there on the streets, that's where they got their own back. He sighed.

'Seriously guv,' said Charlie. 'I'm not just being prejudiced. The room filled with laughter. 'I'm being rational.' That made them laugh even more.

'You have got a point Charlie though I do doubt your motives. Winston would have defended Maggie if Mick *did* turn up at the house and started on her. Watch him for me Charlie, but don't talk to him, not yet.'

Charlie nodded. John Paradise turned towards two other detectives.

'Scottie and Doug. I want you to be at the crem for the funeral service, you're not from this area so they shouldn't recognise you. If anyone asks, you worked with Billy down the docks and you wanted to pay your respects. They'll all be in *The Kings Head* afterwards and they'll all be talking about it so see what you can pick up, just keep watching and listening. Just see if anyone is acting suspiciously or mentioning any names.'

'And I'd give you ten minutes at most before they suss out you're coppers,' Charlie laughed.

The murder team began to look a little more lively, it was a result of sorts. Now they knew what to do and how to go about it.

'The rest of you, we're leaving Churchill Street alone tomorrow but we'll have a car there all day, just watching. And remember, we probably can't blame this one on the Krays.'

There was some laughter around the room.

'Give him a bloody medal when we do find him,' said one of the team. 'Mick Tyler was a bastard.'

***

Jimmy was sitting in May and George's kitchen. His mum and May were looking at old photos. Funny, he couldn't remember George taking photos but he certainly had. Every few seconds, his mum kept saying, 'Ooh look Jimmy there you are.' They were all black and white of course. Grainy, blurry photos and quite a few of him and his dad wearing their West Ham scarves.

'You can keep that one if you like Jimmy,' said May kindly.

'Thank you May,' he swallowed and bit his bottom lip. It still felt strange calling her May instead of Mrs. Pattinson.

'Oh, I've upset you both now,' she said.

Jimmy put his arm around his mum as tears slid down her face.

'No. I want to see them,' Kate said, 'we *need* to see them.' She looked at Jimmy. 'And we're not going to listen to Auntie Molly, Jimmy. Your dad *will* have his ashes scattered at Upton Park and I'll be there even if she won't, that team meant a lot to him.'

'Tonk goes to watch them every week,' said May.

She saw the puzzled expression on Kate's face.

'Our grandson. Sally and our Joe's lad. Funny how things work out isn't it? Me and Sally almost related.

He didn't stop with her long, Joe. I suppose taking on someone else's kids isn't easy but we were disappointed with him. He hardly ever comes to see his own son now, too ashamed I think.'

'Good job you're here then May.'

'I met Tonk,' said Jimmy, looking up from the photograph album. 'He's quite a character.'

May sighed. 'He's kept us going, Jimmy, with everything that's gone on, he's a lovely lad. Mind you I suppose I would say that wouldn't I?' She smiled.

They heard footsteps coming up the path. The door flew open.

'We were just talking about you,' she grinned. 'Good day at school love?'

'Yeah, nan and I'm starving. Whatcha Jimmy.' He threw his cap on the table and ripped his satchel off his back.

Jimmy smiled at his mum and his memory slipped back through the years again, after school. Sugar sandwiches, he mouthed to her and she laughed.

'Tonk, I want you to meet one of my best friends. This is Kate, Jimmy's mum.'

Tonk put his hand out and shook his mum's firmly. 'Pleased to meet ya missus,' he said 'and 'er - sorry about your trouble.'

Tonk helped himself to three slices of bread from the cupboard. He turned to Jimmy. 'If you're still here when the season starts,' he said, 'you can come down the chicken run wiv me an' me mates if you like.'

'Thanks Tonk, I might just do that.'

‘And where are you off now young man?’ May laughed as Tonk headed for the door.

‘We’ve got a murder to solve nan. The coppers ain’t never gonna find out who done it.’

Jimmy laughed. ‘How do you know he was murdered?’

Tonk shrugged his shoulders. ‘Didn’t dig an ‘ole an’ bury himself did he?’

‘Good point,’ said Jimmy. ‘Wish I was nine again, I’d come and help you.’

‘See ya, wouldn’t wanna be yer,’ Tonk shouted as he slammed the door.

Jimmy smiled at his mum then looked at May. ‘Think I’ll just get up to my room for a bit if that’s OK.’

May nodded. ‘You just make yourselves at home,’ she said. ‘Clive would want you to have his room,’ she sniffed. ‘He’ll be out of prison soon Jimmy.’

‘I need to go and see him May,’ said Jimmy, ‘After all this. I can’t believe -’

‘He won’t see anyone Jimmy, only me and his dad, but I’ll ask him. He might talk to you, he must feel so guilty.’

Jimmy sighed. ‘Legsy – I mean Clive - wouldn’t hurt a fly deliberately, we all do daft things sometimes especially if we’ve been drinking. I know that.’ He had thought it best not to mention the drugs.

He had left May and his mum then to go upstairs. He kept thinking back ten years as he opened the top drawer of the chest and saw the letter his dad had left for him. Staring at the shaky, childish writing brought tears to his eyes. His dad had written this when he was dying. Jimmy tried to hold back the tears but they flooded his eyes and dropped, smudging the letters on the envelope.

YOU'LL KNOW WHEN TO OPEN THIS. Those were the words. How would he know? The envelope was simply addressed to 'THE TOP COPPER AT PLAISTOW STATION.'

What the hell had his dad been mixed up in? Did it have anything to do with the discovery of the skeleton? Jimmy stuffed it quickly into the drawer with his underpants, sat down on the bed and wept, for his dad, for himself and for what had to be faced tomorrow.

6

This Old Heart of Mine – Isley Brothers

There was a knock at the door, the front door. That didn't happen very often these days. Sally sighed. She had just finished her stint at the factory. All the boys were out, Josie and Del had gone to the shops for her and a freshly brewed cup of tea was waiting on the table. She had just been looking forward so much to sitting down and putting her feet up.

'Alright, alright,' she shouted as she made her way through the tiny hall.

It was the police. Well, it would be wouldn't it. Not just a policeman though. In front of him stood Tonk, Nessie and Jason.

'Caught these three interfering with a crime scene,' said the policeman. Sally glared at her son. He just grinned back.

'We ain't done nothing wrong mum,' he said. 'We was only trying to help.'

As Sally looked at them all a memory crashed through her mind. She remembered when someone else had brought three children to the door. Ten years ago. Josie, Jimmy and Legs. They'd all been out on the waste only it had been one o'clock in the morning and it hadn't been the police who had brought them home, it had been Jimmy's dad. Billy. The man she had never forgotten. The man they were cremating tomorrow. She felt a catch in her throat and her eyes filled up. He had never loved her, she had known that but she had never quite been able to get him out of her head. Her relationship with Joe, Tonk's dad, hadn't lasted long. Oh, she had wanted it to. She just wanted to be like everyone else really. Every man she had loved, except Billy, had just left her with babies and she honestly didn't know how all that had happened. She felt an incredible sense of self-pity trembling through her body. Always the same when one of the kids caused her grief.

'Don't cry mum,' Tonk was panicking. 'I'm sorry.' He touched her arm and she shook it off.

'Seems to me,' she sniffed and stared straight into the policeman's eyes. 'You should be out trying to find out who it was that was buried there an' who bloody killed 'im, not wasting your time rounding up little kids.'

'I ain't a little kid -'

'Shut up Tonk and get inside. I ain't taking the others, I've got enough of me own to cope with.'

'Actually, Mrs – no, sorry it's not Mrs is it. *Miss* Evans. We could have done your son for assault. He knocked my helmet off.'

Sally laughed. She couldn't help herself.

'No he never,' said Nessie. 'It weren't him.'

Jason slid behind Nessie. 'Weren't me neither.'

Nessie turned and pointed an accusing finger. 'You liar Jason,' she shouted.

'Well it was only a little stone,' he mumbled.

'Right,' said Sally. 'I'll have words with Tonk but I can't keep him inside. He's a boy.'

'Boys are like dogs my mum says,' said Jason cheerily. 'We have to be put outside.'

Sally slammed the door and marched through to the kitchen. The pot of tea had gone cold.

***

'Alright Jimmy?' Josie squeezed his arm as he moved past towards the funeral cortege. He smiled down at her. The whole street had turned out to say good bye to his dad. He had a flashback then. It was the same as when they had left for Australia. Everyone had gathered in the street. He looked across the road briefly and saw the unmarked cop car. He didn't know why they bothered. Everyone round here recognised a copper whatever he wore or drove around in.

His mum clung to his arm tightly, she had been very brave all the way through this. He smiled at her and saw her lips starting to quiver. 'We need to hold it together now for dad,' he said gently.

She nodded. 'I know. I don't think I realise yet, that he's gone. I think it'll happen when I get back home. It's not fair this Jimmy, he was so young. I just wanted to grow old with him, that's all.'

They slid into the funeral car and Jimmy passed her a hankie before putting his arm around her shoulders. He saw her glance towards the police car. 'They have to try and spoil everything don't they?' she said angrily. 'You'd think they could just leave us in peace for today.'

'Do you know who it is mum?' Jimmy asked. 'Who was murdered?'

Should he tell her about the note his dad had left behind? No, not now, he thought. He had been so tempted to open the letter but something had stopped him. He would have a word with George. He would know what he should do with it. And whether this had been what his dad had meant, this skeleton from ten years ago.

'No love, I don't know. Let's just get through this. Molly's meeting us at the crem.'

***

Jimmy could feel his voice shaking as he stood up to speak. He didn't much like standing up in front of people. The tutors at university had recognised that and tried to help him. He took a deep breath.

'I just want to say a few words, about my dad.' He cleared his throat. 'He wasn't a sloppy, sentimental man and he wouldn't have wanted a lot of fuss but he would have loved that he ended up here in Plaistow. He enjoyed Australia but this was always his home. He never forgot it and he never let me forget it either. Every Sunday morning he'd wake me up to tell me how West Ham had got on.'

He stopped and looked around the room. They were all here, his dad's mates. All the people from his childhood. Loopy, Arthur, his dad's drinking partners. All the neighbours, all his football pals and workmates from the docks. It was almost as if Billy Potter had never been away to the other side of the world for ten years. There were plenty of tears but also some smiles at his last remark. Yes, Jimmy thought. My dad would have wanted me to make them laugh.

'He was a good man, most of the time,' Jimmy smiled. 'He once said to me in Australia that all this poncing around swimming and sunbathing was OK but it just wasn't the same as having a pint in *The Kings Head*, or watching West Ham score at Upton Park. He was an uncomplicated man, just liked simple pleasures and he believed in things. Even if I didn't always agree with him, he was always true to himself.'

Jimmy could feel himself slipping away, the words choking him. He looked at his mum, she was smiling through her tears.

'I just want to try and say, if I manage to get it out,' he tried to laugh, 'that I'm really going to miss him. May gave me a photo yesterday.' He smiled at her across the field of sad faces. 'It was me and my dad in our football scarves, just as we were setting off for a match. It just reminded me of one of my best memories. How proud I used to feel of him when I was a little kid and we were walking to football together. There was always crowds of people and he always held my hand. I can still feel his hand -'

Jimmy stopped, that was enough. He coughed.

'Anyway,' he said. 'You're all welcome back at May and George's and then to *The Kings Head*. We're going to give him a good old cockney send-off. But before that I know he would have loved it if everyone just sang a chorus of '*I'm Forever Blowing Bubbles*' before we leave. He loved West Ham United. They were in his soul and every bone in his body.'

The funeral directors looked bemused as everyone started singing.

***

'That was lovely Jimmy,' a weeping Maggie Tyler flung her arms around him as he walked in to May and George's kitchen. Instinctively, he recoiled but when he realised that she didn't stink of booze like she used to, he hugged her back. 'Your speech was just right love. I know you're all posh now but you're still the same little kid. You was always the sensible one.'

'I was the sensible one mum,' Del came over, grinning. 'It was Jimmy that always led me astray.'

Josie came up behind Del and put her arms around his waist. 'Well, from what I remember, it was me that kept you all in order. Things would have been a lot worse if I hadn't been there.'

She looked lovely in black, Jimmy thought. Suddenly, he wanted her arms around *his* waist. He didn't want to be having these feelings about her but he couldn't seem to stop them. Somehow, the scar on her face made her more vulnerable. He wanted to look after her, for her never to be hurt again. Still, he thought, at least his old pal seemed to be treating her well. His old tearaway mate. He wished for a moment that *he* was Del. That had certainly never happened before.

He moved away towards the front room where his mum, Auntie Molly and all the ladies were drinking sherry and talking about the old days. Memories drifting through the conversation like old smoke rings. Cosy and warm recollections, it made him feel like he belonged. Families, friends, dead and alive, they were all getting a mention. May came towards him and patted him on the back.

'Have you got a drink Jimmy? I know you men will probably be off to the pub soon but there's loads of food in the kitchen. Help yourself love.'

'Thank you May and thank you for doing all this.'

'No-one ever forgot your dad,' said May. 'You've all been missed.'

Jimmy suddenly remembered something. 'Where's George?' he asked her, feeling for the letter inside his pocket. Yes, it was still there.

'Where do you think?' she laughed.

Jimmy struggled to know what she meant and then it came to him. 'In his shed?'

May nodded. 'He was very close to your dad, he's very upset. Looked on him a bit like a substitute son really, he was never like that with our own. Tonk worships the ground he walks on though.' She laughed. 'He often sits in the shed with him when he needs to get away. No, that's where you'll find him this afternoon.'

Jimmy walked out into the garden and knocked quietly on the shed door. George opened it, Jimmy could see that he had been crying.

'Come in lad,' said George. 'It'll be good to talk to you.'

He shook Jimmy's hand and ushered him in to one of two battered old armchairs. The smell of his pipe was comforting.

'I need to talk to you about something George,' he said. 'I need your advice.'

George took a deep breath. 'Yes, I think you do lad.'

‘Do you know about the letter?’ George nodded. ‘Has it got anything to do with the skeleton on the waste?’

‘Yes Jimmy.Yes it has. The body was Mick Tyler. They haven’t announced it officially yet though a lot of people will have guessed. You need to give that letter to the police and prepare yourself for a nasty shock. I think it’s best that I don’t say anymore.’

Jimmy gasped. ‘Del’s dad? Jesus, I remember him. Where is he now? Del?’

‘Maggie’s just taken him home to tell him and all the other kids. It’ll be in the papers tomorrow. I’ll come with you if you want. To the station.’

‘Thanks George but I’d rather do it on my own.’

George got up and took two bottles of beer from a shelf. ‘Well, let’s forget about that now. We’ll have a drink together and remember your old man. I can tell you a few stories now you’ve grown up,’ he laughed.

***

DI Scottie Campbell and DI Doug Richards tried to mingle in *The Kings Head* after the funeral. It soon became pretty obvious to them that some of the locals had guessed who the victim was. They heard his name mentioned several times in hushed tones but not much else.

Of course they had been spotted, they knew that coppers were always recognised round here, but in the few minutes before the landlord had cast his beady eyes their way they had heard a few bits and pieces of information that could be useful. There were a few suspicious mutterings aimed at Winston who was standing quietly at the bar chatting to others who had been to the crem. Maggie, of course, was the butt of a few jokes. How she must have finally got her own back, that sort of thing.

‘It’ll be one of those two,’ said Doug.

‘We don’t even know if she was seeing Winston then. Not definitely anyway,’ muttered Scottie.

‘My bet’s on him.’ Doug glared across the pub at Winston’s back.

‘Careful Doug,’ said Scottie.

‘Sorry mate, I can’t help it. I just hate ‘em.’

Scottie could see the bitterness in his workmate’s eyes. It didn’t help that his girlfriend had just left him for a man whose father had come over from Jamaica on the *Windrush* in 1953. Scottie sighed. He was tiring of being in the police. He wondered if it was too late to start again, to do a job where you met good people. There was just too much hatred everywhere and he couldn’t stand being labelled all the time. Like now. He sensed the hostility and they were right to be angry really, he thought. It had been a funeral, someone they had all been close to and him and Doug were trespassing, invading their territory. Trying to get information about the murder of someone ten years ago who no-one could stand anyway. Sometimes, Scottie thought, none of this made any sense.

He looked over to the far end of the bar and saw his snout watching him intently. He remembered now that *The Kings Head* was his local. The snout was swivelling his eyes towards the lavs, he must know something.

‘Just going for a Jimmy Riddle Doug,’ Scottie whispered, passing him a crumpled pound note. ‘Get us another one in will you.’

He walked past the snout without looking at him and went quickly into the toilets. There was no-one in. This was risky and he was surprised at his snout, he was usually pretty careful. As Scottie undid his zip and stood at a urinal he heard the door opening. There was a slight touch on his back and a voice whispering urgently in his ear.

‘There’s a note in your back pocket with some info. Now just get out both of you or they’re all gonna suss me out. Phone me.’

Scottie resisted the urge to remind his snout who was the boss here, but in the end he decided to go quietly. As he came back into the bar he saw that there was an argument going on between Doug and the landlord. It looked as if it was about to get physical. He pushed his way through and tapped Doug on the shoulder. ‘What’s going on?’

Arthur the landlord turned his face from Doug and stared, almost sincerely, into his eyes.

‘Your mate,’ he said smiling, ‘has just barged into my mate,’ he nodded towards Winston who was stood at the bar, grinning, holding onto an empty beer glass.

‘Now it might not be the custom where you come from sunshine and we have no idea where that might be do we lads?’ The pub erupted with laughter and cheering. ‘But,’ Arthur continued, ‘when we *accidentally* bump into someone and spill their drink we buy ‘em another. It’s just an old cockney tradition.

Now this mate of yours seems to have a problem wiv that.'

Scottie took one look at Doug's face and could see that he was about to erupt. He grabbed him by the shoulders. 'We're going Doug. Right now.' He passed another pound note to Arthur and tried to smile at Winston. 'I'll have to apologise for him mate. Get yourself another beer.'

'Watch him,' the landlord shouted after them. 'There's good cops and bad cops and he ain't a good one.'

As Scottie pushed Doug out into the street, Doug turned on him. 'You should have backed me up in there. I'll have that Winston. I'll have both of 'em.'

Oh shit, thought Scottie.

***

'That was very brave of you Arthur,' Jimmy laughed as he bought himself a pint.

'Brave or stupid,' said George. 'They won't leave you alone now. No more lock-ins.'

'I'll be alright. Clean as a whistle me. Anyway, I'm retiring next month.'

'You've bin saying that for seven years,' George laughed.

Winston appeared next to Jimmy. 'Oh Arthur, you can't leave now. Just when we've become real good mates. I was quite touched by what you said to the copper, man.'

'Fuck off,' said Arthur. 'I just hate them more than I hate you lot that's all. Don't you be thinking I'm soft.'

Winston laughed. 'I'm just so grateful I'm allowed in to your cosy l'il pub Arthur. I'll be indebted to you all my life. You is mah hero.'

'And there's more good news for you Winston,' George chuckled as he lit his pipe. 'They've overturned the 'black ban' at Euston Station. You can go and drive trains now.'

Winston looked up and put his hands together. 'My cup runneth over Lord,' he grinned.

Arthur also raised his eyes to the ceiling. 'I'm coming to Australia wiv you Jimmy,' he growled.

'Ah,' Winston wagged his finger at him. 'The all white policy is changing soon too man. That would be funny Arthur. You get your papers through for Australia and end up for six weeks on a ship full of wogs. Ha ha.' Everyone started laughing then, even Arthur.

'Hey, you ain't allowed to use that word, not when it's about you.'

'Ah, but I live in a free country now. I ain't no slave no more. I must be gone, I have to go beat the drums. It's that time honky.'

He threw his arms around Jimmy. 'You take care man. Your dad was a good guy and don't you ever forget it.' He lowered his voice. 'An' if you need a bit of ganja to get through it all, I'm your man. Well, once the coppers have stopped sniffing around anyway.'

'I like Winston,' said Jimmy to Del as he joined him at the bar. And then he remembered.

'I'm sorry Del,' he spoke softly. 'George just told me. About your dad.'

'How would he know?'

Jimmy realised that he shouldn't have said anything. 'I think one of the coppers let it slip,' he answered quickly.

Del shrugged his shoulders but Jimmy noticed that he had been crying and there were dark shadows around his eyes.

'Winston's been a better dad to me than *he* ever was, he was a bastard Jimmy. I don't wanna talk about it.'

'Bet you gave Winston a hard time at first though,' Jimmy tried to lighten the mood.

'I bloody did an' all,' Del chuckled. 'Still it's worked out alright. I went a bit mad for a bit, you know, after you'd left.'

'You were always a bit mad Del. We all were really but we were just kids.'

Del leant in to Jimmy and whispered urgently in his ear.

'All hell's gonna break loose tomorrer, it'll be in all the papers. About me dad.' He stopped, picked up his pint and downed it in one go.

Jimmy could see that Del's eyes were filling up. He put his arm around his old friend's shoulder but Del shrugged him off.

'He *was* a piece of shite anyway,' said Del. 'Don't know why it's got to me.'

He looked down at his shoes.

Should I tell him about the letter, Jimmy thought. The letter that George didn't tell him anything about. Just that he must take it to the coppers.

'Your dad wouldn't have written that out when he was dying for no reason Jimmy,' George had said. 'You *must* take it to the police.'

George had told him not to say anything to anyone about the letter but, bloody hell, him and Del had been through a lot together when they were kids. The old gang, the old loyalties. Did they ever end? All those times when they were kids and they looked out for each other. Well, most of the time anyway. His mind took him back again to the witch's house. They had been spying on her and he had climbed an apple tree and fallen on to the ground. They had all run in to help him even though they had been really scared of Mrs Broncowiez, the witch. He smiled to himself.

'Jimmy,' George was shouting at him across the bar. 'Your mum's just phoned wondering how long you're going to be. Your Auntie Molly's drunk, she needs your help.'

Everyone laughed.

'Are you sure?' Jimmy laughed. 'Auntie Molly's never been drunk in her life.'

'Well,' said George, grinning, 'apparently, she's singing rude songs.'

'Come on Jimmy,' Del chuckled, grabbing his arm. 'We've got to see this.'

The pub began to empty as the news spread about Auntie Molly and there was a trail of men all wearing black, ties askew, making their way back to Churchill Street.

By the time they got back, Molly was past her best but still trying to hold down a tune.

She livened up again when she saw her great-nephew. 'There's my little Jimmy!' she screamed as he came in to the lounge. She ran haphazardly towards him and fell into his arms. 'He's a little treasure ain't he Kate?' she slurred. Jimmy couldn't suppress a smile. His mum had always told him that she hadn't always talked posh but he couldn't believe it. Well he did now. Cockney Auntie Molly. Well I never.

'Come on everyone,' she shouted and began to sing *'Roll Out The Barrel'* in a very determined way. Soon, everyone was joining in. They didn't have much choice. If she noticed they weren't singing she gave them a sharp prod in the back.

'I'll go an' get me drums,' Del shouted.

May had sat herself down on the piano stool.

'May!' Auntie Molly exclaimed. She put her arm around May's shoulders. 'You're my friend,' she slurred, squeezing her shoulders and kissing her on the cheek. 'Now give us a good old East End tune. 'What about '*Henry VIII?*' We can have a little dance an' all. The Beatles ain't got nothing on us.'

As they all began to sing and dance Jimmy looked around the room. Where had his mum gone?

He found her in the kitchen sitting on her own with a cup of tea. Jimmy sat down beside her and squeezed her hand.

'I can't believe Auntie Molly in there,' he laughed. 'How did she get like that?'

His mum smiled. 'I think it was Tonk. He kept slipping more sherry into her glass when she wasn't looking.' She sighed. 'I'm so angry Jimmy,' she said.

'Why did she have to wait until Billy died to get drunk? He would have loved it. He often used to say she should loosen up a bit. He would have laughed his head off.'

They heard a tinkling of glass and a loud thump coming from next door as the music and singing faded. There were a few oooh's and ahhh's and plenty of laughter as well.

They heard May's voice. 'Put her in Clive's bed, she'll be alright. And don't forget to leave a glass of water and two aspirins.'

Del began to play his drums.

Jimmy saw a tear running down his mum's cheek. He wiped it away with his finger and she smiled sadly at him. 'Why can't he be here Jimmy? He'd have had such a good time.'

'Well, perhaps he's watching from somewhere, somewhere where the beer's free.'

'Do you really believe that?'

'No mum, sorry.'

'It's alright, I don't either. Well, we've given him a good send-off. Tomorrow, we start again.'

Jimmy doubted that tomorrow would be a better day what with all the dead body stuff going on. Laughter and tears. That's what you get if you live in the East End, his gran had always said to him. Ho hoped there was a God, it was an outside chance, but for his dad's sake and his gran. She would have been made up to see him again.

7

Wild Thing – The Troggs

'*Plundering porpoises*, it's all happening out there mum!' Tonk came crashing in at the back door. 'Even the telly cameras are here. Good job it's summer holidays, don't think I'd have time to go to school today.'

'Oh I think you would,' Sally laughed, putting a bowl of cornflakes in front of him. 'Well, it's just been on the news. It was definitely Mick Tyler, your skeleton, and obviously it *was* murder.'

'They'll be looking for a weapon then,' said Tonk. 'That'll be our job today.'

Sally sighed. 'Just don't go getting in the coppers' way. I don't want 'em bringing you home again.'

Tonk went racing upstairs and reappeared with a notebook and pencil. He sat down at the table next to Pete.

'You're clever Pete,' he said, passing the book to his older brother. 'We need to write some clues down. Mum?' He turned and faced Sally. 'Tell me all you know about Mick Tyler please.'

'I've only got twenty minutes before I go to work,' she grumbled as she got up and made her way over to the sink. Tonk followed her and guided her back to her chair.

'We'll do the washing-up when you've gone to work mum. Chris, make mum another cuppa.' Chris, who was heading for the door, turned round and stuck two fingers up at his little brother. 'I'm going to see what's going on,' he said. 'Ain't got time to make tea.'

'Well be careful what you say to reporters,' Sally shouted after him. 'In fact don't say nothing at all. No winding them up.'

'I'll do the tea,' said Pete getting up and putting the kettle on. 'Go on mum. What was he like?'

'He wasn't very nice,' said Sally. 'That's about all I can say really. He used to hit Maggie a lot an' he was always drunk.'

'She could have done it then,' said Tonk, beginning to scribble on his first page.

'How could a woman have dragged a body all the way up to the waste?' said Pete. 'She'd have needed some help. Come on mum, there must be more you can tell us. Did he have loads of enemies?'

'Not really,' said Sally. 'No-one liked him but I don't think anyone hated him enough to kill him.'

'Well, someone did,' said Tonk. 'It might take us some time but we'll find out who.'

'He was in prison quite often,' said Sally. 'Maybe he upset someone in there. Anyway, enough of all this, I'm going to work. If I can fight me way through coppers and reporters. They seem to forget that we all have our own lives to lead.' She ruffled Tonk's hair. 'Please try not to get in to trouble. Pete, keep an eye on him.'

Pete sighed. 'Well, I was going to the library mum -'

'Just wait till Josie gets back from work. She's been on nights so she'll be here in an hour.'

Pete nodded and began to trudge upstairs. Just as Sally was setting off for work, Chris and Jason burst through the back door. 'We know who done it!' Jason gasped. 'They've took Maggie – I mean Mrs Tyler away - and Winston.'

'Well she didn't even know Winston when this happened. What are the coppers playing at?' asked Sally angrily.

'Dunno,' said Chris. 'But they're searching the house now.'

Oh dear, Sally thought, here we go again. Another drama in Churchill Street. Raking up the past. She remembered back to that night. The night when Mick Tyler had set fire to Greta's house because he believed she had performed the abortion that had killed his daughter. The shame of that night passed through Sally as it often did. She had known the truth. She had gone with Julie to the abortionist in Green Street who she'd heard was 'safe'. She'd not said anything about it except to George but the guilt sometimes wrapped itself around her and wouldn't let her be happy. It was the price she had to pay.

Despite what she had said to the boys she was sure that the police would find quite a few people who Mick Tyler had upset over the years. She hoped to God that they hadn't arrested Maggie and Winston for his murder. No, they would just be taking them in for questioning, that's all.

***

'Right you two,' John Paradise was furious.

Doug took one look at the guv's narrowing eyes and the grim set of his mouth and took one step back. 'Now why d'you think I've called you in to this very private office of mine?'

Scottie shrugged his shoulders. 'Something to do with the murder guv?'

'Yes. You could say something to do with the murder.' He was holding a small package wrapped in blue plastic in his hand, he threw it straight at them. Scottie ducked but it hit Doug on the left ear.

John Paradise watched the reactions. It didn't take long for him to work it out. Scottie looked completely bemused and vacant. Doug looked like he'd been expecting it. He nodded at Scottie. 'You can go,' he said. 'I'll be down in five minutes to interview Maggie Tyler.' He glared at Doug.

Scottie walked slowly to the door and closed it behind him.

'Guv, I don't know what -' Doug spluttered.

'You don't know what I'm on about? You've got guilt written all over your fucking face.'

Oh shit, Doug thought. The guv rarely used the 'f' word. He knew what this was about.

'Right Doug,' John Paradise had lowered his voice considerably. 'Let's be honest here. We *might* bend the rules a bit sometimes to get our man if we're one hundred per cent sure it was them but we're not sure are we?'

'No guv.'

‘You never, ever do anything like this because you don’t like the colour of a person’s skin. That is abuse of power.’

‘But guv -’

‘No Doug, you are bang out of order here. If I hadn’t had a quick look round before they searched the house - ’

‘But guv, he does do drugs and they *do* kill people.’

‘We’ll get him for the drugs Doug but that is not what this investigation is about. And he’s cleverer than that, Winston. He would have known we’d be sniffing round today. There won’t be anything in that house. No Doug, you’re trying to frame a man for murder because he’s black. That is what I’m objecting to. You’re off the case.’

‘But guv – you can’t do that.’

‘I could do a lot worse believe me. I’m sending you on a drugs course. No-one will know.’

‘But how did *you* know? How did you know that it wasn’t his?’

John Paradise undid the tape and opened the package. ‘Because Doug, this is shite. You’ll learn all about this on your course. Winston isn’t one of the major players in the drugs scene. Just buys it for his mates but he *is* a connoisseur of marijuana. Probably been smoking it since he was a kid in Jamaica and he wouldn’t touch this rubbish with a bargepole.’

He glared at Doug. ‘Now just get out of my sight and Doug,’ he added as his DI walked towards the door. ‘Just like you’ve heard in *‘Z Cars*,’ this conversation never happened.’

***

Jason, Nessie and Tonk stood at the corner of Churchill Street, watching all the action. It was like their little road had been taken over and been turned into a police station. There were coppers everywhere and reporters asking questions.

'We need a base,' said Jason, 'for our operations. I really miss the den already.'

'Me an' all,' Tonk agreed. 'How can we solve all this without somewhere to work from?'

'We need to interview people,' said Nessie. 'We need to prove that me mum and dad didn't do nothing.' She sniffed and wiped her nose on her sleeve. Tonk put his arm around her.

'Yeah, you might get taken into care,' said Jason unsympathetically. 'If they've both been charged wiv murder.'

'Shut up turd,' said Tonk, slapping him around the head. 'Don't worry Nessie,' he said kindly. 'They won't take you into care anyway. Del's old enough to look after you.'

'Right,' said Jason. 'We need to talk to old people, people who remember Mick Tyler.'

'Just that name gives me the creeps,' said Nessie. 'Del might remember some stuff about him.'

Just then they saw Jimmy Potter coming out of May and George's house.

'Hey! Jimmy!' Tonk shouted, running over to him. 'You got a minute?'

Jimmy looked to Tonk like he was in a hurry.

'Not really mate. I've got to go somewhere.'

‘Where you going then?’ asked Jason.

‘None of your business,’ Jimmy laughed.

Tonk produced the notebook and pencil from his back pocket. ‘We need some info about Mick Tyler. They’ve just arrested Nessie’s mum an’ dad. We have to sort it an’ you knew him. You might remember something.’

‘They haven’t been arrested, just taken in for questioning. I’ll be back soon so I’ll see you then.’

‘Hang on,’ said Nessie. ‘Who would remember him from the old days? Except my big brother? Someone older?’

They all watched Jimmy thinking. ‘You could try Greta Broncowiez, up in the big house, she always seemed to know what was going on. She would remember stuff.’

‘She’s scary,’ said Tonk, ‘an’ I think she’d be too old to remember *anything*.’

‘She looks like a witch,’ said Jason.

Jimmy laughed and turned back to face them. ‘We all thought she was a witch when we were kids too. Turned out she wasn’t of course, because there’s no such things, but, I’ll tell you something, Mick Tyler tried to kill her once.’

Nessie gasped and her hand flew to her mouth.

‘*Swashbuckling Sailors!*’ Tonk exclaimed

‘Revenge,’ said Chris, who had just walked up to join them. ‘Could have been her then.’

‘She’d have had to have help,’ said Tonk, writing furiously in his notebook.

‘Well,’ said Nessie. ‘I think we should get up to her house now an’ see what she has to say. She gave me some biscuits once, I remember.’

‘Well,’ said Chris. ‘I’m gonna follow Jimmy. That’s gonna be my job, shadowing people. It’s what I’m best at. An’ I’m older than all of you. You can do all the kid’s stuff.’

They all looked at Jimmy disappearing into the distance. ‘We need to know what everyone in the street is up to,’ he shouted as he rushed up the road to follow him. Jimmy turned round and waved. The three left behind laughed as Chris tried to hide himself behind a lamp post.

‘He can’t be in our gang,’ said Jason. ‘He’s too old.’

‘We’ll just keep sending him off following people,’ said Nessie. ‘That’ll keep him out the way.’

‘An’ we need to keep stuff secret from the grown-ups,’ said Tonk. ‘Chris don’t know how to keep a secret.’ He tapped his pencil on the notebook. ‘It’ll all be in ‘ere. An’ only us three can look at it.’

‘How can we keep it secret if we’re interviewing them all?’ Nessie asked.

‘Yeah but they won’t know what we’re asking everyone else will they or what everyone else tells us or,’ he tapped his fingers on his cheek, ‘what we see wiv our mince pies. ‘An we’re gonna guard this notebook wiv our lives.’

***

Jimmy made his way to Plaistow Police Station. He had noticed that Chris was following him. He had turned round before he had got off the estate and seen him quickly disappear behind a privet hedge. He remembered him and his twin brother when they were babies. It all seemed a very long time ago. He couldn't help laughing to himself. It was the sort of thing *they* would have done when they were kids. He did think for a minute of going on a detour and trying to lose him but why spoil his fun. He wasn't bothered if they knew he had been to the coppers. He would have opened this letter yesterday but George had persuaded him not to.

'If your dad sent it to the police that's where it has to go. What good would it do if you saw what was in it eh? You might have to make decisions. You might decide not to. No, your dad would have known what he was doing. He was dying, not senile.'

The sergeant at the desk didn't seem too impressed.

'Right, just take a seat mate,' he yawned. 'It's DCI Paradise who needs to see this. He's around somewhere. Relevant to the Mick Tyler case you say? I remember him, he was never gonna be an old man was he?'

He saw the sergeant pass his dad's letter on to someone. They were whispering and nodding, looking at him. Why did he always feel guilty when there were coppers around? He hadn't done anything . They had never done anything to hurt him or his family but there was still this feeling that he had sinned whenever he was in their company.

He had only been sitting there for five minutes when a tall, distinguished looking man walked up to him and smiled. He put out his hand. 'DCI John Paradise. You must be Jimmy Potter. Come on through.'

Firm handshake, Jimmy thought. A confident man with a face he wanted to trust. Jimmy, intuitively believed, that he was a good cop.

He ushered Jimmy into a seat on the other side of his desk and sat down himself. He took the letter from his pocket and Jimmy followed it with his eyes.

'So. Doesn't look like anyone has tampered with this. We'll need to check the handwriting but I do believe your dad wrote it. He just sounds – genuine.' He smiled. 'And his spelling is crap.'

Jimmy could feel tears welling in his eyes. 'I just need to know what it says please,' he muttered.

'Must have been a temptation to open it,' said John Paradise. 'I'm sorry about your loss Jimmy. I do remember your dad. He was a cheeky bugger but quite an honest one.'

Jimmy almost laughed, remembering the amount of baccy his dad used to smuggle out when he had worked down the docks.

John Paradise stood up and came round to where Jimmy was sitting. He passed him the three sheets of paper. 'I think it's easiest if I let you read it for yourself.'

The sergeant appeared at the door. 'Cup of Rosie Lee for you mate.' He put the tea down in front of Jimmy. There were two ginger biscuits he had put on the saucer. They were going soggy where the tea had spilt.

Jimmy nodded his thanks and began to read.

***

TO THE POLICE

THIS IS A CONFESHUN THAT ON 22ND MAY 1956 I BILLY POTTER OF 4 CHURCHILL STREET PLAISTOW E14 KILED MICK TYLER AT ABOWT 11.30 AT NITE.

THIS IS HOW IT HAPEND.

I was walkin bac from the Kings Head and I wasnt pissd I was walkin back wiv old Bones I dont even no his reel name but you know who I meen

I saw Del Tyler cum runin out of his howse crying and he told us his dad had cum bac and was hiting his mum I run into the howse and left Bones wiv Del

Mick was kicking Maggie lookd like she was nocked out I tried to pul Mick off Maggie but he nocked me down I got the poker and just hit him over the hed

I dint meen to kill him I thort he was goin to kill her I reelly did I thort they was both ded I dint no wat to do

Bones cum in he had sent Del to bed thro the front door so he woodnt see nothin we puled Micks body outside I dont no y we jus panicd Mick Tyler was just lay there ded and coverd in blud we both just stod luking at Mick for ajiz then I remembrd abowt Maggie

We went bac in the kichin and she was stil nockd out she cum rownd wen we got her upstars we got her to bed and Bones checkd her he was a medic in the war an he said she was OK

Bones sed wat to do he sed we had to beree Mick on the waste there was no one abowt we dragd him up to the waste I went and got some spads out of his shed and we dug an hole and bereed him

I'm sorry it was an axidunt I was trying to look owt for Maggie he wood hav kild her I was just scard

Wen it was dun it was dun an I coodnt undo it ther hasnt been a day wen it hasnt been in me hed plees excus speling I no its shit .

SIGNED : Billy Potter

WITNESS TO CONFESSION: George Pattinson, 6 Churchill Road. Plaistow E14

DATE 30th July 1966

***

John Paradise had watched Jimmy closely while he read the letter. He knew instantly that the boy had not seen it before. His face was losing colour with every second that passed. By the time he reached the end there were tears in his eyes.

John Paradise was a fair but tough cop and everyone knew it. To show his soft side was not something he often did. He couldn't, not in this job, not in this part of London. He knew that even evil criminals had a soft side. He had met the Krays. Ruthless killing machines but they loved their mum, their families and their mates.

He had a son, the same age as Jimmy Potter and his heart went out to the boy. If it had been *his* son he would have wrapped his arms around him and given him a hug but he had to hide all that. He was a top copper. He cleared his throat and passed Jimmy his hankie, it was the best he could do.

Jimmy blew his nose and handed the hankie back. 'Ta,' he said. 'That was just a bit of a shock.'

‘You’ve not had an easy week,’ said John Paradise. ‘And I’m going to make it just that bit harder for you. I’m taking this confession seriously but we’ll have to talk to everyone involved, everyone in the street. What do you think Jimmy? What’s your gut reaction?’

‘Can’t imagine my dad killing anyone,’ he said quietly.

‘Not even in those circumstances?’

Jimmy shook his head. ‘No – yes but he wouldn’t have meant to kill him. He would just have been trying to help Maggie.’

Maggie, thought John Paradise. She had already admitted that she had lied about not seeing Mick that night. She had told them now that she *had* seen him but that she hadn’t seen anyone else in the house at all. That he had knocked her unconscious and when she came round she was in bed. She thought she must have just dragged herself upstairs and that the bang on her head had made her forget.

They had checked out Winston’s alibi and it was solid up until ten thirty that night. He had been at the greyhounds with about six other men and had come straight back to his rented room with three of them. The landlady had seen them all come in. He *could* have gone out again and after so many years they had no official time of death.

Winston said that he had remembered the date clearly because he had taken Maggie to A&E the next day, she told him that she had fallen down the stairs. They had checked with the hospital and the injuries she had come in with could well have resulted in her losing consciousness for some time. John Paradise knew that it would have been unlikely that she could have found the strength to kill him. However there were different rules when it came to murder and self-defence, theory went out the window. Over the years he had been amazed at the strength people could magically possess when they were fighting for their lives or for those they loved. He certainly couldn't rule either Maggie or Winston out as suspects.

Scottie had spoken to the doctor who had attended her that morning. The hospital records had shown that was the last time Maggie Tyler had been seen for 'unexplained' injuries. She had refused to be admitted to the hospital. The doctor said that wasn't unusual for her.

John Paradise had let them both go for now. There was motive but no evidence. The poker had long gone, the one that Billy had mentioned as the murder weapon. The council had put in gas fires during the intervening years.

He certainly *was* going to take this confession seriously and it seemed, to John Paradise, to be quite genuine. He could understand how Billy could have panicked and then it was too late. Old Bones, real name Theobald Harrison, had helped him bury the body. Who would give a baby such a dreadful name, John Paradise thought.

No, that *could* have been how it had happened. It just seemed rather convenient that the murderer *and* his accomplice were both deceased and that Billy didn't confess until he knew he was dying. The next person he

would have to talk to would be the witness to the confession. George Pattinson. He must know something
.

He glanced up and saw that Jimmy was shaking all over.

'Let's get you home son,' he said quietly.

8

The Sound of Silence – Simon and Garfunkel

Tonk and Nessie were sitting with Jason on his bed.

'It's weird,' said Jason. 'That we had a den in the same place as that bloke from Australia.'

'And my Del was in their gang an' all,' said Nessie.

'And my sister,' said Tonk.

Jason smirked at him. 'And your murderer uncle. He was one of 'em weren't he?'

'It was an accident,' said Tonk angrily. 'Anyway it was a really old lady that he run over, she'd have been dead soon anyway.'

'Tonk!' Nessie exclaimed. 'That's an' 'orrible thing to say, you'll be old one day.'

Tonk went bright red and looked down at the floor. 'Sorry Nessie,' he muttered. 'But you ain't got no right to slag my uncle off Jason,' he shouted.

'Just saying that's all. He wouldn't be locked up in the Scrubs if he didn't do nothing.'

They heard a voice floating up the stairs, Jason's mum. 'Come on you lot, it's a lovely sunny day. Get yourselves out there.'

There was a lot of moaning and grumbling amongst the gang. Suddenly, the door opened and Chris came in.

'Glad you're 'ere,' said Tonk. 'I ain't taken your statement yet.' He opened the book and got his pencil out of his pocket. 'Go on.' He nodded at his older step-brother.

‘Five minutes mum,’ Jason shouted.

‘Well, Jimmy went to the police station. He was there for about an hour. While he was there,’ he nodded at Nessie, ‘your mum an’ dad come out an’ walked down to the bus stop. Then about twenty minutes later, Jimmy come out. I hid well behind a wall. I don’t think any of ‘em saw me. There was a copper wiv him. They shook hands an’ then Jimmy started walking back to Churchill Street. That’s all I’ve got to report.

Is that it, cos I’m off wiv Stuart and Dave now?’ Chris left as suddenly as he had arrived.

‘How do you spell Jimmy?’ Tonk asked. Jason took the notebook from him. The handwriting was completely illegible. ‘Oh Tonk,’ he laughed, ‘how we supposed to read that? Who’s good at spelling?’

‘I ain’t bad,’ said Nessie.

Tonk looked as if he might argue but handed the notebook over to Nessie without too much fuss. ‘You can be my secretary then,’ he laughed. ‘We’re trusting you to look after that book Nessie,’ he added seriously.

‘Why don’t we go an’ see that old woman now?’ asked Jason. ‘You know, the one Jimmy told us about. She might know who his enemies were. Who might wanna kill him.’

‘I’ll write some questions down for her,’ said Nessie scribbling away. ‘Course she might not let us in. Perhaps we should take something, you know a present.’

‘We’ll pick some flowers on the way, I know where she lives,’ said Tonk, heading for the door. ‘Our Josie goes to see her sometimes. She lived with Old Bones, he was a right good laugh. The coppers found him dead in the river.'

'Yeah, he was pissed,' Jason added. 'I remember me mum telling me that. He just fell in the river pissed as a fart, she said.'

'Your mum swears too much,' Tonk laughed.

They heard footsteps on the stairs again. Jason's mum came in. Nessie hid the notebook behind her back. Jason's mum stood with her hands on her hips her dyed blonde hair stuck out in wisps. She looked hot and flustered, a cigarette dangled from her mouth.

'Now come on you lot an' get outside,' she said crossly. 'I told you ages ago. Wish I had a chance to sit out in the garden. Go on, piss off.'

Jason sighed as she went back down the stairs. 'Five minutes mum an' we'll be gone,' he shouted after her.

Nessie was looking at her notes. 'Come on then,' she said. 'Let's go an' see Mrs. Bron – Greta. Might as well, seeing as we're being chucked out.' She glared at Jason.

'What do we know about her?' Tonk asked. 'Remember Jimmy said that Mick Tyler tried to kill her.'

'That'll be one of me first questions for her then,' said Nessie. 'She was in one of them concentrating camps in the war, me mum told me that. She was nearly dead when they rescued her.'

'We done it in school last year, didn't we?' said Jason.

'Well she won't mind us asking about dead bodies an' stuff then,' said Tonk. 'She'll be used to it.'

***

The Kings Head was quiet. Jimmy went straight over to George who was standing on his own at the bar looking morose.

'Hey Jimmy, want a beer?' George put his hand in his pocket and put the coins on the top of the bar. 'Here you are Arthur. Another pint for me and one for the young 'un'. Reckon he'll need it today.' He turned towards Jimmy and lowered his voice to a whisper. 'You did go didn't you Jimmy?'

Jimmy nodded. 'Bit of a shock,' he said, knocking back half of his pint in one go. George patted him on the back.

'It was to me as well. He never said anything before you went to Australia. The first I knew was when he wanted me to witness the letter. I've just told the coppers that but I don't think they believe me.'

'He never said *anything*?'

George looked him straight in the eye. 'No. Just said the less I knew the better. He told me it was just instinct. Mick was really laying in to Maggie and he just got the poker and hit him. I don't know Jimmy, I just can't believe it. Like I can't believe my son is in jail for murder.'

'What's all this whispering about?' Arthur joined them.

'Bugger off Arthur, there's a good lad,' said George.

'Er – excuse me mate but this is my pub if you hadn't noticed.' He put his hands up. 'Alright, I'll move along and talk to meself down the other end of the bar. I don't mind if everyone thinks I'm a sad bastard. Might just go and play Vera Lynn on the jukebox.'

Jimmy gave him a forced grin as Arthur moved away still muttering and then turned back to George. 'When did you sign the letter then?' He asked him.

'Your dad called in, morning of the Cup Final. He was only here for ten minutes. Got a shock when I saw him I can tell you. I knew he was very poorly. Made sure he got a taxi back to you.'

'Oh, so that's where he was. Told me he wanted a look round Upton Park on his own.' He scratched his head and thought for a moment. 'I can understand how it could happen though George. From what I remember of Mick, he was a big man. I doubt my dad could have stopped him any other way. But why bury him? He'd have got away with it wouldn't he? He was just trying to protect Maggie.'

George shrugged his shoulders. 'I don't know,' he whispered fiercely. 'I don't know what made him do that. He was probably in shock, that's all I can think. I thought about all the questions I wanted to ask him after he'd gone and he wouldn't talk about it when I saw him in *The Kings Head* later.'

'We'll never know why now,' Jimmy whispered. 'He's taken it to the grave with him.'

George sighed and began to light his pipe. 'Think I might come to Australia with you,' he laughed. 'Must be more peaceful out there.'

Jimmy looked thoughtfully at his glass and then knocked the beer back in one go. 'I'm not going back to Australia until this is all sorted George,' he said. 'I just can't believe my dad did it and I want to see your Legs as well. Try and get him to let me visit him won't you?' He patted George on the shoulder and looked at the clock. 'I'm off to Upton Park now, to see about the ashes, I'll tell mum about the confession when I get back.'

George nodded. 'Haven't you got anyone waiting for you back in Australia? Good looking lad like you.'

'No,' Jimmy replied. 'No-one important.'

George looked over towards the door. Josie had come in with a couple of her friends from the old people's home, they still had their uniforms on. Navy and white overalls, way above their knees. George wondered if girls had any idea how much mini-skirts turned men on. There'd be some very happy but frustrated old men in that old people's home, he thought. He turned to Jimmy to tell him that Josie was in but he had already seen her. George saw the way he was looking at her. His whole face had become alive and soft. Oh no, George thought. More trouble.

***

The three walked up the path to the big house. It had always seemed a bit creepy. Tonk had always run past it quickly when he'd been little. There were old stories from the past about Mrs. Broncowiez being a witch. Of course he didn't believe all that sort of stuff now.

'You knock Nessie,' he said. 'You're a girl, she'll be more friendly to you.'

'She ain't a witch anymore,' said Nessie, 'Jimmy said so. No need to be scared.'

'I ain't scared,' said Tonk fiercely.

Suddenly the door opened and they all took a step back.

'I'll just open the door,' said Greta. 'Then you don't need to decide who should knock.'

They all gasped. How did she know? Perhaps she really was a bit of a witch.

Nessie coughed and held up the notebook. 'We're investigating a murder Mrs. Bron – Bronky,' she said, 'an' we thought you might be able to help us cos you was here when it 'appened.'

'I see. Well you can call me Greta children, I think I know all your names. Would you like to come in and have a biscuit and some orange juice?'

They hesitated for a second. 'I think she'll be alright,' Tonk whispered. 'And there *is* three of us.'

'I must warn you though,' she spoke softly. 'I will be trying to dissuade you from your investigations.'

'What does that mean?' Jason muttered as they were shown into a cosy sitting room. They all got comfy on the settee while Greta went out to the kitchen and came back with a plate of chocolate fingers and a jug of squash.

'I was expecting you,' she smiled at the gang. 'That's why I got biscuits in.'

Jason and Tonk looked at one another in shock.

'*Bleedin' barnacles*,' Tonk whispered

'Er – how did you know?' Nessie asked. 'That we were coming?'

Greta smiled again. 'Just a little talent I have,' she said. 'No, it's just my attempt at English humour. I saw you coming when I looked out of the window.'

The children weren't sure whether they were meant to laugh or not so they stayed silent.

'Now,' she carried on, 'please tell me what you have come to find out. I presume you are talking about Mick Tyler.'

They all nodded. 'Well, I'm not going to tell you much but I will say that he was not a pleasant man when he was drunk.'

'Was he as bad as Hitler?' asked Nessie. 'Sorry but we know you was in the concentrating camps. I'll bet you was glad to get out of there.'

'It ain't concentrating Nessie,' Jason whispered fiercely, 'it's concentration.' He looked at Greta. 'I expect it was even worse than school.'

They saw a faint smile pass over Greta's face. 'Yes Jason – it is Jason isn't it? – It was much worse than school. But I thought you had come to talk about Mick Tyler. Badness or evil is in most of us you know. It might surprise you all that most people put into certain situations are quite capable of murder, that's what I believe anyway.'

'Like in wars?' Nessie asked.

'People kill in war because they have no choice and they see it as a duty to their country. They will kill to protect their families and friends. Many of the guards at Auschwitz knew that their families would die if they did not obey orders. I forgave them. People may kill because their hearts have been blackened and beaten until they have no humanity left inside. Others are what we call sick. Maybe they are born like that, maybe not but they are probably the most dangerous because they plan their destruction.'

'Like Hitler?' asked Nessie, scribbling furiously in the book.

Tonk shook his head and wondered why she was trying to write all this stuff down. It didn't seem to make any sense to him. It had nothing to do with their skeleton. They were just wasting their time with this nice but mad old woman.

'Yes,' said Greta. 'And Mussolini, Stalin and many others who were seen as our friends, not our enemies at that time.'

Tonk sighed. 'Can I have another chocolate biscuit please?'

'I'm sorry children. I don't see so many people now, I tend to get carried way. This is probably very boring to you.'

'Not to me,' said Nessie. 'I love history an' stuff.'

The boys looked at each other and rolled their eyes.

'Nevertheless,' said Greta, 'I must stop. I am really just trying to warn you not to get too involved, it can be perilous. You are just children and you take things at face value but there are just as many dangerous people out there as there always have been. Now, you may ask your questions but I warn you I will probably refuse to answer some of them.'

Nessie flipped back through the notebook. 'Who hated Mick Tyler enough to kill him?' she asked.

Two minutes passed before Greta answered. Blimey, thought Tonk. We'll be 'ere all bleedin' day.

‘There are quite a few people who wouldn’t care much if he died but there are not so many who would have a definite reason to kill him.’

‘Could it have been an accident?’ Nessie asked.

‘Yes, I think that is a possibility.’

‘Is it true that Mick Tyler tried to kill you once?’

The boys gasped as Nessie asked the question confidently.

‘He was grieving when he set fire to my house and very drunk. His daughter had just died. He wasn’t a total monster, it was a case of mistaken identity. He believed that I had caused her death.’

‘So you did have a motive to kill him,’ said Jason.

‘Jason!’ Nessie exclaimed.

Greta put her hand up. ‘No, Nessie, he is right. I did have a motive and I am sure the police would have me on a list of suspects. I would have found it difficult at my age and you must decide that for yourselves but please, take my warning seriously and don’t get too involved. Remember that the murderer may still live around here and may do anything to stop the truth getting out.’

Tonk shivered.

‘Can I ask a question?’ asked Jason nervously. Greta nodded. ‘Is it true that your um - boyfriend drowned because he was drunk?’

‘No Jason,’ said Nessie, ‘that ain’t a fair question and it ain’t nothing to do wiv this.’

Tonk was watching Greta’s face. It went as white as the milk they had seen on the doorstep when they came in.

‘We’d best go now,’ said Nessie quickly. They all jumped up in unison. ‘Sorry to upset you, he ain’t lived here long.’ She nodded at Jason.

Greta seemed to compose herself and showed them to the door. ‘Call in anytime,’ she said, calmly, ‘and don’t forget to be careful.’

As they were leaving through the door Nessie stopped and hesitated.

‘Do you know who did it Greta?’ she asked quietly.

Greta looked into the eyes of the young girl and knew immediately that there was something there. Something she recognised and understood. Completely.

They smiled at each other in peace and immediate friendship. Greta lowered her voice so that the others wouldn’t hear. ‘I think so,’ she said, ‘but believe me I will never tell a soul. And Nessie,’ she added. ‘If you ever need me I will be here for you. You understand that don’t you?’

The girl nodded and smiled. ‘Yes I understand. Thank you.’

***

Greta sighed as she watched the children stroll away down the road. Her eyes were especially drawn to the little girl. Half black, half white. Strange, when that connection happened but it had done occasionally throughout her life. Even in the worst times. When she had flown her brother’s body home to Warsaw, two days before the Nazis invaded Poland, she had met a customs official at the airport. They had recognised each other too.

‘Get out,’ he had said to her. ‘There’s a flight back tonight. I’ll deal with your brother’s body, you must get back to England.’

‘No, Greta had answered. ‘I must see that he is buried properly.’

‘Then you will die,’ he told her. ‘This is not a place for Jews. Not now, but then you know that.’

He had touched her arm then. ‘My name is Harald and I think we will meet again,’ he had said sadly, ‘though I wish that wasn’t true. Good luck and never give up hope.’ He looked at her name on the papers. ‘Greta Broncowiez.’

And so had begun the worst time of Greta’s life. Though now, looking back on it she could see that Harald’s life had been infinitely more destructive than hers. The years in the ghettos in Warsaw had been terrible. She had lived, although survived would have been a better word, with her sister and family in one room, overrun with rats and cockroaches. There were seven of them altogether and one by one they were taken away or died. Greta instinctively knew that they would never be seen again. Rumours trickled through. Whispers of trains, so crowded that if you fell asleep you might be suffocated. And at the end there was only death. At first when people were taken in the middle of the night they would fight against it. They would just be shot. Her uncle had been one of those. Anyone who tried to leave the ghetto would also be killed. There was no escape and, after the first couple of years, the Jews in the ghetto barely spoke, even to each other. No-one smiled. Even the fear was no longer there because there was no hope. No doors opening, no future. But Greta still felt something. Just a spark, a survival instinct. And then she had met Dr. Grupel and had recognised him just as *she* had just recognised Nessie. They were all from the same place and there were no borders.

Dr. Grupel was a Polish doctor, he was not Jewish. Sent in to the ghetto to look at the conditions, not that the Nazis really cared about that or wanted to improve anything. They just wanted to know any gossip. He had smiled at Greta and it was almost as if the sun had come out, just for a few seconds, lighting up the hovel that was their only home. There were tears in his eyes as he looked around.

'This is dreadful,' he said gently. 'Dreadful.'

He turned to Greta. 'I must try to help you all. I don't know how but I *will* try.'

He put his arms around Greta and she felt tears rolling slowly down her cheeks. She couldn't remember the last time she had cried. There were no emotions left now. Hitler and his friends had taken them away, they were all like empty shells. With the visit of Dr. Grupel she realised that she was still alive. There was some hope. The other Jews barely noticed him, they were too far gone.

Dr. Grupel had tried to improve conditions. He brought them in food every week but he could do nothing else. The night that the last of the Jews in the ghetto were taken he knocked loudly on their door.

'You must come with me now,' he said to them all. There was just Greta and her two nieces left .'I will hide you. I know this is bad but where they are taking you is a hundred times worse. Please. They're coming for the rest of you in one hour. I have only just heard.'

Greta's nieces wouldn't go. They huddled into a corner and clung to each other, their minds gone. Greta was torn but when Dr. Grupel came over to the corner where she was trying to make her nieces get up and follow, he put his hand on her shoulder.

'Come Greta,' he said quietly. 'They have to make their own decisions. They are younger, they may survive. Believe me, if you stay you will die. If you come with me there is still hope.'

And so Greta had gone and lived in Dr. Grupel's cellar with ten other Jews he was hiding. There were no rats, no filth, he found them warm clothes. For two whole years they had almost full bellies. Sometimes, very quietly, they even laughed.

Dr. Grupel, who was shot when they were all discovered, had saved Greta's life. By the time they arrived in Auschwitz they were no longer skin and bone. He had given them time and he had given them back some strength.

By now it was 1944 and Greta knew instinctively that the war must end soon. She kept telling herself to hang on but she was a woman approaching middle age and was of no use to the Nazis. It was only her fluent English and the Gestapos need for interpreters that had saved her so far. Dr. Grupel had told her about the gas chambers so she had known when she first saw the smoke in the distance at Birkenau, exactly what it was. The stench when the wind blew their way was appalling and made them all gag. He had also made her promise that she would never tell another Jew that they would probably die. 'It is impossible for most people to comprehend,' he had told her. 'Just let them believe what they want to.'

At the time Greta could not understand why the Jews, homosexuals, coloureds and gypsies in the camp believed that their family and friends had just been taken somewhere else.

'*This* is the worst one,' they would say, teeth chattering with the constant, numbing cold. 'They have gone somewhere better.'

Of course now she understood. It would have destroyed them if they had faced the truth.

And then she had seen Harald. Harald, who she had met at the airport in what seemed like a lifetime away. He knew about the gas chambers. Harald was a Nazi now and he was one of the ones who flicked the switches.

At first she ignored him and her mind was full of hate. When she passed him in the exercise areas she deliberately turned the other way. Then one day, he spotted her.

'I know you,' he said. 'You were at the airport.'

At last she looked into his eyes. The pain in them was unbelievable, her hatred withered away like a deflating balloon.

'Harald,' she heard herself say. 'What is it that you do in here?'

He told her that he was responsible for releasing the gas in to the showers. The gas that had already killed millions of people and she wept. In the middle of the freezing outside area, her shoes worn, her body blue with the cold.

'If I refuse to do my job,' he said, 'I will die and so will my family. I'm sorry, so sorry.'

Greta desperately wanted to touch him, his pain was so much greater than hers, but she knew she couldn't.

'I will help you,' he said. 'I have a friend in a very high position here. The war will be ending soon. Those of us with the gift must help one another. Believe me, if Hitler could identify our powers, I would be in your position too. I have done this for others, it is all I can do to help.'

Greta looked around. No-one seemed to be taking any notice of them. She looked at Harald and knew that he was a low ranking Nazi by his uniform. 'How can you manage to protect anyone, to save people Harald?'

'One of the senior Gestapo officers is in love with me. He allows me some – favours. Of course, I have to pretend to return his feelings and let him do whatever he wants to me sexually but, believe me, it is nothing compared to the other things I have to do in here. Now, I must go or we will arouse suspicion. Have a good life Greta.' He smiled sadly. 'We won't meet again.'

She ached again to touch him, looked into his face and knew that he felt the same. They embraced but only with their eyes. Then he moved away and he was a Nazi soldier again.

For the second time since she had returned to Poland, Greta had been saved and simply because she had the gift. It was like anything else in life, she thought. It can bring good things or it can bring bad.

She had a feeling that Nessie was going to need *her* help. And she would be there for her just like Dr. Grupen and Harald had been there for *her* in Poland. There would be a price to pay but she was an old woman and suddenly she was no longer afraid.

9

Out of Time – Rolling Stones

John Paradise stood in front of his investigations board. They weren't getting anywhere fast with this old murder. The people round here were clever, he thought, they knew how to lie. It was funny, in his experience, it was the toffs and the working classes who were best at it. They had more in common than they realised and didn't feel any sort of guilt when they lied to the police. They weren't intimidated, it was all a game to them. Take the Krays for instance. To the good, law-abiding citizens of the East End, they were often seen as protectors. They were kind to old ladies, soft with kids, they just killed the filth. The Eastenders believed what they wanted to and the police were seen as the baddies. They hadn't seen the dead bodies, the blood and the gore. The pain of the families of those they had killed. Innocent kids deprived of their fathers, weeping mothers. The ruthlessness of their sick minds and lust for power. Yes, thought John Paradise, we all see what we want to see.

Mick Tyler, by all accounts had been a bit of a baddie so no-one really cared that he was dead. He knew that most of his men wanted to believe the confession written by Billy Potter.

The Murder Team filtered in, most of them smoking and some munching on bacon butties. They sat casually in a circle around the room, sitting on desks or chairs.

Someone farted loudly and the others laughed and held their noses. John Paradise had never understood that sort of humour, it made him feel different. That used to bother him but not now.

'Right,' he banged his empty coffee mug on the table. 'Let's crack on. I want this crime solved by tomorrow morning.' There was some laughter, not as much as the fart got though, he grinned to himself.

'Let's sort out what we know. Feel free to interrupt if you know anything that's relevant to what I'm talking about.'

He pointed to an old blurry black and white photo of Mick Tyler which was placed in the middle of the board next to that of his skeleton. 'This photo's the best we've got I'm afraid. It's from the Merchant Navy Pool and would have been the same as the one in his Seaman's Discharge book. It was taken a few months before he died. We've got the copies back from the printers so you'll all get one to flash around and it'll be in all the papers tomorrow.'

'No oil painting was he?' one of the detectives quipped. They all laughed.

'Anyway,' John Paradise spoke louder. 'Let's just sort out possible suspects, motives etc. or we're going to be here all day. The World Cup's over now so let's get serious.'

The mumbles and laughter faded away.

'Right. The confession first. It seems genuine and we've checked the handwriting. It *was* written by Billy Potter.'

The confession was pinned to the board next to a photo of a smiling, tanned, good-looking man.

'He reminds me of someone -' Scottie began. John Paradise glared at him.

'Is it relevant to the investigation?'

'No, sorry guv. It's just a film star or something.'

There was silence. Most of the team realised now that the guv was not in the mood for anymore gentle banter.

'I've questioned George Pattinson, his neighbour who signed the letter as a witness,' John Paradise continued, 'and he says he had no idea that Mick Tyler had been murdered until Billy showed him the letter. He hadn't noticed any change in Billy's behaviour, it had been just before the family had left for Australia. He *did* say that Billy hadn't really wanted to go but as the time got nearer he seemed to have changed his mind. That could be very relevant. I will be questioning his wife and son.'

'James Dean,' Scottie shouted excitedly. 'That's who Billy Potter looked like.'

'Well, they've got two things in common now then haven't they?' John Paradise said crossly, 'They're both dead. Can we just get back to the murder now please?'

'What about the old bloke who he says helped him?' asked Charlie, trying not to laugh.

'Theobald Harrison, known locally as 'Old Bones'. Died a couple of years ago, fell in the river drunk. They found him at Tilbury.'

'I remember that one,' said Charlie. 'No suspicious circumstances.'

Scottie put his hand up, everyone laughed. Scottie was the only one who ever put his hand up.

'I'm just getting to that Scottie,' said John Paradise. 'Give me a chance.' He sighed.

'Scottie's snout was in *The King's Head* after Billy Potter's funeral and he passed him a note. Tell them what it said Scottie.'

'It said,' Scottie stood up. '*A rumour is going round the pub saying that Old Bones' death was not an accident and that it's got something to do with this enquiry.*'

There were a few mutterings around the room. Scottie coughed. 'My snout's told me since that Old Bones had told Arthur the landlord that he thought his life was in danger. Arthur didn't take it seriously.'

Scottie paused and allowed this information to sink in. 'We've spoken to the old girl he lived with,' he added. 'She said that he was teetotal, hadn't had a drink for about thirty years. Strange woman but I believed her. I think it could have something to do with all of this with him being mentioned in the letter as an accomplice.'

'Greta Broncowiez,' said John Paradise. 'That's her name, no photo I'm afraid. Seventy five years old, bit of a fortune teller, you know the type. Eccentric would be the kind way to describe her I suppose. Lives on another planet from what I've heard, certainly not in the real world anyway. Reads cards and palms, healing powers that sort of thing. I think it's unlikely but I *am* including her on the list of suspects. Mick Tyler set fire to her house eleven years ago and he believed that she was in there. She certainly had her reasons to see him dead and she was younger then.' He turned to face Scottie.

'Right, you keep going with that one, find out what you can and have a word with Arthur the pub landlord.

Now, let's move on to other potential suspects. If the confession is false and I'm not sure if it is, our main suspect has to be Maggie Tyler. He beat her up regularly. We've only got her word for it that she was unconscious. Medically speaking she could have been but she's already lied to us once so we need to keep an eye on her.'

'What about the darkie?' asked another cop.

'Maggie has admitted now that she had just started courting Winston then and he only has an alibi up to 10.30 pm. We need to talk to all the Tyler kids again as well, the ones that were old enough to remember anything.' He nodded towards the only female in the room, the only woman on the Murder team.

'That'll be your job Jenny,' he said.

'Thought it might be,' she smiled.

'Del Tyler was the one who they say raised the alarm. He was only a little kid at the time but he might remember things. Won't be easy for him so softly softly.'

Jenny nodded. 'Right guv.'

John Paradise picked up a sheaf of papers and started handing them around. 'Now all your instructions for the day are here. Get round your snouts again, interview locals on the estate. Keep your eyes and ears open. He wasn't a popular man and I think there'll be a few more suspects soon. He quite possibly owed money. I want to know everything about him down to how many times a week he had a shit. Alright?' They all nodded. 'Yes guv.'

'Scottie, can you stay behind a minute?'

When the others had gone, Scottie came over and stood next to John Paradise.

'I've sent Doug on a drugs course,' John Paradise told him, 'so he's off this case. Jenny will be busy interviewing the Tyler kids today but from tomorrow you'll be working with her.'

He saw the look of dismay on Scottie's face.

'She's a good detective Scottie and she hasn't had it easy being the first woman on the Murder Team, just give her a break.'

'But – but I haven't ever worked with women guv. I don't know what to expect. What about when she has her monthlies and all that? My wife throws stuff at me then.'

John Paradise laughed. 'Not all women are like that. Put it this way. She won't burst into tears if she sees a dead body but she'll probably tell you off if you fart in the car. Now piss off and just do your job.'

'Yes guv,'

John Paradise smiled as Scottie left the room. Oh, it was going to take a long time for things to change around here, he thought.

***

Del and his half-sister Nessie were sprawled on the chairs in the lounge watching Tom and Jerry.

‘What’s that?’ asked Del as he saw her writing in the notebook. Nessie quickly hid it behind her back. ‘Just school stuff,’ she said.

‘No need to hide it then is there,’ said Del turning back to watch Jerry get the better of Tom as usual.

‘Actually Del,’ Nessie spoke hesitantly. ‘Would you talk to me about your dad? Don’t matter if you don’t want to.’ The expression on her step-brother’s face didn’t change at all.

‘What do you wanna know?’

‘Just – just who might have wanted to kill him that’s all.’

Del got up and turned the TV off. ‘An’ is that what you’re writing about in your book?’

Nessie nodded. ‘Don’t tell no-one. We’re just trying to find out who done it. I’m trying to help mum and dad. I don’t want the coppers thinking it was one of them. They might put them in prison.’

Nessie felt tears pricking at the back of her eyes. Del came over and put his arm around her shoulder. ‘That’s a good thing you’re doing Ness,’ he said gently.

‘You can’t see it Del, it’s only for us, no grown-ups.’

Del laughed which surprised Nessie. ‘I thought you might have got angry,’ she said.

‘Nah. I don’t wanna talk about him but you just reminded me of when we was kids. We didn’t tell the grown-ups nothing either but be careful. I know what you’re doing is a good thing but you might upset some people going round asking questions.’

‘You mean the murderer?’

'Yeah, if you was questioning the murderer they might get upset.'

'They might kill us,' said Nessie fearfully.

'I'm only joking,' Del laughed. 'Yeah, if it helps mum an' Winston see what you can find out. I'll let you know anything I hear.'

'We'll be careful Del. Who would be a good person to find out things from? We've been to see Greta.'

'And what did she have to say?'

'Nothing much but she told us a bit about the concentr – ation camps.'

Del moved away. 'Be careful of her,' he warned. 'Trouble follows her around. I've known her since I was a little kid. There's something wrong wiv her head, I wouldn't go back there if I was you. Anyway, I'm off to me group practise. Big night tomorrow, we're playing at *The Royal Oak* down Leytonstone. Goin' upmarket,' he ruffled her hair. 'Giving up the job at the factory this week an' all thank God. Music's gonna make me rich now Nessie, feel it in me gut.'

He watched her as she put the notebook back in her pocket. 'An' put that away in the drawer by your bed or something, don't leave it lying around. Might be vital evidence in there.' He winked at her and laughed as he left the room. As Nessie got up to switch the TV back on, her step-sister Marilyn came in and threw herself on to the settee. She patted the seat next to her and Nessie sat back down.

'Hey Ness,' Marilyn whispered. 'Have you seen that Jimmy who's staying at May and George's? He's groovy. Put in a word for me if you're over there with

Tonk won't yer? Mum says I used to sit on his knee when I was little. I'd do more than just sit on his knee now. Cor, he's fab.'

Nessie smiled. Marilyn wasn't her favourite sister. She didn't understand her really. Always on about boys and lipstick and clothes, oh and Paul McCartney. She hoped that she wouldn't be like that when *she* was fourteen. Ava came in, sat on the other side of her and cuddled up. Nessie had one of those true moments of happiness, of belonging. She knew from her dad that her step-brothers and sisters had had a hard time when their dad had lived here but, apart from Marilyn, they had all been kind to her, stuck up for her when she had been called names at school and accepted her. They often fought with each other but never with her. She wasn't sure why they were so protective but sometimes, like now, it warmed her heart.

Nessie wondered what Del had against Greta Broncowiez. She knew that Greta was the same as she was and understood the secret thing that she never told anyone about. How she sometimes knew what was going to come next. Who would be knocking at the door, who would be hurting inside. She sometimes even saw what was going to happen to people in their lives. Usually people she didn't know very well but she always remembered the first time it had happened.

She had been seven years old and Old Bones had stopped to have a chat with her. As she had smiled at him and looked into his eyes, she had seen a picture in her head, as clear as a bell. Old Bones was floating in water, smiling. He didn't have any teeth in. And the very next week, he was found dead in the river. That had really frightened Nessie. She had tried to talk to Ava about it but she didn't seem to understand, so she *needed* to talk to Greta Broncowiez, whatever Del said. She had to know what to do when she had these pictures in her head. Perhaps she could have warned Old Bones and maybe he would still be alive.

***

There was a knock at the door, Kate got up and went through the tiny hall. She had quite a shock when she opened it. This wasn't the same person she had known ten years ago. She had been so young and vibrant and pretty. Kate had been quite jealous of her then, she hardly remembered seeing her at the funeral. Mind you she hadn't really noticed anyone. Now, Sally looked worn down and there were fine lines around her mouth and eyes. She could only be in her mid thirties. 'Hello Sally,' she said. 'I'm sorry, May and George have gone to see Legs, and Jimmy-'

'Has gone to Upton Park to see about the ashes,' Sally finished the sentence for her. They laughed together, almost embarrassed and then Sally moved towards Kate, threw her arms around her and gave her a warm squeeze. 'I'm so sorry about Billy,' she said. 'I didn't get to speak to you at the funeral, I just wanted to say that really.'

'Well, come in Sally, I'm sure May won't mind. I'll put the kettle on.'

They both walked through to the kitchen. Sally sat down at the table while Kate made the tea.

'You're looking well Kate, nice and tanned. Is it lovely out there?'

'It was hard at first,' said Kate putting the cups on the table 'but I love it now. Well I did – it won't be the same without -' she stopped as she felt the familiar lump in her throat.

Sally put her hand over hers. 'Sorry - you know me, always putting my foot in it and saying the wrong things at the wrong times.'

'No, it's fine Sally. Anyway, how are you getting on? I met Tonk. He's a lovely polite boy, reminds me of Jimmy at that age.'

Sally sighed. 'Bet you weren't surprised to see I had another kid wiv another man that walked out on me.'

'Oh Sally,' Kate smiled sadly. 'I don't know how you do it.'

They both burst out laughing. Kate thought about when they were back here before. How she had thought Sally was a slut for having illegitimate children. How she had shunned her – no, that was all in the past when she wasn't herself, when she was still struggling with her memories of the war and the loss of her baby. She looked at Sally, smiling now. She *was* still beautiful.

'You ain't half changed,' Sally laughed. 'You were such a stuck-up cow in them days but I know now, I know what you went through. I think you did the best thing getting away. I should have got away years ago, too late now.'

'No!' Kate exclaimed. 'Never say that. What do you want to do? What were your dreams when you were younger?'

‘Meet a nice man, marry him. Live in a nice house in Ilford and have a load of kids who would all be happy, never have snotty noses and always say please an’ thank-you. They’d grow up to be doctors and solicitors an’ look after me in me old age. Weren’t much to ask was it?’

They laughed.

‘Well, I’ve heard that Ilford’s gone downhill in the last ten years,’ said Kate. ‘Please don’t tell me you’re still at the factory Sally.’

‘Yeah,’ Sally sighed. ‘I *am* still at the factory, I’m a supervisor now though. Bit more money, comes in handy. Oh, I don’t know. I suppose I just belong round here, probably be like a fish out of water anywhere else. Going to Lloret de mar next April though, first time abroad ever, me and Dianne. Do you remember her?’

Kate nodded. ‘She couldn’t stand me either.’

‘She’s a bit older and wiser now. She got married, lost three babies and gave up after that. He left her for a Brazilian stripper but Dianne punched her lights out before they ran off together. She’s alright now, back at home with her mum.’

They both sipped their tea, deep in thought.

‘We’re going to *The Royal Oak* in Leytonstone tomorrow night to watch Del playing in his group. They’re really good Kate, you could come with us.’

Kate smiled, ‘I’m still a bit old-fashioned Sally, I don’t really understand The Beatles or The Rolling Stones. Jimmy played all that sort of music before he went to university, too loud of course,’ she laughed. ‘I’m still more of a Frank Sinatra sort of person really. I like that new singer though, Englebert Humperdinck. Ridiculous name but that's my sort of music.'

'Your Jimmy's done well, getting to university, I'm pleased for him. He was always a great kid. It's just -'

'What?' asked Kate.

'Well – I think, call it women's intuition – I dunno but I think he's a bit in love wiv my Josie. I just saw him looking at her at the funeral in that sort of way, d'you know what I mean?'

Kate felt herself stiffen. She had always liked Josie but if that was true, Jimmy might want to stay in England. She didn't think that she could cope with losing him as well.

'I think you're wrong Sally,' she said. 'I know they were very close as kids but that was a long time ago. Anyway, Josie's with Del now isn't she?'

'Yeah but oh, it's probably just me being silly, imagining things. I'm still a bit of a romantic Kate.'

'You might meet someone in Spain.'

'Well, if I do meet some bullfighter or other at least this time I'll be on the pill. Best invention ever that is. I definitely ain't having no more kids.'

As Sally left still laughing, Kate closed the door and began to worry because *she* had noticed Jimmy and Josie, after the funeral as well. Just a couple of glances between them. A slight touch when Jimmy had brushed her shoulder. She had just tried to put it to the back of her mind but she knew instinctively that Sally was right.

Just another worry on top of everything else and Jimmy had told her that he needed to have a word with her when he came back from Upton Park. She wondered if that would be what it was about.

There was a sharp insistent knock on the door which made her jump. It could be Molly, she said she might pop over to Churchill Street for a cup of tea but it wasn't her. It was the police and they weren't looking happy.

'Mrs. Potter?' She nodded.

'I'm DCI John Paradise and this is DI Charlie Bolt. Can we come in for a minute please? It's to do with the investigation into the death of Mick Tyler. There's something we need to tell you. Has your son spoken to you yet?'

'No,' said Kate trembling, 'but I think he was just about to.'

10

When a man loves a Woman – Percy Sledge

Jimmy stood behind the chicken run wall and looked out over the vibrant, green turf. It wouldn't look like that for long once the season started, he thought. Him and Josie had discussed the scattering of the ashes with a West Ham official and he had let them wander around the ground afterwards.

It was strange, Jimmy thought, so quiet, no claret and blue cheering crowd. He could even hear birds singing, it didn't seem right somehow. He had thought that all the memories would come rushing back, him and his dad watching the Hammers lose again. No atmosphere he supposed. Josie touched his arm.

'Are you alright?' she asked.

He nodded and smiled at her. He had been pleased when he had seen her in *The Kings Head* and she had agreed to come with him. After all those years conversation had come easily to begin with, as if it were only yesterday they had last met. But now, when he looked into her eyes, he knew that he was seeing her in a different way and suddenly he didn't know how to talk to her anymore.

'How's Del?' he asked eventually. 'You know - about his dad?'

'He don't say much Jimmy. Never know what he's thinking, not really. The coppers are interviewing him today.'

Yes, Jimmy thought to himself, it had been Del who had got his dad to come in that night, to help Maggie. It was all in the letter. The letter that he hadn't told his mum about yet. He had to when he got back but how do you tell your mum that your dad had probably committed murder ten years ago. He wanted to tell Josie about it. Needed to talk to someone but he had to tell his mum first and before it was all in the papers.

'He told me,' she said simply. 'Del told me after they found the body – you know, what happened that night. I can't say no more.'

'Well,' said Jimmy. 'I can't yet either so we'll talk about something else. It began to rain, just lightly. They talked of the past, things they remembered and laughed about.

'Shame we had to grow up,' Josie said, 'wish we could have stayed like that forever, in our own little world. I was gutted when you went you know,' she blurted out. 'It left me all empty inside, for a long time.'

Jimmy looked down at his feet. He didn't trust himself to look at her again. 'I thought about you a lot too Josie. I was bullied out there a lot at first.'

'Probably till you got your Aussie accent,' Josie laughed. 'I keep expecting you to start saying 'G'day''

Impulsively, he took her hand. 'Josie -' he began, looking deeply into her eyes. She turned away.

'No Jimmy, it ain't gonna happen. Please don't look at me like that, I'm with Del now. He needs me an' he's been so good to me since -' She touched the scar on her cheek. 'I can't hurt him Jimmy.'

'But do you love him?'

‘That’s a sort of love isn’t it?’ she replied. ‘Caring about someone. And he’s your mate Jimmy, he thinks the world of you.’

Jimmy felt ashamed. He knew that if she hadn’t said any of that, if he had kissed her and she had responded he wouldn’t have thought about Del at all. What sort of mate did that make him?

‘Come on,’ he said, jumping over the wall and helping her over. ‘Beat you to the other side.’

They ran across the pitch, down the tunnel, out of the ground and only slowed down as they walked out through the entrance. They looked at each other and laughed. It was alright, Jimmy thought, it *would* be alright.

A horn sounded loudly behind them. Jimmy pulled Josie out of the way as a smart sports car bore down on them, the driver waved as they stood back.

‘Bleeding hell,’ said Jimmy, laughing and waving back. ‘Hey Bobby! Bobby Moore!’

He turned to Josie. ‘That was -’

‘Bobby Moore,’ she finished for him. ‘I don’t live on a different planet you know. An’ you men go on about us screaming about The Beatles, you’re just as bad. At least we get excited about the *opposite* sex.’

They ran, laughing towards Upton Park station. It was only when they were sitting on the tube that Jimmy suddenly felt empty. He had just almost got run over by Bobby Moore, his dad would have loved that. But he wasn’t here anymore so he couldn’t tell him.

***

‘She’s upstairs,’ said May crossly as he came in to the kitchen. ‘The police have been. You should have told her, she’s a bit upset.’

Jimmy walked slowly up the stairs and knocked on the door of the room his mum was sleeping in. She was sitting on the bed, staring into space. She glared at Jimmy. He put his hands up and sat down next to her. ‘I’m sorry mum,’ he said. ‘I didn’t know the coppers were coming to talk to us, I was going to tell you tonight.’

She said nothing, stood up and moved over to the window.

‘Your dad might have killed him if it was to save Maggie’s life, some sort of accident,’ she said, ‘but he would have confessed at the time. He was an honest man Jimmy.’

Jimmy shook his head. ‘I don’t understand any of this,’ he said.

She came back and sat next to him on the bed. Jimmy put his arm around her and she leant her head on his shoulder. ‘You should have told me before,’ she said, ‘but at least you’re here now. I’ll have to phone Molly, we were going to fly back next week. I don’t know -’

‘Mum if the coppers don’t need you there’s no need for you to hang around here. I’m staying on for a bit -’

He saw her panicked face. ‘Just until this is sorted out,’ he said. ‘I need to know the truth.’

‘Well, they asked me all sorts of questions. I can’t remember what happened one night ten years ago. If your dad had been to *The Kings Head* as usual I'd have been asleep by the time he came back.'

Jimmy looked at her. She couldn't keep her hands still. Twisting them in her lap, her face had gone a deep shade of red.

'You're lying mum,' he said slowly. 'Aren't you?'

'Damn that man,' she said, picking up her hairbrush and throwing it forcefully across the room. 'I'm so angry with him Jimmy for leaving us with all of this and not saying a word. Now I'm even lying to my own son and the police, it isn't fair.'

It wasn't him she was angry with, thought Jimmy. It was his dad and she was right. Whatever had happened that night, he should have said something to them.

'So what *do* you remember?'

His mum took a deep breath. 'I woke up one night,' she began. 'I couldn't tell you what the date was or anything. I heard the creaking of the stairs. Your dad wasn't in bed. '*Is that you Billy*?' I called out. He grunted and I heard him go into the bathroom. I thought he was just back from the pub but when I turned the bedside light on and looked at the clock it was 3.30 in the morning. I had a bad feeling so I just turned the light off and pretended to be asleep. I'd had enough of all the dramas in Churchill Street, I couldn't have coped with anymore. To be honest I thought he might have been with another woman. He was ages washing himself in the bathroom. Then he came in, opened the wardrobe really quietly and took some clothes out. The hangers clanged and I heard him swearing under his breath. I knew he was standing over me then and I kept my eyes closed. Then he went back into the bathroom. Five minutes later I heard him go back downstairs, he was moving around in the kitchen and then I heard the back door closing. Oh, he was very quiet but I heard it, he had gone out again. I got up then and looked out of the window in your room, facing the street. I couldn't see him, it was all quiet out there. I remember it was a really still night. Then I went into the bathroom. I looked in the sink and it was full of water, but red Jimmy, the water was red. It was blood.'

Jimmy held her hand, she was shaking all over.

'I panicked then because I thought he had been in a fight or something, thought he'd hurt himself. I went back to bed, I didn't know what else to do, I was scared. I thought about phoning the police but I didn't know what had happened. Then he came back and went straight into the bathroom, I heard him swearing again and the taps running. He came into the bedroom, I pretended I'd just woken up. I had to know he was alright, whatever had happened. I opened my eyes slowly but he wasn't looking at me, just putting his pyjamas on. Then I put the light on.

'*Jesus Kate, turn that light off, it's four o'clock in the morning.*'

'*Where have you been*?' I asked him. There were no signs of any injuries or anything on his body.

He jumped into the bed then. '*Just been to the lav or ain't that allowed*?'

I should have asked him, demanded to know what had gone on but I was just so glad he was home and safe. He never mentioned that night but suddenly he got quite excited about Australia. I'd even say that he was looking forward to going after all his whinging and moaning before.

After that night, he started having nightmares, just now and then. He'd wake up, sweat pouring out of him and he couldn't breathe. He just said he felt scared and then he would cry. He never cried, your dad.'

Jimmy remembered too when she said it. A couple of nights, when they were in Australia, he remembered being woken up by his dad crying.

'The doctor gave him some tranquilisers. I told *you* it was the war when you told me you'd heard him, that it happened to a lot of ex-servicemen. I even tried to believe that myself, until the police showed me the letter today. So, it wasn't really a surprise Jimmy. I think I always knew something dreadful had happened that night, I suppose I just buried my head in the sand and now, now I've admitted that to you, I know he *did* do it. He did it for us, for our future. What would have happened if he'd confessed? He might have been in prison for a long time. There'd have been no Australia, no money. It would have been the end for all of us.'

'We all bury our heads in the sand sometimes mum,' said Jimmy, 'but I'm not coming back to Australia until this is sorted.'

'But – university Jimmy. You mustn't -'

'I've got a month before the next term starts mum. May and George won't mind if I stay on a bit longer.'

'Well, May and George know all about it and I think it's going to be in the papers tomorrow, about the confession. He was nice, that policeman, very kind. He said there might be some reporters around. They suggested we move back to the hotel but May and George won't let us go.'

'They might not agree with that tomorrow,' Jimmy grinned, 'when the press are all parked outside.'

His mum touched his arm as they got up to move downstairs.

'Do you think he did it Jimmy?'

'If he did mum, it would have been because Mick was trying to kill Maggie. It might have been the only way to stop him. He was a bloody, big man, I remember that. But no, I don't think he did it. It doesn't ring quite true to me.'

'Nothing that happened in Churchill Street was ever simple,' she sighed. 'Oh and I forgot to tell you Jimmy. Clive – I mean Legs - wants to talk to you. May said he's always refused to let anyone except them visit him.'

'Right,' said Jimmy. He had a feeling that he might soon be dreaming about golden beaches in Australia where the sun always shone and problems seemed so much easier to solve.

'I'm going to get us a brandy mum, I think we need it.'

She nodded and tried to smile. 'We'd best phone your Auntie Molly, before she sees it in all the papers.'

***

The three friends stood looking out of the window in Jason's bedroom, their new headquarters. Churchill Street almost seemed under siege this afternoon. There had been police and reporters around since the skeleton of Mick Tyler had been unearthed, but the news of Billy Potter's confession had brought them all out of the woodwork again. The children had enjoyed chatting to the reporters. Winding them up and giving them false clues but now they just wanted their road back. They all laughed as it began to pour with rain and the reporters all ran for cover.

'I wouldn't mind a job on a paper,' said Jason. 'Ain't like proper work is it? And they earn loads of dosh.' The others nodded in agreement.

Nessie produced the notebook from her pocket.

'We don't need that no more,' said Jason. 'We know who done it now don't we? It's all in the papers. You stupid darkie.'

Tonk shouted at him angrily. 'You leave her alone or you can just sod off.'

'Well we're in my bedroom so it's you two that can sod off,' Jason shouted back.

'It's alright Tonk,' said Nessie. 'It don't matter, he'll grow up one day. Anyway, I'm only half a darkie so there.' She stuck her tongue out at Jason.

She wasn't bothered by his remarks. She was nine years old and she was tough. She'd had to be. It was easier now, there were more mixed race kids like her at school. They stuck together in class and in the playground, it was easier that way. She grew to realise that words didn't have to hurt you, not if you didn't let them, her dad had taught her that. She had been so happy this morning when she had heard about Billy Potter's confession. She wouldn't have to worry now, that her mum and dad might go to prison but, for some reason, her dad didn't believe that Billy could have done it. She owed it to him to find out the truth. Even if it meant putting up with prats like Jason Armitage. They needed his bedroom. He was an only child and there were too many eyes and ears in hers and Tonk's houses. Del had promised that he wouldn't tell the grown-ups what they were doing. She was worried about Del, the police had been and questioned him, Paddy and Marilyn yesterday. He had cried at teatime and gone up to his room.

'The coppers have upset him,' her mum had said. 'They always upset people.'

'They have to find out the truth Maggie,' her dad had said. 'I'll go and talk to him.'

She wouldn't tell the others that bit. It wasn't in the notebook, it was private.

She cleared her throat. 'Right,' she began. 'Now we have the confection – I mean confession so Billy Potter is our number one suspect.'

'Could be a false one,' said Tonk. 'Someone might have had a gun to his head.'

'I know that, I was just gonna say it,' said Nessie. She was just about to carry on when the door opened suddenly. She didn't even have time to hide the notebook. It was Jason's mum carrying a tray with juice and wagon wheels on a plate.

'There you are kids,' she smiled. 'What are you doing up here anyway? I thought I heard you shouting. I thought you was having a bloody fight or something.'

Nessie slid the notebook behind her back. Jason's mum was still talking, the permanent dangling cigarette in her mouth.

'I know it's raining out but there's loads of games on your shelves Jason. What about a game of ludo or battleships?'

Jason looked embarrassed. 'We're fine mum, ta for the biscuits.'

She put the tray down on Jason's bedside table and shrugged her shoulders. 'Please your bloody selves,' she said, 'only trying to help. Don't want you getting bored.'

'Oh we're not bored,' said Nessie, grabbing a wagon wheel. 'Ta for these.'

Jason's mum shook her head and went out leaving the door open.

'We'll have to put a notice up,' said Nessie.

While she tore a page from the notebook and wrote 'DO NOT DISTURB' in large letters she thought how nice it might be to have a bedroom of her own, somewhere just to shut herself away. Then she thought about the fun she and Ava had sharing a room. The whispered confidences in the dark, the giggles, the stories, someone to cuddle up to. It hadn't been like that when Marilyn had been in there as well though. Stirring things up and talking about stupid stuff all the time. Telling lies and having teenage tantrums. No, it was lovely now Marilyn had moved out into Paddy's old room, Del had agreed to share with Stuart and it was just her and Ava in a bedroom together.

'Are we gonna get on with this or what then?' asked Jason when they had put the notice on the door and closed it again.

'Where was I?' asked Nessie. 'Oh yeah. So we know now what Jimmy was doing with the coppers. He must have taken the confession in. The one that's in the papers today. So,' she paused, pencil poised. 'As I said suspect number one is Billy Potter.'

'Well, that's it then,' said Jason. 'Don't see as we need to look no further.'

'Well, that's a bit boring,' said Tonk. 'What are we gonna do till we go back to school then? Play ludo?'

'We can't just accuse people if we already know who done it,' said Jason. 'Just cos we're bored.'

Tonk coughed. 'Well, I still say it might be a false confession,' he said knowledgeably. Happens in '*Z Cars*' all the time.'

'Let's just carry on wiv our list of suspects then,' said Jason, yawning, 'though I can't see the point. I s'pose we ain't got nothing else to do. We'll have to put your mum an' dad on the list Nessie. Sorry.'

Nessie passed him the notebook and pencil.

'You can write their names in then cos I ain't,' she snapped.

'And the next one has to be the old lady. Remember,' said Jason. 'Mick Tyler burnt her house down. She must have hated him.'

'I think she knows lots of stuff an' all,' said Nessie, scribbling furiously. 'I don't think she did it though.'

'What about her lover?' Jason asked. 'You know the one who drowned.'

They all giggled.

'What's so funny?'

'People that age can't be lovers you silly sod,' said Tonk, 'they can hardly move.'

'Old Bones,' said Nessie thoughtfully. 'Nah. I think they were both too old. I'll put their names in anyway though.'

'Well, I still think it was that Billy bloke,' said Jason predictably. 'But if it weren't him – that old girl told us to be careful didn't she? Said the murderer might come after us if they know we're on the trail.'

'Scared are you Jason?' Tonk mocked.

'That ain't fair,' said Nessie. 'We're probably all a bit scared. It'll be alright, we'll look after each other.'

'Well I ain't scared,' said Tonk. 'Most exciting thing that's ever 'appened here. Well, since the World Cup anyway.'

They all laughed.

11

All or Nothing – The Small Faces

Josie sat in front of the mirror in her bedroom. She could hear her mum and Auntie Dianne laughing and giggling downstairs, she didn't really want to go to *The Royal Oak* tonight at all.

She sighed as she applied the concealer over her scar. It didn't worry her too much now. It wasn't nice when people stared though, like they had just seen someone out of a horror film. The first time she had been out and that had happened she had run back home and hadn't left the house for three months. Eventually Del had managed to coax her out and little by little she had gained confidence. She touched it gently with her hand. It didn't seem as bad now, she was sure, or was she just getting used to it? Most people were fine about it after their initial shock. Jimmy had been stunned, she had seen it in his eyes. Oh, he had recovered himself well, but she knew what was going through his head.

Jimmy. She had to stop thinking about him. She wished that he would just go back to Australia with his mum. She had always loved him when she was a child. She didn't know whether he knew that but it had broken her heart when he had left.

She laughed to herself. Ten years old and a broken heart, but it was true. You just forgot the feelings you'd had as a kid. They were just as real as when you grew up, she thought and she had never forgotten how she had felt for Jimmy because those feelings had never gone away.

'Well, you've got his cat to remember him by,' her mum had said. Well that hadn't really helped. Poor Precious had been launched into a house where there were two lively twin boys who kept trying to pull his tail and whiskers off. He soon found a friendlier home to move into about half a mile away. No, that hadn't worked at all.

She applied her mascara and Peppermint Pink lipstick and looked at herself, shoulders back. Not at all bad, she thought. At first she had tried to cover the scar with her hair but she soon got fed up with trying to see through it. And her life *was* getting better. Next year she would take her 'A' Levels and then she could start on the road to being a social worker. Her mum had really stood by her and encouraged her.

'Don't you end up like me,' she had said. 'Get some qualifications and then if a man dumps you, you can still manage.'

Yes, life had been better until Jimmy had come back and this murder business had upset Del.

'Jose!' her mum called from downstairs. 'Del's here. And he says to make sure you ain't wearing your mod gear. It ain't that sort of place.'

'Shit,' Josie swore out loud and looked at herself in the mirror. White boots, purple mini-skirt and suede jacket. That was all wrong then. And she'd have to back-comb her hair now as well. Why couldn't people let you wear what you wanted?

'Won't be a minute mum, I'll have to change now.'

Why hadn't Del told her before? He was really getting on her nerves at the moment. She knew why and it wasn't his fault.

If her mum had said that it was Jimmy waiting for her downstairs she would have felt passion and desire flooding her body because it wasn't just an 'in love' feeling she felt for him, she had wanted him to kiss her so badly yesterday, to touch her. What was she going to do?

Stop it, she told herself. Del needs you now and Del was the one who got you back from drowning in all that self-pity. And she knew that he had been devastated when he had heard that his dad was dead even though he made out he didn't care. Oh God, she thought. And now we know that Jimmy's dad probably killed Del's dad. This is going to be a real fun night out. Just bugger off back to Australia Jimmy Potter.

The needle was scratching on the record player. Josie stopped it and put another disc on.

She had been playing the Otis Blue album, one of hers and Del's favourites. She picked up a pile of 45's and picked one.

'*Oh please say to me, you'll let me be your man, oh please say to me, I wanna hold your hand...*'

Josie heard Del's voice, bellowing up the stairs. 'Stop winding me up Josie and get your arse into gear, I ain't in the mood. You know I hate *The Beatles.*'

***

Winston pressed down hard on the horn for the third time. Jimmy sat next to him in the front of the van, there was a knock on the window.

‘Oh no,’ said Winston. ‘That’s all we need.’

The door was sliding back and Jimmy saw Marilyn standing there. Her green mini-skirt barely covered her bum. Her make-up looked as if it had been plastered on and her bleached blond hair was sticking up in a very amateurish beehive. She stunk of hair lacquer and cheap perfume.

‘Whatcha Jimmy,’ she smiled grotesquely.

‘Go home Marilyn, you’re not coming,’ said Winston sternly. ‘You’re too young.’

She completely ignored him and jumped into the van, squeezing herself against Jimmy. He tried desperately to move towards Winston in the driving seat.

‘Bet Jimmy would like me to come wouldn’t you? What a fab night that could be.’

There were loud guffaws from the back of the van where the group were all sprawled over the equipment.

‘Get out now Marilyn,’ Winston said. ‘You look like a tart an’ you’re acting like one.’

Marilyn glared at him. ‘You ain’t my dad,’ she screamed, right in Jimmy’s ear. ‘You ain’t got no right to tell *me* what to do.’

She slid her hand down Jimmy’s back.

‘I think you should do what Winston says Marilyn,’ he said. ‘They won’t let you in the pub.’

Marilyn tried to flutter her false eyelashes at him but one of them was coming unstuck and Jimmy couldn’t help laughing. ‘Go on,’ he said. ‘Del and Josie have got to fit in here yet.’

Moaning and mumbling she slid off the seat, showing her purple knickers as she jumped out of the van. There were wolf whistles from the back.

'You can't fight it Jimmy,' she said, chewing her gum voraciously. 'I know you fancy me.'

'Yeah, alright Marilyn, I'll see you around,' he laughed as he slid the door across after her.

Winston hooted the horn one more time.

***

Josie switched off the record player and marched downstairs as well as she could in her mum's high heels. Her mum and Auntie Dianne, who were getting the tube later to *The Royal Oak*, were still in the sitting room laughing and drinking.

Del was standing in the kitchen, smoking and looking sorry for himself.

'I know you're having a bad time Del,' she said coldly, 'an I'm trying to help you but don't you ever, ever shout at me like that again.'

Del looked down at his feet. 'Yeah well, sorry Jose but Winston's got the van here. We're all waiting on yer.'

'Right well I'll be there in a minute, I'll just say tara to mum.'

She burst into the sitting room where her mum was just opening two babychams.

'I'm off now mum,' said Josie. 'See you there. Don't forget to come will yer?'

Auntie Dianne screamed with laughter. 'Oooh did you hear that Sal? We're both gonna come tonight. Be the first time in years for me.'

That set them both off giggling.

'Sorry Jose,' her mum laughed. 'An' don't be so serious, lighten up a bit. You look good as a rocker, well except for the hair perhaps.'

Josie had changed and was now wearing tight jeans and her brother's old leather jacket.

'What wiv everything going on in the street at the moment?' she scowled. 'How am I supposed to lighten up?'

'You 'ave to darling,' giggled Auntie Dianne, 'if you live round here.'

She lifted her glass into the air. 'An' this helps a bit an' all.'

'Don't worry, Jose,' said her mum sitting down again. 'We'll get there, we've got hours yet and we promise we'll behave.'

That remark made them go into a fit of giggles again.

Josie couldn't help smiling. That would really make her night. Not only was there Jimmy and Del to keep happy but it looked like she was going to have to look after her drunken mother as well. At least her mum was a funny drunk, she thought. It could have been worse.

***

As they made their way to Leytonstone in the old Ford van a joint was passed around. Jimmy, Josie and Del were impossibly squashed next to Winston in the front. Jimmy looked into the back. *The Red Dragons* they called themselves, the group. They were all cracking jokes, excited. *The Royal Oak* was the best gig they had ever been booked for. There was talk of agents and talent spotters often calling in there, they couldn't wait. The Beatles had started it all off and it seemed now that boys all over the country were desperately struggling to learn chords so they could be someone, be famous, have all the girls screaming at them. Not to mention the money.

Jimmy looked at Del, sitting on the other side of Josie, his arm around her protectively. Jimmy tried to forget that he was sitting so close to her, their legs touching. A warm rush infused his body and he closed his eyes. He wouldn't smoke any dope tonight. It would have made it much harder to try to ignore her closeness.

'You having a toke Jimmy?' Winston was passing it to him. He shook his head.

'Pass it here then,' said Del.

Those were the first words Del had spoken to him so far tonight. Josie had told Jimmy about the coppers questioning him. If his dad's confession was true then *his* dad was responsible for the death of Mick Tyler, Del's dad. It wasn't easy for either of them, he thought. He didn't know what to say and he supposed that Del felt the same.

Anyway, after Del had inhaled a couple of drags he seemed to cheer up a bit and joined the general banter. What they were going to play, what order.

'You doing any of Del's songs tonight?' Winston asked them.

'Yeah, thought we'd do '*Take it or leave it*' and '*The End of the Game,*' said one of the group.

Jimmy was astonished and looked at Del. 'You write songs Del?' he asked. 'Bloody hell, you kept that quiet. Not like you to be modest, I'm impressed.'

'You ain't heard 'em yet,' Del laughed at last and Jimmy breathed a bit easier. Perhaps it was going to be alright.

'They're very good,' said Winston, grinning from ear to ear. 'You'll be surprised Jimmy.'

Winston slowed down as a police car overtook them, lights flashing. Jimmy wondered what they would say if they saw inside. A van full of stoned people, including the driver. Jimmy sometimes indulged himself at university but he didn't think driving as well was a good idea. Still, Winston seemed to know what he was doing.

They got to the *The Royal Oak* unscathed and everyone helped to carry the equipment inside.

'You'd better be good,' said the landlord, puffing on his cigarette. 'I heard you was, that's why I booked you. An' no drugs in here, this is a respectable pub.' He looked around at the excited faces and tell-tale red eyes. 'Looks to me like you've had enough already anyway. Stick to the beer now lads please, I've made you some sandwiches in the back.'

The pub soon filled up. It was heaving and stunk of beer, fags and sweat but, unlike *The Kings Head*, it was mostly young people and mainly rockers. Jimmy had been quite unnerved when he had seen on the news about the mods and rockers in his old home country. He wondered why people always had to hate someone. When he had seen footage on telly of the fighting between the gangs in Southend and Brighton it had saddened him. Now he knew why all the group and Josie were wearing leather jackets. Still, it was a good look, he thought and there were a few middle-aged men standing around the bar, just watching.

'Do you work as their manager Winston?' he asked him.

'No, man,' said Winston. 'But I keep an eye on them. They're good Jimmy an' I don't want to see them get ripped off.'

Out of the corner of his eye he saw Sally and Dianne weaving their way towards them. Dianne threw her arms around his neck. 'This can't be little Jimmy,' she slurred.

'Here you are mum, I got you both a seat,' said Josie. 'They're just about to start.'

'Don't worry darlin' I ain't planning on sitting down, except maybe on your knee,' Dianne tried to look sexily at Jimmy. He smiled back uncomfortably.

'Leave him alone Auntie Dianne,' Josie laughed. 'He ain't into old women.'

'Oooh did you hear that Sal? Your daughter's calling me an old woman. I ain't thirty yet I'll have you know, bet I could teach him a thing or two. You look just like your dad.'

Everything suddenly went quiet.

'Oh, trust me an' me big mouth, sorry Jimmy an' sorry about your dad.'

He smiled. 'It's all right Dianne except I think I'm a bit better looking than he was actually.'

They all laughed and Sally and Dianne moved over to stand with other friends they had just spotted.

The music started with some raw rock. Old Eddie Cochran numbers. Josie looked at him and grinned. They were electric, Jimmy thought and Winston was right, he *was* amazed. They were exciting and tight, not a chord or a drumbeat out of place. Before he realised what he was doing Jimmy was up on his feet and jumping around like everyone else. The music just seemed to take over his whole body. He had seen a few groups in Australia but nothing like this, they were just so - alive. Del's drum solos almost raised the roof. The cheering and the music all became a part of the whole night, the whole room. For the next hour, nothing else seemed to matter. He forgot everything, it seemed like this was his whole life.

And then Del got up on the mike and one of the guitarists took over on the drums.

'I just wanna sing this,' he mumbled. 'It's called '*The End of The Game*' 'specially for me dad,' he coughed and looked straight at Jimmy. 'And for me mate Jimmy's dad. Wherever they are, hope they can hear it.' He paused. 'Perhaps not,' he added. 'They'd probably throw stuff at us.'

Everyone laughed but in an embarrassing way. Those that hadn't read the papers had heard all about the murder and the confession and the news had travelled fast as bad news always does.

What the hell is he doing, Jimmy wondered. This wasn't the Del he remembered at all. Sentimental? Soft? Not Del, ever. He thought that perhaps this was going to be a joke, that he was going to get up and sing '*I'm a Pink Toothbrush*' or something stupid like that.

Then he began to sing. His voice was raw and soulful. Jimmy tried to remember if he had ever heard him singing when he was a kid. All he could remember was *Davy Crockett*. That had been Del's favourite for months. His voice reminded Jimmy of Joe Cocker, one of his heroes. The words of the slow rock song brought tears to his eyes.

It's the end of the game, you're not here by my side
When I touch you I know that it's all in my mind
And my last words weren't good and you drifted away
I never could tell you how much you should stay
Now it's the end of the game and you're not gonna see
All the rest of my life you'll be just haunting me...haunting me

Jimmy could feel a lump in his throat and then tears sliding slowly down his cheeks but he didn't care. He felt a hand on his arm and then Josie was hugging him. Over her shoulder he could see Sally and Dianne across the room, dabbing their eyes with their hankies and then Winston was there putting his arms around him and Josie. When all three of them looked up at the stage they could hear Del's voice break and they saw that he too was overwhelmed, he couldn't sing anymore. The music stopped and Del just stood there. Josie left them and ran over to where he stood. She threw her arms around him but he didn't respond. He just grabbed her hand and pulled her through the bar and out of the door.

'Right Jimmy, get off me now man.' Him and Winston were still locked in a bear-hug. 'Don't want no-one thinking I'm a queer, bad enough being a dumb nigger. Man that was some singing. If I'd closed my eyes, I'd have sworn he was a black man.'

'You ain't got the monopoly on soul mate. It ain't just black music,' said a young, sweaty, leather-clad rocker who was standing next to them. Jimmy felt his body taking a sharp intake of breath. How would Winston take that? He was grinning.

'Yeah,' Winston nodded. 'You're right man, ain't just Otis who's got it.'

'That was very restrained of you Winston,' Jimmy tried to smile as the rocker moved away.

'I'm just a bit in the minority here,' Winston grinned. 'It's all about survival man.'

'Is Josie gonna be alright?' Jimmy asked him. 'Del didn't looked angry or anything as they walked out but-'

'She's fine but I'll go and check it out.' He stopped for a second and looked at Jimmy seriously. 'She's Del's girl Jimmy, they're going steady. You have to accept that man.'

So, it was that obvious was it? He would have to try and be careful about showing his feelings. Josie had made it quite clear when they had stood in the chicken run yesterday that she wasn't leaving Del. He looked around him. Some people seemed quite stunned by that performance, of course a lot of them were Del's mates.

Jimmy half recognised some of the faces from when he'd been a kid and he could see that a lot of them had been genuinely moved. There was no doubt in his mind that Del Tyler, his old mate, was going to be a household name.

Josie and Winston came back and walked towards him.

'Del wants to speak to you Jimmy,' said Josie.

'Is he alright?'

'Yeah, he's just outside the front door.'

So, Jimmy thought. That's what this is all about. Winston had spotted his feelings for Josie, probably Del had too. This was going to be awful. What was he going to say? He took a deep breath and went outside.

Del was standing, leaning back against the wall smoking a cigarette.

'That was amazing Del,' Jimmy said nervously. 'You made everyone cry you bastard. What is it? I know I've upset you I can tell.'

Del turned his face towards him. There was anger and pain in his eyes. 'D'you remember when we was kids Jimmy, in the gang?'

'Yeah, course I do.'

'How we all stuck together and looked out for each other?'

Jimmy nodded.

'An' how we always told each other *everything?*'

'Well, not quite everything Del. Everyone has *some* secrets. Look, this isn't easy for us. If my dad *is* telling the truth, then he killed your dad. I don't blame you for being angry.'

'I ain't angry wiv you for that,' said Del quietly. 'My old man was a bastard. I loved him because he was me dad but I ain't blind to what he was like an' why would I be stroppy wiv you? You ain't your dad an' I ain't mine, 'an' loads of people could have killed him. No it ain't that, it's the confession, the letter. All in the papers today. You must have known about it, in fact I heard it was you that took it in. So why didn't you tell *me*? We're supposed to be mates, no secrets, not in our gang.'

For a few seconds Jimmy was relieved. This wasn't about Josie, thank God for that.

But what Del had just said was well out of order, he wasn't being fair. Jimmy could feel his temper rising. He was ten years old again and Del was winding him up.

'So why did you tell me that you hadn't seen your dad since he burnt Greta Broncowiez's house down?' he shouted back at Del. 'You lied to *me* first. OK, I didn't tell you about the confession but I know you saw him the night he died. It's all in there, and yeah I have seen it.' Jimmy took a deep breath. 'If it's all true that is. Is it Del? Did my dad kill him?'

All the energy seemed to leave Del's body. He looked exhausted, Jimmy could see tears in his eyes. 'I'm sorry mate,' he said, 'I don't know, I just didn't see nothing.'

He spat on his hand and held it out to Jimmy. After a few seconds, which seemed like hours, Jimmy did the same.

Josie appeared at the door, hands on her hips. ‘Bloody hell,’ she said. ‘It’s just like when you was kids. At least now you can shake hands without me telling you to. The group are waiting for you Del, landlord says you ain’t done long enough.’

Del grinned at Josie and then at Jimmy. ‘Mates again?’

‘Yeah,’ said Jimmy. ‘Let’s hear you do some more. Tell you what Del, think I’ll have to get your autograph before I go back to Australia.’

‘I’ll never understand men,’ Josie sighed as they piled back in to the pub.

12

I Feel Free – Cream

'Mum, don't worry about the coppers asking more questions.'

'Jimmy, I've lied and lies catch up with you, always. I just don't want to believe that your dad killed anyone, I don't want his name darkened that's all.'

They were sitting outside in May and George's back garden.

'They upset Del yesterday,' she said,' swatting a wasp away with her hand. 'Well, it was him that asked your dad to help, brought it all back to him I suppose.'

'I think he's alright now mum. The group he's in are really good you know, we'll be reading about them in Queensland before too long.'

His mum smiled. 'Probably about ten years after they've had a number one hit here,' she said. 'You know how long it takes things to get to Australia.'

They could hear George pottering about in his shed and the sounds of May washing the dishes in the kitchen behind them. She lowered her voice.

'Did Del say anything to you – you know about that night?'

'No,' said Jimmy firmly. 'No, he didn't see anything mum, let's just forget it now eh? With a bit of luck the coppers won't come here again and you and Molly will be back home next week, sunning yourselves on the beach.' His mum slapped his arm.

'Don't you be so cheeky,' she laughed. 'I don't have time to sit on beaches, you know that.'

Her expression changed. 'I just wondered if he remembered much that's all. He was used to seeing Mick beating his mum up but -'

'Mum there's a lot of whisperings going on, you know what people are like, gossiping, exaggerating, pretending they know more than they do but that copper *will* get to the bottom of it, I know he will. You'll feel a bit better when you're away from here and back in Australia.'

'And you'll tell me the truth, whatever happens? Whoever they blame?'

God, Jimmy thought. The truth thing again. He knew that everyone lied sometimes so would he ever find out the exact truth? He doubted it. They all seemed to be lying at the moment, himself included. If all those lies caught up with them, there'd be hell to pay.

'I think you'll feel better once we've done dad's ashes tomorrow,' he said.

She smiled weakly. 'Even Molly has agreed to come now. I think she thought there was going to be thirty thousand people there, spitting and swearing and singing '*I'm Forever Blowing Bubbles'*. Not to mention twenty two hairy footballers trying to play a match.'

***

There hadn't been thirty thousand singing '*I'm Forever Blowing Bubbles'* in the rain at Upton Park the next day but there were a good few. All his dad's mates from football were there including Loopy and four of his six children and Arthur the landlord had taken time off from the pub. Almost everyone from Churchill Street was there, even Winston came.

'Thanks for coming mate,' said Jimmy shaking his hand. 'I know it's difficult for you.'

'Well, me an' Maggie have agreed not to talk about it, she wasn't happy about me coming. It's hard for her – you know. Mick was still the father of her kids so she just can't face going when your dad is responsible – you know what I mean? Your dad was my best mate down the docks. He stuck up for me when no-one else did. Oh, I didn't mind the name calling, I got used to that. A lot of them tried to get me sacked, they was devious bastards man. He saved my skin a few times.' His voice began to break. ' For what it's worth man I don't believe he did it. Broke my heart when I saw him after the Cup Final, to see him looking so ill. One day we'll sit down an' I'll tell you everything he did for me -'

'Yeah, I'd like that,' said Jimmy. He patted Winston on the back but he was angry inside. Winston was the only one who thought his dad was innocent. Everyone else believed that confession, even his mum. And the more he thought about it, the more he just knew that they were all wrong.

He walked away from the others for a minute as they waited for the vicar to arrive.

'You bastard,' he muttered under his breath. 'What have you left us all with? Didn't bloody think did you? Why? Why did you have to say anything at all? And why didn't I just read the confession, tear it up and burn it? Hindsight was a wonderful thing, he thought.

As he walked towards the vicar and his mum, he saw Josie and Del standing at the back. They were both staring down at the ground but that didn't matter. They were here, it was more than he could ever have expected.

When the vicar had said a few words and the ashes had been scattered on his dad's sacred turf in front of the chicken run, they all sang *'I'm Forever Blowing Bubbles'*.

Sally's sons Chris and Tonk blew bubbles that soared and then burst on black coats and jackets all around the chicken run. Jimmy had to laugh when he heard them arguing.

'You ain't doing it properly,' said Chris. 'Give us it here.'

'Gerroff,' said Tonk, hanging onto his little bubble tin. 'Just cos you've used all yours up. You ain't having mine, piss off.'

Jimmy wanted to be that age again. To not have to worry or to feel so alone. He didn't think he had appreciated it at the time though.

Arthur came over and shook his hand. 'I'll have to get going an' open up,' he said. 'This lot will be gasping for a beer. He'd have loved that Jimmy, well done son.'

'Thanks for coming Arthur, I know you were a good mate of his.'

Arthur looked around furtively, there was no-one nearby except Chris and Tonk. 'Least there ain't no coppers here this time,' he lowered his voice. 'I don't think any less of your dad you know,' he said, 'for what he done. If it weren't for his confession I know they'd be after me for it.'

Jimmy was stunned, but before he could say anything Arthur, the landlord of *The King's Head*, had gone, walking quickly across the Upton Park turf.

He shook his head. Yes, he *had* said what he thought he had. What could he have meant?

He saw his mum coming over and looked over quickly to where Del and Josie had been, they had gone.

His mum slipped her arm through his. 'Let's get home and have a cup of tea Jimmy,' she said, blowing her nose on her hankie.

He smiled at her. 'Sorry mum,' he said, 'but I think mine will have to be a beer.'

***

'Well,' Jason spat out his chewing gum on to the pavement. 'Did you find anything out youse two?'

'We ain't talking out 'ere,' said Tonk. 'Me granddad says we can use his shed today.'

The rain was that fine drizzle that can make you shiver even in the last days of summer.

The three children ran to May and George's house, round to the back and into the shed.

'He said he might put another shed at the bottom of the garden just for us,' said Tonk.

'Why would he do that?' Jason asked. 'To keep an eye on us I suppose.'

'Don't think so,' Tonk replied. 'Just said he feels sorry for us, that's all. Nowhere to build a den no more.'

‘That’s kind,’ said Nessie who had got the notebook out from her pocket.

‘You’re such a *girl,*’ said Jason. ‘You have to be careful of grown-ups you know, can’t trust ‘em. Right, what we got that’s new Nessie? In our book?’

‘Well, nothing since our six suspects,’ she said. ‘I’ve counted Greta an’ Old Bones in. I asked me mum about him an’ she said that he was found at Tilbury wiv loads of booze in his blood but then she said something weird. That he didn’t even drink.’

They all fell silent.

‘Remember how pale she went when we asked her about him?’ said Tonk. ‘*Slumbering salty sailors* – you don’t think –’

‘Are you saying,’ Jason interrupted, ‘that someone killed *him* an’ all?’

‘Yeah, but how could you put drink down someone’s throat if they didn’t want it?’ asked Nessie. ‘He must have wanted to drink it or he’d have just spat it out.’

They all shrugged their shoulders. Tonk stood up and started shuffling around the shed, a quizzical look on his face. He turned to face Nessie. ‘I think *you* need to go and see that old Greta again though. It sounds like she knows more than she’s saying and, I think we’ve got another suspect. We found something out,’ he said, ‘at the Ashes thing.’

‘Go on then,’ said Nessie.

‘It was fab,’ Tonk’s eyes lit up. ‘Ain’t never been to Upton Park when there’s no-one there. It’s huge, that’s where I wanna go when I die an’ all.’

'Might not be too long if you carry on like this,' said Jason. 'I still don't know why we're bothering anyway. If that bloke says he done it then he done it.'

'That's what everyone at the ashes thing was saying an' all,' said Tonk, 'except old Arthur. We heard him say something, me an' Chris.'

'Just tell us what he said,' said Nessie impatiently.

'He was talking to Jimmy, we was earwigging behind him. He said,' he paused dramatically. 'He said *'Good job Billy confessed to the coppers or they'd soon be after me.'* Something like that anyway.'

'Arthur who's the landlord at the pub?' Nessie asked. Tonk nodded.

'Mick Tyler must have done something to upset *him* then,' she said. 'Suspect number seven.' She began writing again in the notebook. 'Something else we have to find out about. Why did *he* hate Mick Tyler?'

'Oh I give up wiv you lot,' said Jason. 'I'll be glad to get back to school an' talk to some normal kids.'

'But if Billy didn't do it,' said Ness. 'Then there's a real murderer round here an' we have to find out.'

'We've got two weeks,' said Tonk, 'two weeks until we're back at school.'

'You're just making stuff up as you go along,' said Jason. 'An' we could get hurt if we keep nosing about.'

'It's OK to be scared Jason,' said Nessie looking up from the notebook.

Jason looked as if he was about to burst with indignation. 'Will you stop saying I'm scared?' he shouted. 'I ain't frightened, ain't nothing to be scared about. I just think it's a waste of time.'

‘You’ll be jealous,’ Tonk laughed, ‘when we’re out solving a murder or two an’ you’re on your own.’

Jason shrugged his shoulders. ‘I suppose I’d better help you then. I knew it would be all different wiv a girl around.’

‘No more whinging now,’ said Tonk, ‘or you’re out of the gang. You’re worse than an old woman.’

‘Might be you that solves it Jason,’ Nessie smiled.

‘It’s already solved an’ I don’t understand why you wanna do it Ness,’ he replied. ‘Your mum and dad are both in the clear wiv that confession.’

Nessie had thought about that and she really did want to believe the confession but she just had a feeling, deep inside that it wasn’t true.

***

‘Come on in Maggie, we’re in the sitting room, I’ll get you a cuppa. Me and Kate are just watching the ‘*Black and White Minstrel Show’.’*

‘Ta May, for asking me over.’

‘Well, I knew Winston would be out with *The Red Dragons* and Kate wanted to see you.’ She put her hand on Maggie’s arm and noticed that her neighbour was trembling. ‘It’s a difficult time for both of you. Would you like a sherry instead of a cup of tea?’

Maggie nodded. ‘Yeah, that’d be nice. I ain’t gonna have a go at her May but if she starts being all hoity toity, I’m pissing off. Alright?’

May put her hand on the door handle. ‘She’s changed Maggie,’ she said, opening the door into the sitting room, ‘it’ll be fine.’

Kate stood up and the two old adversaries smiled at each other across the years.

'I'll get you both a sherry,' said May quickly, turning the TV off. 'Do you know,' she laughed. 'Everyone else from this street has aged, except you two. You both look ten years younger than you did in 1955.' They all laughed as May left the room.

Maggie moved towards Kate and lightly touched her arm. 'I don't blame you or Billy for what 'appened,' she said. 'I want you to know that Kate. Whatever we might say to each from now on.' Kate smiled. 'I mean, well if it was your Billy what done it, if it *was* like he says in that confession, he was only looking out for me.'

Kate looked at the woman standing in front of her. When she had last seen Maggie she had been probably in her mid thirties but May was right. She had lost a bit of weight, her hair, shiny and clean was cut into a smart page boy style. She was wearing jeans and a tee-shirt, she even had a bit of mascara and subtle eye shadow on. She looked, not smart but clean and modern. And there was a softness about her face. Oh, the old scars were still there, Mick's legacy. But over the years they seemed to have faded into the background. She looked almost pretty, Kate thought.

'You're happy with Winston aren't you?'

'I am love, yeah. He's a good man, ain't never been treated like that before. It's like living in a different house now. I don't know why I put up wiv it, all them years. Mind you it weren't easy at first, there's a lot of prejudice out there Kate.'

'From your family?'

Maggie chuckled. 'No, *my* family weren't bothered, his were. They still don't speak to me. What hurts me more is they won't have nothing to do wiv Nessie neither. Still, it's their loss ennit?'

'Billy always thought a lot of Winston,' Kate whispered. She could feel the lump in her throat that was happening all the time. She hoped that someday soon she could mention his name without needing to cry. She coughed and Maggie put her trembling hand over hers.

'I'm so sorry gel,' she said. 'I liked your Billy, he was a good man an' all. An' I'm sorry about all the trouble I caused you before.'

'We were both very unhappy Maggie, I know I was a pain in the arse. Don't be too nice to me, it makes me worse.'

'Oooh,' Maggie laughed. 'Never thought I'd hear you use the 'arse' word. I always called you Mrs Snotty-nose you know.'

They both laughed as May came in holding two sherries.

'You're too honest for your own good sometimes Maggie. I'd have kept that one quiet,' she laughed, handing them their drinks.

'I weren't honest to the coppers though,' Maggie blurted out. 'Well, not the first time they come round anyway.'

'Have you told them the truth now?' Kate asked.

Maggie nodded. 'Yeah, well, what I can remember anyway. I'm glad we're alright Kate, I mean that, wouldn't have wanted you going back to Australia us still being old enemies.'

'And I think we'll all need each other,' said May. 'I don't know if the police are convinced by your Billy's letter Kate.'

'Well, let's talk about something else now,' said Maggie. 'All this doom and gloom. You should have brought Molly tonight Kate. I heard she was a real good laugh at the funeral. I missed that bit, had one of me headaches.'

Kate giggled. 'I don't think she's got over it yet,' she said. 'I think she's got the longest hangover in history, she's been very quiet.'

'Has Jimmy gone to see the group again?' Maggie patted Kate's hand.

She nodded.

'Me and George went to see them a couple of months ago,' said May. 'Bit noisy for me but they're good aren't they Maggie? You must be proud of him.'

'Yeah, he's doing alright,' she said. 'Not my sort of music though. Tell you what Kate, your Jimmy had better watch out. My Marilyn's after him, fourteen going on twenty that one.'

'She liked him when she was little,' laughed Kate. 'Do you remember that Christmas when the tree fell over? She wouldn't leave him alone then and she was only four.'

'She's been hanging around the house a lot all dolled up,' May laughed. 'Now I know why.'

By the time Kate got to bed she felt much more relaxed about everything. They had had a lovely evening reminiscing. Perhaps they were all looking back and remembering the good bits but why not? What good did it do to dwell on the negative things and that feeling of community spirit *had* been there all the way through her bad times. It had been real, even after ten years it hadn't faded away. She knew that everyone was there for her and Jimmy. She wondered and was amazed that she had just been drinking sherry with the woman whose husband had probably been murdered by hers. It seemed unbelievable. And then it came back to her, like someone had just kicked her in the stomach.

It wasn't only Maggie who hadn't told the police everything.

13

The Pied Piper – Crispian St. Peters

John Paradise felt a surge of energy, at last he felt that they were getting somewhere. He had called the Murder Team in to tell them all the latest.

'Scottie,' he shouted when they were all reasonably present and correct. 'Come and tell us what you've got.'

'Right guv,' he began. 'I've had a good natter to my snout. First off he's told me that there's a lot of talk about Arthur the landlord. Apparently, him and Mick had a fall-out just before Mick disappeared. All my snout knows is that he'd barred him from the pub, which wasn't the first time and that Mick had something on him. He did let him back in pretty sharpish after banning him. I'm -' He glanced across to where Jenny Finch was sitting. 'Sorry I mean *we* are trying to get to the bottom of it. One thing did happen to Arthur just after Mick disappeared, his wife left him. Left the older kids behind, took the younger ones with her. She came back about September 1956, well after the murder. It's probably just a coincidence guv but for some reason – well, I don't know. Anyway we're hoping to crack it soon.'

'Thanks Scottie,' said John Paradise. 'Jenny? How did the interviews with the kids go?'

She stood up, looking nervous. Come on girl, John Paradise thought, hold it together.

'The second eldest boy Patrick doesn't live at home anymore but he says he heard nothing,' Jenny began. 'He only remembered it at all because Winston had come round to take her to A & E. He said it was a pretty normal occurrence when his dad had been at home and that things had been much better since he'd been gone. He remembers feeling worried that Winston might have been knocking her around even though he didn't think they'd been seeing each other long. In fact it was the first time that he had met him, another reason why he remembers. When Winston had taken his mum to the hospital he said that Del and him made a vow that if Winston *did* start beating his mum up, they would '*get rid of him'* quote. He admitted that they didn't fancy a black man as a stepfather.'

She paused for breath. 'I think he was telling the truth guv.'

'Remember what I said last time,' said John Paradise. 'Don't ever assume that any of them are telling the truth. Families, they'll lie for each other till the cows come home. Carry on Jenny.'

'He also said that no-one in the family had mentioned seeing his dad that night. That the first he knew he had been at the house was after the news about Billy Potter's confession had got out. His mum hadn't even bothered telling him.'

John Paradise put his hand up. 'Have Patrick or Del Tyler ever been in trouble with us?'

'Del was involved in a stolen car crash a couple years ago guv, his mate was driving. The car hit and killed an old lady on the crossing in Green Street, they didn't try to make a run for it or anything and were arrested at the scene. Clive Pattinson's still doing time for it in the Scrubs.'

'George Pattinson's son, yes, I do remember that. Carry on Jenny.'

'Marilyn Tyler was only five at the time and remembers nothing. She wondered if we could put her photo in the papers though, she's a bit of an attention seeker guv. I wouldn't mind betting that we'll be bumping into her at some point in the future. The other two were even younger, Stuart and Ava. They were just babies.'

There was silence in the room as Jenny carried on reading from her notes.

'Now, for the only one who does remember much, Del Tyler. He was ten years old at the time, remembers hearing a noise downstairs, came down and saw his dad, who, remember, he hadn't seen for about six months, hitting his mum. He says he shouted at him to stop and tried to pull him off her. He was pretty upset guv while he was telling me all this, we had to keep stopping.'

'So you're saying you think that he was telling the truth as well,' laughed an older detective. 'Women are too soft for this job.'

There were mutterings around the room and some laughter.

'That's enough,' said John Paradise. 'She didn't say that at all. Carry on.'

'Thank you guv,' said Jenny, 'but I *can* stick up for myself you know. I was brought up round here and I happen to think that I'm a pretty good judge of character. In my opinion he wasn't putting it on, he was genuinely upset, more than that really. At some points he was almost hysterically crying.'

A chorus of 'wooooooooooooh' went round the room.

'Oh, fuck off,' Jenny shouted. 'I'd rather have a load of little kids than you lot.'

'Time of the month is it darlin?' asked one of the team.

'That's *enough*,' John Paradise shouted above the hubbub. 'We're trying to solve a murder here, no more interruptions.'

He saw Jenny take a deep breath, he also noticed her eyes watering. No, he said to himself, don't whatever you do let them make you cry because that will be the end. She seemed to gather herself together.

'He says that he ran out into the street to get help and he saw Billy Potter and Theobald Harrison, Old Bones as he was known, coming up the road. He told them that his dad was hitting his mum. Billy went running round to the back of the house. Old Bones told Del to get to bed and took him in through the front door. Says he had no idea what was happening with his mum and dad, he doesn't remember hearing any noise. He just went upstairs to bed and Old Bones headed through to the kitchen. Said he remembers feeling relieved and that he thought they would sort it all out, he just hid under the bedclothes.

After a while he says he heard voices on the stairs and thumping noises but he didn't move. He said he wasn't sure how much later it was but everything had gone quiet. He got out of bed and went into his mum's room. He turned the light on and saw her in bed, she had a bruised face but she *was* conscious. He asked her if she was alright and she answered him, said she could do with a glass of water, so he went and got her one from the bathroom.'

She stopped and took a sip of water from her glass on the desk.

'Then he admitted seeing something out of his mum's bedroom window,' Jenny continued. 'Maggie sleeps at the front. He saw *three* men carrying his dad up the road. Billy, Old Bones and -' She stopped, she had their full attention now, there was total silence in the room. 'The other one was Winston Jackson.'

There was a sharp intake of breath around the room.

'He says that he didn't know his dad was dead, he didn't notice any blood. It was dark guv. He thought his dad was probably just drunk and they were helping him up the road, then he went back to bed.'

'Any of the adults speak to him after that?' Charlie asked.

Jenny shook her head. 'He said that Billy saw him the next day and told him that his dad was going back to sea, that he wouldn't be bothering them again.'

'Could he be just out to get his step-father?' John Paradise asked her.

'I don't think so guv. They seem to get on really well, he didn't want to tell me about Winston, that was when he got really upset.'

'And had he met Winston before that night?' the guv asked.

'Yes guv. Said he'd met him a couple of times, he'd come round quite late at night and his mum had sent him, that is Del, to bed both times.'

'He plays in that group *The Red Dragons*,' said a young DI. He saw the puzzled look on John Paradise's face. 'Del Tyler guv, they're a great group. He plays the drums and sings sometimes. Saw them down *The Royal Oak* couple of nights ago, Winston was there. I think he's their manager or whatever, they seemed quite close. He was upset though, Del Tyler. Sang a song for his dad, couldn't finish it.'

'Right,' said John Paradise. 'Well, thank you Jenny, excellent work. It just so happens that we've got two sightings of Winston Jackson, on that night, walking past *The Kings Head* in the direction of Churchill Street at about 10.55 pm. Billy Potter was leaving the pub at that time and the witnesses say that they both walked up the road together.'

There was a low whistle from one of the Murder Team. 'That's it then,' said Charlie, 'bet it's him.'

'We don't know that,' said John Paradise, 'don't know how reliable witness statements can be after ten years. One of the two men says he remembers because when he got home that night his nephew had been killed in a motorbike crash. It does check out, so I'm taking it seriously. We're bringing him in.'

***

Jimmy shivered as he looked up at the imposing gates of Wormwood Scrubs. He remembered seeing the turrets at either side before somewhere. *Billy Liar*, that was it, the film starring Julie Christie. He'd had a real crush on her a couple of years ago.

Dark, black clouds rolled across the sky, the heat was stifling today.

He joined the small, shuffling line of visitors as the side gates creaked open. The little crowd weren't the happiest bunch he had ever seen, most of them had a defeated, empty look on their faces. Maybe it was shame, he thought. He was already beginning to feel the oppressive atmosphere and *he* was just a visitor. What must it be like to come in here for the first time as a prisoner?

They were ushered in to a small, grey room where a prison officer ran his hands over Jimmy's body, quite roughly. Jimmy managed to resist the urge to hit him.

'Turn out your pockets,' he grunted.

Jimmy watched as the officer put his wallet, keys and a small bar of Cadbury's Whole Nut into a small, plastic bag.

'Now Pete,' the prison officer actually spoke to the next visitor he searched. 'What have you brought in for your dad today then?'

'Ain't got a clue what you're on about mate,' said Pete. 'Hey, gerroff me balls!'

'Not your balls I'm bothered about,' the prison officer muttered, holding up a rusty Stanley knife that he had extricated from Pete's underpants.

Jimmy laughed nervously, trying to lighten the mood. He nudged Pete. 'You're very brave or very daft keeping it down there.'

Pete smiled at him but the prison officer didn't. He glared at Jimmy. 'Think it's funny do yer?' he growled.

Jimmy shook his head as, eventually, they all followed the prison officer back in to the wide, bleak corridor; his steel capped boots echoing on the hard floor. Jimmy couldn't see where the corridor ended but he counted numerous sets of gates at intervals along it. The walls were covered in grey paint, peeling off in places. The prison officer didn't speak, just grunted at them all to keep moving. He unlocked the first set of gates and Jimmy shivered as they were ushered through. The officer's eyes avoided all contact and his expression was set in stone. The clang of the gates echoing behind them made Jimmy jump, he hadn't been expecting to feel like this. It was almost as if *he* was the criminal. God knows how Legs had felt. Jimmy couldn't imagine what sort of state his old friend was going to be in, he had always been such a wimp. Every gate clanged and echoed the same, each one seeming to make more noise than the last, deeper and deeper inside. By the time they reached the last one, all sorts of smells were invading Jimmy's nostrils. Urinals and overcooked cabbage, he almost gagged. And there was an acid taste in his mouth, he could feel panic rising through his body. This was not a good place to be.

They were led into the visiting room and Jimmy sat down at a small table, he couldn't believe it when Legs came bounding in smiling. He recognised him right away. Jimmy rushed up and shook his hand.

'No touching!' a guard shouted at them. Jimmy glared at him.

‘Good to see you mate,’ said Legs grinning, ‘can’t tell you how good it is.’

‘You’re looking – really well Legs, looks like prison suits you.’

‘Keep my nose clean Jimmy, get loads of privileges. I can’t say it’s much fun but I’ll be out soon.’

Jimmy looked into the eyes of his old pal, he wasn’t any different, just a couple of feet taller than ten years ago.

‘I just can’t believe that you could kill anyone Legs, I know it was an accident.’

‘Bet you never thought your dad could either,’ said Legs quietly. ‘Sorry about him Jimmy, he was a good man.’

Jimmy looked down at the scratched formica top of the table. ‘I don’t really believe he did it Legsy but whatever he knew about it must have been eating him up all these years. Anyway, enough about my problems. How are you coping in here?’

He looked around, even in this large, anonymous room the atmosphere chilled him. Surrounded by guards watching, listening, some of them shouting at prisoners and visitors, he could sense the hostility.

He saw tears threatening in Legs’ eyes.

‘What happened to you was an accident mate, you didn’t set out to kill anyone.’

Legs shrugged his shoulders. ‘I know that Jimmy, so does God.’

Oh shit, Jimmy thought. Legs has found God.

‘So why did you agree to see me Legs? Your dad says you’ve refused to see anyone except them before.’

‘Might be the last time, you’ll be going back to Australia. Once in the gang always in the gang eh? And you were a good mate to me. You were the first one to talk to me at school when we moved from Blackpool. I remember feeling shit scared and you lent me your pencil. I’d lost mine and that old teacher would have hit me with his ruler. You were the first one who was kind to me but I just want to warn you to be careful with all this Mick Tyler business. If you start poking around it could be dangerous, just don’t draw attention to yourself.’

Jimmy lowered his voice. ‘You mean you think it might have been someone else who killed Mick?’

‘I don’t know. I think you’re just best leaving it alone that’s all.’

Suddenly there was chaos in the room. As if from nowhere, the guards were surrounding a table and shouting at a prisoner.

‘Drop it now Williams,’ one of them shouted. ‘Whatever it is you’ve got in your hand.’

The noise grew louder as the prisoners began banging on the tables.

Legs grabbed hold of Jimmy’s arm urgently. ‘Listen to me,’ he whispered fiercely. ‘While they can’t hear us, they’ll take us all out in a minute. I need you to tell mum and dad something.’

Jimmy tore his mind away from the violence erupting around him and looked into his old friend’s face.

‘I need you to tell them that I’m – I’m a homosexual, you know a nancy boy. I don’t know how else to say it, please Jimmy – can you do that for me? They need to know before I get out and you know me, I'm a coward.'

The guards were still trying to pin down the prisoner who had just received a package from his wife. The other prisoners and some of the visitors were cheering and booing, bells were ringing and an announcement on the tannoy was telling all visitors to leave.

Jimmy looked at Legs, no, he couldn't believe it. Oh, he'd met queers at university so he wasn't naive but surely not Legs, not one of the gang. He shook his head as a prison officer came up behind Legs and jerked him out of the seat.

'Please Jimmy,' he pleaded.

The troublesome prisoner and all the others were being escorted back to the cells, reinforcements had arrived.

Jimmy nodded. 'Yeah,' he said, 'I'll tell them. And I'll be back to see you mate.'

They grinned at each other.

Now that he had got over the shock of Leg's confession and the chaos in the visiting room, Jimmy smiled to himself as he walked back through the prison and out of the gates.

Well, fancy that, he thought. His old mate was a woolly woofter, he wondered what Legsy's God would think about that one.

Jimmy took a deep breath, the air tasted fresher and cleaner somehow, the dark clouds seemed to lighten. The weight that had been smothering him since his dad had died just floated away and he wanted to run across flowery meadows and Australian beaches.

For a few seconds, he just felt giddy with being free.

14

Eight Miles High – The Byrds

Nessie and Tonk slid into the shop doorway as they saw Arthur the landlord turn around.

'We must have walked miles already,' Tonk moaned. 'Where the hell is he going?'

Nessie sighed. 'Will you stop moaning Tonk? That's what we're trying to find out. We need to know if he's got anything to do wiv the murder. If he goes to places we don't know, the people there might be able to tell us more about him. We just need to know what Mick Tyler did to upset him.'

'Must have been something bad,' laughed Tonk, 'if Arthur reckons the coppers might think he done the murder.'

The children ran across the busy road, between the cars. They saw Arthur turn down a small side road, he was whistling and walking quite fast. The children hid on the corner and Nessie peered around the wall. They were just about to move on to the side street when she saw him turning around again. 'Get back,' she pushed Tonk so hard that he fell over.

'*Shivering seaweed*,' said Tonk, ' I'm fed up wiv this. It was supposed to be Chris's job, shadowing people.'

'Well where is he then?' Nessie asked.

'He ain't interested now. Says there's no point if Billy Potter has confessed. Anyway, me mum's taken him to get his new school uniform. Pete's already got his for the grammar, proper posh it is.'

'He must be really clever,' said Nessie.

Tonk shrugged his shoulders. 'Well, I just think he's boring,' he said. 'All he ever does is read books, he don't have no fun. Hey, have another look Ness. Where is he now?'

As Nessie peered around the corner again she saw Arthur, the landlord, disappearing through a purple front gate, about halfway down the road. She told Tonk.

'Well, I suppose we'll just have to wait here now until he comes out.'

'He could be hours,' said Nessie stroking a small mongrel dog that had come up to her wagging his tail.

'There's a garage just past that gate,' said Tonk, 'Looks like we could hide behind it. I'll go and get us some sweets, that'll keep us going.'

'What if he comes out while you're gone?'

'Well, just hide till he's out of sight, then we go an' find out who lives there.'

Nessie was still standing on the corner when he got back with a bag full of blackjacks and milky chews. They ran down just past the house with the purple gate and, sure enough, there was a space between a privet hedge and the garage that they could stand up behind and still not be seen from the house. Nessie made a couple of holes in the hedge so they could get a perfect view of the front door. The red paint on it was peeling and the whole house had a neglected air. The front garden was overgrown and full of empty coke cans and used cigarette packs.

Tonk produced a crumpled pack of Players No. 6 from his pocket. 'D'you want one Ness?' he asked. She shook her head, she had tried one of Del's once and it had made her feel sick.

'Why is there a red lamp on in the window?' Nessie asked.

'Dunno, but it's a bit of a waste of electric,' said Tonk. 'There's one in that house over there an' all.'

'There's loads,' said Nessie. 'Hey, someone else is going in the purple gate.'

They saw a man in a smart blue suit and heard the bell ringing. The door opened.

'Oh hello love.' It was a lady's voice. 'You're a bit early today but she won't be long. Come in and wait.' The door slammed shut.

For the next half hour they waited, Tonk got through two cigarettes. They saw half a dozen men knocking on various doors, not just the purple gate one. There was no traffic though. Nessie wondered how this road could be so quiet except for a few men walking up and down. The road that they had turned off was busy and crowded with shops.

None of the men going by seemed to notice them as they walked past, they all looked quite happy, Nessie thought. One of them had seen them and laughed at Tonk coughing on his fag. 'You need to give them up mate,' he had said to him.

They were just beginning to get really bored when the front door of the purple gate house opened and there was Arthur, stood there laughing and chatting to the lady they had heard before.

‘See you then Arthur. Same time next week?’

Arthur laughed. His face was all red and his stomach was wobbling under a too tight teeshirt.

‘Yeah, see you next week darlin’, look after yourself.’

He looked in their direction with a huge grin on his face before opening the creaking purple gate. He turned left and walked back up to the main road whistling and puffing on a fag.

‘Well,’ Nessie whispered. ‘Wherever he’s been, it’s made him very happy Tonk and he ain’t usually a very happy man.’

‘Mmm,’ said Tonk who was beginning to suspect that this could have something to do with things that his mum had tried to tell him about a few weeks ago.

‘Right, come on,’ said Nessie when Arthur had disappeared from sight. ‘Let’s go an’ knock on the door.’

‘What are we going to say?’

Nessie shrugged her shoulders. ‘I’ll think of something.’

She pushed the bell on the door and they waited for what seemed a long time. Then the door opened and they saw the owner of the voice they had heard. They both gasped.

‘*Plundering porpoises*!’ Tonk exclaimed

She was massive. She filled the whole doorway and the smell of her perfume almost made Tonk feel sick. She wore a tight black skirt that clung to her huge thighs and the rolls of fat on her tummy were squeezed into a tiny red blouse that revealed her ample bosoms.

Her face was caked in make-up and she wore false eyelashes and bright pink lipstick, silvery, blonde hair was piled on top of her head like a beehive. When she grinned at them they thought she was going to eat them alive. Nessie and Tonk both took one step back.

'Now then,' she said, putting her hands on her hips. 'What would you two be after I wonder. Bit young for this sort of establishment I would say. Here, Ruby, come an' see what we've got.'

Another lady of huge proportions joined her at the door and started laughing. She wobbled all over.

'We're looking for our uncle,' Nessie said above the raucous laughter. 'Uncle Arthur.'

They both stopped smiling. 'Why are you looking for Uncle Arthur?' asked the false eyelash lady.

Nessie didn't know what to say. Tonk stepped forward. 'He's supposed to be looking after us,' he said, in what he hoped was an appropriate child-like whimper. He nudged Nessie who promptly burst into tears.

'He ain't give us nothing to eat all day,' she sobbed, 'an' we're starving. We just seen him come in here.'

'Oh, I don't think you did darlin',' said the false eyelash lady. The other one, Ruby, was looking angry.

'Do you know, I hate that Annie. You know, when they're meant to be looking after the kids an' they just -'

'That'll do Ruby,' said Annie firmly. 'Fetch me purse.' She turned back towards Nessie and Tonk.

'I'm sure you'll find he's back home you two, wherever he's bin.' She took two silver sixpences from her purse and passed them to Nessie. 'Get yourselves something to eat wiv this, poor little mites. Off you go now.'

Ruby was still looking angry as Annie began to close the door on them .

'Ain't all fun running a knocking shop is it?' the children heard her saying. 'Those poor kids.'

Nessie and Tonk ran up the road laughing. 'That was funny,' giggled Nessie, 'and scary but at least we've found out that he was just shopping. But what's a knocking shop? What was he buying and we still don't know why Mick Tyler upset him.'

'It could have something to do wiv it Nessie. I reckon whatever he's buying in the knocking shop might not be the law.'

Nessie nodded. 'Anyway,' she laughed, 'we've made a whole bob out of it. That's fab, let's get back an' tell Jason.'

***

When Tonk and Nessie got back to Churchill Street they saw Jason hanging around on the corner looking for them.

'Where the hell have you two bin?' he shouted. 'Don't see why I couldn't come. It ain't fair. I *knew* this would happen when we let a girl into the gang, I ain't happy you know.'

Tonk sighed. 'You can't have three of us following someone, Jason, we'd be falling over each other. Anyway, it was well into Stratford where he went. It was miles an' we ain't learnt much except that he goes to a knocking shop in Palisades Road, full of weird people.'

'Long way to go to buy doorknobs,' said Jason.

'Kind though,' said Nessie, 'giving us a shilling.'

They saw Jason's eyes light up. 'An' whole shilling? I'll have my share then,' he said, trying to get into Tonk's jeans pockets.

'Get off Jason!' Tonk pushed him away and Jason turned his attention to Nessie.

'Don't even think about it.' She glared at him, 'you weren't even there, you didn't do nothing. Anyway, we've spent it on ice creams now.'

Jason spat on the ground angrily.

Nessie sensed the dark thoughts in his head. 'We *do* need you Jason,' she said quietly. 'We're all in this together and at least you know what a knocking shop is, but why would it take him so long to buy a doorknob an' we didn't see him carrying nothing did we Tonk?'

Tonk shook his head. 'It was probably just a little one,' he said. 'He could've just put it in his pocket.'

'I don't know if that's what a knocking shop really is, I'm only guessing,' Jason admitted.

'Our Chris'll know,' said Tonk. 'Let's go an' find him.'

'They ain't back from shopping yet,' said Jason, 'an' me mum says we ain't allowed in my house today, she's just cleaned it.'

'Let's see if we can use me Grandad's shed,' said Tonk. 'He won't mind. We need to get all our facts together. Have you got the notebook Ness?'

'I've always got it,' said Nessie patting the left hand pocket on her blouse. 'You seen me writing in it when we was outside that garage.'

They ran quickly up to May and George's house.

***

'I wonder how Jimmy's getting on at the prison,' said May tearfully as her and Kate sat having a companionable cup of tea at the kitchen table.

Kate put her hand over hers. 'It won't be long and he'll be out May. It was an accident wasn't it? Alcohol is a dreadful thing when it's abused, especially when they're young and not used to it.'

'I don't know Kate but I tell you what, the sooner you get back to Australia the better it will be for you. I don't know what's going to happen with this Mick Tyler murder but I just have a very bad feeling.'

Kate suddenly felt an overwhelming urge to confess to May what she knew but she managed to push it aside. What good would it do? How would it help anything? No, she was sure that the confession would be believed by the police eventually. They didn't need her memories of that night.

There was a loud knock at the back door. May and Kate looked at each other, before May could say 'come in' Maggie had rushed into the kitchen.

'They've taken Winston in again,' she gasped, 'for questioning.'

'Oh, for goodness sake,' said May. 'Why can't they just talk to him at home?'

Maggie sniffed and blew loudly into her hankie. 'Said they've got new evidence,' she said. 'I say it's a set-up cos he's black. You could see it on their faces. They was made up, Winston wouldn't hurt a fly.'

'But they haven't charged him or anything Maggie have they?' asked Kate.

'Not yet but I don't s'pose it'll be long. They'll have put in some fake witnesses. I know what they're like, bastards. An' that solicitor of ours is bleeding useless. Hardly ever sober, he ain't gonna do nothing.'

'Well at least I can help you there Maggie,' said May firmly. She went over to a kitchen drawer and gave Maggie a card.

'I know she didn't get my Clive off,' she said, 'but that was his own fault for not co-operating. Now, she's a woman, but she's a bloody good solicitor.'

'They won't take no notice of a woman,' Maggie wailed.

'The world's changing Maggie,' said Kate whose whole world seemed to be changing and crumbling as the implications of what she had just heard penetrated her mind.

Maggie threw her arms around May. 'I'm sorry love. I know you're trying to help but we can't afford a posh solicitor.'

'She's not a posh solicitor Maggie and me and George will pay for it.'

'I'd like to help as well,' said Kate quietly. 'I don't believe for one moment that Winston did it.'

'He weren't even there,' Maggie wailed. 'Oh girls, thank you. I don't know what to say.'

She collapsed on to a chair.

'I'll get you a cuppa,' said May, 'and then I'll phone her.'

'I've just got to go out for a bit,' said Kate quickly. 'I said I'd pop up to Greta's this afternoon, I won't be long.' She patted Maggie on the head as she went upstairs to fetch her handbag. She had really just needed to get out of the house and gather her thoughts together but as she walked out through the gate she found herself heading in the direction of Greta's house. *She* needed a friend today as well. And it just couldn't be May or Maggie.

***

The gang went straight to George's shed. The window was open and the smoke from his pipe was wafting through it.

'Ooh, I love that smell,' said Nessie.

They recognised the muted sounds of the Beatles coming from inside.

'Does your grandad listen to pop music?' Jason asked.

Tonk nodded. 'He listens to most stuff, he's got one of them new tape recorders an' all, says you can't criticise something unless you've tried it.'

'If he's in we ain't gonna be able to have a meeting,' said Nessie.

'I might be able to get him out,' said Tonk, knocking on the door.

'Can we come in Grandad?'

George opened the door. 'Hello nippers,' he said. 'Wanting to get me out are you? Well I'm not shifting until Maggie's gone.'

He noticed Nessie standing at the back. 'Sorry love,' he said 'but your mum scares me a bit.'

They all laughed, including Nessie. 'Don't worry Uncle George,' she giggled. 'I always keep out of her way when she's off on one an' all.'

George smiled as he knocked his pipe out in the ashtray and turned his tape recorder off.

'Go on then,' he laughed as he picked up his mug of coffee and moved towards the door. 'I'd best find out what's going on anyway, I'll give you half-an hour.'

'Thanks Grandad,' said Tonk. 'Oh, and granddad, do you know what a 'knocking shop' is?'

George almost dropped his coffee and his eyes looked startled.

'Er –er.'

They could see that he was trying not to laugh. 'Ask your mum Tonk,' he said eventually but his eyes were merry and glinting.

He almost ran up to the back door and as he opened it, they heard him laughing.

'You'll never guess what those kids have just -'

Then he stopped and they heard Maggie crying and the door slammed shut.

'Someone needs to go an' listen at that door,' said Jason. 'Something's going on.'

'I hope it ain't me dad,' said Nessie. 'I hope he's not in trouble.'

As she ran away from the gang and up to the house, she knew. His face had just appeared in her head, he was crying. She knew that her dad *was* in trouble and she knew that he needed her.

***

John Paradise sat on the edge of the table, surrounded by the Murder Team. There was a buzz in the room this afternoon. They all knew that Winston had been brought in that morning and rumours had been building up all day.

‘Right,’ John Paradise shouted. ‘Shut up you lot and listen.’ You could have heard a tap dripping ten miles away. ‘First of all I want to thank you for your hard work on this case. It’s only because of that we’ve at last managed to get somewhere. Not information that proves anyone committed murder or manslaughter though, not yet.’

There were some groans and sighs around the room, not as good as they had hoped.

‘But, we can now place Winston Jackson at the scene of the crime or thereabouts. He has admitted that he lied to us and that he *was* in Churchill Street that night. To be fair to him he did admit that *before* I told him we had three witness sightings although Del Tyler insists that he wasn’t there until well after Billy and Old Bones.’

‘Did Winston say why he was there guv?’ Scottie asked.

‘Yes, he did. He said he hadn’t known Maggie long then but they’d already slept together. He’d got back from the dogs, made a bit of money, had a few beers -’

‘And a few joints I expect,’ one of the team interrupted. ‘Sorry guv.’

‘Basically,’ Charlie stepped forward,’ he just thought he might get his end away.’

There was some laughter.

'Thank you Charlie,' said John Paradise. 'Can I carry on now? Anyway, he denies having anything to do with the murder and then -'

'His solicitor arrived,' Charlie finished the sentence for him. 'And she's good guv.'

There were a lot of moans and groans around the room.

Charlie opened his mouth to say something and then thought better of it. John Paradise glared at him. 'One thing I've learned about this particular solicitor is that it doesn't help if you give her a hard time so please try to be polite and civil. What you say behind her back as long as it's to each other, I don't care. Anyway, she's advised Winston not to say anything else. We're holding an identity parade tomorrow morning and the two witnesses who claim they saw him walking up to Churchill Street with Billy Potter that night are going to try and identify him. I don't hold out too much hope. It *was* ten years ago and it was dark.'

'And -'

'Don't even think about saying what I know you're going to say Charlie,' John Paradise interrupted. 'Anyone who shows any sign of racism in this team from now on will be off the case and I won't defend them.'

'How did you know what I was going to say guv?'

'It's a talent of mine. I was right though wasn't I?'

Charlie nodded.

'I mean it,' said John Paradise. 'I can't change your private thoughts and what you do when you're off duty but you're here to do a job and that job means you treat everyone the same, whatever they look like, whatever they may or may not have done. We're here to keep the peace not to cause a war. I shouldn't even have to talk to you like this but it scares me lads, it scares me what I see. Those of you who didn't fight in the war need to do some reading up about it. Hitler was one of the worst racists ever born and just look at what he did and not just Jews. Anyone who was different, born different. Something that no-one can change about themselves. A master race, that's what he believed in. Do you really want to be in some sort of Gestapo because that's how some of you will bloody end up if you're not careful. Have you got that?'

It had been a short but powerful speech and the room fell completely silent. From the back there was even some clapping. They recognised the goodness and honesty in this man. Even if they didn't always agree with him, they certainly respected him after that speech.

DI Jenny Finch had tears in her eyes.

'Jenny's off,' said Charlie. 'Look what you've done to her guv.'

They all laughed.

'Oh piss off and get me a tissue you bastards,' she said before joining in the laughter.

John Paradise smiled. She was going to be alright, now she'd proved that she could swear as well as them.

'What did the guv do in the war?' Scottie whispered to Charlie.

Charlie shrugged his shoulders. 'He never talks about it. That's the closest we're likely to get.'

There was a knock at the door and the sergeant from the desk came in.

'Sorry guv,' he said, 'but there's a lady downstairs, she's in a bit of a state, says she needs to see you straightaway, about the Mick Tyler case.'

'Who is it Joe?' asked John Paradise, gathering up his papers.

The sergeant looked at the piece of paper he held in his hand. 'Kate Potter,' he said. 'I think that's right.'

Oh blimey, what now, thought DCI John Paradise.

15

Needle in a Haystack – The Twilights

Kate had made her way quickly to Greta's, *she* would tell her what to do, she knew herself really. From what Maggie had said the police must have found witnesses that placed Winston at the crime scene. Billy hadn't mentioned him in the confession so, if that part of it wasn't true, his whole confession was probably a lie. Kate thought back to that night, blood in the sink, disposing of his old clothes. She never saw them again. Oh, she knew Billy had been there, been a part of it but had he been the one who had killed Mick Tyler? All these thoughts were racing through her head as she rang Greta's doorbell.

Greta made her a cup of tea and they sat together on the settee. A large black cat, greying at the edges now, plonked himself on Kate's knee.

'Is this the last one Greta?' she asked stroking the purring feline.

Greta nodded. 'Yes, it doesn't seem fair to take on any more at my age. They would only end up fending for themselves or being put down.'

She looked hard at Kate and noticed the hands that wouldn't keep still. Always so much trouble in Churchill Street, she thought, perhaps it was cursed. She wondered what had been here before. What old souls were still wandering and trying to find their way.

'So,' she said. 'Is this to do with the murder Kate?'

Kate nodded. She told Greta everything she knew and also about that night. The night that Billy had come home with blood on his clothes.

'It seems to me from what you've said that everyone is lying or shall I say omitting the facts. By not telling them what you knew about that night Kate you are lying as well. You're all covering up for what you think are good reasons but -'

'Cherry pie lies,' Kate whispered. 'That's what my mum called them, it's just come back to me now. '*Lies told for good reasons can still come back and bite you in the bum Kate'*, that's what she used to say. Cherry Pie Lies. Fancy me remembering that, it's almost like she's talking to me now, in my head.'

Greta smiled affectionately at her friend.

'Old Bones *was* there that night though, wasn't he Greta?'

'Yes. He told me that Mick Tyler was dead and that he would never tell me or anyone anything else about it. He was frightened, he had bad dreams for a long time. Yes, he *was* there Kate.'

'And you don't think his death was an accident?' Kate asked. 'You don't think he just got drunk and fell into the river?'

'No, I don't. I'm frightened now Kate for these children. Oh, to them it's just a game but trying to solve a real murder is not a game. I don't know what they might find out and yet I know that the truth has to come. If everyone starts being honest with the police it will be solved. Everyone, including those who have crossed over, have been trying to protect others. The whole incident is struggling to get out of a thick gnarled forest of lies and loyalty.'

Kate looked down at the worn carpet covered in fading pink roses. 'I just want to go home Greta,' she whispered. 'All the ghosts are coming back.'

Greta patted her hand. 'Of course they will Kate,' she said. 'All those bad memories. Your mum and your sister dying in the Bethnal Green Disaster. Do you know false rumours are still spoken about that night? No-one wants to accept the blame or to say sorry. So they just blame the victims. Oh, it was just wartime, they say now, it doesn't matter anymore. All those families who lost someone, it still matters to *them.* Conspiracies of silence.

And your baby, your little girl, the other things that happened to you. But they made you strong Kate. Once you faced those demons and talked about them. Once you told the truth, your truth. We live with those conspiracies all our lives, all buried deep in that forest.'

Kate smiled through her tears and looked into her old friend's crinkly, wonderful face. 'So, what you're trying to tell me Greta, in your own roundabout and complicated way is that I need to go to the police and tell them everything.'

Greta laughed. 'Yes, I do go on a bit I suppose, it's just the way my mind works. It has to be you Kate who decides but I do really believe that unless someone starts telling the truth this will all get buried -'

'In the forest,' Kate smiled.

'Metaphorically speaking, yes.' She patted Kate's hand again. 'You'll be home soon. They'll have no reason to detain you I'm sure. Come and see me again, let me know what happens.'

'With your talents Greta, you probably know already.'

They both laughed as Kate walked out into the muggy, cloudy afternoon.

***

Sally sighed as she opened the back door. The dirty pots were still in the sink. Josie had finished work at two o'clock but she hadn't made a start on the tea. Goodness knows where the boys were, it was all too quiet.

'Josie! Where are you?' she shouted.

She kicked off her shoes and slipped into her cosy, pink, fluffy slippers by the door as Pete thundered down the stairs.

'Where is everyone?' Sally asked him. 'It's like the Marie Celeste in here.'

'Josie's upstairs crying mum. Winston's been arrested. They think it was him that did the murder, she's just been to see Del. They're all pretty cut up about it over there.'

Sally stood absolutely still and in shock. 'No, Winston weren't even there. Was he?'

'Seems he was mum.'

'Right, well you make a start on the tea, it's only sausages and chips and watch that chip pan. Nearly caught light last time you used it. I'll go and talk to her.'

'But mum I really -'

'Look Pete. I know you're clever, you've got into the grammar an' I'm proud of you but it don't mean you can just forget about real life. I need you to cook the tea right now so just do it. You're eleven years old, if you can't cook a few chips then you can piss off an' go an' live somewhere else.'

'Right, that's what I'll do then.'

'Well I don't think anyone would have you, do you?' She shouted as she walked out the door.

'I didn't mean that,' he grinned. 'I meant I'd do the tea.'

Sally turned and smiled at him. 'Ta love, I'm sorry I shouted.'

She walked slowly up the stairs to Josie's bedroom. Sally couldn't understand why her daughter would want to be a social worker. All the ups and downs of her own life should have put her off that but she had always been a kind girl beneath her tough exterior. She wasn't crying for herself now, she was crying for Del. Sally sighed and knocked quietly on her daughter's door.

'Come in mum.'

Josie was lying on the bed, facing the window. The scar on her cheek was a livid red. It always seemed worse somehow when she was upset. She always knew when Josie was out of sorts.

'How did you know it was me?' Sally laughed.

'Can hear you shouting a mile away,' said Josie, turning around to face her.

She wasn't crying any more but her eyes were red.

'Pete told me,' said Sally, 'about Winston being arrested.'

‘He hasn’t been arrested, just held for questioning.’ said Josie. ‘Del’s upset though.’ She sat up on the bed and Sally sat down next to her. ‘If I tell you something mum, please don’t say nothing to anyone.’

‘I promise.’ It was like talking to a little girl again except that her and Josie had never been able to talk then. Before the attack on her daughter they had fought constantly, for all of Josie’s life in fact. For some reason they had just never got on. Sally had always believed that it had been her fault. When the four of them were all young she had just never had time. She stroked her daughter’s hair and Josie rested her head on her mum’s shoulder, they were all right now. Sally felt a moment of pure peace and love even though such dreadful things were happening all around them.

‘It was Del that told the coppers, about Winston being there.’

‘Oh.’

‘There’s two other witnesses an’ all though, that’s why they’ve taken him in. They were putting Del under a lot of pressure mum and it just slipped out. He feels really bad about it, he didn’t mean to grass on him.’

‘So the rest of the family don’t know?’ Sally asked. ‘That he’s told the coppers?’

Josie shook her head. ‘You won’t say nothing will you?’

Sally shook her head. ‘No, of course I won’t.’

Josie stood up. ‘Thanks mum, he’s gone off to rehearse with the group now. There was a bloke at *The Royal Oak* the other night who works for a record producer, he wants to take them into a recording studio next week, just to see how they sound. He ain't promising nothing but at least Del's got that to think about. I'll be down in a minute mum.'

'They are very good,' said Sally as she headed towards the door. She stopped at the top of the stairs and went back in to her daughter's room.

'I don't like interfering Josie and it's your life, but do you really love Del?'

Josie looked down at the floor. 'He needs me mum.'

'That ain't what I asked you.'

They were interrupted by a shout from downstairs. 'Mum! Come quick!'

'Oh shit,' Sally raced downstairs, expecting to see a flaming chip pan. Instead, her son was carefully plating up the tea and grinning.

'Ha,' said Pete. 'Got yer.'

***

Jimmy took a deep breath as he opened the back door. George and May were sitting at the table. When they turned to look at him he just knew that something had happened.

'What?' he asked, his arms outstretched.

'Your mum's down at the police station Jimmy,' said May, getting up to put the kettle on.

'Why? What's happened now?' he asked.

'Sit down lad a minute,' said George.

'No, I need to get down there -'

'Just sit down and I'll tell you what's happened.'

Jimmy sat and May plonked a mug of steaming tea in front of him.

'They're holding Winston overnight. He's admitted that he was in Churchill Street, the night Mick died.'

And then Jimmy knew exactly why his mum was at the station. 'Didn't she say anything to you, about going down there?'

'She'd just been to see Greta,' May said. 'She must have gone straight from there. A policeman just phoned to tell us.'

'Right I'll get down there now.' Jimmy scraped his chair back, taking a quick slurp of his tea.

Jimmy looked into their kind, compassionate faces.

'How is he?' May asked quietly, 'our son?'

Of course they wanted to know about Legs, of course they did. He sat back down again.

'He seems really good, looking forward to getting out.' Jimmy didn't want to pile it on, he thought, but it was the truth, Legsy had looked much better than he had expected. He knew he had to talk to May tomorrow, if they got a quiet moment together, to tell her that her son was a homosexual, but not now. It had obviously been a stressful day in Churchill Street and he wasn't sure how she would take it.

'Go on now son,' said George. 'Go and find your mother and let's just hope that she hasn't confessed to the murder.' They all laughed.

'Bet you're really glad we've come to stay,' Jimmy smiled. 'I'm sorry about all this.'

'Nowt to be sorry about lad. Thank you for going to see our Clive today, it means a lot. We'll get you some tea when you come back.'

As he walked down the road, Jimmy marvelled at what a wonderful couple they were, George and May. Never asked questions, never interfered. They were just *there*.

He heard someone coming up behind him, running and crying. He turned around and saw little Nessie, clutching a piece of paper in her hand.

He put his arm out to stop her. 'Nessie?' he asked. 'Where are you going?'

She was sobbing, her face all tear-stained, her nose running. She sniffed and took in great gulps of air. 'I'm gonna get me dad,' she said angrily. 'They ain't gonna keep him in that place, I ain't gonna let 'em.'

'Does your mum know?' Jimmy asked, putting his hand on her shoulder. 'Where you are?' She was shaking and trembling. Partly with anger, Jimmy thought but mostly it would be fear. 'Does she know where you're going?'

'She's on the piss,' said Nessie matter-of-factly, accepting the hankie Jimmy offered and blowing her nose loudly. 'So she don't care where I am. Anyway, I'd best get going and I ain't coming back without him. Ta for the hankie Jimmy.'

'Look, I'm going down to the police station as well, we could go together.'

'What you going down there for?'

'My mum's there, talking to them.'

'They ain't arrested her an' all have they?' Nessie asked wide-eyed.

'No, well, I hope not.'

They walked quickly to the station.

'Nessie,' said Jimmy. 'I don't think they'll let you see him you know, your dad. They might let you leave him a message though.'

She stopped and looked at him as if he was mad. Her face was twitching, her whole body was tensed up and ready to spring. No, he thought, she wasn't going to go quietly, she was Maggie's daughter.

'We've got loads of suspecs you know,' she shouted, 'not just me mum an' dad, it's all in here.' She produced a small notebook from her pocket. 'We're getting more evidence all the time, ain't fair that they've picked on me dad.'

Then she just took off down the street, he couldn't have kept up with her. My God, she could run, he thought. He almost felt sorry for the sergeant on duty, he smiled to himself. She was a feisty little girl, a bit like Josie had been. Josie, there she was again. At the unlikeliest moments she would just pop into his head and make him smile.

Before he even got through the doors to the station he could hear Nessie shouting. He couldn't believe such a dainty, tiny little girl could be so transformed. That's what love could do to you, he thought.

'I'm staying 'ere till you let me see him you bastards!' she was screaming. 'He ain't done nothing.' As she said it she spat at the sergeant behind the desk.

'You little mucky mouthed shit,' he bawled back at her. 'I'll -'

'Nessie!' Jimmy was shouting now. 'Stop this right now. You're not helping your dad, you'll end up getting arrested yourself.'

‘Good, I can share a cell wiv him, he don’t like the dark.’

Then her whole body seemed to sag, her face crumpled. She ran over to Jimmy and threw her arms around him, he stroked her hair until she stopped trembling.

‘He’ll be scared Jimmy, all on his own,’ she sniffed.

At that moment his mum appeared through a door with the chief copper, John Paradise.

‘What the hell’s going on here?’ he roared. ‘Sergeant? Are you upsetting little girls now?’

The sergeant was wiping the spit from his face with his hankie in a rather exaggerated manner.

‘She’s not a little girl guv, she’s a monster. She just spat all over me.’

Jimmy could see that the DCI was trying not to laugh.

‘She’s just upset,’ said Jimmy. ‘You’ve arrested her dad, they’re very close.’

‘That’s no excuse and she fucking swore at me guv. Little kid of that age, mouth like a bleeding sewer.’

‘Right,’ said John Paradise, looking at Nessie. ‘Come with me and we’ll have a little chat. Marilyn isn’t it?’

‘No, I *ain’t* Marilyn,’ she answered indignantly. ‘I’m Nessie an’ I ain’t going nowhere till I see me dad, I’ll sit in here all night if I have to.’

John Paradise put his hand out, Jimmy gently pushed her away towards him.

‘Go on Nessie, he won’t hurt you, I’ll wait here until you come out. He’s alright.’

'Didn't know me bleeding name though,' she muttered as she shuffled over to where the DCI was standing. John Paradise turned to his mum who was looking worried. 'Thank you for coming in Mrs. Potter, I'll be in touch very soon.' He nodded at Jimmy. 'We won't be long.'

He held out his hand to Nessie but she immediately crossed her arms and looked down at the floor.

'Right, come on then,' he said, 'follow me.'

Jimmy and his mum watched as the little girl monster shuffled reluctantly after DCI John Paradise.

The sergeant behind the desk was clucking, he came out to the front and picked up a piece of paper.

'Oh, that's Nessie's,' said Jimmy. 'She was carrying it when I bumped into her.'

'Kids today,' he muttered, 'chucking litter about everywhere.'

A memory came back to Jimmy then. Him, Del, Legs and Josie. The old gang, walking past the witch's house. Del throwing a bubble gum wrapper down and her coming out, shouting at them. They had only been about seven. They thought she had flown. He remembered the fear and he shivered.

'Oh, leave her alone,' he said angrily, snatching the bit of paper from the sergeant.

He opened it out. Nessie had drawn a picture for her dad. It was their house and in the front garden stood seven stick figures, she had labelled them all. There was her mum, her dad, Del, Marilyn, Stuart, Ava and herself.

He took it over to the sergeant, who had reclaimed his space behind the desk, and passed it to him.

'Could you at least give this to her dad?' he asked him.

The sergeant looked at it and Jimmy saw his face soften. Only slightly, but it did.

'Bloody kids,' he said. 'It's always them isn't it? It's always them that suffers. Then they turn into little shits and produce more little shits who do exactly the same. I'll get it to him. Now, you just sit down nice and quiet while you're waiting, I can't handle any more dramas tonight. It's not even seven o'clock.'

Jimmy smiled at his mum. Now he had to find out what she had been saying to DCI John Paradise.

When was this all going to end?

***

Kate and Jimmy were sitting round the kitchen table having their tea with George and May. Jimmy had made sure that Nessie had got home. All they had managed to get out of her was that DCI Paradise *had* taken her to see her dad. She said that he had seemed OK but she wouldn't say any more.

As they all finished their shepherds pie and baked beans, Kate began to tell them everything that had happened to *her* at the station.

'I was in a bit of a state when I got there to be honest. It was when you said that Winston had been arrested May. I knew I had to go and tell the truth and Greta agreed. I – I lied the first time I spoke to them.' She looked at George and May.

She told them about Billy that night and how she had just put it all out of her mind.

'What did they say?' George asked. 'At the station?'

'It was that Paradise man,' she said. 'He seemed quite understanding, though he did make it quite clear I should have told them about it before and that really what I saw only confirms that Billy was there. At some point he was in contact with Mick Tyler's body, it doesn't prove that he actually killed him.'

May put her hand over hers. 'Did he say you could go back to Australia next week?'

'He said that I might as well. He seems to think that there are people who know the truth but they're all trying to protect someone. He said he was always doubtful about the confession. That it was just too convenient that Old Bones was dead and Billy was dying. And of course, now that Winston has admitted being there, I expect it's him the police think everyone is trying to protect. Oh, I don't know but I do know that the confession just doesn't hold water anymore. I don't think they're very confident of finding out who did it, to be honest. He said, of course, if there is a murder trial, I'd have to come back. So that's what I'm going to do. Me and Molly will be going home next week.' She looked at Jimmy and he shook his head.

'Could Jimmy stay on with you for a bit?' she asked quietly.

'Course he can love,' said May quickly. 'He can stay as long as he likes.'

'Well just make sure that he gets on a plane by the end of September, so he's back for university.'

They all laughed.

'Is it alright if I give Molly a quick ring now George?' she asked.

He nodded.

As Kate scraped back her chair there was a loud banging on the door, they could hear Maggie shouting.

'Oh no,' said George. 'Maggie's on the drink, doesn't happen so often these days. I think I'll be off to my shed.'

'I'll get it,' said Jimmy.

He opened the door to a furious Maggie. This was how he remembered her, she was spluttering and swearing.

'Evening Maggie.'

'I'm looking for your mum, Mrs. Snotty- Nose. Where the bleedin' hell is she?'

'You'll have to get past me first Maggie,' said Jimmy. 'If you calm down a bit I'll let you in – if that's alright with George and May of course.'

'An' who the fuck are you,' she slurred. 'Jumped up little tosser.'

She drew her fist back as if to punch him but he put out his hand and she couldn't get past it. He could see that she had been crying, her face was all red and splotchy.

God, he thought. Mother and daughter all in one night.

'I wanna know,' she was pointing a finger at him now. 'I wanna know what she's said to the cops.'

'I'll tell you tomorrow Maggie.'

Jimmy's mum had come up behind him. 'I'll tell you tomorrow,' she repeated. 'But it's nothing against Winston, I thought it might even help him. I'll come and see you in the morning, I promise.'

'I ain't going nowhere,' said Maggie firmly.

Oh, not again, Jimmy thought.

'Let her in,' May called through from the kitchen. 'Come into the sitting room Maggie but behave. If you don't then I'm throwing you out, I'll get you a sherry.'

'Well, I don't mind if I do.'

Maggie seemed to calm down a bit and Jimmy guided her through to the sitting room where she plonked herself on a chair. As Kate and May sat down on the settee opposite her, Maggie glared at the woman she had never really liked.

'Well Mrs. Snotty Nose what have you got to say for yourself?' she slurred menacingly.

May sent her a warning look. 'I mean it Maggie. If you start, you're out.'

Kate told Maggie about that night and what she hadn't told the police before.

'I lied Maggie,' Kate said. 'I lied to the police. I didn't tell them about it the first time I spoke to them.'

Maggie shrugged her shoulders. 'There's only you who would worry about that. Everyone lies to the coppers, they expect it.'

'But don't you see Maggie that it isn't going to get sorted until people start telling the truth.'

'Perhaps the truth's so bad no-one wants to see it,' said Maggie. 'An' if your husband hadn't done that confession, none of this would ever have come out an' my Winston would be at home wiv me now.'

'Whatever reasons Billy did that for were good ones, I'm sure of it,' said May.

'They were lies though,' said Kate. 'He didn't say anything about Winston being there. What else wasn't he saying? And he's left us with all of this. I'm angry with him too Maggie. If he wasn't already dead, I'd probably kill him.'

They heard a banging on the back door. Jimmy, who had been sitting quietly on the arm of the settee, got up but as he got to the door, Del came bursting in.

'Right mum,' he said. 'Come on, I'm getting you home. Stop terrorising the neighbours,' he laughed. 'We need to get you to bed.'

Maggie tried desperately to get out of the chair. 'Don't know what you've got to be so happy about,' she grumbled.

'Might be getting a record deal tomorrow mum. I might buy you an house in Torremolinos or something.'

Maggie burst into tears. 'I don't want no house in fucking Torrem – whatever it is. I just want my Winston home,' she slurred.

'Come on Maggie,' said Jimmy. Between him and Del they managed to get her up and out of the door.

In his shed, George sat thoughtfully puffing on his pipe. All this talk about who did what and when, all these lies.

'Well,' he said out loud. 'You've left us in a right pickle Billy Potter. What do I do now? Does the person who did it deserve to be protected any longer?'

He wondered if anyone else had worked it out yet or was he the only one alive who had guessed what had happened that night ten years ago?

16

Nowhere Man – The Beatles

John Paradise smiled as he thought about the little girl he had met for the first time last night.

He was waiting for the Murder Team to come in and had poured himself a cup of coffee that his wife always put in a flask for him. That muck out of the machine tasted of nothing. Now he had ten minutes to savour it and enjoy his ham sandwich before they would all come rambling in, coughing and moaning. The euphoria that had followed England's World Cup win had faded like magical snow turning to slush. He sighed and thought about Nessie again.

He had taken her in to his office last night, called Jenny in to sit with them, and sat Nessie down in a chair on the other side of his desk. She had been sniffing and trembling but still defiant.

'We've got five suspecs,' she said to him, 'because I ain't counting me mum an' dad.'

She took a small notebook from her pocket and started looking through the pages.

'Go on,' he had said to her trying to keep a straight face.

'I ain't gonna tell you everything,' she said firmly. 'I ain't a grass but I can tell you a bit about Arthur – if you let me see me dad.'

'Is he your chief suspect?'

She had shaken her head. 'He's the only one I can talk about,' she said.

'OK Nessie, tell me what you've got.'

She had told him what Tonk and Chris had heard Arthur say at Upton Park.

'We followed him,' said Nessie. 'Yesterday, me and Tonk.'

'Where did he go?'

'Are you gonna let me see me dad?'

'Yes Nessie. I *am* going to let you see your dad.'

'He went to a 'knocking shop' in Palisades Road.'

John Paradise had spluttered his cup of coffee all over the desk. He had just taken a gulp and started coughing violently. He tried to prevent the laugh that he knew was about to escape.

'It ain't funny,' Nessie said indignantly, 'we do need your help though,' she added. 'We don't really know what a 'knocking shop' is and no-one will tell us but we know it's something that ain't quite right. There was some weird people, nice though. A big, fat lady give us a shilling.'

John Paradise had recovered himself sufficiently enough to put his serious face back on.

'You shouldn't be hanging around Palisades Road Nessie, it's not a nice place for little girls.'

'I ain't a little girl, I'm nine and a quarter,'

'I'm not going to tell you what a 'knocking shop' is Nessie. You can ask your dad but that information could come in very handy, thank you.'

He tapped his pen on the desk. ‘Do you know anything about Theobald Harrison? ‘Old Bones’ I think you called him.’

Nessie was looking at him suspiciously. ‘When am I going to see me dad?’

‘Soon,’ said John Paradise. ‘Well, I just wondered if anyone has ever mentioned his death. You see Nessie, we’ve been told that his death was not an accident.’

Nessie’s eyes widened and she clapped her hands to her mouth.

‘You mean someone might’ve done him in an’ all?’

He nodded.

‘Well,’ Nessie began. ‘Me mum and Sally Evans was talking about him the other day. They said it was strange that they found him drunk because he didn’t drink and that everyone in Churchill Street knew that and,’ she added, ‘my friend Greta would never have lived wiv a drunk man.’

‘So you and Greta are friends?’

‘Yes, we’re special friends.’

She looked deep into his eyes which, for some reason, made him feel uncomfortable. ‘You could be a special friend an’ all I think. Anyway,’ she changed the subject. ‘How could someone force him to drink beer?’

John Paradise sighed and leant back in his chair. Their eyes met again. He saw her fear and her courage and felt that he had known this little girl all his life, but he had no idea why. It wasn’t a feeling he quite recognised, it frightened him. Sometimes, he knew things that were going to happen before they did but he didn't believe in all that stuff. He never spoke about it, these feelings he had about people. He shivered.

'Sometimes Nessie,' he said, 'people we call alcoholics, once they realise that they can't stop drinking, stay sober for years then they just get a craving, you know like you might do for chocolate.'

'I don't like chocolate.'

'Well, what sweets *do* you like?'

'Lovehearts, they're me favourites but me most favourite thing is ice cream. Dad always buys me ice cream. Can I see him now please, you promised?'

'I just want to try and explain this to you first Nessie. I do believe that this is what alcoholics are like. You might not eat ice cream for years. Then one day something bad happens and you can almost taste it when you walk past the ice cream shop. All those little cornets and the ice cream in the machine and you can't resist, you just have to have one. You think it'll make you feel better.'

'Well it would.'

'But for an alcoholic Nessie, once they get that feeling and they start drinking again, they just can't stop. One is never enough. And alcohol changes your brain, makes you out of control. He was an old man, we think he was just sitting on a bench by the river and fell in because he was so drunk.'

'I suppose if I couldn't stop eating ice cream I would just be sick,' she said seriously. 'Anyway I want to see me dad now. You said.'

'Come on then.' He held the door open and she went ahead of him, almost skipping.

‘Is this normal procedure guv?’DI Jenny Finch asked him as they followed Nessie out.

‘Not really, but there’s no rule that says she can’t see her dad for a few minutes, as long as you stay with them. I’ll get him into the interview room. Sorry Jenny, I know you’re meant to be off duty but it’s important.’

Winston had been sitting on the bed, head in his hands, when John Paradise had walked in. He looked up.

‘When am I going home man?’ he asked

‘Not yet Winston, but I’ve got someone to see you up in the interview room. I’ll just warn you that she might ask you some awkward questions about prostitutes.’

When he had taken him up to the interview room, Winston had opened his arms wide and Nessie had run and thrown her arms around him. She had clung so tightly to him, as if she would never let him go.

John Paradise smiled at Jenny over their heads, he felt a lump in his throat.

‘I’ll leave you to it,’ he said to Jenny. ‘I’ll be back in ten minutes.’

He drank the last of his coffee and wondered why this little girl had made such an impression on him. When he had come back to collect her Winston just told her to be brave and she was as good as gold. With only one backward glance at her dad she had walked with John Paradise down the steps.

‘I still don’t really understand,’ she said, looking up at John Paradise.

‘What don’t you understand Nessie?’

‘Well, me dad told me what a knocking shop was but I just don’t get it.’

‘Perhaps when you’re a bit older.’

‘Oh I know about sex and stuff but why don’t he just do it wiv his wife? Arthur. He wouldn’t have to pay *her* would he?’

John Paradise grinned as he took Nessie back to where Jimmy and Kate were waiting for her.

She had looked at him with those beautiful strange dark eyes. ‘Ta,’ she had said. ‘You’re the only copper I ever liked.’

And then she was gone.

***

As the Murder Team all filed in, John Paradise stood by the board and watched. He shuffled his papers and cleared his throat.

‘Right gents,’ he began ‘and Jenny.’ he nodded at her and smiled. She looked so young or was it him just getting old?

‘First of all, Winston Jackson. We’ve still got him here. Identity Parade at 2 pm. The PC’s will bring in some volunteers later.’

‘That won’t be hard finding a few w – black men around here guv,’ Charlie laughed.

John Paradise gave him a withering look.

‘Did the witnesses know Winston before guv?’ Jenny Finch asked.

‘We can’t find any connection,’ he said. ‘At that time Winston never drank in *The King’s Head*. Neither of the witnesses had worked down the docks. They’re brothers and they knew Billy Potter because their mum had been to school with theirs, it was him they recognised, not Winston. Both of them moved down to Kent shortly after the murder to work on the ferries and they're still there.'

'He's admitted being there though guv?' said Charlie.

'I know,' said John Paradise, 'but only after Mick Tyler was dead. It would help if they could ID him being there earlier. Anyway, just the fact that he's changed his statement and admitted he was there at all is enough to hold him a bit longer, we can get him remanded in custody. Be interesting to see what effect that would have on some of the others in Churchill Street. If we hadn't taken him in, I doubt if Kate Potter would have changed *her* statement.'

'Does that affect anything guv?'

'Not really. Just that Billy Potter was there and was a part of it. Doesn't prove he did it. I'm letting her go back to Australia next week, I really don't think there's any more she can tell us. She'll have to come back if we get someone to trial.'

'Scottie and Jenny.' He paused and pulled his eyebrows together. 'Have you got any more on Arthur, *The Kings Head* landlord?'

'Yes guv,' said Scottie beaming. 'Met my snout last night. Arthur and Mick Tyler fell out after Arthur barred him in October 1955, he'd caused a big fight apparently. According to my snout, he tried to blackmail Arthur into letting him back in. Said he'd tell his wife he was playing away, you know, had other women. Well, Arthur did let him back in but, unfortunately for him, Mick had already told his wife and then he disappeared after that fire. Arthur's wife Polly left him after Christmas, didn't come back for eight months. He was pretty devastated by all accounts.'

'He was heard by countless witnesses saying that he would '*kill the bastard'* if he ever came back,' Jenny added. 'Sort of thing you'd say though isn't it guv? Doesn't mean you'd do it.'

'Get him in for questioning Scottie. His alibi stands up for that night but he visits a prostitute in Palisades Road so he hasn't changed his ways. We can use that to get info out of him if we have to. Landlords hear all sorts of things.'

'Will do guv,' said Scottie.

'Charlie,' John Paradise looked over to where his DI was sharing a joke with someone. 'Tell them about Theobald Harrison.'

Charlie sauntered out to the front of the room and stood next to the guv.

'Right, we've investigated the death of Theobald Harrison, 'Old Bones' as he was known locally. The autopsy confirmed that there were huge amounts of alcohol in his blood. No signs of any injuries or any attack. He was alive when he went in to the river, drowned when he came out. No suspicious circumstances and before anyone suggests it, we can't dig his body up, he was cremated.'

'So we can't prove anything there then?'

'No guv. The woman he lived with said that there was no way he would have willingly started drinking but he had been classed as an alcoholic when he was young and, as we all know, it can happen any time.'

'Thanks Charlie. I think I'll pay a visit to Greta Broncowiez, I haven't actually met her yet. I know she had reasons to hate Mick Tyler but I can't see it. I do think that whoever did this was just trying to protect Maggie, not deliberately setting out to kill him. It's just a question of finding out who.'

There were mutters of agreement around the room.

'Right, that's all for now lads – and Jenny. You all know what lines of enquiry you're on. Anything interesting let me know immediately. Oh, and there's a gang of kids trying to solve the murder. Watch out for them, I don't want them getting hurt but also I don't want them getting in our way.'

'Is it true you let Winston's kid visit him last night guv?' asked Charlie.

'Yes. It's not against the rules Charlie, she was very upset.'

'You're just an old softy aren't you guv?' said Jenny laughing.

'She just caught me on a good day,' he replied. 'You all know I can be a ruthless bastard so let's get to the bottom of this before I'm picking up my old age pension, alright?'

They all muttered and chuckled as they slowly left the room.

***

Ten men lined up at the station. All shapes, sizes, ages. All black. Some looked nervous, some defiant. Winston bit his lip and tried to stop shaking.

The first white man came in with a sergeant by his side. All the men in the line-up could hear what he told him.

'If any of these men is the one you saw on the night of 22nd May 1956 just put your hand on his right shoulder, then walk away. You can take your time, don't rush it.'

The white man looked terrified. There must be a better way than this, Winston thought, for everyone. He didn't remember seeing anyone outside *The King's Head* when he had been walking towards Maggie's house that night and he certainly hadn't walked up the road with Billy Potter. He had been well drunk and full of ganja though. He wished now – too late for all that. The past had happened, he couldn't change it.

The white man stopped in front of him. Winston could see the fear in his eyes as he looked him up and down furtively. As he shook his head and moved on, Winston closed his eyes and took a deep breath of relief, he felt close to tears. As he turned his head he saw the man put his hand on an elderly black man's shoulder. The man's eyes widened in horror, he kept moving his head around in an agitated manner. Winston looked at him and tried to convey sympathy without changing his expression. God, he thought, that must be awful. To be picked out when you weren't even a suspect.

The second white man was a very different proposition. He came marching in, full of confidence.

The sergeant repeated the words to him and he stood in front of them all and grinned. 'Ten wise monkeys,' he laughed.

'That's enough,' said the sergeant. 'It's not a laughing matter, just take your time.'

The man walked cockily up the line. Stopping at everyone of them and smirking. Then he did it again before walking back to where the sergeant stood.

'Sorry sarge,' he said mockingly. 'They all look the same to me, can't tell one from the other.'

The young man standing to Winston's left on the line, jumped forward and shouted at him 'You fucking white bastard.'

Winston went after him and managed to drag him back.

'That's him,' said the white man. 'Recognise his voice.'

He put his hand on the shoulder of the man who was now standing back in the line next to Winston.

'Doesn't say nothing about your hearing his voice in this statement,' said the sergeant.

The white man shrugged his shoulders. 'Don't care which one gets sent down, don't matter to me.'

'Piss off,' the sergeant said, giving him a sharp kick on the backside, 'and get back to wherever you come from.'

The irony of the sergeants words weren't lost on Winston. He chuckled and soon the others joined in.

'What's going on sarge?' John Paradise had entered the room. 'This is not a circus, it's supposed to be an identity parade,' he shouted as he went over to talk to him.

Winston couldn't believe what had just happened. The hostility from white man number two had been totally out of order, he was going to have a word with that Paradise man. He was not a piece of shit and he would not be treated like one. God, this world needed sorting out, he thought.

'You're all free to go,' said John Paradise. 'Except you Winston, over here please.'

'That was a fiasco man,' said Winston angrily.

'I know and someone's head is going to roll. I've just had a phone call from Scotland Yard. Have you heard of a racist group called *Freedom United?'*

Winston shook his head.

'Well,' John Paradise continued. 'It seems that they try to set up black people for crimes they might be connected with. Those two are on Scotland Yards list as belonging to them, we're holding them both for wasting our time.'

'Well they ain't much good man,' Winston drawled. 'The dude that the second witness picked out would have been about twelve years old ten years ago. They obviously didn't even know what I looked like either. Waste of bloody time. Anyway does this mean I'm free to go now?'

'Not quite yet Winston. You've lied to us, we've not finished with you yet.'

'Oh an' there was me thinking I might even get an apology.'

'Don't push your luck Winston. We don't do apologies here.'

John Paradise turned and walked away.

***

The house felt strangely quiet. Jimmy's mum had gone shopping up to town with Auntie Molly before their flight back to Australia tomorrow.

Jimmy had woken up late after another night watching Del's group playing. They were recording today up in London and Parlophone were going to record two of his songs. If they came out alright, the group would be signing a contract with them and their first single would be out within a month. At any other time the group would have been ecstatic at this news but Winston, who had mentored and supported them for the last two years, was still locked up in a prison cell. The celebrations had been a bit muted.

Del had been down to the police station yesterday to see when he was going to be released.

'Don't want to record nothing without him there Jimmy,' he had said. 'They ain't got nothing on him. Both them witnesses picked other blokes. I told 'em it was important but they ain't interested.'

'Get Nessie to ask,' said Jimmy. 'She gets on well with that John Paradise. If anyone can get Winston out she will.'

'I hope she ain't getting too friendly wiv the coppers,' said Del angrily.

'Oh, they're just messing Del, the kids, like we used to. Trying to solve your dad's murder. Have you seen the little notebook she's got,' he laughed, then saw the pain on Del's face.

'Sorry mate,' Jimmy patted him on the shoulder. 'I know I shouldn't laugh but they just remind me of us when we were kids that's all.'

'Yeah I know, thought we knew it all didn't we?' He punched Jimmy lightly on the chest but at least he was smiling now.

'Listen mate,' Jimmy added. 'In a couple of months time you'll be number one in the charts, playing on '*Top of The Pops', 'Ready, Steady Go'* and everything. You won't be worrying about any of us, money to burn and a bird on each arm. Lucky bastard.'

They laughed. 'Yeah, I'll believe it when it happens,' Del had said, 'but I'd never forget Churchill Street. It's roots ain't it, in me blood an' I ain't interested in loads of birds either.'

Jimmy's heart had sunk when Del had said that.

He sat on the edge of the bed now and thought about Josie again. Perhaps if Del did get famous he would just drift away. None of the Beatles had stayed in Liverpool had they? Couldn't get away fast enough. No, he might forget all about her and once he didn't need Josie any more... no, he was in fantasy land now. He was interrupted by May's voice.

'Do you want some breakfast Jimmy? I've got you a cup of tea ready.'

He moved slowly downstairs. May was sitting in the kitchen, no sign of George. Then he remembered Legs, he had to tell May about her son.

'May,' he began, sitting down at the table and pouring himself a cup of tea from the pot. She interrupted him.

'They've let Winston out,' she said excitedly. 'This morning. Maggie was over the moon. Well, until he told her he was going to the recording studios with the lads,' she laughed. 'I think she's given him a bit of a hard time over that, I don't think he'll be getting much for his tea tonight.'

'That's good news,' said Jimmy smiling, wondering whether Nessie had played a part in Winston's release.

'It was that solicitor we got for Clive. I told you she was good, she must have got them to let him go. They've got no proof that he did anything and she reckons that some fascist group paid those witnesses to lie to the police.'

'But who would want to frame Winston like that? There's some sick bastards around.'

'He did lie to the police though Jimmy, he was there.'

Jimmy nodded. 'Yeah, I suppose so.'

He put his hand on her arm gently. 'May, I need to talk to you, about Legsy – I mean Clive.'

May's face, so recently animated, creased into a worried expression.

'What Jimmy? What is it? I knew he would talk to you. I was so glad when he said he would see you. He just always seems alright when we go, you know he seems to be coping. He's not is he? That's what you're going to tell me.'

‘No, he’s fine May,’ said Jimmy. ‘Well, as fine as you can be in there. It’s just – it’s just something he wants me to tell you, he can’t say it himself.’

Jimmy could see that May had begun to tremble, he needed to get this out quickly.

‘There’s no easy way to say it May but Clive is – is a homosexual.’

There was silence for a few seconds. Jimmy looked out of the window.

‘Oh, thank God,’ May said finally. Jimmy saw her muscles relax and her breathing return to normal. ‘I thought it was going to be something serious.’

‘Do you not mind?’

She smiled. ‘I think I’ve always known,’ she said. ‘Thank you for telling me though Jimmy,’ she patted his hand. ‘That must have been difficult for you.’

She got up from the chair, went to the fridge and took out some bacon. ‘You deserve a big fry-up,’ she laughed. ‘Sally’s brother’s a homosexual you know. He has a lovely time.’

Jimmy almost choked on his tea, stunned at her reaction. He hadn’t expected that. ‘How will George take it?’ he asked her.

‘Probably not quite as well as me Jimmy but he’ll be alright.’

‘Do you *really* not mind May?’

The bacon spluttered and spat in the frying pan.

‘No,’ she said. ‘Oh it would have been nice to have more grand-children I suppose but things are changing Jimmy, thank God. It’s going to be legalised soon, George was talking about it the other night, the government have promised. It won’t be easy for Clive but at least he’ll have our support and he won’t spend a lifetime trying to be something he can’t.’

She passed him his plate of bacon, eggs and all the trimmings. ‘Do you know who I was thinking about this morning?’ she said. ‘Julie Tyler. Do you remember her Jimmy? She died because of a botched illegal abortion. That’s all going to change next year as well, all those young girls who have died.’

‘It’s all about timing isn’t it?’ said Jimmy. ‘Life?’

‘And where you’re born and who you’re born to has a lot to do with it as well,’ May smiled.

‘You’re sounding like George now,’ Jimmy laughed.

‘I knew I’d been living with him too long!’

There was a knock on the door and Josie popped her head round. ‘You’re spoiling him May,’ she laughed, looking at the huge fried breakfast.

‘You having a cuppa love?’ May asked her. ‘Thought you’d have gone to the recording studios. Exciting isn’t it?’

‘Well,’ said Josie. ‘I might pop in later but I’ve just come off nights, I’m a bit knackered.’

‘Do you fancy going for a walk?’ asked Jimmy, still wolfing down his breakfast.

Josie nodded as May poured her a cup of tea. ‘That’d be nice.’

She smiled at him and it nearly broke his heart.

17

Sunny Afternoon – The Kinks

Greta looked closely at the detective who had come to question her. She recognised him immediately as one with the gift but also that it was a gift he had not yet accepted.

'I have spoken twice to other detectives already,' she told him. 'I really don't remember that date particularly but I will be honest with you Chief Inspector. I do know that around that time Bones became very agitated, he was frightened. I knew something had happened. When I asked him he told me that Mick Tyler was dead. Nothing else, said I was better not knowing.

'I thought you fortune tellers knew everything,' his eyes twinkled. 'I've read your statements, it's not about that night I want to talk to you, it's about how Bones died. I've heard that you believe his death wasn't an accident. I know you said that at the time but do you still feel the same?'

'I know it wasn't an accident officer. I know that he was coerced into having a drink and once he started he couldn't have stopped, not after the number of years he was dry.'

'And you think it has something to do with Mick Tyler's murder?'

She nodded. 'I knew it was eating away at him, what had happened that night, I should have tried harder to get him to talk about it. I'm an old lady and I just wanted a bit of peace so I ignored it.'

'I know you say you don't remember that *particular* night but would it have been possible that he was there? Did he ever stay out late?'

She nodded slowly. 'At that time we had a ferret as a pet, he was called Chuck – after Chuck Berry.' She smiled. 'Sometimes, he would go missing and if he hadn't come in before we locked up for the night Bones would go looking for him. Often it would be quite late and I was usually asleep by the time he got in. I don't remember a specific night I'm afraid. I just know that he knew something about Mick Tyler's death and that's why he was killed, because he *was* killed officer.' She put her hand on his arm. 'I know you have no proof but I think you believe that too. Tell me Detective Chief Inspector, why are you too frightened to follow your instincts?'

She could see all the muscles in his body tense, her touching him had disturbed him. He stood up with his cup of tea. She watched as he looked around the room. His eyes rested on the deck of tarot cards on top of a small table and then he caught sight of her bare arms. It was a warm day and Greta had taken her cardigan off. He was looking at the number tattooed on her forearm. She followed his eyes and noticed that his hand had begun to shake, some of his tea spilt into the saucer.

He cleared his throat. 'You were in a concentration camp?' he asked quietly.

She nodded and automatically put her other hand over the numbers. 'Which one?' he asked quickly.

'Auschwitz.'

'I'm sorry.' His voice was almost a whisper. 'I'm so sorry.'

'I don't think you're here to talk about me officer but I would like to talk about you, just for a short time. Don't be frightened of things you don't understand,' she said. 'Just let your thoughts come through and your life will be enriched. If you continue to fight it, you will never know yourself properly.'

'And the little girl, Nessie? She told me that you were 'special' friends?'

'Yes, she has the gift as well.'

John Paradise cleared his throat. 'I'm sorry Mrs Broncowiez but I'm a rational man, I can't believe in all this, even if I wanted to. I can't just act on instinct alone, not in this job.'

'You have a very strong psychic presence,' she said softly, ignoring his outburst. 'Everyone has it to a degree when they are born but I'm guessing that when you were a child it frightened you. The premonitions, the unbidden knowledge you could see when you met strangers, the pictures in your head, you rejected it all. There's a cloudiness in your childhood DCI. Paradise. It seems very murky, difficult to see but you still have those intuitive feelings about people. Because you rarely use those skills, they are dormant. Dormant, but not dead. I recognised you the minute I saw you.'

She looked into his eyes and saw a softness before they clouded over and became hard.

'Mrs Broncowiez, I'm here to question *you*. Not the other way round. I haven't got a clue what you're talking about. Now, each to their own I say and if it makes you happy to read cards and palms, as long as you're not doing anything illegal, that's fine. As a policeman, however, I'm afraid I think what you're saying is a load of -.'

'Bollocks.' She finished the sentence for him and they laughed together. Greta smiled at him as he put down his empty cup on the table, next to the tarot cards.

'I think that you should stop being a policeman,' she said, 'just for a few moments and then you might get somewhere. You know who killed Mick Tyler just as I do, your mind just hasn't accepted it yet that's all.'

'God you don't give up do you?' he laughed as he walked towards the door. 'Well, thank you for the tea and your time Mrs. Broncowiez. I think these new teabag thingies might put you out of business.' He smiled and Greta laughed, such an old joke.

He nodded as he headed for the door. 'Well, it's been – interesting to meet you, I'm sure I'll see you soon.' They shook hands.

'Don't leave it too long,' she said softly, 'or we may not meet again and that would be a shame.'

***

It was another warm day in Plaistow. The sunshine on her back made Josie feel unbelievably happy, the fact that Jimmy was beside her made it even better. He kept going around in her head, she just couldn't stop it. So many reasons not to feel the way she did. He was going back to Australia, there was nothing else to say.

Then there was Del. When she had stopped seeing him, before the accident, nothing much had really happened. He hadn't seemed really bothered whether he was with her or not, she knew now how his feelings had changed.

'I've missed you Jose,' he had said when he had visited her in hospital after the attack. 'I didn't know I'd miss you that much. I'm gonna find the bastard who did this and then I'm going to look after you.' That speech had really meant something coming from him, he wasn't the world's most romantic man.

The bandages had just been removed and the wound was horrific to look at but he didn't seem to see it, she had felt such a rush of love for him then and yes, it was love. Not how she felt about Jimmy, a different kind of love. Probably more the sort you would feel for a child. The fact that she had felt herself then to be so ugly and lacking in confidence had made his feelings for her even more precious. They had been fine, until Jimmy had come home.

She looked up at him now. The sun shining on his fair, floppy hair, hands in his pockets like when he had been a kid. He grinned at her as they walked along, they didn't even need any words now.

'Can we have an ice-cream when we get to the park?' she laughed. 'I'm starving. Haven't even had any breakfast yet and it's nearly lunchtime.'

'You can have whatever you want Jose,' he said, 'my treat.'

'I love your Aussie accent,' she giggled. 'You must have a hat wiv corks on back in Australia, bet you have.'

‘Wouldn’t admit it to you if I did,’ he laughed, nudging her arm gently as they walked through the park gates.

Children were playing everywhere, it was the last week of school holidays. Mums with picnics and babies with their nappies hanging down. They headed towards the cafe, bought their ice creams and moved away from the crowds of children and nagging parents towards an oak tree next to the bowling green. It was nice just sitting under the old tree in the shade.

‘I remember climbing this tree when we were little,’ said Josie.

Jimmy smiled. ‘Do you remember when we went to Buckingham Palace Jose?’

‘Yeah, when I got hit by that taxi,’ she laughed. ‘I remember you and Del teasing the guards and one of them told us to fuck off.’

‘I remember being scared that you were dead,’ said Jimmy, taking her hand. ‘Josie -’

She could feel tears in her eyes as she looked into his. ‘When are you going back?’ she blurted out.

‘I’m not,’ he said. ‘I’m going to try and get into university here. I don’t mind if I have to start again but I need you Jose. I need you in my life and if there’s any chance of that, I’ll stay here for ever. There, I’ve said it and I know Del would be hurt and I know I shouldn’t even be thinking it -’

‘Just shut up and kiss me,’ said Josie.

It lasted a long time, their first kiss. By the time they had come back into the real world their ice creams had melted all over the grass.

***

'*Shitting submarines*,' said Nessie as her, Tonk and Jason, hiding behind a convenient bush, watched Josie and Jimmy as they held hands and then kissed.

They had been playing in the paddling pool, just messing about when they'd seen the two of them coming into the park, laughing and giggling.

'Let's follow 'em,' said Jason who had been determined to follow someone after being left out of the expedition to the knocking shops but they hadn't expected them to start snogging.

'Del ain't gonna like that,' said Tonk.

'Well you ain't gonna tell him,' said Nessie angrily.

'I'd want to know,' said Jason. 'If it was me.'

'Perhaps they were just messing,' said Nessie quickly.

'What and leave two bloody ice creams melting in the sun?' said Tonk. 'I'd never do that for a kiss, even if it was Brigitte Bardot.'

Jason laughed.

'Ain't funny Jason,' said Nessie. 'Del's me brother.'

'And Josie's me sister,' said Tonk.

'They're only half brothers an' sisters,' said Jason. 'It ain't the same, me mum says.'

'Keep down, they're moving,' Nessie whispered.

They watched as Jimmy and Josie walked back across the park towards the gates.

'See, they ain't even holding hands now,' said Nessie. 'I think it's alright.'

Tonk nodded. 'Yeah, they was just playing, probably.'

‘Nah,’ said Jason. ‘They’ll have gone somewhere to do sex.’

‘We could follow them again,’ said Jason.

‘Nah, it’s boring,’ said Nessie.

Secretly she felt really upset. She had just got her dad back from a prison cell and now this. Del really would not be happy if he found out about it. ‘I wish that Jimmy would go back to Australia,’ she said angrily.

‘His mum’s going back tomorrow wiv that funny auntie who got drunk but *he* ain’t going yet,’ said Tonk.

‘It’s Del’s dad’s funeral tomorrow an’ all,’ said Nessie quietly, remembering. ‘The coppers have said that me mum can bury him.’

‘The one who was murdered?’ Jason asked.

Nessie nodded.

‘Still it ain’t all bad news Ness,’ said Tonk. ‘Your Del might be famous soon, me mum says.’

‘And then,’ said Jason, ‘he’d have hundreds of women and loads of dosh. He wouldn’t need Josie no more.’

Nessie wasn’t so sure that Del would be interested in lots of women but it did make her feel a bit better to think that he might be on *Top of The Pops.* He would like that, she thought.

‘I think it must be lunchtime,’ she said. ‘Best get back home.’

‘Don’t forget to put all this in the notebook Ness,’ said Jason.

‘I ain’t putting kissing an’ stuff in there,’ she said. ‘That ain’t got nothing to do wiv the murder.’

‘You never know,’ said Tonk. ‘I agree wiv Jason. Hey, I heard that they’ve had that Arthur down the station, asking him questions.’

‘They’re a bit behind us, the coppers,’ said Jason. ‘Got there in the end I suppose though.’

Nessie didn’t say a word as they walked slowly back to Churchill Street.

***

There was a sort of celebratory feel in *The King’s Head* even though Arthur wasn’t in his usual place behind the bar.

‘Is he still down at the station?’ Josie asked Del.

He nodded. ‘They’re playing mind games with them all. That’s what they’re doing wiv Winston an’ all. They ain’t got a clue Jose, no evidence. Just that they was all there and none of ‘em liked me dad much.’

‘I didn’t know Arthur was there that night,’ said Josie.

‘Why else would they take him in? Someone must have grassed him up,’ said Del.

Josie was genuinely puzzled. ‘But why would *Arthur* want to kill him?’

‘Jose,’ Del sighed. ‘Just leave it alone. We’re meant to be out celebrating the group getting a contract wiv Parlophone. Bleeding hell, same label as your sodding Beatles. We could be on telly in a couple of weeks an’ be having a bevy wiv John Lennon.’

Josie grinned at him and he put his arm round her shoulder and kissed her cheek, the scarred one.

‘I ain’t gonna run off and dump you Jose,’ he said seriously. ‘Even if we do get famous. You’ll always be my girl. You know that, don't you? Hey there's Jimmy. Now we can really get the party started.'

Josie shivered and moved over to talk to a couple of the girls she worked with who were in. She didn't really want to see Jimmy tonight. She felt she might give herself away, the feelings she had for him. They'd talked about it all the way back from the park, all she wanted was to be with him and he felt the same. She knew that Del would be hurt but it looked like he was destined for more than just Churchill Street. Josie prayed that fame would turn his head for a while, that he wouldn't be able to resist all the girls that would be hanging around him. She had noticed at *The Royal Oak* that a lot of the girls were looking at him lustfully when he sang. They might be disappointed though if they knew what she did. Jimmy had agreed that they would just have to wait until the time was right, he didn't want to hurt Del either.

She couldn't resist watching him though as he stood laughing and joking with Del. He seemed to sense it and returned her gaze. Then he grinned and she just had to smile back. God he was lovely, she thought and one day they *would* be together, she had to keep that in the back of her mind. Jimmy had promised her that he wasn't going back to Australia. He was taking his mum and Auntie Molly to Heathrow tomorrow and he would tell his mum that he was going to apply for a transfer to London University. Goodness knows how they would manage money-wise but they would get by. Then he would have a degree and she would be a social worker. They would have a lovely little cottage somewhere in

Essex and probably three children, they had decided. God, they had even named them. Molly, Jack and Billy, after his dad. Josie giggled to herself. They had already named their kids and they hadn't even slept together yet, she wasn't sure how much longer she could wait for that.

She had never in her life imagined being so soft and sloppy over a bloke, but it had happened and that was that. It would get her through all the bad bits, all the pretence and the lies. She risked one more glance at him and their eyes met again. God, she thought, I just want to rip his clothes off. She blushed at her own boldness and turned away, the girls were laughing about something that had happened at work and she joined in.

Josie returned to the reality of now. Del, partying and drinking at the moment but tomorrow, tomorrow was his dad's funeral and she would have to be by his side. She knew he was going to be upset and that she had to look after him just like he had looked after her, she owed him that at least.

The pretence started here, the little cottage in Essex was a long way off yet.

***

The kids watched from over the road as Kate, her Auntie Molly and Jimmy got into a taxi to go to the airport. Nessie watched her mum giving the woman she always called 'Mrs Snotty-nose' a hug. Why did grown-ups all do that, she wondered. Say nasty things about people and then be all lovey dovey, she was never going to be like that when *she* grew up.

‘You going to the funeral Ness?’ Tonk asked.

Nessie shook her head. ‘Nah,’ she kicked a stone into the road and looked down at her feet.‘I didn’t know him. Weren’t *my* dad.’ She had never met Mick Tyler and didn’t want anything to do with him, dead or alive. His death had caused that much trouble, her dad hadn’t been the same since he had been locked up at the station, he just looked sad all the time. There was so much stuff she didn’t understand. She needed time to think, especially about earlier this morning and the really scary thing that had happened to her.

‘Well, what we gonna do today then?’ asked Tonk as the taxi set off and they all waved. May Pattinson was crying and blowing into her hankie.

‘Wish *I* could just fly off somewhere,’ said Nessie.

‘What’s up wiv you today?’ asked Jason. ‘You ain’t usually this quiet. There’s sharks in Australia and crocodiles. *I* wouldn’t wanna go there.’

‘And no telly,’ said Tonk.

‘They do have tellies,’ said Nessie, trying to smile.

‘Leave her alone,’ said Tonk. ‘It’s a bad day for her. Come on let’s go down the park.’

Maggie Tyler came over. ‘What you doing today Ness? We’ll be going in a couple of hours and then back to May’s. I’ve left you a sandwich an’ May’s putting a good spread on so you won’t starve. Your dad’s working overtime so he won’t be back till late.’ She took her small red purse from her pinny pocket and gave Nessie a shiny half-crown. ‘Get yourselves an ice cream wiv this.’

‘Ta, Mrs Tyler,’ said Tonk. ‘We’ll look after her, don’t worry.’

Maggie patted him on the head. ‘You’re a good kid,’ she said and then walked slowly back to the house.

‘I’ll come down the park for a bit then,’ said Nessie.

‘Yeah, knew you couldn’t resist an ice cream,’ Tonk laughed.

‘We might find someone else to follow,’ said Jason.

‘Well they still got Arthur,’ said Tonk, ‘down at the station so we can’t follow him, ain’t no-one else. Hey Nessie, we could have a game of crazy golf *and* an’ ice cream wiv that money your mum give us.’

‘Yeah,’ said Nessie. ‘Yeah, let’s do that then.’

After a round of crazy golf they were sitting on a bench eating their ice creams, half watching some very bad tennis players.

‘So is your brother gonna be famous Ness?’ Tonk asked her.

She nodded. ‘Yeah, I think so. They’ve made a record.’

Tonk whistled. ‘*Suffering seahorses*, you will get away from Churchill Street then. He’ll buy you all a big house in the country.’

‘Wiv a fab swimming pool an’ a tennis court,’ Jason laughed. ‘You won’t wanna know us no more.’

‘I won’t go,’ said Nessie.

‘Thought you said you wanted to go somewhere,’ Tonk laughed.

‘Oh just shut the fuck up both of you,’ Nessie shouted. The boys were so taken aback they almost dropped their ice creams, Nessie didn't often use the 'f' word.

She stood up now, trembling, tears in her eyes. 'I'm sorry,' she said quietly, 'but I just need to get away.'

'What – on your own? Why would you do that?' asked Tonk.

'I might go an' see me dad at work,' she said. 'Take me sandwich an' have me lunch wiv him.'

'Alright,' said Tonk, 'but have you got the notebook? We might see something.'

'No, I ain't got it, I forgot.'

'You ain't right today,' said Jason. 'You're acting like a girl. See Tonk, I told you what would happen.'

Tonk shrugged his shoulders. 'You sure you'll be alright?' he asked her.

Nessie nodded. 'Yeah. I'll be OK,' she sniffed.

As she walked away, Nessie knew that she had to have time to think. To work it all out, all the jumbled thoughts that were crashing around in her head. There was one truth in those thoughts among all the rubbish and the scary bits floating around. She now knew, without a doubt, who had killed Mick Tyler.

18

19th Nervous Breakdown – Rolling Stones

'Well, before anyone else says it,' said Maggie, knocking back the large brandy May had poured for her. 'Good riddance to bad rubbish, I'll have another please May an' then that's it, I won't need no more.'

They had all returned back from the crem and most of them were digging in to May's infamous pork pies.

There was an embarrassing silence after Maggie had spoken. No-one could think of anything nice to say about Mick Tyler. Del turned away from his mum. 'He was me dad,' he said quietly.

'I know son an' I'm sorry but I ain't gonna pretend he was a good man. I'll tell you something. I was more upset seeing Mrs Snotty-Nose go back to Australia than I am about – him. And where have you been anyway? We was looking for you when we come out the crem.'

'I just needed to be on me own mum, I've only been gone about an hour and that's Jimmy's mum you're having a go at now,' Del shouted. 'Me best mate. Just shut up mum.'

'It's alright Del,' said Jimmy offering him a bottle of beer. 'Let's get out of here.'

They stood outside the back door, leaning against the wall, drinking in silence.

'I don't know why I'm sticking up for him,' Del said finally. 'He was an old bastard.'

'It was the drink Del, made him nasty. It's an illness.'

Del looked at him in a way Jimmy didn't understand. Like he was already far away, somewhere a lot better than this.

'You need to look forward now,' he said. *The Red Dragons* are good. I mean *really* good, all of you, you're gonna make it Del.'

'Nah, something will happen Jimmy, something bad, it always does. You'd stick wiv me wouldn't you? If things went bad? You and Josie will always be there for me - won't you?'

Jimmy felt sick. Could Del know? No, not possible, he thought. But at that moment in time he felt like he was the lowest of the low. How could they do this to Del? Why did love always hurt other people?

'Course we'd be there for you mate. Anyway, nothing's going to happen, you're going to be a star.'

Josie came out then, she looked pale and drawn. He avoided looking in to her eyes. Del put out his hand and she took it.

'I'll see you inside,' Jimmy muttered and headed back into the kitchen.

People drifted in and out of May and George's house all afternoon. Later on some went down to *The Kings Head* to welcome Arthur back after his night in the cells. A few gathered in George's shed and chatted about football. The sunny weather had broken this afternoon and there were grey skies and showers. Jimmy found himself alone with George in the shed.

'You coming down *The Kings Head* for one George?' he asked him.

George shook his head. 'No,' he said. 'Think I'll just have a night in with the missus. She told me Jimmy, you know, about Clive being a homosexual.'

'How do you feel about it?'

'Not sure really. I've never had any prejudices, I'm lucky like that but when it's your own son...'

Jimmy nodded. 'Yeah, I can see that George.'

'I don't think that May realises how hard it's going to be for the lad because it will be hard, it's not even legalised yet. Oh, I know it's coming soon but I just hope, sounds horrible, but I hope he moves away, because people will talk and that'll upset May more than anything.'

'It would make sense, but you will still go and see him won't you?'

'Course I will, he's my son Jimmy.'

Del appeared at the shed door. 'Have either of you seen Nessie anywhere?' he asked. 'Me mum's getting a bit worried. She ain't seen her all day.'

George looked at his watch. 'I saw her walking down towards the docks at about one o'clock, five hours ago. She was on her own.'

'I'll just check wiv the other kids,' he said. 'She was in a bit of a funny mood this morning that's all.'

'I'll come with you Del,' said Jimmy.

They all moved back towards the house. 'She'll be just playing somewhere,' said George. 'Perhaps she's met some kids from school and forgotten the time.'

They moved into the lounge where Maggie was standing looking worried. 'I think something's happened to her,' she said. 'I can feel it in me gut. Can I use your phone May? I need Winston here now.'

Oh, no, Jimmy thought, not another drama. He thought about his mum and Auntie Molly on their way back to Australia. If it hadn't been for his dad and Josie he would have been with them.

***

Maggie seemed relieved as she came back through to the sitting room a few minutes later. 'I've just seen Sal,' she said 'and Tonk says that Nessie was going to see her dad. Anyway I just phoned and they ain't seen Winston at work since lunchtime, his overtime was cancelled so he must have taken her somewhere.'

You could almost hear the relief around the room.

'I'll give 'em bloody hell when I see them,' Maggie said crossly. 'Worrying me like this.'

They all began to disperse and wander back home. May and George were left at the sink washing up.

'You should have taken them all up on their offers to help,' said George grumpily, looking at the dirty plates piled high.

'I just wanted the house back to myself,' said May crossly. 'I must change the sheets on Kate's bed after we've done this. Oh, I'm going to miss her you know. I've got used to having her here.'

George put his arms around her. 'I know love. You've just been surrounded by men all your life, it's a pity we never had a little girl.'

‘Well, it’s a bit late for that now love, by about twenty five years.’

‘We could still try,’ George laughed, holding her tighter.

‘George Pattinson!’ May giggled. ‘Are you propositioning me, an old age pensioner?’

She laughed again as she went back to her washing-up and flicked a few soap suds over him. ‘Maybe later,’ she smiled, ‘if you’re good.’

***

John Paradise was getting very frustrated now. Lots of suspects, no concrete evidence. The number of people supposedly at the crime scene kept increasing until he was beginning to think that it might have been like that crime novel he had just read where all the suspects stabbed the victim so that no one person could be charged. Charlie was sitting at the desk next to him working on an unpromising lead. He looked up.

‘We’re not getting anywhere with this are we guv? We’ve brought two people in and held them for questioning, one admits being there, the other doesn’t. I reckon that Arthur is telling the truth. I mean he admitted he couldn’t stand Mick Tyler didn’t he? That he blamed him for his wife leaving him but he’s adamant he wasn’t there and one anonymous witness isn’t going to prove he was. His alibi stands up as well, we’ve just got no proof. I reckon it was the darkie but -’

‘That’s because you want it to be,’ John Paradise snapped. ‘We’ve no proof that Winston did anything either. You’re right, it’s all a mess.’

‘Oh, forgot to tell you guv. That batty old woman phoned this afternoon, you know her that lives in the big house?’

‘Greta Broncowiez?’

‘Yeah, that’s the one. Going to stay at her cousin’s in Bournemouth for a week, thought she ought to let us know. I’ve got the phone number.’

He reached over, picked up a jotter pad and passed the top sheet over.

‘Right, when’s she going?’

‘She was going today. We don’t seriously think she could have anything to do with it do we guv?’

‘No, that’s OK. I would have appreciated you telling me *before* she had gone though.’

For a moment he was tempted to tell Charlie about Greta Broncowiez and the strange conversation they’d had. It had been weird because he *had* felt some sort of connection with Greta as he had with the little girl Nessie. He had felt something, he might just phone his mum. See if she remembered things from his childhood, just out of interest of course.

Don’t be so ridiculous, he thought to himself and chuckled.

‘What’s made you so happy all of a sudden?’ Charlie asked. He looked at his watch. ‘Hey guv, it’s gone nine o’clock, we shouldn’t be here.’

The door opened as they were starting to clear their desks. ‘Sergeant?’

‘Hope you weren’t planning on going home tonight guv,’ said the sergeant. ‘This has just come in.’ He handed John Paradise a note. He read it quietly, his eyebrows shot up.

'It's from Winston Jackson. Shit.'

'What is it guv? What's happened?'

John Paradise felt the blood drain from his face. No please, not this, he thought. He turned to Charlie.

'That was Winston on the phone. His little girl's gone missing. Nessie Jackson, nine years old. Last seen at,' he looked at his watch. 'One o'clock this afternoon, she's been missing for *eight* hours.'

***

'Tell you what Loopy, I was shitting meself in that cell.' Arthur whispered to Loopy across the bar as he passed him his beer. 'I tell you, when that door clangs and the lock goes across.' He shivered and wiped his brow. 'I'm going straight now, I'm doing nothing illegal ever again.'

'You didn't do it though did you Arthur? You didn't kill Mick?'

Arthur looked suitably indignant. 'You're a little shit Loopy,' he said. 'How long have we been mates? Course I didn't do it an' I ain't got no idea who did, but I weren't sad to hear it was him. I was good to Mick Tyler, I must have barred him ten times over the years, always let him back in. Gave false alibis for him an' allsorts. Then he grasses me up to the missus. I shouldn't have mouthed off though, should have kept quiet about it.'

'Anyway, they've let you go Arthur, that's the main thing.'

‘They ain’t got no evidence Loopy. They ain’t got nothing on anyone, not really. Don’t know why they can’t just accept Billy’s confession and leave it alone, everyone hated Mick Tyler anyway but what I really want to know is how they’ve found out where I go on a Thursday.’

‘Why? Where *do* you go on a Thursday?’

‘Ain’t telling you but someone’s grassed me up. It’s like the bleeding Gestapo over here now. Sometimes I think we’d have been better off under the Nazis.’

George came rushing in the door and over to the bar. ‘There’s an emergency,’ he gasped. ‘Something bad’s happened.’

He whispered in Arthur’s ear. He rang the bell on the counter urgently.

‘Hey Arthur,’ Loopy shouted. ‘It ain’t bloody nine o’clock yet, hope this ain’t for last orders.’

One look at Arthur’s face told the punters that this was no sort of joke.

‘Winston just got home,’ he shouted. ‘Maggie thought he had little Nessie wiv him, course he hadn’t, he’s been in here. She ain’t been seen since one o’clock, he’s just phoned the coppers now. Has anyone seen her since then?’

There was silence and a horrible gloom descended on the room instantly. There were punters shaking their heads, muttering and swearing. No-one had seen her, no-one.

Del and Jimmy appeared in the doorway, Del looked haunted.

‘We need to find her,’ he shouted. ‘Me little sister. She ain’t nowhere.’

Punters moved towards Del clapping him on the back, trying to offer some words of comfort.

Arthur rang the bell again. ‘Right,’ he shouted. ‘We’re all gonna get out an’ look for her.’ Around the room everyone seemed to become energised, their whole body language changed, from shock and fear to action.

‘Right we need to do this proper,’ said Arthur grabbing a pad of paper from under the bar. ‘The coppers will be here soon but we need to get out there now an’ look for ‘er.’ He brought out a street map and started dividing it into squares with a pencil. He looked around the room.

‘Right,’ he said. ‘I want you in groups of four an’ I’ll give you an area to search. Well *come on*,’ he shouted at them. ‘We ain’t got no time to waste.’

Loopy shouted above the mayhem.‘We’ll find her,’ he said to everyone but looking at Jimmy and Del. ‘Last time we was looking for kids it was you two buggers. You all turned up, so will Nessie.’

Jimmy remembered. When the four of them had run away to London. The day Josie had been run over outside the gates of Buckingham Palace. But that was different, they had run away because they had known they were in trouble. Why would Nessie run away? What could possibly have made her do that? No, this was far more sinister, this was scary. He looked at Del. His friend couldn’t stop twitching, he had hardly spoken to Jimmy since he had burst in to May and

George's house twenty minutes ago, tears rolling down his cheeks. May had gone straight over to Maggie's and he had dragged Del down here because he hadn't known what else to do. He had wanted to see Josie but she was at work, on night duty.

'Let's go an' look in the park Jimmy, it's getting dark now. Wherever she is she's gonna be scared, I ain't gonna be part of Arthur's magic plan.'

'He's only trying to help Del, and he's good at organising, we all want to find her.' Jimmy snapped.

They heard the police cars approaching as they ran out of *The Kings Head* and down the street.

***

'Tonk, just think,' Sally was sitting on her son's bed. The twins were already snoring, she had heard Tonk crying when she came up to go to the toilet. His grubby, tearstained face was melting her heart. 'Maybe you know something Tonk, that'll help us find Nessie. Just think about everything she said this morning because the coppers are going to ask you anyway. Why was she acting strange? What had happened?'

'Nuffink,' Tonk sniffed. 'Just that she wished she was on a plane to Australia like Jimmy's mum.'

'And she definitely said she was going to see her dad?'

'Yeah.'

Sally put her arms round him and he snuggled up to her like when he had been little, she gently brushed his hair away from his eyes.

'Well, that's a good sign Tonk,' she said. 'That means that she probably *has* just run away. Something might have happened at home, they've always been a – strange family. She'll come home when she's hungry and at least it's not cold at night yet, just try not to worry.'

Tonk shook his head. 'I need to stay awake mum, in case they find her.'

'Nice try mate. You can go an' get in my bed, I won't be long. Just for tonight though.'

He tried to smile. 'I'm scared mum, it might be the murderer. He might be after me an' all.'

'What do you mean?'

'Well we've been trying to find out – you know who killed that Mick bloke. We've been following people an' stuff, we've got it all written down. Well, Nessie had it all written down in a little book. All our evidence and all our suspects.'

'So who do you reckon did it then?'

Tonk shrugged his shoulders. 'Dunno. We ain't getting far wiv it to be honest mum. We think it might be Arthur, he goes to knocking shops you know.'

'Right,' said Sally. 'Well, tomorrow, you might want to give that notebook to the coppers, you never know there might be a clue in there.' She ruffled his hair. 'Anyway don't you be worrying about murderers. Whoever killed Mick Tyler was just trying to help Maggie that's all.'

'So he wasn't a proper murderer then?'

'No love. He or she certainly wouldn't kill little kids. Now, go an' get into my bed if you want to.'

'Ta mum,' Tonk whispered.

Sally went back downstairs and out of the back door to see what was happening. There were quite a few neighbours standing around and three police cars. She walked over to where a policeman was making notes and talking to George.

'Excuse me officer,' she said. 'Will you be wanting to talk to the kids tonight? You know, Nessie's mates.'

'And you are?'

'Sally Evans from number 8,' she said.

'Yes, I know it's late love, but time means everything in this sort of thing. We're sure that she's just run off somewhere but we need to find her, we'll be working our way down the street so we should get to see you in the next half hour anyway.' He nodded at George. 'Cheers mate,' he said as he walked away.

Sally nodded. 'I'll go an' get the kids up then I'm going to phone Josie at the old people's home. She might have seen Nessie somewhere.'

'Winston's devastated,' said George. He's gone out looking for her, blaming himself of course. He was knocked off work early and didn't want to come back until Mick's funeral was done so he went to the dogs at Walthamstow and then out for a few bevies. Comes home and everyone thinks Nessie has been with him and, of course, she hasn't. Maggie nearly killed him. Oh God Sal, I hope she's all right.'

Sally saw that there were tears in his eyes. 'Tonk thinks it's something to do with the murder an' that the murderer will be after him an' all. Honestly, kids an' their imaginations.' She tried to smile at George but his face looked set in stone almost as if he had just seen something that had really terrified him.

'No,' he said. 'She'll have just run away, she'll be back soon.'

***

This was every policeman's nightmare, a missing child. Yes, they were all professionals, John Paradise thought, but they were human too and it was down to him to hold everyone together. Maggie Tyler had been hysterical when they had searched the house, screaming abuse at them and refusing to co-operate. It was only when Winston came back from a fruitless search and the doctor had given her tranquilisers that she finally calmed down.

They had questioned everyone in the street but there was very little to go on. Nessie's friends were obviously upset as well but both Tonk and Jason had told him that she had been in a funny mood that morning.

They had told him that there was a notebook that she kept with her at all times while they tried to solve Mick Tyler's murder. It hadn't turned up when they had searched the house but the kids had told him everything that they could remember was in it.

It wasn't much, John Paradise thought. Surely Nessie's disappearance couldn't have anything to do with a murder that happened ten years ago.

He was sitting on his own in a patrol car parked at the top of Churchill Street. The street was sealed off. He sighed. Tomorrow, if she hadn't been found, he would have to deal with reporters as well. Bastards. He hated them in cases like this. They got in the way, asking the residents all sorts of questions, upsetting people who were already emotionally wrecked. Trying to dish the dirt on anyone they could find, just for their headlines. They'd have a field day round here. What sort of person, he thought to himself, would choose to do that for a job.

He looked at the clock on the dashboard. Three a.m. The street was quiet, unbelievably so. There was a slight wind tonight, it blew an empty cigarette packet across the road in front of him. He could have done with one but he had given up five years ago and he wasn't going to go through that struggle again. He couldn't remember when he had last eaten either. Then he felt guilty that he could even think about that when a child was missing and not just any child. Nessie, who he had formed a bond with in a very short time. A child he knew.

It was still warm outside, thank God. To think of her out there in January or February would have made it so much worse. There were patrol cars out everywhere, searching. Not much more you could do in the dark. If they hadn't found her by morning they would have to start searching the park, dragging the boat lake, searching abandoned buildings. They would do it methodically, starting from here. John Paradise knew that the answer was in Churchill Street. He was also sure that Nessie wasn't far away. He felt it in his bones and in his head, like he always had done. Greta Broncowiez was right about him. He knew, he was so sure that he almost smiled to himself. Nessie was alive, he *knew* that she was still alive.

He called in on the radio.

'Yes guv. Any news on the kid?'

'No, but listen Charlie. Get that crazy woman, as you call her, back from wherever she's gone.'

'Mrs Broncowiez?'

'Yes.'

Greta Broncowiez, he thought, Nessie's special friend.

As he finished the call there was a tap on the car window, it was Jimmy Potter. In his hand was a thermos and he was carrying something in a brown paper bag. John Paradise wound the window down.

'May thought you might be a bit hungry Mr. Paradise,' he said.

He passed him a thermos of coffee and a plate of fish and chips covered in the brown paper bag. The smell was overpoweringly delicious and almost brought tears to John Paradise's eyes. May Pattinson had even sent out vinegar and salt.

'No-one sleeping much tonight then son?'

Jimmy shook his head. 'We're playing cards,' he said. 'You will -'

'We *will* find her Jimmy,' said John Paradise shaking the salt on to his chips. 'And we'll find her alive, if it's the last thing I do.'

'Do you think she's been taken by someone?'

'I can't answer that at the moment, we just don't know and tell May Pattinson that I love her.'

He wound the window back up.

It was little things like this that reminded you, John Paradise thought and when you were a copper you needed to be reminded that there *was* good and kindness out there. His working life was full of the dregs of society. For whatever reason they were like that, they were. Oh, the petty thieves and dodgy dealers were alright, you could even have a laugh and a joke with some of them, wide boys. That's what they called them these days. You could see where they were coming from but anyone that would harm a kid in any way. They were scum and he had no doubt that someone had taken Nessie, for whatever reason. He shivered even though it wasn't cold.

'Where are you Nessie?' he spoke out loud. 'Where the fuck are you?'

***

Jimmy lay on the bed, he looked at the illuminated clock. Ten to four in the morning, he kept dozing and waking up again. He imagined that it was the same for all the residents of Churchill Street tonight or this morning or whatever it was. What an awful night.

Him and Del had searched the park until it was so dark that they could scarcely see each other's faces, they searched in silence, calling her name over and over again. The only people they saw were police and others from *The Kings Head* who were all looking too. Sometimes Del would sob and Jimmy would try to console him and then he would be alright for a bit. The darker it got, the worse he was.

'She's out there somewhere all on her own,' he sniffed. 'She's just the same age we was remember? When we was in the gang? She's just a little kid.'

They talked about the old days, about everything that they had done together and even though Jimmy knew that it wasn't appropriate to be thinking about himself at a time like this, he vowed that he could never hurt Del by going off with Josie now. It just wasn't going to happen, he would be fine. He would go back to Australia and live his life alone.

It was almost midnight by the time they got back to Churchill Street, it was choked with patrol cars and police moving from house to house.

'They'll be questioning us now,' said Jimmy.

'Best go an' see how me mum's doing,' said Del. 'See you mate.'

They spat on their hands and shook them.

'They'll find her Del,' said Jimmy as he watched his friend walk slowly back to his house.

'Fucking pigs,' Del turned to him and spat on the ground. 'Couldn't find a tart in a brothel. First thing in the morning Jimmy, we'll go looking again.'

Jimmy nodded. Del had always hated the police, he remembered.

He lay in bed now, everything going around in his head.

'Where are you Nessie?' he whispered to himself. 'Where are you?

19

The Sun Ain't Gonna Shine Anymore – The Walker Brothers

So, it's begun, my final chapter. The end for me. It has to be but I'm gonna make sure I take a few with me, they won't catch me for a while. I wasn't wanting this, not yet. It's not really a good time and I hate things happening at the wrong time. You know? It makes me feel all kind of edgy but everything has moved so fast in the last couple of days, I've had to think quick. Done pretty well so far, though I say so myself. Not sure about the shooter though. Bought it when I heard Billy Potter was coming over, just in case. Soon as I saw I him I knew I wouldn't need it. Just put a note in his pocket. That frightened him half to death I expect. Wouldn't have taken much to blow him away. I've never used one before, a shooter that is. Oh, that ponce in Romford showed me what to do but it's not the same. Thought I'd have more time you see. That I could have gone to a shooting range or someplace. Nowhere round here you can shoot without being noticed. It'll be OK though. I'll make it OK. I think I've done alright so far. Everything's under control. And I'd know wouldn't I? If everything was going to go wrong. You know, if I was going to die.

***

Nessie wanted to be sick, but she couldn't because there was a gag tied around her mouth. She was lying on what she guessed was a mattress and she couldn't move. Wherever she was it was pitch black dark. The fear came slowly, at first she felt nothing. She was just alive and that was enough and then, through the groggy awakenings in her mind, she began to remember. She was right in the middle of a nightmare, it had begun even before she had decided to go and see Greta. Whenever that had been, because she had no idea how long she had been here, tied up and gagged.

She tried to cry out but it just came out like a whimper. And then, in the dark she heard a groan. Someone had answered her, she wasn't alone. It must be Greta. It gave her some comfort to know that she was here too, even if she was in the same position she was in and at least Nessie knew now that *he* hadn't killed her – yet.

When Greta had answered the door to the murderer, Nessie had been sitting on a chair by the back window, looking out at the apple trees dotted around the garden, gnarled and twisted with age. She had heard a stifled scream and, as she jumped up, she saw him dragging Greta into the room with his hand over her mouth. When she saw who it was she gasped, *the murderer*. The murderer was here, in this house.

She had run towards him instinctively armed with nothing but her fists. He had thrown Greta to the floor violently. Nessie had heard a dull thud when her head had hit the carpet. She moved towards Greta but, as she did so, *he* had grabbed her in an armlock, smothering her face with a cloth of some kind that stunk. That was the last thing Nessie remembered. He hadn't spoken a word or uttered a sound.

Everything had seemed to happen so fast and now she had no idea how long she had been lying here, but her arms were really hurting and she could barely feel her legs. They must have been here for a long time. She started to rock her body and found that she could move a bit by rolling. Trying to get some momentum going, she fell on to a cold, stone floor. Where were they? Were they still in the house? She had to get to Greta somehow, make sure she was alright. The blackness in the room kept going round, she was so dizzy. Nessie made another sound and Greta answered. The sound came from her left. She rocked backwards and forwards until she managed to sit up. Greta kept groaning and Nessie shuffled on her bottom towards the sound. Every move hurt her beyond imagining but then, at last, she felt Greta's body, she could hear her breathing. Greta was lying on the floor and Nessie lay down beside the old lady so that their sides were touching. It was such a comfort that she felt tears on her cheeks and somehow she knew that Greta was crying too.

They hadn't been lying together long when they heard a door slam and footsteps. It wasn't as dark now, Nessie thought, it must be daylight outside. They must be in Greta's cellar. There was a strange smell of sweetness mixed with mould and coal dust. She could see that the room was full of cardboard boxes of all shapes and sizes. She didn't want to die in here.

Maybe it wasn't him, perhaps it was the police. That nice one that she had met, he might have worked it out. Where they were.

The door was flung open and the lights went on. He was standing at the top of the stairs. They must be in Greta's cellar and it wasn't the police. It was *him*. When he saw them he laughed.

'That was silly Nessie, all that effort and I even gave *you* a mattress.'

He shook his head. Nessie took a look at Greta, she was awake and her eyes smiled. It's alright, she was saying, it'll be alright, but she had a huge bruise on her head and she didn't look well at all.

Nessie looked back at him and was filled with a great anger. Why was he doing this to them? How dare he? If she could have spat at him she would.

He took something from his pocket and moved towards Greta. 'I'm gonna undo your gag Mrs B.' He was speaking in a weird American accent, like in cowboy films. Why was he doing this to them, Nessie thought, but then she realised she was glad. It made it easier for her to hate him especially if she closed her eyes.

'I need you to make another phone call now,' he was saying. If you try anything stupid I'll shoot Nessie and don't think I won't.'

Nessie realised what he had taken from his pocket. He had a gun, a real, proper gun. Not a pretend one like you'd get in Woolworths. He began to wave it around in the air, then he put it down on the floor while he removed Greta's gag. She coughed, spluttered and spat in his face. Nessie tried to smile at her friend.

The murderer slapped Greta hard around the head.

'Careful,' she croaked hoarsely. 'I'm no good to you at the moment if I'm dead.'

He jumped up manically, picked up the gun and held it to Nessie's head. She closed her eyes, screaming inside and tried to think about yesterday. If it *had* been yesterday. Anything at all except the reality of the cold steel which had the power to splinter her brain into little pieces. She tried to remember being in the park and feeling the sun on her back, warming her and making her feel alive. *He was going to kill her*. The children running around on the grass, laughing. *The gun clicked.* She saw the squirrels up and down the trees like they didn't have a minute to waste. Oh, how she wished she was a squirrel getting ready to hibernate, she almost laughed at herself but it came out as a strangled sob.

'Stop!'

She heard Greta. 'I'll do whatever you want, just don't hurt Nessie.'

The pressure of the gun against her head disappeared and Nessie took a deep breath.

'Don't do anything stupid,' Greta whispered to her urgently.'Help will come, trust me.'

The murderer slapped her across the face again. 'Shut up,' he growled. 'Just shut the fuck up. Right, this is what's going to happen.'

'We're gonna go upstairs Mrs B,' he drawled beginning to undo the ropes on her legs. 'And you're gonna make another phone call. You'll say exactly what I tell you to, then you'll put the phone down. If you try anything I'll come back down here and I'll shoot her. Have you got that?'

Greta nodded and glanced across at Nessie. Nessie shook her head, she knew that Greta could read her mind.

He won't kill me, he wouldn't kill a child, especially me.

Greta held her gaze. *I'm not going to take that chance*, her eyes replied.

As Nessie watched her friend painfully climbing up the stairs of the cellar with a gun at her back, she had no idea what to do.

***

Jimmy was downstairs in the kitchen making himself a cup of tea. He had managed a couple of hours of fitful sleep, he looked at the clock, five thirty. The sky was lightening but only slightly. As he looked out of the window, the rain began to splatter. He couldn't stop thinking about Nessie. Was she getting wet? Wherever she was, whether she had chosen to be there or not, she would be frightened. He decided that he would give Del a ring in half-an-hour. He was sure they wouldn't be sleeping much in that house.

As he thought about it the phone suddenly rang. Every nerve in his body jumped.

'Jimmy? Jimmy Potter? Is that you?'

'Yes, speaking.'

He thought he recognised the voice. It was very distinctive, guttural and precise.

'It's Greta. Greta Broncowiez here. Jimmy you must come to my house right away. Be very careful that the police do not see you and you must not tell anyone where you are going. If you do, Nessie will die.'

'But where -'

The phone went dead. Oh my God, he thought but he didn't hesitate. Grabbing his mac, he slipped out of the back door and jumped over every fence up to the end of the road. He skirted around the waste, hiding behind the diggers and up to the footpath which lead to Greta Broncowiez's house.

His mind raced as he ran. Did this mean that Greta had taken Nessie? Why would she do that? The rain grew heavier and thundered onto his mac. He ran up to the door and rang the bell. The door opened and he nearly passed out, his legs buckled beneath him.

'What the fuck are you doing here?' was all he could say.

***

Josie couldn't believe all the activity in Churchill Street when she arrived back from her night duty. Her mum had phoned and told her what was going on, she had been really upset.

Josie had phoned her bosses but they couldn't find anyone to do her shift and she couldn't just leave twenty elderly residents to fend for themselves but all night her mind had been racing. Surely Nessie must have just run off somewhere.

It was only half-past eight in the morning but the street was closed off and full of police cars. She had just passed *The King's Head* which she could see was being used as an incident base. She almost couldn't take it all in, it was like something from an American film.

'You can't go in there,' said a policeman, standing at the barriers which straddled the street. 'It's a major incident scene.'

'I live here,' said Josie. 'Number 8.'

The policeman consulted a list. 'Josie Evans. Just done a night shift at an old people's home, right?'

He grinned at her and then she saw his face change as he noticed her scarred cheek, she was used to that now.

'Who have you been having a fight with love?' He laughed. 'God, you know how to have fun in this neck of the woods don't you?'

'Have you always been a complete arsehole?' she shouted, trying to push her way through.

'Hey love, remember, I'm a police officer, I was only having a joke with you.'

Josie pulled her hair right back from her face. *'This*, officer is *not* a joke. I realise you must be bored out of your brains stood here but there ain't no need to take it out on me.'

'They'll want to talk to you,' he said.

'Well they'll just have to wait. My boyfriend's little sister is missing an' I need to go an' see if he's alright. I don't suppose you've found her yet, judging by all this going on.'

He shook his head.

'Excuse me dear.'

A tall, slim young girl wearing a trouser suit was heading towards her with a microphone. Following her was a sweating bald-headed man carrying a huge camera.

'BBC News. Do you live here? Do you know the missing girl?'

Josie soon found herself surrounded by men with notepads and pens all firing questions at her.

'Is it true that she's a coloured girl?' one asked.

'Oh why don't you all fuck off,' Josie shouted at them as the policeman let her go through the barriers.

'Don't think we can use those shots,' said the cameraman laughing.

They all joined in. 'Well that's what you can expect from the people round here, rough as guts,' said a reporter from the Daily Sketch.

'Hang on a minute,' said another. 'These people are worried sick. A little girl they know has gone missing. Now I grew up round here and I can imagine what they're going through so why don't you lot fuck off back to Fleet Street and carry on getting pissed in your posh pubs.'

'Don't you slag us off like that. You'd chop your arm off for one of our jobs, Stratford Express wanker.'

A slight scuffle broke out then but Josie didn't look behind her to see what was going on. She went straight to Maggie's house, knocked on the back door and let herself in.

Maggie and Winston were sitting at the kitchen table. Winston had his arm around her.

'Oh, Maggie,' she said, taking a seat next to her and holding her hand. 'They'll find her, I know they will.'

‘They think one of us done it,’ she sobbed, looking at Winston. ‘They think -’

‘No, Maggie,’ said Winston. ‘They don’t but they have to eliminate us first, they have to.’

‘Oh stop sticking up for ‘em,’ Maggie shouted. ‘They come in here, tear our house to pieces again as if we’d hide her in the wardrobe or something. Why do they have to do that? Just tell me.’

‘They’re looking for clues,’ said Josie gently. ‘They need to find out where she might have gone. She might not have been taken, she might have just run away from something. They need to try and find out.’

Maggie blew her nose. ‘I know, I’m sorry but there ain’t nothing I can do, just sitting here waiting, thinking about my little girl and where she might be. Out in that rain, she’ll be getting wet.’

Winston stood up and moved over towards the kettle. ‘Cup of tea Jose?’ he asked her.

Josie nodded. He must be devastated, she thought. His eyes were full of pain.

‘Is Del around?’ she asked.

‘No, I think him and Jimmy are out looking for her,’ said Winston. ‘Thanks for coming Jose, it means a lot.’

Josie suddenly realised how tired she was, it passed through her in a wave. Too much happening. God, she needed this cup of tea.

***

When George told May who he thought Mick Tyler’s murderer was she had slapped his face, hard.

‘You stupid man!’ she shouted. ‘Why didn’t you tell me this before?’

They were sitting up in bed, the teasmade was whistling next to them.

He had been stunned by that slap. In all the years they had been married there had not been one single moment when he had been tempted to harm her in any way. Oh, there were the usual moments of irritation and arguments that you get in any marriage, he thought but nothing physical like this. Ever.

'Can you not imagine what I'm going through and have been going through since I realised? he shouted. 'I didn't know this was going to happen, Billy can't have known either. He thought that if he took the rap for Mick's murder -'

'It would help the real murderer,' May finished the sentence for him, before bursting into tears. She threw her arms around George. 'Oh George I'm sorry,' she cried. 'But you of all people, the truth has always been so important to you.'

'I know love, it's alright. Don't take on, you haven't broken 'owt.' He touched his cheek gingerly. 'You can pack a mean punch though,' he laughed.

'I'm glad *you* think it's funny and do you really think that Nessie disappearing has got something to do with Mick Tyler's murder?'

George nodded. 'The more I think about it, the more I'm sure. Those kids have been pretending to be The Famous Five trying to solve a murder. I think Nessie must have found something out, probably by accident.'

'But he wouldn't hurt her surely,' said May.

'If you'd asked me that yesterday, I'd have agreed with you.'

He swung his legs out of the bed and moved over towards the chest of drawers.

'Anyway, I'm off to the station now. Time I told them who Billy and Old Bones were trying to protect. You'd think they might have worked it out for themselves by now.'

'Well I certainly didn't,' May whispered. 'Now it all makes sense even though it doesn't bear thinking about.'

'The police have set up an incident room at *The Kings Head,* that'll please Arthur,' said George, doing up his trousers.

'Do you want me to come with you?'

'No love, I'll do this on my own. I don't want to be worrying about you as well as everything else. No, you stay here.'

He finished dressing, kissed May on the cheek and walked out into Churchill Street towards the barriers. He saw Josie surrounded by reporters. He could see that she was agitated and any other time he would have stopped but he knew that this morning he couldn't. George carried on walking, past the barriers, towards *The Kings Head.*

***

John Paradise had called a briefing in the bar. The detectives were all gathered around except Jenny Finch who was with the Tylers.

'Charlie,' his DI was just coming in the door.

'Yes guv?'

'Did you get hold of Greta Broncowiez? We really need to talk to her.'

'No guv. What would she know anyway, she's just a dotty old woman?'

John Paradise would probably have thought the same not long ago.

'Charlie. Are you sure it was her on the phone? You know, when she told you she was going away?'

'Yes guv. She's got that sort of German accent. You know, sounds all her words out. Proper English, not like how we talk and I'd interviewed her before you did hadn't I?'

'And why can't you get hold of her?'

'Wrong number.' He pulled a scrap of paper from his pocket. 'They'd never heard of her.'

'Let me look at that,' said John Paradise, grabbing it out of his hand.

'1703 15679' he said out loud. 'I thought you said she'd gone to Bournemouth.'

'That's what she said.'

'Are you sure?'

'Hundred per cent guv. Why?'

'Because this is the code for Southampton. Bloody hell Charlie, you should have known that.'

'Oh, so I'm supposed to know every telephone code in the country now am I?'

'You should have checked it out. Sorry Charlie but I think she was trying to tell us something by giving you the wrong code. Have we called at that house yet? Have we tried her home number since Nessie disappeared?'

'I did try her phone number guv but there was no answer and we haven't been to her house for two reasons. One, we didn't think she was there and two we're still working through all the houses on the estate.'

John Paradise looked at all the bemused faces around the room.

'I think Nessie has been taken by the person who murdered Mick Tyler. I think she found out and I think he's got her. Somewhere. She knew the old lady and I want that house searched. That telephone number was a cry for help, that's what I think.'

'Do you know who's got her guv?' asked Doug.

'Yes. Call it gut instinct but I know who I expect to see there. Just think lads. Who is the one person who we know was at the scene of that murder who everyone would want to protect? The one person in all of this that we haven't even thought about?'

A police constable came bustling through the front door of the pub.

'Guv,' he called. 'George Pattinson wants a word.'

'Send him in.'

He looked around at his detectives. He could see that the brains were working overtime and that one or two had got it already, they looked horrified.

George Pattinson came in. He was sweating as he made his way over to where the detectives all stood.

John Paradise put his hand up. 'If you know who killed Mick Tyler Mr.Pattinson just give me the name. If not, we're busy.'

'I know who killed Mick Tyler officer. It has to be him.'

20

Bang Bang – Cher

'Well, hi there Jimmy, come on in *mate*, you'll be getting wet out there.'

Jimmy walked in to Greta Broncowiez's house completely confused.

'What are you doing here Del?' he asked.

Del was so fast drawing out the gun that Jimmy barely saw him move. He could feel his whole body shaking as he felt the metal in the hollow of his back.

'Why the fuck shouldn't I be here?'

'Why? What are you doing? Have you gone mad or what mate?'

'Just shut up and get over there, on that settee. *Mate*.'

Del pushed him through to the sitting room, prodding the gun in his back. Only this wasn't Del, Jimmy thought. This was someone else in Del's body, Del's head.

'Don't think I won't use it,' he said. 'Because I will, I might anyway. Depends how I feel.'

He kicked Jimmy on to the settee and sat down opposite him in a chair.

'Now then,' he said. 'We'll have a nice long chat *mate*, just you and me.'

'Where's Greta?' Jimmy asked. He was starting to work things out in his head and none of it was very good.

'Ain't important, stupid old cow.'

Jimmy gulped and took a deep breath. 'And Nessie?'

'Ain't got a clue *mate*.'

He pointed the gun at Jimmy menacingly.

'Well,' said Jimmy taking another deep breath. 'What's this all about Del?'

He forced himself to talk gently. His friend was on the edge and he knew it.

Del settled himself back into the chair.

'I think you know Jimmy,' he said, 'but I'll start at the beginning shall I? Remember when we was kids? When we was little? Oh, you were alright, you had a mum an' dad that looked after *you*. Little nancy boy. '*Don't go out without your cap on Jimmy'*, your mum was always saying. '*Don't go out without your cap or your ears will get cold'*. Well, my mum an' dad couldn't have given a toss whether I got cold, caught bloody pneumonia or even died.'

He spat on the carpet. 'That's how much they cared. Fair Jimmy, is that fair? An' don't you start tellin' me that the world ain't fair because I ain't listening.'

'I just want to know if you've got Greta and Nessie Del, I just want to know they're safe,' said Jimmy quietly. He had to stop this somehow. He just had to. How should he talk to him? What was best? He was insane, there wasn't a best way.

'I don't want you to interrupt me,' Del shouted. 'This is *my* story now. Ain't about you or your new *girlfriend*.'

Jimmy desperately tried to stay calm and took a deep breath. 'Del, you can walk away from this,' he said. 'If you haven't hurt them you won't get charged with anything. I won't grass you up. Listen mate, you've got a lot going for you at the moment. *The Red Dragons*. You're going to be famous, mate, I know you are. You've got a recording contract. Jesus, this is not the right time to throw all that away.'

'Don't even think about calling me your mate after what you've done to me,' he screamed waving his hands around in the air. 'An' I said don't interrupt me, so just shut the fuck up. I know this ain't a good time. Don't you think I don't know that? It wasn't in my plan, not yet. Do you think I don't want to be rich? To be famous, on *Top of The Pops*? But now this has started, I just can't stop it.'

'What do you mean?' Jimmy felt his stomach churning, his head thumping.

'That's what I'm trying to tell you,' he shouted, his spittle flying everywhere. 'Just shut up will yer. You always had too much to say.'

Jimmy closed his eyes but it didn't make anything go away. When he was little and his mum told him off for something he had always closed his eyes. It hadn't worked then either. He cold feel a huge lump of fear in his gut, tears were coursing down his cheeks.

'I ain't hurt them. Alright? I ain't killed them, now can I get on wiv this? I know I ain't got all day. They'll work it out soon. Was it fair that I got a bastard for a dad? He's the one who started it. Did you know it was me what killed him?'

Jimmy recoiled on the settee in shock. 'But – but you were only a kid ten years ago,' he gasped.

‘Oh yeah, that was me and don’t say nothin’ cos this is *my* story now. *My* turn. *My* life. Right?’

Jimmy nodded. This was even worse than he could ever have imagined.

***

Nessie still lay next to Greta in the cellar, they shivered and tried to get some warmth and comfort from each other’s bodies.

She could hear shouting upstairs, someone else was in the house, but there’s nothing we can do, Nessie thought to herself, pulling against the ropes that were tightly bound around her body. Tears of anger and frustration sprang into her eyes.

She took her mind back to whenever it was, she had lost track of the time. It had started the morning before she had gone to the park with Tonk and Jason. Had that been just yesterday? It seemed like another time, another world. A safe, secure world.

She had woken up suddenly, early. She was on her own. Ava was sleeping at her mate’s house but there was someone sitting at the bottom of the bed. For some reason she didn’t want to open her eyes. When she did, she saw that it was only Del. Then she looked at his face and she knew that it wasn’t really him. His eyes were wild and as black as night and in his hand he held their notebook. He began to bang it up and down on his knee.

‘So,’ he had said. ‘You’ve been very clever Nessie, ain’t yer? Finding all this stuff out. Haven’t got to the truth yet though. I’ll just help you a bit with that shall I?’ He smirked and in a sudden movement he grabbed her violently by the shoulders and hissed into her ear. 'I'll tell you,' he said. 'I'll tell you who killed my dad shall I? I've been laughing at you. All this time.' He put his hands around her neck and squeezed. 'An' I'll tell you something else,' he hissed. 'If you breathe a fucking word, you're dead.' He had shaken her so hard that her teeth had rattled. Then he had let her go and grinned. 'There, I think you've got that message Ness.'

She had heard footsteps then. Her dad, off to work. Del had put his hand over her mouth. Her dad was whistling. Frustrated tears erupted from her eyes, Del was really hurting her.

When she had heard the front door slam he released his grip.

'There,' he said. 'Now, remember what I said Nessie. You be a good girl and don't say nothing. Alright?'

He had stood up, still smiling. She had shivered and kept nodding her head. The shock seemed to have stopped her moving or calling for help. Her muscles just wouldn't work and she had never felt so terrified in her whole life, she could scarcely breathe. Eventually her voice had come out, like a cracked whisper. 'You killed him didn't you?'

'If you say so,' he had laughed, putting the notebook in his pocket.

'No - no,' Nessie protested, forgetting her fear for a moment.

'Oh yes,' he smiled. 'It's mine now. Finders keepers and remember Ness. From now on, I'm gonna be right behind you. I'm gonna know what you're doing every second of every day.'

He had moved towards her as she shrunk away from him. Then he had patted her on the head, very gently.

'Sorry Ness,' he had said, softly. 'I didn't mean to hurt you but you see how important it is don't you? To keep it a secret? I know you will, won't you?'

She had nodded and shivered as he left the room. She had heard him in the kitchen, heard the kettle whistling. A bad dream, was it just a nightmare? But when she pinched herself on the arm it hurt. This was no dream. Her mum had popped her head in and Nessie had frozen. All she could see was Del's face, she couldn't speak.

Her mum spoke. 'Alright Ness? Come and have your breakfast love.' Del's voice had floated up the stairs. 'Wanna cuppa mum?'

A voice had screamed inside Nessie's head. Tell your mum, go on tell her. Her mum was closing the bedroom door. She had no idea why she couldn't say anything. It was like her brain was frozen. She just couldn't believe what Del had turned into, some sort of monster. Like in *Doctor Who* when she had to hide behind a cushion but there was nowhere to hide here and no switch to turn him off. This was real. Perhaps it was all a big joke. He would come running upstairs, grinning all over his face, and give her the notebook back. 'Only messing Nessie,' he would say. She had put her hands up to her neck where he had tried to choke her. No, that had been real. For a few moments she had thought she was going to die.

She heard them downstairs, chatting. She would have to tell her mum later, when Del wasn't around. Anyway, she would probably just laugh. Why would she believe *her*?

Her mum had gone upstairs to get ready for the funeral. Marilyn, Del and Stuart were in the kitchen, Radio Caroline on in the background. They were all laughing as Marilyn danced around to *'Reach Out I'll be there' by the Four Tops*. It was just like a normal morning. She looked at her oldest brother and he smiled at her, like he usually did. There was no menace, he was just Del. *Could* she have imagined all that?

No, she told herself firmly, it hadn't been a dream. She had to go and tell her mum what she knew, now, before he hurt anyone else. She slipped out from the lounge to the bottom of the stairs but he had seen her and in seconds he was behind her, breathing down her neck.

'You weren't thinking of having a word wiv mum were you? That would be silly, wouldn't it Ness?'

The doorbell rang.

'Saved by the bell,' he laughed. He pulled her down the stairs and pushed her towards the door. She could see through the glass that it was Tonk.

'I think you should go out now Ness, but remember. Not a word an' wherever you are, I ain't gonna be far behind. We'll have a chat later.'

She had gone straight to the docks when she had left the boys in the park to tell her dad about Del but he had been knocked off early. One of his workmates had told her that he'd gone out somewhere so that he would miss the funeral. There was only one other person she could talk to and that was Greta.

'*If you ever need me*,' Nessie remembered her saying it. Well she certainly needed someone right now. As she had passed her own home on the way to the old lady's house she thought she had seen a shadow. A glimpse of something or someone. It must have been Del, he must have followed her and now here they were locked up in this nightmare. How was it going to end? She tried to snuggle into Greta's body for comfort. Greta's skin felt colder.

***

'I always liked blood. Remember our Julie, when she died? The blood all down the stairs. I had to try hard not to laugh when I seen it. Silly cow, getting pregnant. He always loved her best, me dad. Why couldn't he have loved me like that Jimmy? Anyway, I saw him off, got me own back and got away wiv it. I was a little kid, no-one thought about me. The only ones who knew I done it was your dad and Old Bones. Me mum was out for the count, she don't remember nothing.'

Something else clicked in Jimmy's brain. Old Bones. No, he wouldn't have done that, would he?

'You killed Bones.' Jimmy felt like he was in a trance. 'You did didn't you?' He could hardly believe himself what he was saying. 'And my dad protected you. Would you have killed him as well? If we'd still lived here?'

Del was screwing his eyes up and moving the gun up and down in a manic way.

'Ain't gonna tell you again Jimmy boy, shut the fuck up. I got this shooter to kill your old man. Didn't need it though did I? And I didn't kill Bones, well, not really. He was the only one who cared, he was kind to me that night, when it happened. He took me upstairs, cleaned all the blood off me later. I was covered in it so he washed me an' put me to bed. An' afterwards, he used to talk to me, always asking me how I was. Telling me it was just an accident an' I wasn't to feel guilty, that I'd just been defending me mum. Then, as the time went on, he changed his tune a bit. Said he was having bad dreams. *He* was having bad dreams. What the fuck did he think was happening in *my* head, I was the one that had killed me dad, not him. He started talking about us going to the coppers. Telling them what had happened an' where the body was. You know, that sort of stuff. I had to get rid of him Jimmy, he was too dangerous an' wiv your dad in Australia he was the only one who knew the truth. I got him pissed, that was just so easy. Told him I got messages from his dead little girl. You know, his little girl choked and died when he'd gone on the piss years ago. I just happened to have a bottle of whisky on me when I told him, he believes in all that stuff you see, living with the witch. Remember her Jimmy? Our witch, when we were just kids in the gang? Anyway, I took him to a bench by the river and we sat there, just talking and him drinking. Seemed hours before he passed out. Then I just pushed him into the river, easy peasy. No blood though, so not a proper murder.'

Jimmy knew there was going to be more, he felt sick. It came over him suddenly and he vomited all over the carpet. When he looked up, Del was crying.

'You shouldn't have done what you did Jimmy. You were my mate. An' I didn't mean to hurt all them people but they hurt me. Something happened in me head after I'd killed me dad and I had to kill him. He was hurting me mum but then it started something off an' I couldn't stop, hurting people.'

He was still vulnerable, Jimmy thought. Some of the Del he knew was still there.

'You need help Del, you need to talk to someone.' said Jimmy gently. 'Can I clean this up?'

'Oh, no you don't get me like that. You see, I ain't never gonna be soft again. No, we'll just have to smell it for the rest of my story.'

'And Legs? Did you have anything to do with that?' Jimmy asked fearfully.

'You see Jimmy, he hurt me an' all. I thought the gang meant something to all of you, like it did to me, you was all my proper family. You and Legsy well, you had everything at home. I hated my house, hated going in there. Well, I'll tell you something about Legs shall I Jimmy boy,' he drawled. 'Legsy is a queer.'

'I know that, I went to see him in prison.'

Del's face changed. He spat fiercely at Jimmy, his whole body trembling.

'You never told me!' He screamed. 'Do you see what I mean Jimmy? You leave me out all the time. You don't tell me stuff. That hurts me, all that stuff really hurts me.'

'What did he do to you?'

Del began to cry again and then he breathed in very deeply. Jimmy could see that he was desperately trying to control himself.

'He was pissed one night, we both were.' He was speaking quietly now. 'In the park. We'd been smoking some dope, I nicked it from Winston. We hadn't never tried it before, made him feel horny I suppose. He started kissing me, trying to get my clothes off, trying to – you know – what they do. I was that pissed I nearly let him. Started saying he loved me an' all that. Tell you what, I could have killed him but I'm clever now you see, I stopped. I stopped the red mist coming down that time, held on to it and thought about it. I pushed him off and said that perhaps we should go an' nick a car. I told you the rest, except I lied about who was driving.'

'*You* were driving. It was *you* that killed the old woman?'

'Yeah, she was ancient anyway, did her a favour really.'

'So why did Legs take the blame?'

'I told him I'd tell his mum and dad and the coppers what he'd tried to do to me in the park and he loved me Jimmy. He would have done anything for me, straight up. I let him think I felt the same about him, even let him kiss me a few times. Uggh. Just until he was locked up of course. Scared little Legsy, would rather go to prison than tell his mum an' dad he was a queer.'

The phone rang and they both jumped. It seemed to ring for ever.

‘They’re on to me now Jimmy. It won’t be long.’

***

‘*Plundering porpoises*, where are them cop cars going?’ Tonk shouted. He watched out of the front window as half the cars pulled away, blue lights flashing but no sirens, silent approach. There were other policemen running towards the footpath at the end of the road. Reporters and cameramen ran through the barriers and followed them.

Sally shivered as she crossed herself and stood behind her son, her hands on his shoulders. She had already been to St. Joseph’s this morning to pray that they would find Nessie safe and well, it was always peaceful, sitting in the church. Sally wasn’t overly religious, she didn’t go every Sunday or anything like that, but she had always believed and at times like this she was so glad that she did. She had looked up at the smiling face of the Virgin Mary, surrounded by candles, they were in yellow glass containers and gave her an orangey glow. Please, she had whispered, please let her be safe. She had felt better when she had left.

When Sally had arrived home she heard on the radio that the police believed Nessie had been abducted. Who would do that? Who would take a child?

‘You ain’t going in to work are you mum?’

‘No love, I’m not leaving you, not until they’ve got someone locked up.’

‘I’d say something was happening now. Wouldn’t you mum?’

***

The detectives who hadn't guessed that Del Tyler was the man they were looking for were shocked when George Pattinson gave them his name.

'But he was just a kid. Ten years old guv for Christ's sake,' said Scottie.

'It must have been an accident,' said George Pattinson. 'He would have been defending his mum. They didn't want his life to be ruined, he was just a kid.'

John Paradise coughed. 'Well, you've confirmed what I thought Mr. Pattinson. I understand everyone protecting him but he's not ten years old now is he and when you've killed someone, whether it's an accident or not, it changes your life for ever.'

'Brilliant drummer like him an' all,' said one of the officers shaking his head.

'They can get another drummer DI Parks,' John Paradise snapped. 'We can't get another Nessie.'

He turned to face all his officers. 'Now let's go and get this nutter and get that kid back. I'll bet you everything I own that he's holed up in that house with Nessie and Mrs Broncowiez. Charlie, keep trying that home number. He hasn't got a gun or anything that you know about has he Mr. Pattinson?'

'God, no,' said George. 'What sort of people do you think we are in Churchill Street?'

'Right, well it should be relatively simple then.'

***

The phone ringing had unnerved Del, Jimmy could see it. With one hand still holding the gun that was pointed at him, Del walked backwards to where the wires were and ripped them out.

'That's better Jimmy. Now we can have a bit of peace, I'll just carry on with my story.' His face changed as he looked at the phone wires, he started to bang his head against the wall. 'Shit,' he shouted. 'Shit. I needed that fucking phone. I need to get Josie here. Right now. *My* girl Josie, remember her Jimmy? She ain't getting away wiv this either. Shit.'

Jimmy felt a slim ray of hope. If that *had* been the police maybe they had worked something out. He had to try and delay Del, he had to stop him getting to the end of the story because he knew what that would be about. Somehow he had found out about him and Josie and that was why he had flipped. Jimmy was in no doubt.

'Are you listening to me?' Del was shouting, waving the gun around. 'Because I ain't far from the end now.'

Jimmy closed his eyes and thought about Josie. Thank God Del had messed up with the phone, at least she would be safe. Please just let me live to see her face again. Her face, Josie's face.

'You bastard!' Jimmy shouted as he leapt up and lunged towards Del. 'It was you who cut Josie wasn't it?' The anger had come from nowhere but it was like a ball of red fire that coursed through his body.

The shot rang out and echoed around the room. Jimmy felt a pain, like someone had thumped him really hard in the shoulder.

'Sit back down Jimmy,' Del roared and then he was still. He hadn't moved from the chair he had sat down on, his gun was aimed at Jimmy's head.

Holding on to his injured shoulder with his other hand, Jimmy staggered back and collapsed onto the settee.

'That was naughty Jimmy. Just cos I always made you be an injun when we was kids.' He was talking quietly again, back in control. 'You always wanted to be the cowboy but I'm the cowboy today and I ain't got to the end of my story. That's very rude of you.'

'Why did you do that to her?' Jimmy was shouting now, he couldn't stop himself.

Del shrugged his shoulders and then his body seemed to slump. Jimmy watched as tears began to erupt from his eyes. There was silence for what seemed like an age. Apart from Del's sobs.

'I loved her,' he said at last. 'She dumped me Jimmy, just like I was a piece of shit. She said we were too young, some rubbish like that. People are always hurting me. Can't you understand that? I had to cut her so that no-one else would want her. She was *my* girl and if you hadn't come back I could've looked after her for ever.'

He began to shout again and pulled something from his pocket. 'She's just a tart Jimmy. A fucking tart but that ain't what's hurt me this time.'

Spittle was spewing from his mouth as he threw Nessie's notebook over on to the settee next to Jimmy. 'Read it. The last page. Now!' he screamed waving the gun around again and pacing around the room.

He's lost it, Jimmy thought. He's really lost it and he's going to kill me. He removed his hand from the injured shoulder, blood was seeping through his shirt. Grabbing the notebook and wincing as he did so, he found the last page and began to read. He scarcely recognised his own voice, it was shaking so much.

Nessie's writing was neat but was obviously that of a child. He found the final entry.

'Read it!' Del shouted again.

'*Went to the park with Tonk and Jason. Didn't do much -*'

There was a loud banging at the door.

'Police! Open up!'

Del jumped and turned towards the hall that led to the front door but he still kept the gun trained on Jimmy. Sweat was dripping off him and he was twitching all over. 'Fuck off!' he shouted. 'I'm in the middle of my fucking story, I ain't finished it yet.'

He turned back towards Jimmy. 'Finish it! Finish reading it as if you don't know already what it's going to say.'

Jimmy had to shout over the sound of the hammering on the door.

'We followed,' Jimmy gulped when he saw the next words. He looked up. Del was staring at him, his eyes were spewing hate.

'Go on,' he said quietly. 'Go on my best *mate*. My *pal* since we was two years old. Fucking say it you bastard.'

'*We followed Jimmy and Josie,*' Jimmy read, his hands shaking. *'We saw them kissing.'*

Del cupped his hand over his ear in an exaggerated manner. 'Sorry mate, didn't quite hear that. Shout it out you bastard. Repeat it. Every - fucking - word.'

'*We saw them kissing,*' Jimmy shouted, his own anger erupting and then he sobbed as he finished the sentence, '*but I don't think it's important so I ain't going to write any more about it.*'

And then the front door caved in. Jimmy recognised the sound of another gunshot. Then a roaring in his ears followed by silence and no more pain.

21

A Well Respected Man – The Kinks

As the police approached the big house they could see that the curtains were all drawn, it was then that they had heard a gunshot.

'Phone for armed back-up,' said John Paradise. 'Now! We need to get in there.'

'They'll only be a few minutes guv, we shouldn't do anything stupid,' said Charlie. They had all crouched behind the privet hedge when they had heard the shot.

'I think we need to get in there, that could have been Nessie,' said John Paradise. 'Have we got an ambulance on the way?'

Charlie nodded. They could hear shouting now, coming from inside.

'Who's that in there with him guv?' asked Scottie, shuffling up behind him.

'I can't tell,' he whispered. 'But Del Tyler sounds out of control, we're going in.'

He signalled silently to three of the police constables also behind the hedge to follow.

'Come on Charlie, Scottie. Let's get in there.'

'Guv,' Charlie argued. 'We need to wait. I think you're wrong here, he could kill one of us.'

John Paradise drew a revolver from his inside pocket. 'I'm not that stupid Charlie,' he said. 'And I'm going in first.'

He led the men out from behind the hedge in to the front porch of Greta Broncowiez's house.

As the door finally collapsed under the weight of six policemen he took in the scene in the sitting room in a fraction of a second. It was what he was trained to do.

Del Tyler was pointing a gun at Jimmy Potter who was lying on the floor, bleeding heavily. Most murderers who were cornered would have used their potential victim as a shield but not this one.

John Paradise had hesitated for just a thousandth of a second. Del Tyler had a maniacal grin on his face and was moving towards him. As the guv realised what was about to happen, he whipped out his gun. At the same time he heard a shot and, as if in slow motion, his body seemed to be flying through the air. There was a whooshing sound, a thump in his chest. The pale, green carpet, covered in faded, pink flowers seemed to be rising gently to meet him. It seemed to take forever but he wasn't frightened, he sort of knew that this was the end. That when he hit the pink flowers he would be dead but why was everything moving so slowly? There was a rushing noise in his ears. He was aware of people around him and yet he couldn't see anything at all anymore.

And then he heard *him.* Laughing. He heard his voice echoing through the clanging sounds in his head.

'Good,' Del Tyler was shouting, 'I always wanted to kill a copper.'

He tried to tell them not to shoot Del Tyler but he didn't have any energy left now. It was sort of like that feeling when sleep just had to come and you just had to let it. He gave his wife one last cuddle.

***

Del Tyler had thrown his gun down on the floor and put his hands up in the air, he was still laughing. Charlie had just checked that the guv had no pulse. As he shook his head he threw the guv's gun to Scottie.

'Keep the bastard covered,' he shouted.

'I'll do more than that,' said Scottie angrily. 'Did anyone see him throw his gun down?'

They all shook their heads.

Del Tylers face was frozen in horror. 'You can't shoot me,' he cried. 'It ain't the law.'

'No!' Charlie roared. 'No, you can't do it Scottie. It's the last thing the guv would've wanted, the last thing.' He stood up, walked over to where Scottie stood and took the gun from him.

'He'll get fucking nothing now!' Scottie screamed. 'We can't hang him anymore, he'll end up in Broadmoor watching fucking telly all night and getting a roast chicken dinner every Sunday. Where have those bloody ambulances got to?'

Del Tyler stood still while he was handcuffed and charged by Charlie. There was a look on his face that was inexplicable to those around him. He looked as if he was in a moment of pure ecstasy. Every copper in the room just wanted him dead. Right now.

'Where are they? Where are they you arsehole? Nessie and Greta Broncowiez?' Charlie shouted.

'In the cellar. I ain't hurt 'em.'

They heard Jimmy Potter begin to groan over on the floor near the settee.

'Check him out Scottie. Try and stop -'

He looked up as the ambulancemen raced through the front door.

A young PC came running up from the cellar. 'We've got them,' he said. 'They were tied up down there but they both seem alright.'

'We'll get the ambulance crew to check them out,' Charlie shouted, 'but first of all let's get rid of this fucking arsehole quick and get him down the station. I don't want them to have to see him again.'

Out of the corner of his eye he saw the guv's body being placed in a body bag and it was then that the little girl came running towards them.

'No, Nessie, I don't want you to see all this.' He stopped her and tried to guide her away.

'Nessie,' Del Tyler called out to her as he was being manhandled out by two policemen. 'I wouldn't have hurt you. You know that don't you?'

She stood silently and stared at him. Then she walked slowly towards him and spat all over his shoes. 'I hate you,' she spoke quietly. 'I'll always hate you now.'

Then Del Tyler burst into tears, great gulping sobs as he was led away.

'Too late now to make out you're a softy mate,' said Scottie, giving him a quick kick in the balls. 'You just killed one of the best coppers I've ever met and your life is going to be hell, I'm going to make sure of it.'

Charlie watched Nessie as she watched her brother being taken away. The anger in her had seemed to melt away. She looked up at Charlie, there were tears in her eyes.

'He's right,' she said. 'I knew he'd never have killed me.'

The room was almost silent. DI Charlie Kingston stopped for the first time since they had entered the house and suddenly realised that the guv had gone. He couldn't take it in. One minute he was large as life, now he was in a body bag. His eyes were drawn to the clock on the mantelpiece. Ten minutes. That's all it had been. Ten minutes ago his boss had been living and breathing and trying to save the life of a little girl. How could that happen? He wanted to throw something at the clock. Turn back the time. Stop it fucking ticking because he knew that his life would never be the same again. He thought about the guv's wife and kids. How would they ever get over this? He blinked back the tears. He still had work to do but they would come later he knew. Unknowingly, he vowed that he would get this bastard locked away for life and he would do it for the fairest, best copper he had ever had the privilege to work for and then he would carry on doing it. He was suddenly very aware of why he had wanted to be a policeman.

'Did my mate get shot dead?' Nessie asked him.

He nodded.

'He was alright for a copper,' she said.

'Come on Nessie,' he put his arm around her shoulders. 'I'm going to take you back to your mum and dad.'

He knew instinctively that it was exactly what Detective Chief Inspector John Paradise would have done.

22

Blowin' In The Wind – Stevie Wonder

Jimmy sat, propped up on his pillows in the hospital bed, Josie by his side. His right arm in a sling, the bullet had fortunately only grazed his shoulder.

'You can tell Del had never fired a gun before,' she tried to laugh as she squeezed his left hand.

'Got it right the second time though, bastard. That man was a good cop you know,' said Jimmy. 'I still can't believe all that, it's like I've just had the worst nightmare ever. Doesn't seem real, it wasn't Del. Not the Del I knew anyway.'

'There was always things about him that were weird,' she said. 'I think I just ignored them. Remember, when we were kids and how he had a thing about blood? I cut me knee once and he wanted to lick it. He loved my scar an' all, he was always touching it, kissing it, I just didn't see it. He could be very funny as well though. And gentle, sometimes he was so kind. I really thought he'd turned out alright.'

He saw her shiver and squeezed her hand.

'I could never forgive him for hurting you,' said Jimmy. 'He's just sick. If the law hadn't changed last year, he'd have been hung. As it is -'

'He'll be put away for life Jimmy, that's all I care about. Mum says she thinks killing his dad probably set it all off. I can't believe what he did to Old Bones, poor Greta. And Legsy. I just – I just can't believe any of it.'

'And you felt sorry for him.'

Josie looked at him, tears in her eyes. 'So did you. It's our fault isn't it?' she said. 'It's our fault that copper died.'

'No,' said Jimmy firmly. 'No, you've got to stop thinking like that. Nessie came to see me this morning, she's blaming herself for writing about us kissing in her notebook. When she woke up the next morning he was sitting on her bed. He'd taken the notebook out of the drawer, threatened to kill her. Had his hands round her neck, poor kid, she was terrified. That's why she went to see Greta, she couldn't find her dad and she didn't know who else she could talk to. They had some sort of – connection. I think she'd guessed then, that Del was the one they had all been looking for.'

Josie was crying. This was going to be hard, Jimmy knew. Everyone was going to be blaming themselves but they'd all get through it, they would have to.

***

Acting DCI Charlie Kingston stood by the board. This was the last meeting. The last time the Murder Team would have to discuss Mick Tyler's death and Del Tyler's arrest. The last time.

At least that scum was locked away now, crying like a bloody baby half the time now. '*Too late for tears*,' he had said to him. *'Won't wash with me, won't wash with anyone. Your hell begins now mate'.'*

Between the sobbing episodes, Del Tyler had told them about that night. The night of the murder. His first one, his dad and then he had told them about the second one, Theobald Harrison. The weird old lady had been right all along, perhaps she hadn't been so dotty after all.

He had told them about Legs taking the rap for him when the old lady had been run over. That it had actually been him, Del at the wheel and, finally, he had admitted to cutting his own girlfriend's face. How he had managed to get away with all that was unbelievable, Charlie Kingston thought.

He had just told George Pattinson that his son was going to be released very shortly as Del Tyler had just confessed that it had been him who had driven the stolen car.

'But why?' George asked him. 'Why would my son have taken the blame?'

Charlie Kingston had shrugged his shoulders. 'I don't know Mr. Pattinson, you'll have to ask him that.'

'Well, that's good news anyway,' George grinned. 'Can I just phone my wife and tell her? It'll really perk her up. We need something good to happen in Churchill Street. It's been a nightmare for all of us. I should have seen it before, should have realised.'

'Don't blame yourself, he was a clever manipulator Del Tyler. He fooled a lot of people.'

Charlie Kingston brought his mind back to the present. 'Right,' he didn't need to shout, there was a hush around the room. No jokes in the ops room this morning, no laughter. A lot of anger though.

'You should have let me shoot him guv,' said Scottie.

There were mutters of agreement, others shaking their heads. Someone kicked a chair over.

‘That’s enough!’ Charlie Kingston shouted. ‘Do you think I wouldn’t like him to be dead? Is that it? I would like Del Tyler to be hung upside down where I could disembowel the fucking little bastard, but I can’t do that. I’m a copper and all I can think about and all you should be thinking about now is what the guv would have done. I can’t get him out of my head, it’s almost like he’s haunting me and that’s it. That is how we have to remember him, by doing what *he* would have done. All the bloody time, because he was a good cop, a fair cop. For Christ’s sake, even the people in Churchill Street are mourning for him. I can’t say any – take over Scottie.’

Charlie Kingston couldn’t carry on. Jenny Finch ran after him as he headed for the swing doors, his hands over his face. Scottie put his arms out and stopped her.

‘No Jenny. He won’t want anyone seeing him like this. Right,’

He walked slowly towards the board and took a deep breath. There was absolute silence in the room. ‘This is what the bastard told us about the night Mick Tyler was murdered.’

***

‘You are Derek Charlton Tyler?’

‘Yes.’

‘Please proceed with your statement as regards your first offence. The murder or manslaughter of Mr. Michael Tyler on 22nd May 1956.’

‘Don’t know where to start,’ Del Tyler sniffed.

‘The beginning, and don’t stop until you’ve got to the end. I don’t want to know how you felt, how hard done by you are, who's upset you in the past. I just want the facts please Mr. Tyler and slowly and clearly, everything you say is going to be written down and then typed up immediately. We don't want any mistakes on this one.'

'There's no need for that tone Detective Inspector,' Del Tyler's solicitor spoke to Charlie Kingston. 'And I would like it noted down that the accused has bruising on his face.'

'Yes, he had a bad fall as we were taking him down to the cells,' said Charlie straightfaced.

Del was shaking but the tilt of his head and the way he glared at Charlie Kingston reflected the arrogance of his body language. They saw him take a deep breath.

'Well - me an' me mum was in the kitchen. She was getting me a cocoa before I went to bed an' then there was this knock on the door, quiet like.'

He stopped, tears welled in his eyes.

'Go on and stop snivelling.'

'Well it was me dad, he was just stood there. '*Leave us alone Del*,' he said to me. '*Get to bed. I need to talk to your mum*.' He was sober an' all, he weren't drunk. He hadn't seen me for six months, didn't even ask me how I was doing. Just told me to go to bed.'

'What did I say to you?' Charlie Kingston asked him. 'I don't want to know about your dad not loving you, just tell me what happened next.'

'Well, I didn't go to bed, just sat on the stairs listening. At first they was talking quiet an' then I heard a thumping sound against the wall an' I knew he'd hit her. She shouted at him to stop.'

Del Tyler picked up the glass of water that was in front of him, his hand was shaking.

'Go on,' said Charlie.

Del took a deep breath. 'I ain't feeling so good.'

'You'll be feeling worse if you don't carry on, we've only just started.'

The solicitor gave him a warning look.

'Look Del,' said Charlie Kingston. 'The sooner you get it all out the sooner you can have a nice cup of tea and a fag. Alright? Now, just get on with it.'

'I run back in the kitchen. Me mum was on the floor, there was blood.'

'Did your mum see you?'

'Yeah – no, I ain't sure. Her eyes were looking all glazed over and then he really punched her, right in the face. She didn't see nothing after that, she was out cold. I run past him, got the poker. He was bending over her an' I just hit him on the head, hard as I could. I thought he'd killed her.' He started to sob.

'My client needs a break,' said the solicitor.

Charlie Kingston nodded to Scottie. 'Get him some water and a fag.'

Ten minutes later when Del seemed to have calmed down again Charlie coughed.

'Right, where were we? You've just hit your dad with the poker. What about the other kids, didn't they hear nothing?'

Del shook his head. 'It weren't noisy. He didn't make no sound when I hit him first, just slumped down and sort of crumpled up. There was a cat, I heard a cat crying. That's all.'

‘So what happened next Del? How many times did you hit him?’

‘He got up. I couldn’t bleeding believe it but he got up an’ he staggered over to the door, he was just grunting a bit that’s all.’

‘What were you doing?’

‘I couldn’t move. I was just – I just couldn’t move. I was stood there holding the poker. There weren’t much blood on his head, I remember that. Then he fell out the door, collapsed just outside. I went a bit mad. I just kept hitting him. I wanted him dead then, I wanted to see him bleed.’

Charlie Kingston tried to hide his disgust. The solicitor looked horrified and put a hand on Del’s arm. He shook it off.

‘And at that time there was no-one in the kitchen except you and your mum?’

Del nodded.

‘Was your mum still unconscious?’

He nodded again. ‘She didn’t know nothing, honest she didn’t. She weren’t moving and her eyes was closed. She was breathing though, I could see that. I didn’t know what to do. I just jumped over his body. He weren’t moving, I knew I’d killed him. I felt like I’d gone mad. I run round to the front of the house an’ I heard Bones whistling, he was always whistling. He was coming up the road wiv Billy Potter. They was laughing, I remember that. Bloody laughing. I just stood there until they saw me. They come running over then, shaking me, asking me things. What was I doing out in me pyjamas? Why was I covered in blood?

Where was me mum? That sort of stuff. I didn't know how to talk no more. The words wouldn't come out. I just pointed to the back of the house. Then, when I could talk, I told 'em'. I told 'em what I'd done.'

'Go on,' said Charlie. 'What happened next?'

'Billy told Bones to wait wiv me while he checked round the back. When he come back he was crying, told Bones to get me to bed but to take me through the front door so's I wouldn't see nothing. Bit late for that I thought. Bones took me up an' left me in the bedroom before he went downstairs again. He come back up and started cleaning all the blood off me in the bathroom, I still couldn't talk. He told me that me mum was alright, they'd put her to bed. '*She's a bit confused Del*,' he said to me '*She thinks Mick has just gone off. She don't know he's dead*.'

I felt all this panic in me then. *'He ain't dead*,' I shouted. '*He got up. After I hit him he got up*.' Bones told me not to worry. He said they would sort it and that I weren't to say nothing about it. Ever.'

Del gulped and drank some water greedily.

'Was Winston there then?'

'No an' I don't think they told him nothing either. He never knew it was me who had killed me dad, I would have known. He must've have wondered though, who had done it. I went into me mum's room. I got her a glass of water an' I looked out the window. That was the first time I seen Winston that night. Him and Billy was one on each side of me dad, holding him up an' walking up the road. Bones was behind them, carrying a spade. I knew then for definite, that he was dead. I was glad.'

Del Tyler met Charlie Kingston's eyes and held them defiantly.

'Billy come to see me the next day,' Del carried on. 'Told me that me dad had just gone back to the Merchant Navy, said he wasn't hurt as bad as I thought, but I knew. I knew he was dead. Bones was the only one that told me the truth.'

'First Interview with Del Tyler finished at,' Charlie checked his watch '11.30 a.m.'

'I ain't finished yet,' said Del.

'Oh, I know you haven't Mr. Tyler. There's a lot more we need to talk to you about. This is just for starters.'

Del Tyler started to laugh then, hysterically. 'I'm fucking glad I killed him,' he shouted. 'I hated him.'

As Del Tyler was escorted from the room Scottie, who had been writing Del Tyler's statement, shook his head. 'Stupid, stupid people. Thought they were doing this kid a favour and look what's happened.'

'He'd have got away with it,' said Charlie. 'Defending his mum. There was no need for any of this. If they'd all told the truth in the first place, the guv would still be alive.'

'I suppose they thought it was for the best, he'd have done something anyway. I think he's just sick.'

Charlie shook his head. 'Might not have come out though if that hadn't happened, he was on the way to being a big pop star by all accounts. What a waste of a bloody life.'

‘Don’t deserve to live though does he guv? Should have kept that death penalty. We’re all going to get shot at all the time now. Those three coppers that died last month, I knew one of them. You’re not going soft on him are you?’

‘No, and don’t call me guv, not yet, I’m not ready for that. I hate him for killing the best boss I ever had and I always will but think about it Scottie. He was a ten year old kid, he’d just killed his dad and he was left with all those nightmares. On his own. No wonder he went loopy.’

‘You *are* going soft on him. You’re starting to sound like the guv already.’

‘Nicest thing you’ve ever said to me Scottie,’ Charlie’s smile was fleeting. ‘If it had just been what he did to his dad I could probably have forgiven him. Understood it even. But he’s done a lot more than that to other people. He’s admitted it all. So yes, I’d love to see him hang but I’m a copper and so are you. We’re not here to judge or be political but he was just a kid Scottie. There was no-one looking out for him. He never asked them all to lie did he? Hadn’t even got to secondary school, just a little kid.

He shook his head and they walked slowly out of the room.

23

Try A Little Tenderness – Otis Redding

'So you really didn't know?' Maggie sniffed and blew her nose into her hankie. Her and Winston were sitting in the kitchen. He had been very quiet ever since Del's arrest two days ago. It was the first time that they had had the house to themselves since then.

'If I'd known,' he said between gritted teeth. 'I'd have sorted it, for Del's sake. That kid needed help, they wouldn't have locked him up. He was trying to stop his dad from killing you. Billy was my mate but I'll never understand why they covered it up.' He sighed.

'When I got there they'd already put you to bed. There was no sounds anywhere in the house. I didn't know any of the kids had been up. I didn't even think - he was just lying there, outside the door, Mick. Blood everywhere man. Made me sick, I just threw up all over the path. I asked Billy if they'd phoned the cops. He just said, '*We ain't phoning the coppers Winston. You trust me don't you?*'

'Well, I did trust him Mags, he was me best mate. He'd looked out for me down at the docks. I was in some kind of shock, I just nodded. He told me what they were going to do wiv the body but he didn't say why. Bones just stood there shaking. I thought he might have a heart attack or something.'

'Ain't telling you nothing Winston an' you wasn't ever here,' Billy said to me,' *but we need your help.'*

'I owed him Mags, after all he did for me. I just tried to shut it all out my head, I think it was just instinct. For Christ's sake, he was only a little kid. If I'd known -'

'They was just protecting him,' Maggie sniffed. 'I ain't a brilliant mum, I know that.' She squeezed Winston's hand. 'I don't remember nothing that happened but if I *had* known I'd have done the same as them and lied. An' I think you would an' all.'

He shook his head violently. 'No Mags, no I wouldn't have. That's where we're different.'

He stood up and moved towards the door still shaking his head.

'Winston, we're all right though ain't we? You ain't gonna leave us or nothing – are you?'

'I don't know Maggie an' that's the truth. I love you, you know that, an' whatever happened when Mick was living here – well, that's in the past. You've been a good mum to Nessie but I don't know that I can do all this stuff anymore. We need to get away from here, just for a break. You, me, an' Nessie.'

'How can I?' Maggie screamed. 'How can I leave Del locked up in that cell wiv no-one? Someone's got to be here for him.'

'Well, you've never cared much about him before,' Winston shouted back. 'You've always been hard on him. Or did you know what he was like? Had he ever done bad stuff before? Because he nearly killed our Nessie. And if you know something -'

He saw Maggie's face begin to crumple.

'I'm sorry Mags,' he said. 'I shouldn't have shouted at you. It's just when I think of what he could have done to her -'

He moved towards Maggie and tried to put his arm around her, she pushed him away violently.

She stood up then, tears streaming down her face. 'Well fuck off then,' she screamed. 'You fucking black bastard an' take your fucking half-breed wiv yer. I'll be happier on me bleedin' own!'

Winston could feel his heart thumping, he had never felt such misery. 'You don't mean that. I love you so much it hurts but I just can't breathe anymore in this house. I need to get away, just for a couple of days. I'm taking Nessie to Southend whether you come or not. She needs it after what she's been through.'

As he closed the door the teapot just missed his head. The tea leaves slid down the door as the china crashed and splintered on to the floor.

***

'I'm going to Southend,' said Nessie.

They had all gathered in George's shed. Nessie, Tonk and Jason. Jason had brought the *Stratford Express* with him and was reading the headlines.

'Bleeding hell,' he exclaimed.

'Put the paper away Jason,' Tonk hissed at him, nodding towards Nessie.

'Don't matter,' said Nessie. She tried to smile, but it was hard, her whole body just felt full of sadness.

'Says here,' said Jason excitedly, 'all about the group.' He read the paper to them slowly.

TEN YEAR OLD MURDERER LOSES CHANCE OF STARDOM

LOCAL GROUP, 'THE RED DRAGONS', HAVE LOST THEIR SINGER AND DRUMMER DEREK TYLER WHO, AS ALREADY REPORTED IN THIS PAPER, HAS BEEN ARRESTED FOR KILLING A SENIOR POLICE OFFICER. IT IS ALSO BELIEVED THAT HE MURDERED HIS OWN FATHER IN 1956, WHEN HE WAS JUST TEN YEARS OLD.

A spokesman for 'The Red Dragons' said yesterday. 'The group are all devastated. They have just released their first single 'The End of the Game,' composed by Del Tyler which has entered the charts this week at number 72. They are now considering whether or not they have a future without him.'

Lead guitarist Les 'Chalky' White said 'We are all in shock. Del was our undisputed leader and a great bloke. We always had a laugh with him, we just can't believe it...'

'That's enough,' said Tonk, grabbing the paper from Jason.

'It's alright Tonk,' said Nessie, taking the paper from him.

Above the writing was a photo of her half brother Del when he had been her age. He was smiling. There was a dark smudge on his cheek and his hair was sticking up all over the place. She thought his eyes looked really dark, *they* weren't smiling at all. Just like when he had looked at her when he had read the notebook...

Next to that was a photo of the group. The face was still the same, he was smiling but not properly. She had never noticed that before.

'Don't cry Nessie,' Jason said quickly. 'I'm sorry.'

She stood up. 'I'd best get moving, I need to see Greta before we go to Southend, me dad thinks the sea air might be good.'

The boys looked embarrassed as she moved towards the door.

'We'll be here for you,' Tonk shouted. 'When you get back.'

'Ta,' she said, through her tears. 'I know you will.'

***

'Oh it's lovely to see you Nessie. Do your mum and dad know you're here?'

Nessie burst into tears when she saw her old friend. She threw her arms around Greta and they clung to each other for a long time. Nessie cried. Heaving sobs, while Greta softly stroked her hair.

'Let it all out,' she whispered. 'It's the best way.'

Greta waited until Nessie grew quieter and then she gently pushed her away.

'You'll need a drink now,' she said. 'Sit on the chair, I'll get you some orange juice. Do you feel alright – being in this house again?' she asked.

Nessie was sitting dwarfed in the huge flowery green armchair. She looked comfortable and relaxed.

'Yeah, I'm OK,' she laughed. 'As long as I don't have to drink me juice in the cellar.'

Oh, to be a child again, thought Greta, making her way towards the kitchen.

'I can't stay long,' said Nessie, drinking her juice slowly. 'Me dad's waiting outside. We're going to Southend for two days.'

'Just what you need,' Greta smiled.

'Can I just ask you something?' Nessie asked.

'I can't promise to answer you but yes, of course.'

Nessie took a deep breath. 'When we was in the cellar, you know, when the coppers came in and untied us I noticed – I saw boxes an' boxes of biscuits. They was everywhere.'

'I keep them for visitors,' said Greta sharply. 'Just for visitors.'

Nessie could see that her friend's eyes were beginning to fill up.

'I'm sorry, I didn't mean to upset you.'

Greta's face paled and she began to tremble. Nessie watched as she took a deep breath.

'No, I will tell you the truth,' she said quietly. 'When I was in Auschwitz we were starving. You will never have experienced that Nessie, I hope you never do. When people say they're starving because they've missed a meal it still makes me angry. None of us had any meals for years. You never forget that pain because it *is* a pain, physically and mentally. That's why my cellar is full of biscuits, it makes me feel safe. Now, let's talk of other things and leave it at that.'

'Are you – OK?' Nessie asked.

'Oh yes, I'm fine. Takes more than being tied up and having a gun to my head to frighten me.' She laughed and soon Nessie joined in. 'I'm sorry about Del,' she said. 'I know you loved him and it's hard when someone you love becomes a different person. I do think that he was born – different. If his life had been kinder it may not have come out but we'll never know now.'

'Can you forgive him for killing Old Bones?'

'I'm going to try,' she said. 'He would never have hurt you though Nessie, I know that, I felt it. I'm just so sorry about the policeman. I'm going to go to his funeral, I don't think he had an easy life either.'

'I liked him an' all,' said Nessie. 'He let me see me dad you know, when they locked him up. I'll come wiv you, to the funeral.'

'Well, that's up to your mum and dad. It's good to say goodbye to people you cared about though. Remember all the especially good people Nessie because sometimes and some days, it feels like everyone is bad.'

'You know when funny things happen to me, like when I know what's going to happen an' stuff? It's a bit scary.'

Greta smiled at her new friend. 'Yes, it can be and when you see things you usually only get half the story, it's easy to jump to conclusions. All I can say is that you shouldn't be frightened of it and if you are, come and talk to me. Any time.'

Nessie nodded. 'An' I can help you throw out the mouldy biscuits an' all.'

There was a knock at the door.

'That'll be me dad. Him an' and me mum have been shouting all the time today.'

'It's very hard for them Nessie but I'm sure they'll be alright, it's been a dreadful shock for everyone.'

Winston smiled as Greta opened the door.

He shook her hand warmly. 'Thank you ma'am for looking after my little girl,' he said.

'She's always welcome here Winston, you have an inspirational daughter. It was really *her* that got me through it all.'

She waved as they walked through the gate and for one fleeting moment Greta wished that she had been a mother.

***

Jimmy and Legs had been in the *The Kings Head* for a few at lunchtime, catching up on the old days.

'Remember our bonfire nights?' Jimmy asked.

'Old Bones singing round the bonfire, Del throwing bangers all over the place.' Legs laughed.

'He used to tie 'em to cat's tails as well. We should have seen it Legs, shouldn't we eh? Things in his head that weren't right.'

'You don't understand do you?' Legs asked him quietly. 'You don't understand why I took the blame for him.'

Jimmy shook his head. 'No. No I don't. Oh I know you had a thing about him.'

'Men and women get obsessed with each other and do stupid things. People seem to understand that. Look at Maggie. How many years did she stay with Mick Tyler and he was beating her up every week?'

'Sorry Legsy, but I don't understand that either.'

'It's a sort of madness and it happens to us queers as well.'

'He said you were in love with him,' said Billy. 'That's why you did it.'

Legsy put his drink down on the bar. 'It *was* an accident Jimmy. One minute we were laughing and joking. The next she was just there, in front of us. Del couldn't move. I jumped out and went over to her, I knew she was dead. Her handbag was on the road behind her, the purse was open, pennies falling out everywhere. There was an inhaler and a lacy hankie, that's the picture I always see.'

Jimmy looked at his old friend and saw tears in his eyes.

'I'll get you another beer mate,' he said.

'No, just let me finish. I need you to understand.' He took a deep breath.

'When I got back to the car he was sat in the passenger seat sobbing.'

'Clever,' Jimmy interrupted.

'He wouldn't move. I wanted to run away, they wouldn't have found us. Then people started coming over, someone phoned the coppers. Del just sat there crying and looking at me. He had a cut on his head, blood was trickling down his face. '*Help me Legs',* he said. *' Please help me. They'll lock me up, I couldn't handle that.'* A copper came up and tapped me on the shoulder '*Were you driving?'* he asked me. I looked at Del, his eyes were begging me, begging me to take the blame.

‘*I love you Legsy*,’ he whispered to me. So I did it. I told the copper it was me driving.’

‘That’s not love, that’s obsession,’ said Jimmy. He wanted to shake Legs but it was too late for all that.

‘I don’t know why I did it. It was the worst day of my life and the lies just got worse and I couldn’t see a way out of it.’

‘You could have told the truth,’ said Jimmy.

‘Oh and they’d have understood would they? It’s still illegal you know Jimmy. What I am. He came to see me Del, twice, before I went to court. First time he told me he loved me, he’d wait for me, we’d go and live somewhere where no-one knew us. Oh, he was clever. He even cried. ‘*I don’t know how I’m gonna survive without you’* he said. He just brushed my hand gently, he could be very gentle you know.’

Jimmy grimaced. ‘I don’t want to know all that stuff Legsy, no offence mate.’

‘He came back once more, just before I went to court. I was panicking by then, really scared. I told him that I might have to tell the truth, that I couldn’t handle it. That was when he changed. Threatening, evil. Said he’d tell everyone about me and all the stuff I’d done to him. Called me a little nancy boy. ‘*It’s your own fault Legsy. Doing those disgusting things to me in the park. Made me go mad.’* And I believed him. I really thought it *was* my fault but I’ll tell you what, he bloody enjoyed it.

Then he said he’d start by telling the coppers that I’d raped him and that he’d tell my mum and dad. I couldn’t handle it, I thought I’d end up inside whatever

I did and why would the coppers have believed me? I don't think they took fingerprints or anything, not after I admitted it.'

Jimmy looked up and saw Josie making her way towards them.

'You two are good together,' said Legs. 'I'm happy for you mate and thanks for listening, I needed to talk about it.'

Jimmy patted him on the back. 'You'll be alright now,' he said. 'Now he's gone.'

'Oh I don't feel anything for him now. It was just madness but I can't explain to mum and dad, I just can't.'

'Right,' Josie came towards them smiling. 'There's a tummy bug going round at the home so I haven't had a good morning.'

'Need a drink love?' Jimmy asked.

'I'll get these,' laughed Legs. 'We'll have a toast to old friends.' He winked at Jimmy. 'And I've got the best old friends in the world.'

***

'Well, that wasn't bad Mr. Potter,' Josie laughed as she snuggled up to him in her bed.

'You're such a romantic Miss Evans,' Jimmy laughed as he slapped her bum playfully. 'Oooh,' he winced. 'I don't think all this exercise has helped my shoulder.'

Finally one of them had been home alone and they had been able to make love undisturbed all afternoon.

'Please tell me the earth moved more than once,' he laughed as she sat up on the edge of the bed. 'And where are you going now?'

'Mum will be back from work soon, you'll have to move.'

She looked at him tenderly and stroked his forehead. 'I dreamt of this for years,' she said slowly. 'Even before I knew what it was, it was always you Jimmy. Does that make me weird?'

He shook his head and smiled. 'No, I'd say you have very good taste.'

Her expression changed suddenly. 'You don't think this is wrong do you? I mean so soon after -'

He put a finger on her lips. 'No, it isn't wrong. How could it be?'

He moved reluctantly away from her and began to put his clothes on. 'And tonight,' he said, 'we're going to do something else that normal people do. We're going to the Ilford Palais.'

Josie groaned. 'That is really not a very cool thing to do Jimmy. Can't we go to the Marquee instead? There's some really good groups play there.'

'Ah but *The Small Faces* are playing down the Palais tonight.'

She threw her arms around his neck and screamed with delight. 'Oh, they're fab, I love them. Not as much as you, of course,' she added cheekily, kissing him on the cheek. 'I thought you were doing some nights in *The Kings Head* for Arthur.'

‘Yeah, but I haven’t started yet. Is this our first argument Miss Evans because if it is I’m going to have to put you in your place.’

He took his pants and jeans off again and grabbed her arms. ‘Just get back in that bed now woman, I haven’t finished with you yet.’

They both giggled and loved each other again as if it was the only thing in the world that mattered.

24

My World Is Empty Without You – The Supremes

The church was absolutely packed and not just with policemen and their families, John Paradise had touched many lives.

Greta held Nessie's hand in the back pews. Next to her sat Winston, Josie and Jimmy.

'Can't believe I'm at a copper's funeral man,' Winston whispered for the tenth time.

From the beginning of the service, Nessie had held on to Greta and her dad's hands tightly while they sung hymns and said prayers.

Then a short, elderly man limped towards the front. When he turned to face the congregation, Greta saw the resemblance.

'Bet that's his dad,' Nessie whispered to her. Greta nodded. He had a soft voice and yet from the back of the church they could hear every word clearly.

He smiled. 'We had four children but it was always John who got lost, got into trouble, fell over. In fact the first time he told us that he was going to be a policeman was when he was brought home by one when he was five. He'd met an old tramp passing by and decided to join him for a life on the road.'

The church filled with laughter, John Paradise's dad looked pleased.

'Yes, my son was a great lad, though I suppose I'm a bit biased. He phoned my wife a few days ago to ask about his childhood because he has no memory of it himself and now I want to tell you all a little about John's wartime experiences. They changed him, made him the man you all knew and, I believe, it's a story that needs to be told.'

He stopped, cleared his throat and took some sheets of paper from his pocket. His hands shook as he opened them out.

'John was an RAF pilot in the war. He loved flying, it was his great passion.

'When I'm up there, flying through the air dad,' he said to me once, 'nothing else seems to matter.'

The worst part, of course, was losing his friends. By 1944 he had flown many missions and survived but in that year his luck finally ran out. His plane was shot down over Northern France. Him and nearly two hundred other Allied airmen were handed over to the Gestapo by a French informer. They were *not* taken to a POW camp as they should have been, but to Buchenwald, a slave labour camp. The inmates in Buchenwald were starved to death rather than gassed. When they arrived they found themselves surrounded by emaciated peoples who could barely be recognised as human beings. John only talked about it once to me and, as far as I know, he told no-one outside the family. I encouraged him to write all his memories down because it was so difficult for him to talk about it.'

He stopped, removed his glasses, and wiped his eyes with his hankie. He cleared his throat again. The church was full of silence. There was no fidgeting, no sound except almost silent tears, dappled sunlight played over the congregations heads.

Greta swallowed as her tears fell and she was back in Auschwitz again. Nessie squeezed her hand.

'I'm just going to read you some extracts from his writing,' John Paradise's father spoke again. 'And these are *not* the most harrowing parts.'

'We were lucky,' my son wrote. *'We had a shared discipline and we looked out for each other. If one of us fell over in the exercise areas we would prop him up between us and get him back to the hut. Anyone else who fell over would be sent to the hospital, given a lethal injection and burned. I can still smell the stench from those chimneys every day...'*

'The other prisoners looked barely human. The only thing that they had in common was that they were different. Different from Hitler's Germans. They were outcasts, Jews, homosexuals, gypsies, coloureds, communists, the disabled and they were all alone, they had no hope. Yes, we were lucky but I have never forgotten them and I never will...'

'I can't believe how lucky I am still to be alive. Word had got out that we were in Buchenwald. Some German airmen had stayed over in the camp and they were genuinely appalled when they saw us in there. Although we were no better than the other prisoners there was a common code among all airmen, whichever side we were on, a kind of strange brotherhood. We appealed to them to help us. They hated the Gestapo as much as we did and managed to get us out. Out to a POW Camp. We soon found out that the Gestapo had

planned our execution, we had missed it by only days but I still feel the guilt I did then, as we walked out of there and left all those poor, poor people behind. There was nothing we could do for them...'

Nessie squeezed Greta's hand even tighter and looked into her old friend's face. Tears glistened in her eyes but she smiled at Nessie.

'I knew he understood,' she whispered.

'When I finally got home, I seemed fine but shortly afterwards I had a breakdown and now I have no memory of myself as a child. No memories of anything before the war and what happened but something good did happen during that time which still warms my heart. When we were taken on one of the death trains to Buchenwald, we stopped in a tunnel. A bridge in front of us had been blown up and we had to walk miles through frozen countryside, carrying the Gestapo guards equipment, to meet up with another train. We were weary and starving and quite a few prisoners were collapsing all around us. As we crawled into a little French village the local people forced the guards to stop. They brought out steaming hot soup and bread, they passed around brandy and cigarettes, gave us the blankets off their own beds. They saved our lives...'

'I'm finishing this story here but it will never finish in my lifetime. It has taught me to fight the evil in men and women because there will always be Gestapo out there but I never forget the good. After all, we were saved by German airmen and they weren't much different to us...'

John Paradise's father folded the paper carefully again and put it back in his pocket. He smiled through his tears.

I'm sorry I've gone on a bit,' he tried to laugh. 'He'd be having a right go at me now. I'm just so proud to have been his dad -'

25

Have You Seen Your Mother Baby Standing In The Shadow? – Rolling Stones

'How was it love?' Sally asked her daughter as she poured her a cup of tea.

'Very moving. He was in a concentration camp you know, like Greta was. What did you do mum? In the war?'

'Makes me feel guilty sometimes,' Sally laughed. 'I had a good time. We were young. I was in the WAAF, travelled round the country, had some great mates. I think it was the most alive I ever felt in me life really. You always knew though, that you could be brown bread the next day, everytime there was a bombing raid. Everyone just lived for the moment.'

'And you got pregnant with me?'

'Yeah,' she smiled at her daughter. 'Turned out alright didn't you?' She punched her playfully in the shoulder.

'I've got a confession mum,' said Josie.

'Don't tell me, you've been sleeping wiv Jimmy,' she laughed. 'I ain't daft you know. You never did it wiv Del – did you?'

Josie blushed. 'That wasn't what I was going to tell you mum,' she said, 'but as it happens, no. I don't know why. We tried but – he just couldn't do it, he said it didn't matter.'

'Oh I think it does love,' said Sally. 'I know a lot of girls still wait until they're married but things are changing now.'

'Well, after this -' she touched her scar gently. 'I was scared. I didn't want anyone touching me in that way, you know what I mean? Del wasn't bothered and I suppose I just felt safe wiv him. I knew he wouldn't try it on like other blokes. I know they're making him out to be a monster mum but -'

'He scarred you for life!' Sally said angrily. She saw the look of pain on her daughter's face. 'Oh, I know he loved you,' said Sally, 'in his own way but he wasn't right in the head. I don't understand it neither.'

'It's different wiv Jimmy,' said Josie shyly, touching the scar on her cheek.

'It ain't as bad as it was Jose, it's faded a lot. Anyway what was you going to confess then?'

'That was when you told me about me dad,' said Josie slowly. 'When we were kids and we first found out about sex. The American airman, Rory. Remember? That's actually what I'm trying to tell you about now.'

Sally stopped peeling potatoes and sat down at the table next to her daughter.

'What about him?' she asked sharply.

'He wants to meet you.'

There was a silence in the kitchen that seemed to last a very long time. Finally Josie spoke again. She swallowed and looked at her mum. Her face was white and she was trembling.

'Sorry mum, I knew it would be a shock, I just didn't know how to tell you. Del found him for me. He went to a records office somewhere. There was a list of American servicemen who wanted to contact people from the war. Our names were on there, he was looking for us.'

'I wrote to him,' said Sally angrily. 'I wrote to him when you were born, just to tell him, that's all. That he had a daughter. What the bloody hell were you messing about trying to find him for? He never answered that letter you know, the bastard.'

Josie felt a tremor of anger through her body. 'He's my dad mum. Of course I want to know about him, why shouldn't I? ' she shouted.

Chris came running down the stairs. 'What's going on?' he asked quietly. 'Why are you shouting at mum?'

Josie stood up and pushed past him. 'I'm going to me room,' she snapped. 'Send Jimmy up when he comes.'

***

'Why didn't you tell me before?' Jimmy asked.

'Oh, don't you bloody start,' Josie snapped, jumping off the bed and putting the '*Hard Days Night'* LP on the record player. 'Things have been a bit dramatic round here lately or hadn't you noticed? I haven't had much time to tell you anything.'

He could see that her eyes were glistening with tears. 'Sorry love, come here a minute.'

She sat back on the bed next to him and he held her close. 'Go on then, tell me all about him.'

Josie told Jimmy how she had written to her dad and he had replied immediately. They had been writing for about a year and now he had started talking to her on the phone every Sunday night when she was working at the home.

'He just seems really nice Jimmy. I really want to meet him.'

Jimmy stroked her hair. 'Did he tell his wife? That he was phoning you?'

'They split up, quite a long time ago. He got married again but she went off wiv a roadie who worked wiv Elvis. He just says he wants to see me an' mum. He wants to explain everything to her.'

'How does your mum feel about it? She didn't look too happy when I came in, didn't even offer me a cuppa.'

Josie sighed. 'I think it'll take a bit of time.'

Jimmy jumped up. 'Come on,' he said, 'let's go for a walk.'

'It's pouring wiv rain,' she laughed.

'Put your mac on then. You've turned into a real wimp Josie Evans, I've got something to show you.'

They walked up to the top of Churchill Street to the waste. The diggers stood idly in the rain.

'Should have put me wellies on,' Josie laughed, 'it's like a mudbath. Where are you taking me now?'

He grabbed her hand and sat her down next to him over by the hedge. It was full of bits of concrete and dust, old tin cans and other rubbish.

'This is where we had our den,' she laughed, rain dripping down her hood and face. Jimmy was soaked, he wasn't even wearing a mac. He knelt down in the mud and pulled a box from his pocket. She gasped as she saw what was inside. He took out the sparkly engagement ring.

'Will you marry me Jose?'

She stopped giggling and looked seriously into his soaking wet, wonderful face.

'What would I want to marry you for?' she said, trying to be serious but then they were laughing and clinging to each other in the mud and the rain.

'Course I will,' she shouted at last. 'Where's the ring gone?'

'Oh shit, I've dropped it in the mud. Shut up Jose, this is serious now,' he smiled, retrieving the ring.

'Is that a real diamond?'

'Is that all you want me for?' he grinned. 'For my money? No, course it's not but I will buy you a diamond one day Jose, I love you so much.'

Josie laughed as he tried to put the ring on her finger and it fell into the mud again.

'Suppose it didn't occur to you to check what size me finger was?'

Jimmy looked confused. 'Well, I just guessed,' he admitted sheepishly. 'Come on Miss Evans, soon to be Mrs. Potter, let's go and tell your mum. It might cheer her up a bit.'

They walked slowly back down Churchill Street holding hands laughing and looking like two mud wrestlers.

'That was really romantic Jimmy,' Josie sighed. He stopped, bent down and kissed her gently on the lips. 'It's where it all began Jose,' he said. 'I couldn't have done it anywhere else.'

'You don't think it's too soon -'

'No. I don't. The Tylers will understand.'

***

'They're bleeding engaged?' Maggie Tyler exclaimed as Tonk and Nessie came in with the news.

'Well of all the - my Del's hardly been gone five minutes an' she's in Jimmy Potter's trousers! Little strumpet!'

'Is that like a little trumpet?' Nessie whispered to Tonk. He shook his head. 'Don't think so, she ain't taking this very well.'

Winston was trying to calm Maggie down.

'Well, I'm going right over there an' I'm fuckin' gonna -'

'No you are *not!*' Winston pushed her forcefully back onto the kitchen chair.

Nessie jumped. She had never heard her dad shout like that before. They hadn't been expecting this sort of reaction. Maybe she should have told her dad first. She hoped that as she got older she would know when she should say things and when she shouldn't, she was getting that awful sinking feeling in her stomach. Surely you didn't still get that when you were old.

'Bloody Mrs. Snotty- Nose is still haunting me, even from the other side of the world.' Her mum put her head in her hands. 'An' after the day I've had an' all.'

'Sorry mum,' said Nessie. 'I just thought it was a bit of good news, I mean weddings are always good news ain't they?'

'I think that might just be in fairy tales Ness,' Tonk whispered.

Nessie glanced at her dad. He was giving her that sort of look that meant she should just shut up.

'What happened with the solicitor?' he spoke gently now to Maggie and stroked her hair as she cried.

'They're gonna go for insanity. He'll be locked up in Broadmoor for the rest of his life now.'

'Better than the death penalty,' said Winston. 'That's what it would have been a couple of years ago for shooting a copper. At least you'll be able to see him. How was he today?'

'In his own little world as usual. I told him his song was number 3 in the charts, he really thinks they'll let him out to go on '*Top of The Pops*'.

'Are they on this week? *The Red Dragons*?' Tonk asked excitedly.

Marilyn came flouncing into the kitchen. 'Did you say they was on '*Top of the Pops*' on Thursday? Seriously mum, that is fab news. You have to get Del to do some autographs for me next time you see him. I reckon I could sell 'em for at least a shilling each.' She looked at her mum sitting at the table. 'What's happened now?'

Tonk couldn't contain his excitement. 'Our Josie just got engaged to Jimmy Potter.'

Marilyn looked around at them all. 'Is this some sort of joke?' she asked. 'Jimmy Potter wouldn't touch her wiv a bargepole, she's a slag. Her mum's a slag an' so is she. I don't believe you. He fancies me, I know he does. I can see it every time I bump into him, he just looks at me in that sort of way.'

‘Shut up Marilyn,’ Winston roared, ‘and get up to your room.’ Marilyn looked over to her mother hoping for some support.

‘You’re disgusting,’ Maggie said. ‘Sometimes I don’t know where you’ve come from.’

‘Bloody alky Mick Tyler,’ that’s where she’s come from,’ Tonk was shouting at Marilyn now. He ran over and kicked her in the shins. ‘Don’t you dare call me mum an’ me sister a slag.’

‘Enough,’ said Winston, pulling Tonk away from his step-daughter. ‘All of you just go. Me an’ your mother need to talk.’

As they ran down the path Tonk muttered to Nessie. ‘Is it always like that in your house?’

‘Sometimes,’ said Nessie, matter of factly. ‘Whenever Marilyn kicks off me dad always says ‘*Never mind Ness, just another day in Paradise*.’

‘*Fucking flying fish*,’ Tonk laughed.

They giggled as they crossed the road to seek shelter in George’s shed.

***

‘Oh, I am pleased for you both,’ said Sally, throwing her arms around them. ‘That don’t mean I’ve forgotten I’m still angry with you Jose, about your dad. Can’t believe it,’ she giggled. ‘Me an’ your mum Jimmy, sort of related. We didn’t get on too well in the old days.’

Sally stood looking at their worried faces and smiled. ‘She’s a different person now, we’ll be fine. So, have you thought about when and where?’

Jimmy and Josie looked at each other, dripping wet and covered in mud. 'No, we haven't thought that far ahead Sal,' said Jimmy.

'Just a small wedding I think,' said Josie. 'We need to find out when your mum's coming over. Jimmy, we need to tell her!'

'Alright, don't panic. I think we need to get a bath before we start thinking about anything else,' he smiled.

'Before you even think about it,' Sally wagged a finger at them both. 'Separate baths in separate houses, you ain't married yet.'

'Mum!' Josie exclaimed. 'I'd say that was a bit of the pot calling the kettle black, you were young once you know.'

'I ain't forty yet, cheeky buggers. Go an' get yourselves cleaned up an' then we'll have a long natter about it. I'll have to start saving me pennies.'

'Small wedding mum, not the world an' his wife. Anyway you ain't paying for it all.'

'It's tradition. Bride's family always pays.'

'Well it's a stupid tradition then,' said Jimmy as he headed for the door.

They were interrupted by Tonk who came running in, Nessie behind him. They bumped into Jimmy. 'They've gone mad over at the Tylers,' he said dramatically. 'Maggie's screaming and shouting about Del an' Marilyn thinks you fancy her Jimmy so she's upset an' all, she says you're all slags. What does that mean mum? I knew it was something bad the way she said it so I kicked her anyway.'

'Oh, great,' Jimmy groaned.

'I'll sort Maggie out if Winston can't,' Sally laughed 'and Marilyn will get over it.'

They all jumped in unison as they heard the sound of crashing glass coming from the sitting room. Jimmy got in there just in time to see Marilyn's ample bottom disappearing around the corner. A large stone sat in the middle of the carpet. Sally came up behind him. 'Little cow,' she said. 'We could have been sat in here, I'm calling the coppers.'

'I'll go and have a word with her,' said Jimmy. 'Don't phone the cops till I get back Sal.'

Josie walked out to the gate with him. 'Is it always going to be like this Jimmy?' she asked. 'I'm so tired of all this aggravation all the time.'

'Well at least your mum seems pleased.'

'She won't be,' said Josie.

'What do you mean?'

'I want me dad to give me away.'

'Oh shit. Can I change me mind? About marrying you? We've only been engaged for half-an-hour and look what's happened already.'

'No,' Josie laughed. 'I'll sue you for everything you got.'

'You're all I've got,' he laughed, 'so that's alright.'

'Go an' sort Marilyn out then. I'd move fast, Maggie's on her way.'

'I'm gone,' he laughed, running down the street and still covered in mud.

***

'Please tell me you ain't phoned the coppers Sal,' Maggie's lips were trembling as Sally put the kettle on.

Josie had disappeared upstairs, they heard the sounds of the bath water running.

‘I was going to Maggie. Have you seen the mess? If one of the kids had been sitting in there -’

‘I know an’ I’m sorry. She just had a bit of a thing about Jimmy that’s all, she ain’t a bad girl, not really. Winston’s gone to get some glass, he’ll fix it for you straightaway Sal. It’s just -’ Maggie broke down in tears. ‘It’s just – it’s only been a couple of weeks since they took Del away. I can’t tell him his girlfriend’s got engaged to his best mate.’

‘He knows Maggie. He knew when he went up to Greta’s house, when he shot that copper. He knew that Josie was in love with Jimmy.’

‘There you are you see. That’s why he done it, it’s all their fault. Jimmy and Josie, all their bleeding fault.’

‘No Maggie!’ Sally snapped. ‘He scarred my daughter for life, was that her fault? He killed Old Bones for God’s sake, he would’ve killed Billy an’ all if he hadn’t died anyway. That’s what he’d bought the gun for. No, I’m sorry Maggie. I know you love him, he’s your son but he ain’t right in the head an’ you know that.’

Maggie shuddered and stared blankly into space. ‘It must’ve been something I did then and you’re wrong you know. I don’t love him.’

Sally put her arms around her shoulders. ‘No Maggie. Some people are just born wiv – problems, you probably don’t see it if they’re yours.’

‘Oh, but I did,’ she said slowly, pulling a handkerchief from her pocket and wiping her face. ‘When he was little.’ Her face crumpled.

‘I ain’t never told no-one before Sal, he would have only been about seven. I saw him strangle a cat in the garden. It was old Mrs. Nixon’s, that tortoiseshell, the one that only had one eye. It had been running wild since she’d died, no-one was looking after it.’ Maggie was whispering so quietly that Sally could barely hear her.

‘I saw him out of the kitchen window, I walked away. I don’t know why I did that. I saw the expression on his face, it frightened me Sal, really scared me. I *had* to pretend I hadn’t seen it, I went and sat on the stairs. Then I heard him come in. He was crying.

‘What’s up ?’ I asked him. He come running up and threw his arms around me. *‘Dead cat mum. There’s a dead cat on the grass, I just found it.’* I wanted to push him off. I felt sick and dirty wiv him near me. Couldn’t stand him after that. So it’s all my fault this. You’re meant to love your kids, ain’t yer?’

She stopped and took a deep breath. ‘We buried that cat. Del couldn’t stop crying, even said a prayer. I just put it out me head, what he’d done and that evil look on his face. He enjoyed killing it, just like he enjoyed killing his dad. I saw that an’ all.’

Sally gasped. ‘You *saw* him? You said you were unconscious, that you didn’t see nothing.’

‘I know what I said Sal. I’m sorry but I have to tell someone the truth. I trust you, I know it won’t go no further. I can't tell Winston. I couldn't stand it if he left me and he would.'

She blew her nose noisily into her hankie. 'Mick hadn't been hitting me that night, he was sober. He wanted to come home. Del was excited when he come in through the back door.

'*Dad!*' he shouted all happy like. He run up to his dad but Mick just pushed him away, told him to go to bed. Del weren't happy about that, I could tell.'

'I ain't seen you for months dad,' he shouted at him.

Well, we talked. Me an' Mick. I told him I didn't want him home. We were all happier without him, then he started crying. He was on his knees in front of me, begging, pleading. I saw Del out the corner of my eye passing behind him. The next thing Del's got the poker in his hand and then he's hitting Mick over the head wiv it. That look on his face. The same way he'd looked when he killed that cat -'

'Oh Maggie,' Sally could feel herself shaking all over. 'I'll get you a brandy.'

'I'll have one when I've finished,' she said, 'there ain't much more. I tried to stop him. Mick was crawling towards the door, blood pouring out of his head. I pushed Del over an' he dropped the poker. He turned round and glared at me like he really hated me. He was mad, I saw it in his eyes. Then he punched me, me own son, ten years old. I hit the corner of the table and fell on to the floor. That's how I got hurt. I passed out then, when I come round they were carrying me upstairs. Billy and Old Bones helped me to bed. They just believed what Del told 'em, that Mick had hit me. I lay awake, hearing the sounds, imagining what they were doing. Then Del come in with a glass of water for me, he was crying.

'Sorry mum,' he said. *'I didn't mean to hurt yer. Don't tell no-one will yer? Me dad's alright, he's gone.'*

It was like he was two people. Oh, I never believed a word he said after that but I did think that Mick was alright. I just thought he'd head off back to the Merchant Navy. It was a bleeding shock to me when they found him. I just wanted to forget it but he scared me after that, Del. Frightened of me own son. He'll never get out now an' at least he won't never hurt no-one again. I just couldn't face it then, it should've stopped that night. I knew he was a bad'n Sal.'

Sally said nothing. She put her hand back on her friend's shoulder. 'I think it's time for that brandy now don't you?'

'One thing I want to do first Sal, I'm going to phone the cops about Marilyn smashing your window.'

'You don't have to Maggie. Marilyn ain't like Del.'

'I know but I just want to start doing the right thing, she has to learn. Please Sal, please don't tell no-one what I've told you.'

'I won't say nothing Maggie, you've been through enough and there wouldn't be any point now. There's only one thing I want from you and that's your blessing for Jimmy and Josie's wedding.'

Maggie nodded and tried to smile.

Sally couldn't stop shaking. What would have happened if Josie had married Del? What sort of life would she have had? My God, her daughter had had a lucky escape, it didn't bear thinking about.

And now. Well, there was another secret she would have to take to the grave, along with all the others.

SIX MONTHS LATER ...

Good Vibrations – Beach Boys

May put her copy of the '*Stratford Express*' down as Kate came into the kitchen yawning. She had been so pleased to see her back in Churchill Street again for Jimmy and Josie's wedding. 'You've still got jet lag,' she laughed. 'You look as if you can hardly keep your eyes open.'

Kate laughed too. 'Well, I wasn't going to miss my son's wedding for any amount of jet lag.'

She looked at the paper lying on the kitchen table. 'Is there anything about -?'

'Yes,' said May crossly. 'The papers are all calling for the death penalty to be brought back, all these policemen being killed. Not surprising really is it? Del going to Broadmoor for life seems a bit of a soft option to me Kate.'

'But he must be mad,' Kate said. 'No normal person could do the awful things he's done.'

'Well,' said May, pouring a cup of tea for her friend. 'He's either mad or very clever. He could have killed your Jimmy and look what he did to my Clive. Oh, I don't know. I just want to forget it now. It's been awful Kate, the press and television people hounding us all the time.'

Kate put her arm around her friend's shoulder. 'As long as he's out of the way now that's all that matters,' she said, 'Has Clive ever told you why he went to prison for Del?'

May shook her head. 'He says he can't and that's the end of it. I'll never understand but he's out now and we've all got a wedding to look forward to. I went to see Nessie parading in her bridesmaid dress yesterday, she can't wait to show you. She's so excited.'

Kate smiled. 'I'm so glad Josie asked her after everything she went through. Are you sure you won't come to *The Kings Head* with us all tonight May?'

'No love, it's a family thing. It'll be interesting to meet Josie's dad though. I'll wait up for you coming in, you can tell me all about him.'

'Sally's dreading seeing him again. She knows she's got to put up with him being here for the wedding though for Josie's sake. Don't know if she'll be able to keep her mouth shut. '*If he says one word out of place*,' she told me,' *I'm just walking out.*' Can't say I blame her really. I can't believe I'm going to the pub with her,' Kate giggled 'and that we're going to be related. It's a strange world isn't it May?'

May sighed. 'You're happy about Jimmy and Josie though aren't you? She's a lovely girl.'

'Yes,' said Kate reluctantly. 'I always liked Josie. I just miss him. It's like I've lost him as well as Billy. Nothing in life seems to happen at the right time does it?'

There was a knock on the door.

'Well, there they are, have a lovely time,' said May as Kate grabbed her handbag and opened the door.

***

'You won't leave me alone wiv him will you Kate?' Sally whispered as they sat down next to each other in *The Kings Head.*

'You really are nervous aren't you? No of course I won't.'

'Oh, here he is,' Josie exclaimed, jumping out of her seat, as a tall, attractive middle-aged man came in through the door.

Sally gripped Kate's hand. 'What does he look like?' she hissed at Kate.

'He looks as scared as you do.'

'I can't look at him.'

Then he was standing over them. 'Hi Sally,' he said shakily.

Sally just nodded avoiding eye contact. Josie introduced him to everyone else and the men all moved towards the bar to get a round in.

'Alright Sal?' asked Kate.

'No I'm bleeding not. I ain't seen Rory since 1946,' said Sally angrily. 'Twenty years ago. He knew I'd had a baby, he never got in touch. Now he just swans back over here to walk his daughter down the aisle. Pays for everything so of course they all think he's bloody wonderful.'

'Did you love him Sally?'

Sally blushed. 'Yeah, as it happens, I did. He was the first one who broke me bleeding heart.'

Josie came back from the toilet. 'Well,' she said to her mum.' How's it going? He's alright mum honestly, please don't look like that, just try to smile.'

'Josie, he left your mum, pregnant at seventeen years old. Her mum threw her out and it's been a long struggle, of course it's hard for her,' said Kate. Blimey, she thought to herself. Here's me sticking up for Sally.

'Sorry mum,' Josie sat down next to Sally and squeezed her arm. 'I do know how hard it's been for you. I do understand why you're angry wiv him but I just really want you to like him.'

Sally stood up. 'I'm going to talk to him. On me own. It'll be alright.' She smiled at Kate. 'And was that you sticking up for me Mrs Snotty- Nose?' she laughed.

It was a quiet night in the pub. Mid-week, just a few regulars. Arthur the landlord was regaling Rory with tales from the war and Loopy was telling him about his bad leg when he was ambushed in France.

'You're not still telling that old story Loopy,' Jimmy laughed. 'He's only doing it to get a drink off you Rory. It's not true.'

Rory laughed. 'Hey you guys,' he said. 'You're really something else. What are you having – Loopy? Is that your real name?'

'Oh don't ask him how he got his name. That story's even longer,' said Arthur.

They laughed as Jimmy took the drinks over to the table.

Sally tapped Rory on the shoulder as he stood at the bar. 'I think we need to talk,' she said nervously, 'before we join the others.'

He nodded and followed her to a table at the other side of the room.

'Oh – oh. Trouble at mill.' Arthur laughed. 'I'm gonna miss all this you know, when I retire.'

'You ain't never gonna retire Arthur,' Loopy laughed, 'they'll be carrying you out of here in a box.'

Legs arrived at the bar.

'Nice to see you back Legsy. I hear you're gonna be Jimmy's best man.' Arthur boomed. 'Ain't seen much of you since you got out, bet the food's still shit in the Scrubs,' he laughed.

Jimmy came up and clapped his old mate on the back. 'How's my best man doing, what you drinking?' They moved over to where the girls were sitting.

Loopy whispered in to Arthur's ear. 'Have you heard that he's – you know?'

They watched as Legsy joined the others at the table.

'Yeah, it's the way he walks ennit?' Arthur agreed. 'Can spot 'em a mile off. Poor George, more worry for him.'

'Still,' said Loopy, 'at least that arsehole's locked away now. Can't understand why Billy tried to protect him like that, bleeding madman.'

'He was just a kid,' said Arthur. 'Didn't seem no worse than the others, I certainly didn't spot it. Anyway, all done and dusted now.'

'Saw that group on telly again last night,' Loopy lit up a cigarette. 'They've had two number ones already. He could have been someone you know, Del. Shame.'

They both nodded silently into their beer.

***

'I just want to say I'm sorry Sal. Real sorry.'

Sally could feel the anger screaming through her body, she wanted to hit him. He put his hands up, as if he had read her mind.

'So that makes it all alright then does it?' she whispered furiously. She noticed that he had begun to shake. 'You come over here to give her away at her wedding after all these years. Not a fucking word, no money, no support.'

For the first time that night Sally made eye contact with the man who had flown back to America and out of her life twenty years ago. He looked defeated, as if he was about to burst into tears. Good, she thought. There were deep lines on his face and his hair was greying and thin on top but he still had those eyes. The warm, twinkly ones that had got to her all those years ago. Well, now he was just a sad middle-aged man, she thought. He's not even worth me losing me temper over.

'I had to go home Sally. I had a wife and two kids, I never lied to you about that.'

'Strange how you suddenly had to go when I found out I was pregnant though. Look Rory, I ain't gonna pretend I like you being here but Josie seems to want it an' it's her day. I have to be civilised, I know that but I can't cope wiv any fake, friendly banter, you know what I mean? I'll see you on the day and be polite an' all that but I'm going home now, I'm sorry.' She picked up her handbag.

'You'll upset them if you go now.' He put his hand on her arm. 'Come on, just come over and finish your drink, I'm not the villain you're making me out to be you know.'

He smiled, she did *not* want him to smile, tears pricked the back of her eyes.

'It's not real easy for me either,' he said softly. 'Coming over here into the lion's den,'

'Oh, piss off,' she snapped but the venom had gone. She just wanted to go home and cry now. On her own. 'One drink and I'm off.'

He put his hand on her arm again as they stood up, she pushed it away. 'Don't – don't touch me,' she hissed as they walked back quickly across the bar.

***

'They seem to be getting on alright,' Josie said. 'They're still talking anyway. Wouldn't it be good if they got back together? I'm sure he still loves her you know.'

Kate smiled indulgently at her future daughter-in-law. From where she was sitting Sally's expressions were not friendly ones. Still, we all see what we want to, she thought and she knew that Josie desperately wanted her mum and dad to get on. 'It'll be fine Josie,' she said. 'You just worry about each other, I'll keep an eye on your mother.'

Josie laughed. 'I'll bet you wouldn't have chosen me to marry your Jimmy, Kate. I'll be a good wife to him, I promise.'

Kate touched her hand, just for a moment. 'I know you will,' she said. 'It's hard for me, him being the only one and living so far away.' She laughed. 'Billy was always going on when Jimmy was little, telling me to let go, not to smother him but I did find it difficult. You love your children too much really– it's the best and the worst thing I ever did, having a baby. You'll find out, when it's your turn.'

'Thanks Kate. I've always loved him you know.'

'Yes, I know you have and I *am* pleased it's you, really I am.'

Legs and Jimmy had been laughing. Old memories and childhood days.

'They're coming back,' Josie whispered.

'I'll just get the next round in,' Jimmy said quickly. 'I don't like blood.'

They were all laughing as Sally and Rory sat down.

'Well, you guys sound like you're having a good time,' Rory laughed, taking a long sip of his drink. A startled expression crossed his face. 'I take it this must be warm English beer?'

They all nodded.

'Get used to it,' Jimmy laughed. 'I know you asked for wine but they'll think you're a queer if you drink that in here.' He looked at his best man with a twinkle in his eye. 'Sorry Legsy, no offence.'

'None taken mate.'

They all laughed, even Sally. Kate squeezed her hand. 'It'll be alright,' she said to the woman she had hated ten years ago. The woman who had been in love with her husband. 'You can do this, you've been through a lot worse.'

'Ta Kate,' she sniffed. 'You're a good mate.'

***

Josie snuggled up to Jimmy in her bed. Her mum had reluctantly agreed that he could move in, just until they got married.

'Can't wait to get into our little flat in Stratford,' Josie laughed. 'Don't know why we couldn't move in before the wedding.'

'She doesn't want us living in sin,' Jimmy laughed.

'You'd think she was the Virgin Mary sometimes,' Josie giggled.

'Four more days Josie, that's all. And your mum did well tonight, must have been hard for her. I don't think you realise.'

'Are you telling me off now?'

'Yeah, yeah I am, I just feel for her that's all. Mind you, after the third gin and tonic she seemed to relax a bit,' he laughed.

'Did you notice the two rounds he bought she asked for a double?' Josie giggled. 'She ain't daft, me mum. She don't usually even drink gin and tonic.'

Jimmy kissed the top of her head. 'I missed Del tonight,' he blurted out. 'Is that stupid? After all he's done? When we were sat there, you, me and Legsy. It felt like the end somehow.'

'Well, yeah, it is,' Josie agreed. 'Everything changes, we've all changed, we ain't the innocent little gang we were ten years ago.' She looked serious. 'Jimmy, you won't ever change and leave me will you? Every man that me mum ever loved has left her. I couldn't stand it, I know I couldn't.'

He pulled her closer towards him gently. 'Never,' he whispered. 'I will never ever leave you and we'll have loads of little Potters. We'll make our own little gang, we could start now if you like.

Josie bit her lip and smiled shyly at him.

'Actually Jimmy, I know this is really bad timing – and I'll have to put off being a social worker for a bit and money's going to be tight but - I think the first gang member might already be on their way, I just didn't quite know how to tell you -'

He grinned and she opened her arms to him.

He gasped and laughed. 'I'm never going to get bored married to you am I? Just shut up and kiss me,' he ordered, 'with tongues.'

###

ACKNOWLEDGEMENTS

So many people to thank for helping me with '**Cherry Pie Lies**'. First of all, again to the Jelly Friskers Writing Group especially Jenni Thornley for her technological know- how. Also Hilary Taylor and Shirley Mason who were also good enough to read for me. Gill Garbutt has again been a star for her editing suggestions, support and for coming up with the book title! Many people helped me in my research. Apart from my best mate 'Google' I would like to thank Ross and Laurel Burnett, Sally and Alan Rich, Gill Letcher, Terry and Nancy Bond, Catherine Armistead, Joanne Carradice, Ruth Allen and Graham Woodbridge.

Last but not least I need to thank my anonymous police snout and his anonymous wife. You know who you are and I couldn't have written it without you.

You are all stars!

ABOUT THE AUTHOR

Lynne Whelon lives in a small, friendly village on Morecambe Bay with her cat Minty. Her formative years were spent in Reading and Ilford, Essex.

Lynne began working with children in 1965 and still works at her local primary school. She spent seventeen years in the Merchant Navy working on cruise ships and saw the world but, more importantly, met some fascinating people from all walks of life.

When she left the sea Lynne began to attend writing classes and joined the Jelly Friskers Writing Group. She has had some success selling articles and short stories to magazines before writing her first novel 'The Chicken Run', first published in 2011.

For further information about Lynne's writing please visit her Facebook page www.facebook.com/TheChickenRunNovelNews

Lightning Source UK Ltd.
Milton Keynes UK
UKOW04f2100061213

222513UK00002B/15/P

9 781784 071738